WHEN I SEE YOU

Also By Katherine Owen

NOT TO US

SEEING JULIA

WHEN I SEE YOU

BY

KATHERINE OWEN

The Writing Works Group

Seattle

The Writing Works Group

Visit our website: http://www.thewritingworksgroup.com

BOOK AND COVER ART DESIGN BY: *The Writing Works Group*
Cover art Photo image: Stockfresh Stock photos:
"Footprints on the beach"© Dmitry Bairachnyi (dmitroza)
"Cowgirl in straw" © Dmitry Bairachnyi (dmitroza)

INTERIOR BOOK DESIGN BY *The Writing Works Group*
SPECIAL FONTS: Wallflowers & Alana Pro
by Laura Worthington
Deniart Systems 4 Point Floral™
TEXT FONTS: Adobe Garamond Pro, AR Decode,
Palatino Linotype, Penna-Regular, Sakka Majalla

Discover other titles by Katherine Owen at the website:
http://www.katherineowen.net

This book is available as a trade paperback print edition as well as an e-book
at most online retailers.

Printed in the United States of America

WHEN I SEE YOU

By

Katherine Owen

WHEN I SEE YOU

Part One

My Girl

THE LAST TIME WE DANCE IS nothing special, but I remember
it now.

There's that.

~ Jordan Holloway

CHAPTER ONE

Jordan – Can't help falling in love

THE DISTANT NOTES OF AN UPDATED version of "Can't help falling in love" plays from the stereo speakers, and we move along the grass slow dancing in the moonlight, but really not paying attention to the significance of the song or the romantic light shedding from the full moon or the whispered musings of our friends who watch us. We are in our own perfect world, like always. It's almost our last night together, and I have been a bitch about just about everything since nine this morning. He leaves in two days, and I have decided to make him pay for it on so many levels that I've lost count. Fear of abandonment is one of my character flaws. I tried to be up-front about it when we first met, but Ethan chose to ignore it. Now, almost four years later, I've begun to wonder if he has any idea of what my deepest fear really entails. Or, if he just doesn't see it and loves me anyway.

His lips brush my forehead, now. "Don't be mad."

"I'm not mad."

"Don't be mad, and don't lie to me, either," he says with a laugh. His charm almost undoes my anger, but not quite.

"Fuck you, Holloway." My ability to swear has been one of the biggest character attributes that I've gleaned and honed to perfection over the years from my best friend, Ashleigh.

Ethan just laughs again. "I promise. This is the last tour, Mrs. Holloway. I promise. The last one. Even old Brock is getting tired of it."

I glance around Ethan at his sniper partner, Lieutenant Brock Wainwright, who is busy trying to pick up the very single Ashleigh Blondell. A part of me feels guilty for not warning the man about Ashleigh's black widow ways. Yet, another part is secretly entertained by the thought of the charming Brock Wainwright being unceremoniously dumped on his ass by the end of the weekend by my insatiable best friend. Two notorious sex fiends that will probably outdo each other in short order. Both are legendary for their inability to commit to other human beings, because their idea of a relationship consists of no more than two consecutive dates or a long one-night stand. *Who can outlast who?* A mischievous smile spreads across my face.

Ethan looks at me with raised eyebrow. "What?"

"Looks like Ashleigh and Brock are going to get to know each other better." I nod in their general direction.

"Brock can handle it, and so can Ashleigh."

"Finally, we agree on something."

I fight the urge to actually smile. Ethan doesn't answer. He just lifts up my chin with his finger and kisses me—one of his let-me-show-you-how-much-I-love-you-baby kisses. His kiss threatens to undermine my annoyance with him.

A few minutes later, he's charmed me enough to allow myself to get pulled along into the shadows by him. We make our way down the twelve steps that lead to our little section of sandy beach and the Pacific Ocean.

Half undressed and moving beneath him, I finally let go of some of the reasons why I am angry at him. My insecurities at his leaving drift away in the ensuing minutes of our lovemaking, which I must admit has always worked with me. And, Ethan knows this.

I close my eyes and let him invade all of my senses and give myself up to him. How is it possible to still be this in love with him after so long? The man is the sun to my falling rain. He makes me want to believe in happily-ever-after's, even though I gave up on those long ago. He fills my world with so much love and profound joy; I feel guilty for having and taking so much. These thoughts rush at me, while he satisfies my body in ways that seem almost impossible. His hands run along my sides and caress my breasts. My breath comes in jagged gasps as he pitches into me with his familiar, frenzied passionate ways.

With his explorations of my body, I cannot keep up my guard against him. Again, my mind tries to summon up righteous anger at him for leaving me, but I fail. Undone, I lie back in the sanctuary of the cool sand dune. Under the magical spell of his traveling fingers, I finally give myself up to him.

"Don't be mad, baby," he says to me when we finish.

The last vestiges of the anger, deep inside, I've been holding on to melt away at his words. He truly does know me better than myself and I can only laugh as I process this revelation as he leans down and kisses me again.

Ethan lies in the twilight beside me breathing heavy. Out of the corner of my eye, I watch his chest move up and down as he gasps for breath. I love watching him breathe. I always have. I roll up on to my side and just stare at his fine features outlined in the subtle moonlight. He looks like a Greek god—statuesque, perfect, bigger than life.

Despair at his leaving finds me again. I feel helpless, all at once, engulfed in silent desperation. His leaving feels likes the loss of my parents all over again.

"You win," I finally say.

"I always win," Ethan says back to me.

He looks over at me and gives me this confident smile. I can barely see his face in the diminishing light, but I trace the outline of his face with my finger. "I love you, Jordan, for always."

His words bring tears to my eyes.

"Then, don't go." My begging sounds frantic even to me and I lie back down in resignation. Turn my back to him so he won't see my sudden tears. He moves in behind me and cradles my head in his chest.

"Have to."

He sits up and leans over me, trailing his fingers beneath my dress.

"Want to."

I slide away from him, retrieving my panties as I go and slip them back on. I smooth down the folds of my party dress purchased especially for tonight's event.

"Sometimes, I think you love Brock Wainwright more than you love me. And Max." I bite my lip regretting my words. "Sorry. I shouldn't have said that. It's not fair."

"No, but you don't always fight fair."

"I'm not fighting with you," I say.

It's not fair that I've brought up Max. Ethan misses our son probably more than he does me. He's barely spent any time with our three-year-old. Max, who, right now, sleeps peacefully in his bedroom, despite the party taking place. Ethan shakes his head and looks sad for a moment and then grins at me. I push up to a stand, just out of his reach, and tower above him.

"Don't be mad," he says as if I haven't spoken. "You know I love you. And Max. I'll be back as soon as I can. Just know this, Jordan—"

The clear sound of footsteps coming down the wooden steps has us both glancing over into the darkness and the general direction of the stairs at the same time. "Ethan?" Brock calls out.

"Over here."

My husband gives me a pleading look. I quickly finger-fix my hair, then pull it back, and re-clasp the rhinestone ponytail holder, just as Brock comes up to us.

Ethan's best friend is all smiles. I blush in the semi-darkness, knowing he knows we were fooling around on the beach. What is wrong with me? Why do I care what Brock Wainwright thinks of me?

"Sorry, did I interrupt something?" Brock drawls.

His southern accent is somewhat charming and I find myself half-smiling, despite my embarrassment and general irritation at his ill-timed interruption. Ethan slyly grins over at me. His secretive smile promises that we will take up where we left off when we're alone again. He trails his hand along my bare leg. I automatically respond to his touch with a shudder getting even more embarrassed. My face gets hot.

"No, not at all," Ethan says. "We were just getting ready to come back."

I extend my hand and pull Ethan to his feet. He catches me in his arms and kisses me in front of Brock.

"Baby, don't be mad," Ethan says.

"I'm not," I say quietly.

The truth is I'm getting upset again. At Ethan. At his best friend, just for being here. I forcefully extricate myself from Ethan's tight grip around my waist and step back. All the while, Brock watches this interaction with a raised eyebrow. His quizzical look infuriates me further.

"I'm going to check on the guests."

"Don't go, Jordan," Ethan says.

I force myself to smile, to play it casual.

"Don't go," he says again.

"Have to," I say with a touch of irony. This inner anguish unfurls at his beseeching tone, but I start up the stairs, taking them two at a time. Their conversation drifts upward to me.

"What's wrong with her?" Brock asks.

"She's upset that I'm leaving again."

"Tired of being married to a Navy SEAL?"

I hear Brock's easy laughter and then Ethan's sigh.

"No, tired of the Navy SEAL not being here."

"Jordan, I love you for always," Ethan says.

I reach the top of the stairs, turn, and look down at both of them. His words reach for me. This profound sadness assails me. My eyes sting. I stare down at the two of them. There they are, two courageous men, who consider themselves bigger than life, standing in the fading twilight looking up at me. The eerie half moon bathes the beach and the two of them in trick white light. They seem insignificant and small in comparison to the behemoth almost-black ocean churning behind them. The hundred feet marked off between the three of us seems suddenly ominous.

"Love you, for always," I say to Ethan, blowing him a kiss.

He pretends to catch it with one hand and then smiles up at me in the moonlight. There's something in the way he looks at me then that makes me want to run back down the stairs and straight into his arms, but, I don't.

No.

I turn back towards our beach house as Ashleigh calls my name. I shiver at the eerie feeling that has surfaced inside of me. I shake my head side-to-side to undo this sense of foreboding.

Within minutes, I'm pulled back into the role of hostess. I'm caught up in refilling wine glasses, replenishing the ice bucket, and finding more food for the late night guests that still grace our back patio. They are all here to say good-bye to Ethan before he heads back to Afghanistan with his sniper partner, Lieutenant Brock Wainwright.

Good-bye. He and I have to say good-bye.

Again.

I wipe away a stray tear, put on a fake smile, and rejoin our party guests.

⸎

"I'm heading out," Ashleigh says.

She runs her fingers through her long blonde mane of hair. It's not quite as long as mine. I've always envied her golden color, while she's always admired mine, dark mahogany, like my famous mother's. A shade or two darker though. And, I'm not famous. But, I'm not dead either.

I watch as Ashleigh's hands move down to smooth the pleats of her black mini skirt which barely covers her endless long legs. I grin at this subtle flirtatious maneuver. Her red tank top is low-cut and reveals the tops of her breasts. I know she knows this. I feel this pang of envy at her perfection. The girl leads a charmed life. She gives me her I've-got-this-handled smile. And, I roll my eyes at her and jerk my head over in Brock's direction where he is talking animatedly to my husband.

"With him? Are you sure that's a good idea?" I ask.

I don't normally get involved in her liaisons. I've witnessed too many to count. Ashleigh always seems prepared and carries an endless supply of condoms and can recite the I'm-smart-and-I'm-careful speech by heart. Her moral code is ruled by Venus and she certainly doesn't require my guidance.

"Jealous much?" Ashleigh looks at me in surprise.

"No," I say, uncertain. I grimace and hold up my hands as if to ward her off and turn away. Even I think I sound defensive and I can't really comprehend it myself. Brock Wainwright has been an unexplainable irritation, since he arrived at our beach house four days ago, after spending three weeks of his leave with his own family in Austin. I guess the basic premise is: I don't like sharing Ethan with anybody. Our time together is so limited. Ethan's sniper partner is another person taking my husband's attention away from me.

I busy myself at the counter and measure out a shot of tequila. I haven't really drunk anything tonight, but now I'm in the mood.

Ashleigh comes over and stands next to me.

"Hey." She touches my arm. "What's wrong? Spill it; you've been on edge all night."

"Nothing."

I try to swig the tequila like a pro, but cough a little as I drain the shot glass. Ashleigh hands me the lime wedge and I suck the juice from it.

"He's leaving. *Again*," Ashleigh says.

"Right."

The misery of Ethan's leaving has already begun to seep back in. The heartache creeps into my voice with the use of the word, *leaving*.

"But, this is it, right? The last tour? Then, he'll be home for good."

She puts her arm around my shoulders. I lean against her and sigh. .

"True."

I pull away from her and try to smile, while I pour myself another shot.

"You've forgotten the part where he is gone for the next year—the four hundred and thirty-three days in between now and then."

My best friend looks sympathetic. "I don't know how you do it.

She joins me for the third one and sets out another shot glass. We are busy getting ready for this one, when Brock and Ethan make their way over to us.

Feeling the rush of the alcohol, I openly stare at Brock Wainwright. He is different from Ethan in every way, except height. They are both tall. But Brock is more Calvin Klein underwear model with his chiseled features and dark crew-cut hair; he's got a Henry Cavill look going on. Ethan constantly teases me about my undeniable obsession with The Tudors actor, and now, his look-alike is across the room from me in the real-life persona of one Second Lieutenant Brock Wainwright. Even the man's crooked smile, though incongruent with the flawlessness of his good looks, mirrors the actor's from the photographs I've seen. It's unnerving. *Who is that good-looking in real life?*

Ethan is slighter in build, reminiscent of his wide receiver football days at Yale, tall and lanky. His blonde hair is straight like golden flax. He keeps it short, for the service, in this bristle-like crew cut. I've always wanted him to wear it longer, but I enjoy sweeping my hand over the top of his head and feeling the boar brush softness of his hair beneath my fingers. I do this now and pull him to me as the tequila courses through me and softens the sharp edges of all of me.

"Kiss me."I reach inside his shirt and feel for his heartbeat.

"Jordan, my tequila girl, you know how that stuff makes you do crazy things." Ethan laughs, then lowers his head and brushes his lips across mine.

"Let me show you how crazy I am."

I grin at Ethan and pull him even closer. The taste of his cologne and hint of his sweat arouse me in an instant. I close my eyes and breathe him in and lose myself in his kiss. For now, all is right with my world.

Moments later, I open my eyes, look past Ethan's shoulder, and meet the unexpected gaze of Brock Wainwright. He looks disconcerted, then surprised, as if he's just figured something out.

In my tequila-induced haze, I stare back and attempt to discern what he's thinking. It's confusing. There's just something in the way he looks at me. It's, as if, he understands the secret depths of my terror—my fear of losing the one I love the most. It is, as if, he, somehow, knows my secret—the burdensome inner fear I constantly battle. I shiver and glance away from the man and center my full attention back on Ethan.

My husband's seductive claim on me leaves no doubt as to what we're going to be doing in the next couple of hours, even as I remind him we have guests. I push away the image of Brock's troubled face and cling tighter to Ethan and attempt to halt the proverbial march of fear of losing him that is already attempting to take hold of me.

⚬⚬⚬

A few hours later, the four of us are the only ones left. Everyone else has made their way home. We have an eclectic group of friends these days. Most of them are our neighbors around Malibu—friends with distant ties to my famous parents or some of our college friends that stayed around the area after graduation—affluent, but likable, people. I lost my parents, when I was seventeen, so my only sense of family is Ethan, his parents who reside in Austin like Brock's family, and Ashleigh, of course. Ashleigh has been there for me for more than ten years, when we were still sophomores in high school.

Right now, my best friend is draped all over Brock in a suggestive way. She sits in his lap with her arm possessively curved around his neck. Brock doesn't seem to mind. Ashleigh's sexual conquests don't normally bother me, but even with tequila coursing through me, I am strangely annoyed by her demonstrative intentions with Ethan's best friend. We have imbibed in almost the entire bottle of tequila. Ethan grins over at the amorous cozy couple across from us.

"You should stay the night," Ethan says to Ashleigh, winking at her.

I give my husband a pleading look, but it's too late. Brock is already agreeing that Ashleigh should spend the night, and Ashleigh is already out of the man's lap and pulling him to his feet.

With obvious intent, she pulls him along the hallway, to our guest room, where Brock's been staying. She's stayed in that room, herself, on numerous weekends with me, when Ethan is gone. She winks back at us.

"It's our second to the last night. I want to be alone. Alone, alone."

"We'll be alone," Ethan says, coming to his feet.

He towers over me with a beguiling look. "Now, let me show you what we're going to do, Mrs. Holloway."

In one swift motion, he picks me up and starts carrying me down toward our master bedroom at the opposite end of the hallway. I laugh up at Ethan. He brushes my neck with his lips.

"Night, Wainwright." Ethan turns and calls out to Brock.

That's when I catch another curious look from Brock at the other end of the hallway. An undeniable look of sadness crosses his features. My first instinct is to call out good night, but, before I can, Brock turns away and shuts the door to the guest room with such finality that I'm taken aback.

Contrition travels through me. I don't know why.

"I love you," Ethan whispers.

His lips travel down the side of my neck and then he sets me down and closes our bedroom door with his left foot. I laugh, shaking my head side-to-side as he moves toward me. His intense loving gaze effectively chases away the strange emotions that Brock Wainwright evokes. I center my focus back on the man standing in front of me.

My world. Ethan.

He's all I see.

CHAPTER

TWO

Jordan – Show me what I'm looking for

THREE-YEAR-OLDS ALWAYS GET UP ON TIME, and with Max, it's always been early. I feel the soft tap on my shoulder and self-consciously pull the sheets up over my naked body. Keeping my eyes closed, I smile.

"Momma. Pancakes."

I open one eye and ascertain the time of 6:05 a.m. Shit. Four hours of sleep, and the overindulgence in tequila is a combination that wreaks havoc on all of me now. Max's cherub face comes into view. Ethan stirs beside me. I glance over at him and see him smile even though his eyes remain closed.

"Maximilian, is that you?" Ethan asks.

This is all the invitation our three-year-old needs; he clamors into our bed, jumping onto Ethan, who is unprepared for the onslaught of Max. Ethan groans as Max lands directly on top of him. I start to laugh, but take advantage of the commotion, covertly slide out of bed, and grab my black robe that I unceremoniously cast aside late last night. I tie it around my waist as I go.

"Breakfast," I mutter. My enthusiasm for cooking wavers a little as I say this. My head begins to pound from the tequila as soon as I come to a full stand.

"French toast!" they both say together.

I glance back at Max, the perfect little replica of Ethan, and then the man, himself, and smile. "Fine. Come help me?"

Ethan winks at me and promises to come and help me out in a few minutes. He easily swings Max high above his head. Our son squeals with laughter. Ethan gives me this knowing look over Max's head as he lowers him to his chest. I think Ethan's just beginning to realize just what all he misses when he's away from us. I blow them both a kiss as I leave.

The intoxicating smell of rich coffee reaches me. When I reach the kitchen doorway, I discover Brock is already up. He's made the coffee. Like the perfect house guest, he pours me a cup, and adds a little cream just the way I like it. I'm too surprised to respond. *How does he know how I take my coffee?*

"I saw Ethan fix your coffee yesterday," he says.

"Oh." I blow on the steaming cup and take a cautious sip. "Thank you. Isn't it a little early to be up?"

"I'm an early riser. Always have been. I sleep light. I heard the birds around 4:30 a.m. this morning. I grew up on a ranch, sleeping in was never an option with my father." He winces and then flashes me one of his white smiles.

I shake my head as if to clear it from these wayward thoughts, that begin with the notable silent admission that the man is extremely good-looking and end with, I shouldn't even be noticing. Yet, in the four days he's been here, this is something I've been undeniably aware of, since we first shook hands, when Ethan introduced us. "Jordan, this is Brock. I can't believe you two are finally getting to meet each other. What's it been almost four years since we've been able to make this happen?" Ethan had asked.

It's been almost four years, since we said, "I do," in Vegas, just after I'd found out I was pregnant, exactly eight weeks after we met, just before Ethan shipped out to Germany and on to Afghanistan with his best friend from Austin and sniper partner, Lieutenant Brock Wainwright.

With an unquenchable obsession for bizarre facts, I added it up, once, and still keep track. We've been married for one thousand, four hundred and twenty-eight days, and I've spent a total of two hundred and ninety-seven of them with Ethan, counting today.

Who lives like this? The nagging thought plagues me at odd moments like an endless tape reel. It's the one pervasive thought that I wake up with in the middle of the night. *Too often.* That's when I wonder how I ended up all alone, in love with a Navy SEAL, who is off fighting the bad guys an entire world away from me. After losing my parents, the one thing I told myself I would never allow myself to do was fall in love. Loving someone and losing them is too great of a price; and yet, here I am. In love. Alone. Much of the time. *How did I end up here?*

Some nights when Ethan's away, Max crawls into bed with me. It's the only time that the strange tilt of my world seems as it should be. As Ethan says, "It's not the quantity of time that we spend together; it's the quality." But, there are times when the fear becomes more prevalent, when I do wonder if our time together is too finite. There are those nights when I wake up and give into the relentless terror that all the plans we've made, honed and shined up for our certain future, are no more than a mirage and will never happen.

God knows.

God knows this girl no longer believes in fairy tales and has extreme trouble in believing in happily-ever-afters. The closer we get to ours—the ending of Ethan's last tour—the more fearful I become about never seeing it happen.

Who thinks this way? Who thinks this way and remains sane?

Brock stares at me, now. His gaze so intense I blush, look down at my open neckline, and pull the silk robe tighter around me. I'm suddenly very much aware that I'm standing here in only my robe with nothing on underneath. After fumbling with the robe a little more, I look up.

He has this bemused expression. His lips are parted as if he has something to say. I wait, but he doesn't say anything.

"Where's Ashleigh?" I finally ask. I flip my hair with the back of my hand and look at him.

"Sleeping."

"Worn out." I blush, embarrassed at my impetuous reference to his sexual rendezvous with Ashleigh.

Brock just laughs and shakes his head. "Worn out," he echoes back to me, and then grins. "Something like that."

I hide behind the safety of the Viking's stainless steel door. The cool air caresses my hot face. I welcome it as I procure eggs and milk from the refrigerator. "Ethan and Max want French toast," I say from its depths.

"Well, that's my vote," Brock drawls from behind me.

"I should probably get dressed." I move back toward the hallway, just as Ethan and Max appear.

My husband's gaze openly travels over me; his smile widens. "Get dressed, woman."

He fondles the opening of my robe and trails his fingers along my collar bone. He brushes his lips against my forehead as I pass him.

"Babe, I'll get things started and entertain Brock," he says.

"Don't touch anything. I'll be right back."

I hear Max giggle as the two men set about preparing French toast. I race down the hallway to change, before Ethan turns my pristine kitchen into a complete mess. He has a tendency to spread flour everywhere.

"She's amazing. Right, Brock?" I hear Ethan ask.

"Incredible," Brock says. "I don't see how you're going to be able to get on the plane."

It's probably meant to be funny, but I don't hear either one of them laugh.

An hour later, the household has been fed French toast, and all the adults have been replenished with multiple cups of Brock's strong black coffee. Max is busy showing off his swing set and sandbox to the clearly hung-over Ashleigh and his daddy. I watch my son as he constantly pulls at Ethan's outstretched hand. His unmet need for Ethan's attention brings tears to my eyes, but our child's enthusiasm is contagious. I can't help but smile, when I hear Max call out, "Look at this, Daddy; look at this, Ashleigh," in his sweet, elf-like voice. I gaze at the three of them through the open French door that leads to the backyard and feel this surge of love for my little family.

A half hour later, Brock peruses the *Los Angeles Times*, while I decorate cupcakes for Max. Decorating cupcakes has become my signature specialty within this small community of Malibu. It's kind of a sideline hobby to my real job as head chef at Le Reve.

I look up. Brock watches me with the rapt interest similar to that of a small child. It reminds me of Max when he's mesmerized with a television program like Big Bird or Barney. The newspaper is folded up and lies next to his forearm.

I slip up with the icing under his studied scrutiny and attempt to refocus upon the task at hand by breaking eye contact with our unexpected house guest.

"Ethan tells me you studied at CIA," Brock says. "That you're a head cook, here in Malibu. At Le Reve, is it?"

I glance up from what I'm doing and nod, but looking at him is worse. The man continues to interfere with my ability to concentrate on the cupcakes for some reason. I glance away from him, intent on getting back to looping blue icing across the little cake's surface in a circular pattern, making ocean waves. I'm going for a *Finding Nemo* theme, per my three-year-old's request. He's taking the cupcakes to his play date with his friend, Davey. I hold my breath in an attempt to drape the icing in a steady wave pattern.

"Head chef at Le Reve. Before that, head chef at Rivera," I say. "And before that, I worked at L'Ecole in New York, even a summer in Paris." I lift my chin in defiance and can feel myself blushing. *Why do I feel the need to provide my resume to this guy?*

"*Chef*," Brock says with a wide smile. "Sorry, you gourmets are so touchy about titles."

"It's a big deal in the culinary world to be a head chef. It takes years to get that title and the responsibility that comes with it." I shrug, trying to give off an air of indifference, but even I can hear the edge in my voice.

"Okay," Brock says. "Head chef at Le Reve. Tell me what that's like."

I put down the pastry knife, somewhat disconcerted to be asked about the restaurant. Ethan sees it as a drain of my time away from Max, away from him when he's here. Le Reve is a source of tension between us every time he's home.

"There's a certain energy and excitement in running a restaurant every night. You spend your whole day preparing and planning, and then, the satisfaction of execution on a nightly basis is exhilarating. Almost spiritual." I smile over at him. He gets this disconcerted look. "There's nothing quite like it. Le Reve is small, only eight tables, but people come from all over to eat there. We have a good thing going. My boss, the owner, Louis DuPont, is from Paris. He's amazing and gives me a lot of flexibility. It's close by. Ashleigh or Mrs. Richards watch Max in the evening, and I try to be home by midnight or so." My voice trails off at the thoughtful look on Brock's face. "What?"

"Isn't it kind of hard to juggle all of that with Max?"

"It works. I don't know any other life. Of course, Ethan would prefer me to work part-time and be home with Max more." I hesitate, before saying,

"Running a restaurant, making decisions about food, and preparing it is cathartic for me. I need to do it." I pause, experiencing misgivings about saying anything more, but somehow, needing to. "Ethan was gone when Max was born. He's been home three times in the past three years. I have a life. Here. In L.A. It works."

I sweep the pastry knife across the air in agitation and openly blush, knowing I sound too defensive. I take an unsteady breath. I've given too much away. "We make it work," I say in a low voice.

I look over at him. He's shaking his head. I'm unable to look away.

"You just don't know how rare you are. I think it's great that you have a career and still manage things with Max." He frowns. "Most women wouldn't put up with the long tours away from home. It wreaks havoc on a relationship. It takes commitment. Trust. It's rare."

"Relationships are hard, no matter what the circumstances," I say.

"You think so?" Brock asks. There's discernible disquiet in his tone.

The ground seems to shift beneath me. I reach out for the counter to steady myself. Yet, I'm unable to stop myself from saying more. "We sailed into marriage with all these dreams and made all these promises. We were so naive. Within fifteen minutes of meeting him, I knew how I felt about him and how he felt about me." I try to smile. "He swept me off my feet and I didn't hit the ground, until I was standing at the airport and watching his flight to Afghanistan take off." I smile, but then, it fades.

"At that moment, I'd never felt so alone in my life. And, there have been other times when I have felt pretty much alone." I stop, take an unsteady breath, and close my eyes, remembering the death of my parents and that exact moment when Ethan left the first time. I open them and he's staring at me intently.

"Alone. Eight weeks pregnant. Ashleigh and I had been in L.A. for a couple of years already. Then, I'd met Ethan and everything changed," I say in a low voice. I gaze over at Brock and then shrug my shoulders, attempting to lighten the mood at seeing the disconcerted look on his face. "But nothing really changed. Do you know what I mean?"

"Yes." Brock looks even more troubled.

"What?" I ask with growing trepidation.

"I was engaged once. It didn't work out." A shadow crosses his face. "I dropped out of my last semester of law school and signed up for SEAL training, then sniper school. My father wasn't too happy." Brock gets this bleak look. "Relationships are hard whether you're in L.A. or Austin."

Ethan and Brock both grew up in Austin. I pause in mid-air with my pastry knife, realizing that this is one more thing that Ethan hasn't really shared with me. I don't really know much about his life in Austin, before me. We rarely go there because his time is so limited when he's home.

"I'm sorry. About the fiancée. About your dad," I say.

"I got over it. I moved on." He shrugs and looks indifferent.

"Is that why you go through women like they're an endless supply of shaving razors? To defy your father? To prove you're over her?"

I blush at my bluntness.

"I suppose so." He tries to smile but it doesn't reach his eyes. I sense this profound sadness in him. "But razors aren't as sharp. Never disappoint. Never maim. Not intentionally, anyway; and don't require commitment."

"You and Ashleigh should get along just fine then," I say, tartly.

A twinge of guilt for warning him about Ashleigh's fickle ways surges through me. She's my best friend, but another part of me feels absolution for warning him. He seems like a nice guy. Genuine, even.

"I believe we have a clear understanding of what this is and isn't."

"A fling." *Why am I saying this to him? Why do I need to know?*

"Yes."

"Like I said, you should both get along just fine then."

"Thanks for the warning, though." He gets this thoughtful expression.

I just nod, knowing that Ashleigh has a date with a new guy this very evening. A part of me is intrigued with how she's going to break that news to our house guest, since she's now slept with him and he's probably expecting more of the same tonight, since it's his last night in the States.

It doesn't matter how many times I warn Ashleigh that her insatiable appetite for sex is going to lead to an encounter that turns into something more when she least expects it. She just laughs it off.

"Just be aware of Max. That's all I ask." I give him a knowing look.

"Thought of that," he says. "It does get complicated; doesn't it?"

"Not too often. He's three. He's not adding things up yet, in terms of you both being here when he wakes up and the two of you walking out of the same bedroom. But in another year or two, things will be different."

"Ethan will be home."

"Ethan will be home," I say with such wistfulness that I surprise myself.

Why am I so openly sharing my feelings with this almost stranger? He might be Ethan's best friend, but I barely know him. I shrug, attempting nonchalance, and start decorating the cupcakes again.

"Max is great," he says.

"Max is great. He's the light of my life. Without Ethan here so much of the time, Max keeps me going." I look over at Brock and smile but feel uncertain, all at once.

This conversation has become way too personal. I don't even tell Ashleigh some of this stuff. He intently stares at me. Self-conscious, I tuck a strand of my long hair behind one ear and attempt to hold the cake knife steady and essentially ignore him.

"Your hair," he says softly. "That dark mahogany color—" He gets this squeamish look, as if he's suddenly realized how personal his question is.

"My mother was a true redhead. Mine's a couple shades darker."

"Your mother. The Oscar winner." He nods in understanding. "Davis and Laurel Breckinridge," he says with reverence. "You have your mother's stunning beauty, but your dad's eyes. That amazing green everyone always talked about. People must recognize you everywhere you go."

"It was a long time ago."

"Not that long ago," he says. "You know my mom probably went to school with her in Austin."

"I don't know much about Austin. It's just a weird coincidence that my mother is from there and so is Ethan. And you." I lift my head and give him a pleading look, silently signaling this conversation is over.

"You don't talk about them," he says softly.

"I don't." I sigh and look at him, wary, all at once.

"That's what Ethan said."

Silence ensues. He just watches me work.

"This place is beautiful." He makes a wide sweep with his left arm around the seventies-style Frank Lloyd Wright kitchen and family room. "It's quite a tribute to them. The way you kept the era alive for them."

"Old Hollywood," I say wryly. "I sold the other house, but, this one was always my favorite growing up. Theirs, too. We used to come up on weekends from the other house. They liked the privacy. The beach. The Pacific. It was pretty magical. I want Max to have that childhood memory, too." He looks as surprised by my soliloquy as much as I am. "But as I said, I don't like to talk about them."

"So you said." His lips curve slowly into a smile.

Now, I'm caught up in his penetrating gaze, stopped again by the thought that the man is incredibly good-looking.

"Has anyone ever told you that you look like Henry Cavill? From The Tudors?" I ask.

"Isn't that the Henry the Eighth show?"

"Yes," I deadpan, giving nothing away.

"Do I look like him or *act* like him?"

I flush from head to toe. "Henry Cavill's character is pretty tame. He's married and *good*, most of the time." My voice drifts away. We've gotten into another strange conversation. I bite my lip.

"So. I look like the king's sidekick and behave more like Jonathan Rhys Meyers, who plays Henry?"

"You've *seen* it."

"My twin sister loves that show," he says with a laugh. "She said I looked just like Henry Cavill once, too."

"You have a twin?"

"I do."

"Wow. That's amazing. You seem like such a loner."

He gets this disconcerted look. "Diana looks like me, but she's way different. She's a successful attorney, married to one, has two kids, at almost thirty, she's done it all. Mom and Dad are so proud."

I wince at his sarcasm and feel this modicum of sympathy for him.

"Marriage is misunderstood, overrated," I say airily.

With intention, I fill another pastry bag with orange frosting and concentrate on the task in front of me. He remains silent, but I can feel his scrutiny of me. Finally, curiosity compels me to look over at him.

"So," he says softly. "Which is it? Misunderstood? Or, overrated?"

I'm caught up in his unwavering look. He's *willing* me to say something.

"Depends on what side you're on," I say. "When you're married, you're privy to the misunderstanding. When you're not married, it's overrated." I try to smile. "You rush in, headlong, full of dreams and wishes, so far removed from reality that you never even realize you've married into a family and the Navy. One refers to you as the girl from L.A., and the other refers to you as the dependent spouse." I try to smile, but struggle with the unbearable sadness that attacks me from all sides.

"No," I say with an unsteady breath. "No one tells you about that part."

"No," he says. "No, they don't."

I can't even look at him, too afraid I'm going to fall apart in front of him. I set down the knife and head to the pantry. My whole body trembles. It's difficult to put one foot in front of the other. "Forgot something," I call out to him as I leave. "Excuse me."

Cloaked in the darkness of the pantry, I command myself to get a grip. My heart rate beats out of control and I gasp for breath. I've just revealed to Ethan's best friend my deepest reservations and resentment about this life. *My life. My marriage.*

I sink to the floor and hold my head between my hands. Whiffs of sugar from my hands assail my nostrils while tremendous guilt shakes my body.

What is wrong with me? Why do I feel compelled to tell him everything? I lean back against the closed pantry door, turn my head, and feel the coolness of the wood against the side of my face. I close my eyes.

Breathe. Stop talking to him. What is wrong with you? Why do you feel the need to tell him anything?

After five minutes, I emerge from my contrived sanctuary and re-take my post at the kitchen counter with renewed gusto and contrived nonchalance. My parents were actors. Surely, I've inherited some of their fortitude.

"Are you okay?" Brock asks.

"I'm fine."

I glance over at him. His hair has this unmistakable unruly wave to it, and it's a bit longer than Ethan's. I wonder how far out of regulation it is for the U.S. Navy. It seems to have grown a bit with this last month of leave. He smooths it back with his hand now and catches me staring at him and grins. *Charmer.* I feel the heat stain my cheeks.

"You need a haircut," I say, surprising myself and him.

"Yes. Ethan said you cut his. Would you cut mine?"

"Sure, I guess," I say with an airy wave of one hand. "I mean, if Ethan says it's okay."

I sound like a sappy housewife waiting for permission from her man. Wincing, I look over at him. He gets this bemused smile.

"Sure, I can cut your hair, since you're leaving tomorrow. You're both running out of time."

I sound ominous.

He hears it.

"We're leaving tomorrow," he says gently.

I look down in surprise at the mess I've made of some of the cupcakes. This conversation has taken another wayward turn. I swipe at my face and at the sudden onset of unshed tears with the back of my hand and attempt to concentrate.

❧⯑❧

Minutes later, I direct him to the main bathroom for the scissors and a towel while I try to finish up the cupcakes. He returns with all the supplies, strips off his white t-shirt, and settles down in one of the kitchen chairs, waiting for me. I'm down to the last two cupcakes. He looks thoughtful as he continues to watch me work. I get more uneasy. *Why does he make me so nervous?* I've been around many of Ethan's friends over the years, but there's something about Brock Wainwright that makes him so different from all the others. *He looks too much like Henry Cavill. Any woman in their right mind would be anxious.* I smile at this adept self-analysis.

"Can I ask you something?" Brock asks.

"Uh-huh."

I bite my lower lip, feigning concentration on finishing the frosting masterpiece in front of me, although I'm actually holding my breath in anticipation of his question. A part of me already knows that it will be too intimate or too personal to actually answer.

"Are you happy?"

I look up at him. He looks genuinely concerned. I blush, recalling my deepest thoughts and revelations about marriage to him.

"Of course," I say quickly.

"Really *happy*. It's hard to have this life with Ethan when he's gone so much of the time."

It's not a question. It's a statement. A salvo. *Is he testing me? Or, taunting me?*

"It's hard," I say slowly. "You've been in love, right? The fiancée?"

"Yes. It was a long time ago."

Devastation crosses his features, and then, he shrugs and slowly smiles. "I don't talk about her. Ever." He gives me this challenging look.

I nod slowly in acknowledgement and smile back.

"A long time ago still counts," I say. "Ethan's always here, inside of me."

I point to my heart; then blush again. I'm wearing Ethan's 'Sea, Air, and Land' SEAL t-shirt, but suddenly feel embarrassed at this man's close scrutiny of it.

"But does he really *see* you?"

His question catches me off guard. The disquiet in his voice reaches for me, stirring up all these insecurities about Ethan I harbor.

How does Brock know that I wonder? How does he know that I don't believe in fairy tales or happily-ever-afters anymore? Does he see my pain? Does he feel it? And, if he does, how come Ethan doesn't?

I decide to ignore him. With determination, I set my tools aside and begin scraping the frosting mistake off the remaining cupcakes with a butter knife without answering him, willing myself to get a grip and keep silent.

And, he waits. He just waits.

I have to admit, I've never met a guy who has so much patience with silence as this one. Over the past four days, this is something I've begun to notice. Brock seems to relish silence. He's comfortable with it. Whereas, Ethan and I always seem to be talking, filling in the spaces of quiet with more to say. Maybe, it's because we're always chasing time, savoring the briefest moments because being together is always so finite.

But does he see me?

The need to fill the protracted silence wins out.

"He sees me. He sees what he wants me to be," I finally say.

Now, Brock openly displays this confident look, as if he's just figured out the solution to a complex mathematical equation that I haven't even begun to work out.

"So he kind of ignores the tortured soul that you are."

His amazing insight into my psyche causes me to mess up the final cupcake. I have always had this underlying sense that Ethan disregards my inner turmoil. The grief over my parents all these years later still haunts me, and the incredible fear I carry at being left all alone is something that Ethan is the last to recognize. I scowl at him over the flower vase that sits between us on the counter.

"He doesn't ignore me. He knows who I am."

"When he's *here*," Brock says dryly. "Don't you have dreams, too? I mean, I know you love him, and God knows he loves you and Max, but what about this life and all the time he's away?"

"He knows me," I say again. "We have a good life. I have Max. I'm the head chef at an exclusive restaurant. Someday, I'll run my own place."

He gets this weird look, almost sympathetic. "Your own restaurant."

"Yes. My own place. Here in Malibu. That's the plan." I get defensive. "And, when we're together, it's perfect."

The bleakness of my reality and what I've just said begins to take hold. My hands tremble. I put down the knife again and struggle to regain my composure. Brock's perceptiveness upsets me, and the truth in what he's said reverberates at an appreciable level. It reaches for me. Ethan completely ignores the tortured part of me. And, how does Brock *know* this?

Flustered, all I can do is watch when he gets up from the kitchen table, comes over to me, runs his finger along the bowl of blue icing, and sticks it into his mouth.

All the while, somewhere, deep inside of me, something begins to give way.

"Lady, I don't think even *you* know who you are."

He grabs the cupcake with the ruined icing I had set aside to fix and begins to peel away the paper and plops the whole thing into his mouth.

"Hmmm…good. Perfect, Jordan. Just the way you are."

"I'm not perfect."

I'm uncertain as to why I feel compelled to admit this to him. I blush under his open appraisal.

"I think you are."

His face is inches away from mine. The smell of chocolate cake emanates from him. I stare at his mouth, suddenly fascinated and intrigued by the way his lips move as he slowly eats the cake and brazenly gazes back at me.

The shifting persists. I catch and hold my breath, too uncertain of my visceral reaction to him. Then, an intrinsic thought assails me from out of nowhere. *I'm attracted to him.*

I look down, taken aback that I clench the decorating knife and practically wield it at him as a weapon. I glance back up at him and discern his own bewilderment as it travels across his features.

We step back from each other at the same time.

And, for once, I don't feel the need to say anything.

I dully follow his movements as he picks up his castoff newspaper and heads toward the back deck, calling out for Ethan.

"I'm not perfect," I say to the empty room after he's gone.

⊰⊱

Ethan has taken Max to Davey's house along with the extravagant *Nemo* cupcakes. Ashleigh spent a few minutes with me gulping coffee, provided a few whispered headlines about how great Brock was in bed, and then promptly disappeared. She murmured something about the need to start the laundry. I suspect what she's really doing is sitting in my car in the garage and canceling her date for tonight. When I told her that Ethan and Brock would be having dinner at Le Reve with me, she decided to cancel her plans with this new guy and join us. "Michael will keep," she'd said with a satisfied smile. "Brock is leaving tomorrow." Her introspection lasted a full thirty seconds and must have set some kind of record. Then, she shrugged and smiled at me. "He's fun," she said with a secret smile.

"Like so many of them," I said back to her. She just laughed.

Now, I'm fulfilling my promise to cut Brock's hair. What seemed like a simple favor has turned awkward in the last twenty minutes. We operate in uncomfortable silence.

"It's none of my business," Brock says after a while.

"It's not."

"I'm sorry. I didn't mean to upset you."

"You didn't," I lie.

His lips curve up into a little smile and he shakes his head at me. I comb his hair and concentrate on getting the edges even. My fingers run across his hairline. The radio plays in the background, and the implied closeness of this scene begins to play out for both of us. He fidgets in the kitchen chair, while I struggle to maintain nonchalance.

"You've got to stop moving your head," I finally say. "Or, I'm going to mess up." I grip his chin and direct him to keep his head level. I grin at him, wielding the scissors near his face.

"I'll be good." He starts to laugh and sits up taller.

I attempt to concentrate on getting his hair even. The radio plays the Carolina Liar's song, "Show Me What I'm Looking For." I sing along with the melody as I move around Brock and cut his hair.

While the music tends to relax me, he seems to get more uptight. The song ends and that's when I notice he's holding his breath.

"Everything okay?" I ask.

"Yeah," he says with a tight smile.

"I'm almost done."

"Good."

"Close your eyes."

He closes them, while I trim along his forehead. I blow away the stray hairs from his face, and he opens his eyes and stares straight at me for a moment. A deep crevice forms at the bridge of his nose. A part of me wants to smooth away the tension with my fingertips. The rational part turns away, grabs a hand towel, and wipes down his shoulders and neck.

"Okay, Lieutenant, you're good to go."

He rises from the chair, rubs the back of his neck, and looks around for his t-shirt and pulls it back on. "Thanks, Jordan," he says with disquiet.

"No problem."

I begin sweeping the kitchen floor, but still harbor some unexplainable turmoil. For some reason, I look up at him and glimpse this pained expression as it flits across his features. Then, he smiles over at me and it disappears.

"About the other stuff," Brock gets this apologetic look. "I don't know what I'm talking about." He stops, takes a deep breath and says, "Ethan loves you. You love Ethan."

"Yes."

My answer seems to hold enough conviction for both of us. He studies my face for a few seconds, as if he has something more he'd like to say, but then, he nods and walks away.

.A few minutes later, I hear Ashleigh's familiar giggle from the direction of the guest room. Soon after, the shower is running again, and their shared laughter reaches at me from down the hallway.

The uneasy feelings engendered by Brock are replaced by this incredible longing for Ethan. And, just as suddenly, Ethan's there, walking up the path leading to our front door.

He carries a bouquet of flowers. I gaze at him through the kitchen window and smile wide.

Here's my life. This is what I want, what I need.

I race to the front door, anxious to meet up with him.

"For me?" I ask.

Guilt assails me over the strange conversation with Brock. *Ethan loves me. I know this.*

He kisses me now, leaving no room for doubt to linger. "For you," Ethan murmurs against my lips. He holds my face between his hands and kisses me long and hard. "I missed you."

"You were gone a half hour. Forty-five minutes tops."

"I know, but I missed you. We need to make the most of our time together."

"Don't steal my lines," I say with a shaky laugh. My throat constricts with emotion, and love for him surges through all of me.

"I'm going to steal more than that."

Ethan pulls me along to the master bedroom, despite my protests about entertaining our house guests. "They'll find something to do." He closes and locks our bedroom door. "We've got a few hours before Max needs to be picked up. Let's make the most of it."

And, so, we do.

⁂

I lace my fingers with Ethan's for a few minutes and then hand him his car keys, so he can go pick up Max. Ashleigh has determined she has a few errands to run. I'm pretty sure one of those involves seeing the mysterious Michael, no doubt placating him, in some way, for canceling their evening plans.

I've called the restaurant and made sure everything is in order for tonight's festivities. I'm technically taking the night off, as Louis none too subtly reminds me when I call, but duty and this overriding sense to ensure everything is perfect for the guys' last night in town prevails. Tomorrow, they catch a flight back to Dover from Los Angeles and then on to Afghanistan for parts unknown.

Malibu keeps the winter season, gripping the rest of the nation, at bay, even in late January with its usual gift of upper sixty-degree weather. I've changed into running gear, determined to get a run in along the beach.

It's a rare treat, running the shoreline. With Ethan gone so much of the time, I usually have to load up the baby jogger and run the neighborhood streets because keeping track of Max along the beach is too much of a battle. Living the single parent life much of the time, I'm determined to take advantage of it while I can. I race down the steps of our back deck.

"Jordan, do you mind if I come with you?" Brock calls out.

I mind. This is my time. It's rare that I get to do this without asking Ashleigh or Mrs. Richards for help, which I try not to do too often.

"No. Of course not. Come along." I force myself to smile at him. I stop to stretch at the top of the beach steps and re-clasp my ponytail. "Do you run on regular basis?"

"Not as much as I would like. Afghanistan isn't exactly Malibu, or even L.A.," he says with a wry smile. "I put in the miles when I can."

"Right." My tone is too sharp and part of me doesn't care.

The man continues to put me on edge. But, most of all, it's my last full day with Ethan, and here he is underfoot. I start down the stairs and hear him following noisily behind me. My inexplicable confusion over Brock continues to mount starting with the mere fact that he spends more time with Ethan than I do. The mere fact that he is now physically involved with my best friend. The mere fact that he is interrupting my personal time by running on the beach with me in the first place. And finally, the whole bizarre exchange between us earlier in the kitchen beginning with the disconcerting thought that I find him attractive to my revelation about marriage being overrated and ending with the whole tortured soul conversation. What did he mean by that? Why would he say something like that? All of it weighs me down now. Yes. That about covers it. All my reasons for being disconcerted by him. That about covers it. Those are the reasons.

We've been running for about twenty minutes. I've outpaced him much of the way. My anxiety spurs me on.

We're about three miles up the coast, but I finally slow down because my lungs are aching from taking the run at such a fast pace. I look over for Brock and realize I'm running alone.

I turn back in surprise and discover Brock about a hundred feet behind me. He's lying on the beach, breathing heavy. His right arm rests across his grey t-shirt. I can almost make out the words, U.S. Navy, in black block letters even from this distance as his chest moves up and down at an accelerated rate as he attempts to catch his breath.

Reluctance and shame commingle with me. Guilt at my bitchy behavior assails me as I make my way back to him. *What am I trying to prove to him?*

"You okay?" I ask, attempting to catch my own breath. My hands grip my sides as I bend down toward his sprawled-out frame.

"Am I supposed to be?" Brock gives me an irritated look. "If you wanted to run by yourself, you could have just said so."

"Oh. I…yeah." I hang my head, embarrassed. "Okay. Look. I'm sorry. It's just—"

"He says you're pissed at him for leaving you again."

The tender way he says this catches me off guard. Tears immediately well up. I turn away to wipe at them and then I sink into the sand beside him with a heavy sigh.

"I'm not mad," I say in defeat. "I'm just so sad that he's leaving again."

Brock glances at me sideways. "It's not easy for him, you know. He's not one to say that he's suffering, but he misses you, too. It's there, all the time. I see it."

"I miss him so much when he's gone." I turn to look at Brock.

He nods as if he's heard what I said, but continues to stare straight ahead out at the horizon. I turn away from him and do the same.

"He memorizes your letters. He reads them over and over and recites them back to me, word for word, days later."

"He reads you my letters?"

"Yeah. I think it's cathartic for him. He talks about you and Max all the time. It's hard for him. He misses you both so much."

"It's hard…for me." There's an edge to my voice.

"Yeah. I know. With your parents."

I look at him then. "I *told* you, earlier, I don't talk about them."

"So you did." Brock turns and stares at me. "Look, I'm not married. Like I told you earlier, I came close." His voice trembles. He sighs and runs his hand through his hair. "The kind of pain you both must feel in being apart," he says in a low voice. "It's hard. But, just know, I *see* it." He swallows and gets this anguished look. "In him. In you."

"In *me*? You don't even *know* me."

He gives me a wan smile. "He reads all your letters to me, Jordan. I *know* you."

I look away from him and wipe at the tears that keep falling. Then, I get back up again and look down at him. "Brock," I say. He looks up at me and I'm filled with such intense emotion I can't even speak. I take a deep breath and hold it while he just waits for me to say something.

"Promise me. Promise me, you'll keep him safe."

"Jordan, I—" This conflicted look comes over him. "Okay. I promise."

"It's important. I can't…I can't lose him."

I kneel back down in front of him, grip his hands, and search his face for understanding.

This strange feeling of recognition seems to pass between us. His lips part and he starts to say something, but then stops. I watch him, wary, all at once, taken aback, once again, by this mysterious connection with him.

"Jordan," he says with perceivable disquiet. "I promise. I'll keep him safe. For you."

He reaches up to my face and wipes away a tear from my cheek. The action is so intimate that I think we're both surprised by it.

I immediately stand and impatiently offer him my hand. He grabs it and I pull him up. He towers over me for a moment, just like Ethan.

I look up at him. Sunlight illuminates his face. His eyes reflect both the golden sunlight and the amazing blues of the Pacific. I'm mesmerized for a few seconds.

"Bring him back to me."

"I will."

All at once, I'm uncertain and disconcerted by the way he's looking at me. "I love Ethan," I say instinctively.

"I know."

There's this unease between us now as we both silently acknowledge this unspeakable connection and the invisible line that we've just summarily drawn between us.

"We share Ethan. We both love him," I say.

"Yes."

I stare at him. A shadow crosses Brock's face, just as the sun moves behind a cloud. Somehow, I'm still caught up in this peculiar moment with him and unable to look away.

But then, he turns away from me. This chilling sensation travels through all of me and gets even stronger the farther he gets from me.

Unhinged, I watch as he runs back in the direction we came from.

I attempt to shake off this bizarre reaction and the uncertainty the man stirs up inside of me and race to catch up to him. He glances over at me and tries to smile, but I sense a similar unrest within him as well.

We run in silence, side-by-side, back down the beach towards home, towards my life, towards Ethan and Max.

I'm disconcerted by the depth of our conversations, the promise I've extracted from him, and something else.

The remnants of long-ago grief and the incredible fear of being left all alone stir awake, deep inside, lifeless embers that have just been waiting to catch fire.

Chapter

Three

Brock - Foxtrot tango free bird

At 10,000 feet above sea level with no sea in sight, breathing labors in the thin air. Light-headedness plays a significant role. Minds wander.

Clear thought gets lost in the body's constant, determined search for oxygen. The body knows. It begins shutting down the extremities not essential to survival. Acclimated, these high altitude effects are less noticeable, but they're there, even for two Navy SEALS, like us, surveying the scene from up above.

The rest of the SEAL team below us are far enough away and still enough in their movements that it proves difficult to discern them from among the desolate atmosphere of dust and straggly tree growth that wends its way into being. We no longer even attempt to identify this foreign plant life in this God-forsaken place called Afghanistan. I take an exorbitant amount of time to disengage my eyes from the horizon in front of us, debating my need for movement against the ten dollar wager for doing so. I finally give up and look over at Ethan.

He keeps his left eye steady on the scope of his rifle.

"What?" Ethan asks in an unhurried tone.

The man is The David—a statue of extreme patience and marble stillness. He smirks, while still looking straight ahead. He's been this way, since we were kids fishing at Logan's Pond in Austin.

"You giving up, Wainwright?"

I have lost so much money to Ethan I will have to pay for Max's college education. We make constant bets on who can stay still the longest. I always lose, but I still wager with him on a daily basis, if only, to better pass the time.

"Ten bucks," I concede, gratefully moving my head and stretching my body. My back aches from being on my stomach for this long. No matter the five hundred sit-ups I do every morning and every night. Being motionless for this long is always a battle between willpower and physical discomfort for me. Not for Ethan. He can go hours without doing more than blinking and exercising his trigger finger with only the slightest of movement. I've concluded he is more machine than man. I can tolerate the silences, but not the stillness.

We have been doing this mission for almost five hours. The light of the day has changed. Soon, the twilight will wreak havoc on our ability to sight anything within ten yards of us, let alone a thousand yards out.

We lay side-by-side, like two people married to each other for too long, not exactly touching, but singularly aware of the other. I see his mouth curve up into a familiar grin as he feels my continued stare. Having served together for the past three years, we're known as the best snipers on our team. We've become somewhat revered among our Special Forces unit and always draw the short straw for sniper duty. If I'd had a brother, I would have wished for someone like Ethan. I know he feels the same. We're close. We have been since we were eight and found ourselves sitting next to each other in Mrs. Clausen's third grade class.

From my perspective, Ethan has it all. He tells me I have it all. He seems to admire my stamina for the coveted rest and relaxation that always includes plenty of alcohol and sex with beautiful random women, while I envy him for his life back home in California, most of all, his wife and son.

Since our return from the States, this last tour has been different from the ones before. Something's changed. Everything's changed. Most of all, the two of us.

I know he struggles with missing them too much; it's affected his concentration in the mundane things that we have to do every day. Since spending part of our last leave together at his beach house, I can understand now how much he misses Jordan and Max. Being so far away from them must make it worse. Having finally met them, I envy him, even more, for everything he has. His life back home is everything I secretly want.

We never talk about Annie. I forbid it, but I'm reminded of her now. Jordan Holloway has brought everything back for me.

Ethan and I spend the better part of each day together. Our constant conversations about his life back home and my escapades, infrequent, as they are in this foreign part of the world, keep us going. My liaisons seem insignificant now. I've begun to live through Ethan's daily correspondence with Jordan, fully appreciating her total devotion to him and his to her. Remembering my promise to her to bring him back safe sends a tremor through me now. God knows I would take a bullet for him and I know he would do the same for me, but, something's different. Something's changed. I cannot name it, but I *feel* it. But, I need to concentrate and stop over-thinking everything. A lack of focus on the battlefield is what can get a Navy SEAL killed. I chastise myself for drifting and re-situate my scope on the dead-looking scenery of Afghanistan in front of us.

We pass the next hour talking about Max. Jordan has enrolled him in a new pre-school, and Ethan is upset that he's missed his kid's first day at the new school. The pictures that Jordan sent along with the email seem to just make him feel worse instead of better. He moves impatiently beside me, and I'm a little alarmed at his unusual lack of concentration. Ethan doesn't normally let life in California affect him at all, and especially not on a mission. His growing edginess becomes more obvious as the minutes tick by. I watch his uncharacteristic restless movement.

"What's up?" I finally ask.

"She's thinks she's pregnant. She missed her period. I mean, I knew she was talking about it, and God knows we weren't overly concerned with contraception when I was back there. It's just..." Ethan stops and gives me a bleak smile. "I'm not going to be there."

"We've got another leave in six months," I say slowly. "Mid-September."

"Yeah. But I'm missing *all of it*. I don't know if I can do this anymore."

Ethan glances back at me one more time. His stern look telepaths that this conversation is over. He readjusts his rifle and looks into the scope again. I sigh heavily, finally letting go of the deep breath I've been holding since his news and refocus my eyes on my sighting scope and scrutinize the landscape. Then, I look deeper, pulling my eye even closer to the scope and try to determine if the puff of dust I just saw is real or not.

"Congrats, bro," I finally say.

"Am I terrible for hoping she isn't pregnant?" Ethan asks.

I'm hoping she isn't, too, for these completely selfish, secret reasons. Visceral jealousy roils through me. Jordan might be pregnant. Ethan is always the lucky one. And, what am I? The one living vicariously through my best friend's life and fantasizing about his wife every other God-damn minute. My time at Ethan's home in Malibu has stirred feelings inside of me that I haven't allowed myself to feel since Annie all those years ago. And now I have them for Jordan, Ethan's wife, a woman I can never have.

I wallow in the memory of her, remembering how incredible she looked on our last night there. Jordan's cheeks, flushed, as she lithely moved in her sexy black dress and oversaw the serving of all this amazing food at the restaurant, Le Reve, where she works. "The dream, that's what Le Reve means in French," she'd said to me with a laugh.

We toasted that night to her and Ethan as they celebrated their fourth anniversary a little early. We drank to Jordan as head chef, the fabulous food, and the evening itself. It seemed all of us imbibed in the expensive champagne, but probably me, most of all. I attempted to drown my lust for a woman I could never have in California's finest sparkling wine. I turned Ashleigh Blondell down that night, feigning I was too drunk to perform and needed my rest for the flight out. The truth was I spent a miserable night on Ethan's living room sofa, feeling sorry for myself, regretting my brief liaison with Jordan's best friend, and suffering with the dawning revelation that I wanted Jordan, herself, most of all. My best friend's wife. I couldn't stop thinking about her that night or every night since then.

Now, I've missed something Ethan's said. "What? What did you say?"

"Where did you go, Brock? I think you just missed the last five minutes of everything I just said."

"Maybe." I give him a sideways glance. "Fill me in?"

"Nah. I shouldn't keep talking about her. It just makes it worse."

"You should have told her about Austin. The jewelry," I say in a low voice.

"I know," Ethan says miserably. "In a few months, I can work out the funds and she'll never have to know."

"She'll eventually have to be told you're moving her and Max to Austin," I say.

"Yeah."

"She wants to open a restaurant of her own. At least, you got that right." I sound accusatory. I take my eyes off the scope and glance over at him with an apologetic look.

"I just wasn't planning on a second kid right now. She's not going to have time to run a restaurant if she's pregnant." Ethan says. He gets this anxious look. "And, we'll need the money to keep things going in Austin."

He takes his finger off the trigger and rubs his eyes. I look over at him in surprise. His lack of concentration is more alarming than mine.

"Can we just *not* talk for a while?" Ethan asks, irritably.

I just nod, because, frankly, I can't talk about his wife with him anymore today. I'm struggling with the dreams I had of her late last night. I wish I'd never met her. Then, maybe, I could take up my normal escapades in this foreign place and forget all about Jordan Holloway. Maybe, she wouldn't invade my every waking thought or my dreams at night, if I'd never met her. Ethan is talking, and I've missed what he's said again.

"I should have told her," he says now. His remorse is unmistakable.

"Can we just concentrate on the God-damn mission?" I ask, adjusting my scope, and attempt to focus upon the landscape in front of me again.

"I don't know. Can you?" Ethan's irritation matches mine.

"If you can, I can."

We retreat into an unusual, stony silence.

"Here we go," Ethan whispers fifteen minutes later.

Most people could barely hear him, but I do. Most people would miss the sudden anxiety in his tone, but I hear it.

"Fuck," he says beside me.

I re-sight my scope, again. And, there it is, the slight swirl of dust and the unfamiliar black boots among the dark shadows of the brush to the north. I quickly sight the advancing movements of the rest of our small team, but know they're still oblivious to the danger just to the north of them. With my right hand, I grab the radio positioned at my left hip to let the unit below us know there is trouble coming right at them.

"Foxtrot tango free bird. There's movement to the north of you."

The radio comes back with nothing, but static. Ethan swears again, even before I finish the radio call. I look through my scope, make my spotter's analysis, and rattle off the coordinates to him.

Ethan dials them in on his rifle with fast urgent clicks.

I frantically try the radio again. "Foxtrot tango free bird. Movement to the north."

"God damn it. God damn it, Brock," Ethan says, a few seconds later. "Get the hell out of here!"

I hear his rifle shot. At the same time, I feel the air slice between us. It takes another second to realize we're under heavy fire as shots come from everywhere all at once.

I push back for a second and see Ethan slumped over his rifle. I grab him by his left forearm and deftly pull our gear along with us as I go crashing back down the side of the mountain with everything and both of us. When I reach a flat hidden spot, I summon all my strength and lift him up over my shoulder, ignoring the knifing pain that rolls through me and then, judiciously make my way down the treacherous terrain.

Bullets zip from all sides, as if we're metal duck targets in an arcade game, but I keep to the shadows and hide behind the giant boulders scattered across the landscape and map the way in my mind back to camp.

As per our training, I utilize the terrain as cover and go radio silent to protect the rest of the team. The danger fades along with the daylight and the ping sounds whirring through the air get farther from us.

I'm talking to Ethan the entire time about how we're going to make it back, ignoring the relentless pain knifing its way through my shoulder and chest. There's all this blood mysteriously cascading down my right side like an uncontainable oil stain.

"It's going to be okay," I say, trying to catch my breath. "I'll get you back to Jordan and Max. Hang in there, buddy. "

Four hours later, in total darkness, I barrel into camp with Ethan. I yell for help. "Get a medic. Now! I need a medic for Holloway!"

I gasp for air, realizing I've been holding my breath on and off for hours. I feel light-headed, but elated because I've managed to save everything. Everything. All of it. Both of us. I feel this immense relief for keeping my promise to Jordan.

One of the medics races towards me. *Finally. I can let go.* I gently set Ethan down on one of the barrack's cots and watch the medic dive in, ready to demonstrate his medical feats on Ethan. The medic, right beside me, shines a flashlight across Ethan, and says, "He's dead," at the exact same moment that I grasp this truth in looking at my best friend's face.

Ethan's right eye is open. The other—a fatal chasm—hemorrhages blood and brain matter.

The darkness closes around my own sight and extinguishes the last of what I know as standard operating procedure. The mission all but finished. The earthquake of painful loss deep inside of me opens up, and the once stable ground of my life crumbles inward.

Chapter

Four

Jordan Wonder woman

It was an ordinary day on the Phuket beaches of faraway Thailand, the day after Christmas 2004. The sun rose, heating up both air and sand on the bleached white beach. It was the promise of another perfect day in the middle eighty degrees Fahrenheit where bikinis, sandals, sun hats, and sunglasses would be the norm. The long Palm branches made a reed-like swishing sound in the gentle breeze, while birds chirped familiar notes much like the high keys on a piano delicately played. The tourists combed the coffee shops in search of morning coffee, croissants, and trinkets to remember the holiday season with. Thai natives embraced the normalcy of another day—another ordinary one poised for its predictability, even in paradise. All unaware that change was on its way spawned from a 9.1 earthquake in the guise of a killer wave that had already wasted much of Sumatra and Indonesia.

Some tourists and Thais were curious as the water swept out of the bay at Kata Noi Beach. The unusual ocean life suddenly left behind—an amazing sight to behold for the curious. A gift of nature holding mysterious wonder, some of the tourists and Thai people ventured farther and farther out, exploring nature's surprising bequest on this otherwise ordinary sunny day. But, the birds must have stopped singing and the reed-like rustling sound of the Palm trees must have served as the only prelude to the main event. Soon, a wall of seawater estimated as high as a hundred-feet in some places rolled in from far across the Indian Ocean. Its onslaught toward the shore built with forward momentum was unstoppable. Its destruction unforeseen. Its devastation so final. The tsunami swept over virtually every living being and inanimate object in its path. Death came to the beachcombers first and swept them out to sea. Then, the tsunami took virtually everyone else along the seashore and long into the city of Phuket—five thousand eight hundred souls in all. Later, the world would learn of the tsunami's human toll: destruction over Indonesia, Sumatra, Africa, even as far away as China. The official number of people that died from the tsunami: two hundred, twenty seven thousand, eight hundred and ninety-eight people. One third of the deaths were estimated to be children, perhaps, too small to escape the destructive waves. Fourteen countries were severely impacted by nature's devastation that day. The indiscriminate destruction and loss reverberated around the world touching people in some way, everywhere.

My day starts out, ordinary, just like that one. It is more than six years later. Max plays in the backyard, his blonde head visible from the kitchen window. I pour a good measure of cream into my coffee, take a seat on the back deck steps, and casually watch him. I marvel at his good nature which is so like Ethan's.

He chases down a butterfly and strays towards the white picket fence gate and the beach that leads down to the sand and the Pacific Ocean below. One stern call of his name brings him back and he flashes me a smile as if to say, I know, Momma. I smile back at him and sip my coffee.

There isn't a cloud in the true blue sky and I lean back, resting against the sun-kissed warmth of the steps. Ethan was here just a month ago and I have this twang of heartbreak. Fourteen more months and we are done with this tour. Fourteen more months and he'll be home for good. He promised me this time.

My heart aches for him; I miss him so much. Six weeks together, between tours, is not enough time, not enough time for me or Max.

I bite my lip in vexation and try to forget my varied temper tantrums over his leaving again. How much time did I waste fighting with him? On his last night here, we stayed up all night making love and plans. I told him I was off the pill and he had just smiled and said, "Come here." We worked on future children the entire night. I smile at the memory now. I'm more than a week late. Two days ago, I wrote to Ethan, telling him I might be pregnant. I'm still in shock that I would get pregnant so easily, even though the same thing happened with Max.

Max calls out to me. I smile at my towheaded blonde child and he grins over at me with this mixture of mischief and adoration. The fact is I miss Ethan terribly, but Max makes it bearable. Max saves me from dwelling on the aching loneliness I carry deep inside for Ethan. The recurrent heartbreak I battle, this recurrent heartbreak in missing Ethan on a daily basis and attempt to combat this overwhelming loneliness. The truth is no matter how many people I surround myself with; I still miss Ethan. I look up at the sky and see the misting remnants of last night's moon. Can Ethan see it? Is he thinking of me at this very moment? I blow a kiss at the sky and manage a wan smile, though I can still feel the sadness reaching for me.

I can't decide if it's worse because I might be pregnant, or worse, because of this weird melancholy that I have been unable to conquer for the last day or so.

I glance at my watch. Ashleigh will be here in another four hours. Louis is running things tonight at Le Reve. I have the night off, for once, which is probably why I'm experiencing all these wayward disconcerting thoughts. *I'm not busy enough.* I grimace and look for Max again.

I close my eyes and try to clear my head of this pervasive worry over Ethan. Instead, I try to enjoy the morning sun that attempts to warm me all over. I hear nature's concert with the musical wrens flitting from our Palm tree and the distant crash of ocean waves from the Pacific. The light breeze caresses my face and lifts the tendrils of my hair from my face. I pull the band out of my hair and run my fingers through it and let it hang freely. The reassurance of Max's small voice as he talks to himself stirs me from my reverie and reminds me of what's important.

I am here. I am blessed with this amazing child, Max. And, there may be another on the way. I love a man who loves me back. This is a perfect life. *Almost.* If he were here, it would be perfect.

But does he see you? The strange conversation with Brock drifts back to me.

"Yes. Yes. He does."

I hold Ethan's latest email in my hand and re-read the part where he tells me he loves me, misses me, and reminds me that we only have four hundred and two days to go. He wrote this two days ago. I shudder and chase away the thoughts as to why he hasn't written back to me. *Maybe, he's out on a secret mission. Yes, but he always finds a way to write to me.*

This time he doesn't. I shake my head to clear these menacing thoughts and close my eyes.

"Ethan, where are you?" My whispers go unanswered.

The wind makes an eerie sound. I open my eyes and anxiously watch Max as he carries a bucket of sand up the slide ladder and prepares to go down. Less than a minute later, he's coming down the slide. I keep from crying out a warning to him to be careful by holding my breath and silently chastise myself about being overly protective. I breathe a sigh of relief when he lands on his feet at the bottom. I close my eyes again; luxuriate in the serenity of the warm sun, my child's laughter, and thoughts of Ethan.

❧❧

An hour later, the sound of a car coming up the drive doesn't really register with me, until I hear the subtle whir of the car's engine shut off and then two car doors slam almost simultaneously. I get up from the back steps and peer through the front window. It is the color of the car. A dark blue color with dark tinted windows. The kind of car meant to be nondescript. The black tires without the white stripe. Whitewalls. The absence of whitewall tires is the second clue. The kind of car whose appearance is meant to be unobtrusive and not noticeable and yet, because it is not flashy, because it is dark blue and the tires are plain black—it actually calls attention to itself. People *do* notice it. *I notice it.* I stand behind the screen door now and watch it settle in my driveway and try to ignore the significance of the two men in all full dress white uniforms alighting from this nondescript dark blue car. I glance at the last hint: government-issued plates. I have ten seconds of remaining naiveté before full comprehension comes over me and takes away my smile for good.

I call to Max in a daze. "Mommy has to answer the front door. Stay there, Maximilian."

My heart pounds fast, now. I can't catch my breath because I realize that the fissure from the earthquake inside of me has already opened up.

I open the front door with trembling hands and take in the clean-cut looks of the two full dress white uniformed officers with their white hats in their hands. They don't even have to speak any words because I already know who they are and why they're here and what they're going to say to me.

The we're-so-sorry-for-your-loss speech barely registers. The tsunami wave of heartbreak inside of me is so great it has already done massive destruction and damage to my human spirit. I hear these distant piercing screams that will not stop.

"Make them stop," I say at some point. One of the uniformed officers comes over to me and puts his arm around my shoulders.

"Mrs. Holloway, is there anything we can do? Anyone we can call for you?"

"Make the screams stop," I beg.

"We're so sorry for your loss."

The officer's blonde crew cut looks so much like Ethan's and the blue eyes. He's not as tall, but the reminders are all there.

I reach for his outstretched hand, trying to remain steady, but the tsunami—the giant wave of dark grief just keeps coming. I can't escape it. I fall into his arms in the awkward hug he offers me.

"Is there anyone we can call?" The officer whispers in concern.

"Ethan," I say in a faraway voice.

He repeats his question. I see this sympathy for me in his eyes when I supply him with my husband's name again.

"Ashleigh," I finally say.

Dazed, I look over at my three-year-old, who has come in from outside bearing a yellow pail of wet sand and trailing some sort of sodden blue rope from his swing set and can only stare. One of the officers bends down to him and rescues the pail of sand from spilling onto our bleached hardwood floors and carries it back outside.

I watch all of this from some closed-off place of detachment, while gasping for air.

"Max."

It's all I can say as I suddenly forget how to form words.

I hold out my arms and he runs into them. I bury my face into the crook of my young son's neck and smell the sweet scent of him—the remnants of Johnson's baby shampoo, freshly-cut grass and wet sand from this morning's outside play adventure. I pull him close to me. Then, the wave of grief takes over. All I can see is this dark abyss. It circulates through all of me. I can feel myself get swept away.

Ashleigh drops me off in front of the funeral home in Washington D.C. and promises to be back in a few minutes. Impatient, I gather enough strength to open the front door of the building and step inside. The gloom envelops me in the first thirty seconds. *Fuck.*

I introduce myself to the hovering figure before me and register his first name is Igor. Incongruent with his last name, Dasher. The funeral director.

Perfect.

"Can I see him?" My voice is clear, resolute. It rises above the cloaking din of the mortuary.

"No," Igor Dasher says to me.

"Yes."

I wave my hand. As if, my hand, alone, can intimidate this beady brown-eyed man into helping me. Saving me, really. I have to see Ethan. I have to hold his hand no matter how cold it might be. I have to. I have to see him, so I can make sense of this thing. I have to say good-bye. I've begun speaking aloud, apparently. The little man before me has gone a vanilla shade of white. His pallor is all the more natural in this depressing circumstance.

"The Navy has specific instructions that prohibit such requests—"

"Fuck the Navy. He belongs to me, not them. He's mine. Do you hear me?" My voice goes up by two octaves and Igor Dasher takes a step back from me. He looks me over, taking in the simple black dress I'm wearing, not knowing its significance for both Ethan and me. Our first date. I'm wearing the cocktail dress I wore on our first date. I wipe away a stray tear. Igor Dasher continues to study me.

"Fine," he says with resignation. "Don't say I didn't warn you though. This is not what we normally do for gunshot victims."

I wince at his words, but wave my hand again, convinced now that such gestures give me some kind of superpower with the man. "Fine."

"Fine," he echoes back to me. "Give me a few minutes." His voice is curt. I stare him down as he backs out of the room away from me in his hideous green velvet suit. When he's gone, I fight for breath and sway a little and grab the nearest piece of furniture, which ends up being a wood table with an open coffin on display all done up in white satin.

"Fuck," I whisper in the still room.

The sunlight pierces the dim space through one of the few windows in this front parlor. I watch the dust particles in quiet interest float through-out the room in its stubborn illumination.

"Fuck," Ashleigh echoes as she enters the room. "The God-damn rental car is parked. Only in D.C. would they make you fucking pay twenty bucks for parking ten blocks away."

"Well, it just adds to the happy occasion, don't you think?" My retort is sharp and I immediately apologize by putting my arms around Ashleigh. "I'm sorry. I'm not myself."

"Who would be?"

She hugs me back and I try to draw solace from her embrace. I feel as if I'm living in a strait jacket weighed down by invisible constraints I'm unable to undo and half drowning. I have felt this way, since the first day. The first day of knowing he was gone.

"The guy's going to let me see him."

"What? We talked about this. I'm not sure it's a good idea."

"So you've said." I pull away and cross my arms and lift my head in defiance. "I've got to see him and say good-bye in my own way."

"Jordan, it's not—" Her voice trails off at the sight of the funeral director's green velvet suit. The incredulous look on Ashleigh's face is priceless. Her fashion sense is even more perfected than mine. I begin to laugh in this inappropriate way at the comedy of our circumstances. The mortician continues to make his way towards us and I stop laughing all at once and begin to experience this extreme panic that my husband will be touched by this loathsome man. Has been touched by him.

God, why have you done this to me? My little prayer goes unanswered.

I steel myself against the state of affairs in which we are all held hostage and reiterate my need to see Ethan for both of them. Ashleigh tries to put on a brave front, but when I ask her if she wants to go with me, she shakes her head. Retrieving a cigarette from her purse with trembling hands, she finally escapes outside with contrived casualness about need-ing a smoke. All this from a girl who doesn't even smoke.

I shrug my shoulders in contrived nonchalance at Ashleigh when she looks back at me and follow Igor into the inner chambers of his sanctum. I move with trepidation following behind him down the long predictable dark hallway.

My heart pounds so loudly; I'm sure he can hear it. He gives me a surreptitious look as he opens a door to his right.

We enter a tomb of a room shrouded in red velvet and there is Ethan lying out on a long table. Why bother with a bed for the dead? I cringe inward at the morbidity of my thoughts. *Fuck.*

"Leave us," I command.

"But, the law states I have to be present." I turn and give the man a withering glance and wave my superhero hand again. After a minute, he bows out of the room as he did before. "Ten minutes, Mrs. Holloway. Ten minutes. That's it. This is highly unorthodox."

"Fine."

I spend the first two minutes keeping my distance from the man who lies before me. He's dressed in his best suit, the gray one he was wearing when we met. Not surprising, it still fits. Ethan—the impeccable dresser, the finest athlete, the bravest soldier, the best husband, the most doting father. He did everything well. He exuded charm, grace, and humility in every way. He is god-like, all powerful and mighty, even lying here.

I am drawn in to touch him. I trail my fingers along his hands tucked peacefully across his chest. I ignore the clamminess of his skin, the stiffness of his fingers. I've lain with this man for hours. I've heard the gurgling of this man's stomach too many times in our most intimate moments when we would laugh at the sound and its peculiar timing. I lay my head down and listen now, but hear only lifelessness. The stillness of him is so final.

"Don't leave me, baby," I say in the imposing silence.

I lift my head and stare at his face. Pale. Still. Silent. So, unlike him. I wait an indeterminable moment for him to start talking.

"Say anything. Say anything. Say anything at all. I'm here. I'll wait. I'll listen."

The silence wends its way around me like an invisible spider's web.

"Say something. *Anything.*" I whisper.

His head is partially covered with a white silk handkerchief and I pull it away, before I can think of why the cloth is there in the first place. And, there it is. The clear reason on why Ethan would never be saying anything to me, ever again. His left eye is missing. Part of his skull.

Igor must have done his best to clean up the brain matter and dried blood before he permitted me in to see my husband like this, but no white silk handkerchief was going to be able to cover up the violence that has been done to him.

I kiss his lips, untouched by the brutality imposed upon the left side of Ethan's face.

"I will always love you, Ethan." I stroke his head as I've always done and it's the one thing in touching him that feels the same; his hair moves like the finest boar brush under my fingers. "I will always love you."

My tears fall on him now and the wet trails make their way down each side of his face. I kiss his neck and then his lips, again. After a while, I burrow my head into his left shoulder. For the first time in days, I feel this tranquility come over me. I close my eyes and revel in the closeness of being with him, again.

Reunited, even as we are. The cruelty of our circumstances plays out in the tranquility of the room like a fine mist dissipates into parched earth.

"Ethan," I say, lifting my head from his shoulder and looking into his lifeless face. I can only stare, waiting for him to answer me. I lay my head back down, close my eyes and begin to cry, again, harder now.

"Mrs. Holloway? Are you? Are you all right?"

Igor Dasher has come back into the room. I open my eyes at the sound of his weary voice and look over at the edges of him in his fine green velvet suit. His image swims before me. My sobs fill up the room now.

"Fine. I'm fine."

He seems to smile, if that is at all possible for the man, at my lies.

He glides across to me as if he is on wheels in this slick bumper car motion. One minute he is across the room, in the next, right beside me.

"Your friend. She's looking for you."

He takes my arm and pulls me towards the door. I turn and take one final look at Ethan.

"Love you for always," I call out to the motionless god lying on the table.

I swear I hear Ethan's voice call back to me, 'Love you, for always, Jordan.'

Good. I'm crazy.

Good. That's good.

That's fine. Fine.

Igor Dasher is looking at me in alarm and I fear I've spoken my thoughts aloud, but he refrains from saying anything more. I grace him with a benign smile, as we glide down the hallway together arm-in-arm. The funeral director hands me off to Ashleigh with a fervent wave of his left hand and not another word. The man seems more comfortable among the dead. I give him this beseeching look, attempting to convey my wishes for him to take care of Ethan in the most respectful manner. As if reading my thoughts, the green velvet man makes that promise to me.

"Thank you, Mr. Dasher," I finally say. "Thank you for letting me in to see him and say good-bye."

CHAPTER

FIVE

Brock – A coordinated assault

I OPEN MY EYES AND SEE NOTHING. Nothing, but blackness, as if I am in a cave without a light source. I blink several times, as if, somehow, by doing so, I will dislodge the darkness that surrounds me. I still can't find the light.

I shake at the sudden touch of a hand upon my arm as a sweet voice whispers, "Welcome back, Lieutenant Wainwright. How do you feel?"

"I can't see." I try to control the tremor in my voice and the one that shoots through my body—a fault line shifts inside, causing me to tense up all over.

"I'll be right back," she says.

A few interminable minutes later, I feel the bed move beneath me.

"Lieutenant Wainwright. You're awake," says a new voice. Male. Authoritative. Haggard.

"I can't see," I say again with matched authority that all but commands him to *fix it*.

There is this unfamiliar sensation with panic that stirs to life inside. It threatens to surface as the minutes seem to grind by. A hand touches my eyelids and pulls them back. Looking. Looking. *Looking for what? I can't see.*

My breathing gets labored the longer this goes on. My heart rate speeds up, and this burning sensation stabs at me at mid-chest.

"What is it? Why can't I see?" My words come out harsh, but I keep going. "Why can't I see?"

"Yes. The medic on scene said that you complained of that after you returned to camp. Before that," he pauses. "Could you see before that?"

My mind races, thinking back to what he is talking about. "Before when? What are you talking about?" The terror threatens to surface. I gasp for air.

"Do you remember returning to camp?"

"There was a mission. Ethan and me. We were on a mission. A long hike." Flashing images of Afghanistan roll through my mind. Tall grass. All the fucking dust. I turn my head, as if I can hear Ethan talking to me. My eyes search the darkness and try to make out an image, an image of any kind, but there's nothing. *I see nothing.*

"It was dark," I say in a low voice. My throat tightens. I squeeze my eyes closed and then open them again. "It was all black. Treacherous terrain. Carrying everything. I know I saw the light of the camp." My voice trails off as my mind attempts to deal with the present and nothing but darkness.

My memory must be playing tricks on me; it flashes with the images of a black night of Afghanistan. I lean back against the bed. My head is caught between two pillows. I struggle to gain my balance and reach out and feel the cold steel of what must be the bed rail. My breathing gets more uneven.

"Do you remember anything else?" he asks.

"What? No. I don't remember anything. It's too dark."

The reality of darkness attacks me from all sides. The pain in my chest worsens. Blackness engulfs me. I close my eyes, trying to escape its oppressiveness. I open them, but it's still there. I struggle to catch my breath. *I'm forgetting something. What is it?* Something happened, but I can't remember what it is.

"Lieutenant, we're doing everything we can. You have multiple bullet wounds in your right shoulder and the upper chest. Fortunately, it missed your heart and we were able to re-inflate your right lung." He stops. He just stops talking and sighs heavily before he goes on.

"We can't explain the blindness."

"I'm a spotter. With a sniper team. A Navy SEAL. *I can't be blind.*"

I can't control the fear in my voice any longer. It takes over my whole body and my mind. I groan and put my arm over my face. Sudden exhaustion assails me. I feel helpless and out of control. In response, pearls of sweat spread across the surface of my skin, everywhere.

The blackness swims all around me, like the murky water of Logan's Pond back home. Just thinking of my father, the pond, my mother, and home somehow lifts me up. It's just enough to take a much needed breath.

"It's probably temporary," he says. I detect the uncertainty in his voice.

He will not give me false hope. I open my eyes, discover the blackness, once again, and let out a jagged breath. I close my eyes, then open them again. There is no difference whether they are closed or not. It is all black. *There is nothing. I see nothing.*

A door opens somewhere near. I hear the click clack of a woman's high heels meet up with the linoleum floor. The sound comes toward me, capturing my attention.

"Dr. Smith, I thought I told you to come and get me as soon as the lieutenant was awake?" A different female voice. I hear her heavy breathing, as if she's been running, but sense she's angry.

This modicum of satisfaction at her telling off this Dr. Smith cheers me up. *Tell him, sister. Let's fix this thing. Tell him now how we're going to do it.*

"Right, okay. I'll leave you to it," says the voice I now designate to Dr. Smith. His angry retort sounds insincere.

I take solace at this heated exchange. A minute later, there's the sound of the door closing with a resounding bang.

"Asshole." I start to smile upon hearing her whisper this. She takes a deep breath, and the faint scent of her perfume drifts towards me. "I'm Dr. Richards. Kate Richards. Major Kate Richards, Lieutenant Wainwright," she says. The woman outranks me by one, and I try to control the grimace that automatically travels across my face at hearing her rank.

"Major Richards," I say dryly.

She kind of laughs. I hear the scraping of a chair against the floor. Her scent gets even stronger, and I presume she's brought the chair close to my bedside. Then, she firmly grips my right hand.

"Do you remember what happened to you?"

I sigh heavily and feel growing frustration and this incalculable fear at the same time. *How many times am I going to have to tell them I don't remember anything?*

Finally, I answer, "Carrying a lot of stuff to camp. It was dark. I remember seeing the camp's lights up ahead. It was tough—the trek back to camp. Mountains. Terrain. I think I cut myself up a bit on some of the jagged rocks as I made my way down."

I've run out of words, and I wrack my brain to try to remember more. "Where am I? How long have I been here? Why can't I see?" I tack on all these questions as the panic within me begins to travel outward.

She strokes my hand in regular rhythm; I'm caught up in counting the number of times she does this, while a weird sense of calm comes over me.

"Lieutenant, you've been in this hospital for the past nine days. You've had major surgery on your upper torso. Both your chest and shoulder were hit by gunfire. As Dr. Smith must have told you, you're lucky to be alive."

"I can't see." My retort is harsh and I no longer try to hide the anger and panic. "I need answers, now!"

"You've been through a harrowing experience," she says in a soothing voice. "And, we're trying to determine what has happened to your sight. It seems to be triggered by a traumatic event. Can you tell me anything else you remember? Anything at all. Take your time. Close your eyes and think."

Time wallows. It just wallows there like the mysterious stillness of murky water where something terrible is bound to be lurking. In this case, it's this undeniable fear I succumb to. I'm lost, out of sorts. I can't breathe.

"Tell me anything you remember." Her coaxing is mesmerizing on some level; it brings me back. Her bedside manner is obviously her "A" game.

I don't answer for a minute or two, trying to breath evenly again. I sigh, frustrated with the barrage of the same set of questions from two different doctors now. "All I can remember is this feeling of racing against time. That I needed to do everything I could to get back, taking the terrain triple time. I can't remember anything else."

There's a long silence. I sway in the blackness, feeling light-headed and worn out all at the same time, while Major Richards continues to stroke my hand.

"Okay, I want you to just lie back and rest. Listen to me."

She doesn't talk, though. She stops, while I wait in this utter blackness, silently pleading for her to go on. I hear her sigh heavily and sense her sudden hesitation. I go on high alert. I brace myself, both mentally and physically, for what she's going to say to me next.

"Lieutenant, you were ambushed—under fire with your partner, Lieutenant Holloway. Do you remember?"

"An ambush?" My mind races, but the images are no more than flashes of dark and light. "No."

How can I not remember any of this?

"Ethan? Is he okay?" I ask. She takes another deep breath as if playing for time. Apprehension begins to close all around me and my breathing gets more labored. "Tell me what happened."

"I can only tell you what we have been able to piece together."

Her qualifying statement seems to be some kind of warning for me. I hold my breath and wait for her to continue.

"You and your partner were ambushed. You were under heavy fire. But, somehow, you brought all the gear and Lieutenant Holloway back to camp. You carried it all. All the gear on one shoulder and Lieutenant Holloway on the other back to camp. Ten miles back to camp in under four hours. You called out for the medics as soon as you arrived. Do you *remember* any of this?"

"No. It was pitch black. Rough terrain." My voice is barely audible.

A fear, greater than the one I have about the blackness, begins to swirl around me like an oppressive heat wave.

"Where's Ethan? Lieutenant Ethan Holloway." I enunciate his name slowly, as if she's hard of hearing or merely a five-year-old child. "Where is he?" I choke out.

She sighs again.

I take a jagged breath, then hold it, and just wait.

"Lieutenant Holloway is dead." Her voice is so soft that I strain to hear her words.

It takes a minute longer for them to even register. *Ethan is dead.*

The minutes go by. I breathe in and out and swim with the blackness. My eyes sting; I fight for breath and control. My mind seems to fracture into a million pieces, while my body embraces absolute stillness, like the tectonic plates of the Earth shifting underground, wreaking permanent destruction.

Ethan is dead.

Five minutes? I still haven't said anything. This stranger, this woman, continues to hold my hand, continues to stroke it back and forth. I breathe, matching the rhythm of her strokes. I still don't say anything. The darkness of grief is as unbearable as the one that envelops my sight. My best friend is dead, and I don't even remember how it happened.

"No." I finally say, making sure she understands that I won't accept this outcome.

She grips my right hand tighter. "I want you to know how sorry I am. I understand you two were close. You grew up together?"

How does she know that? Leave it to the Navy to provide a complete history in my case file. Bitterness fills me up.

"In Austin. We grew up together in Austin. Signed on to the SEALS at the same time. Live together. Fight together. Shoot together." I recite our shared motto, as if by doing so, I can undo everything she's just told me.

"What I also want you to know is that we're going to do everything we can to help you get your sight back," she says in this gentle voice. "And, in the meantime, we'll do everything we can to help you cope with the loss of it."

She lets go of my hand. Helplessness invades me. This unfamiliar feeling of being lost and swallowed whole in darkness takes over.

"We'll talk tomorrow," she says.

I scowl at her promise and even more as her voice gets farther away from me.

"We've got a lot of work to do. You need your rest."

"Let's start now."

"No. It's late. We'll start first thing in the morning. Lieutenant, you've got to give your body and mind time to heal. Whether you remember it or not, you've been through a lot."

"Where am I?"

It's a belated question. I should have asked that already. Now, I'm afraid to know the answer.

"Stateside." She pauses. "This is Walter Reed National Military Medical Center in Bethesda. Get some rest, Lieutenant. It's after midnight. I'll be back tomorrow morning, and we'll start our work then."

I hear the click of the door and feel the oppression and combat the sudden fear of being alone. All of it presses down on me.

Two things cause me to shake: I'm not in Afghanistan any longer. Most wounded SEALS are treated in the field and return to the line. This fact implies: this is serious. Secondly, Ethan. Something has happened to Ethan and I can't remember any of it.

He's dead. There's a part of me that cannot even fathom this outcome on any level.

I lay back against the pillows, open my eyes, over and over, hoping to see something, *anything*, but the result is the same every time. Blackness. It's like being a prisoner in solitary confinement trapped in complete darkness—this not seeing thing.

I try not to think the word, but it comes out of nowhere into my head. *Blind. Blind. I'm blind.*

Ethan is dead. Ethan is dead. Ethan is dead. Darkness hasn't just taken my sight; it takes my mind as well. I try to reel it back to a better place, but I can't.

I listen intently for human sounds, but all there is is the endless ticking of a clock and only the intermittent sound of muffled footsteps outside of my hospital door, but nothing more. When I'm relatively certain I'm alone, I allow myself to feel the incredible sorrow of losing my best friend. The tears stream down my face. I don't even make an attempt to wipe them away. My left shoulder and the middle of my chest begin to pulsate with this intense pain, as if this is a coordinated assault on both my soul and physical form.

CHAPTER

SIX

Jordan – Wreck of the day

"BANDITOS." I GRIMACE, REMEMBERING, AND LOOK over at Ashleigh. Her shoulders sag as she acquiesces with a nod and I go on. "That's what they called them there. People that preyed on the tourists. The seamy side of Barcelona. In a country where the laws were different and perpetrators like them were so rare and hardly ever caught. Banditos that lured the tourists out into the countryside. They preyed on couples—oblivious, trusting souls, like my parents, looking for adventure and willing to leave the protected confines of resort life and the safe side of Barcelona and venture out in an unfamiliar and unprotected place. And then, the banditos did whatever they wanted. First, they blindfolded them and told them if they cooperate everything would be okay. Then, they stole their cash and all their credit cards and within hours racked up thousands of dollars with their accomplices. Males. Females. Banditos. They worked in groups of four or five. They stole my parents' virtues and, then, made sure they would never identify them again. Banditos. They left this out of the brochure, when they lured us to Barcelona." My tone is bitter and I do nothing now to hide it.

"How come you never told me the whole story?" she whispers, shocked.

"We didn't want the paparazzi to get a hold of it." I grimace as she looks over at me in disbelief. "What? Scare the shit out of you at seventeen on how cruel and unusual life could be? That would hardly be fair."

I force myself to smile and move from the refrigerator to the counter in a regular rhythm, intent on the task of baking chocolate cupcakes for Max's preschool. This is incongruent to the funeral planning that Ashleigh and I have been doing, but I cannot seem to stop myself from performing this ordinary task. A mother's wish, I guess. The busier I keep myself, the better contained the raging grief inside of me will be. That's my hope, at least.

"And, now? Why are you telling me, now?"

Ashleigh pushes a tendril of her long hair behind one ear. Her face is streaked with old tears. There have been two of those—crying jags. Well, she cried, while I felt nothing, but the pervasive grief. It's invaded my system and taken over. Ethan has been dead for ten days. His funeral is tomorrow.

"I don't know. It's weird. I've never been able to talk to you about it—what happened to them. But now, I can't stop thinking about it, and them, and what I saw then. It's some sort of…well, it's some weird, fucking form of closure, I guess."

I shrug my shoulders in bewilderment. I haven't been able to explain the nightmares I've been having about my parents and all the horrible moments I lived through when I was just seventeen that resurface now.

"Why?" Her gentle tone is almost my undoing. I move abruptly toward the refrigerator, again, turning away from her.

"Ashleigh," I say in a low voice. "Ethan." My voice trembles with just saying his name. "It was just like my dad. I can't get the image of Ethan's face out of my mind. It haunts me. I wake up every day and, for the first minute; I feel fine and then, that horrible last memory of his face rushes at me. I can't get it out of my mind."

"I wish you would have listened to me about that." She waves her hand through the air and then frowns at me. "You don't always have to be so fucking brave, you know." She twists her hair around her finger. A sure sign she's thinking deeply about something.

"Right now, I'm just so empty. I can't feel anything. Sometimes, I wake up and my world seems so ordinary, but then, I remember and I struggle to make it to the bathroom before I'm throwing up, sickened at the thought of him dead and remembering his face and how he looked. His beautiful face."

I sink down in the chair and hold my face in my hands.

"It won't always be like this. You know this. Remember? I was there when the stuff happened with your parents and you picked yourself up and you started over. Look at you. You fell in love and married Ethan. You have Max." Her desperate tone matches the one I continually hide from her. I live in my own private hell.

"I thought I was pregnant. Maybe, I was. I told him I thought I was. I wrote him an email, ecstatic because I'd missed my period. What if that upset him? What if he got killed because of me? Because he was distracted? Because of me," I whisper.

"No," she says, shaking her head. "He would have been thrilled, not distracted at all. Are you pregnant?"

"No," I whisper. "I got my period this morning."

"I'm so sorry." Ashleigh comes over and puts her arms around me.

I cannot find my way back to the surface. Grief is like this turbulent ocean wave that holds me down below the surface of the living. I feel as if I'm drowning most of the time. Ashleigh holds me in her arms and tells me everything is going to be okay. I want to believe her, but I can't.

"He's gone, Ashleigh. He's gone. I can't believe it. I just can't believe it."

"I know. It's so God-damn unfair."

Her swearing makes me want to smile. I pull away from her and she brushes back the hair from my face.

"Jordan, I just want you to know; I'm here. I'm not going anywhere. I'm here for you."

"I know." I try to smile, but the effort is too much. Finally, I swallow back the emotion building in my throat and in a trembling voice say, "Keep the tequila shots coming at the funeral. We're going to need them."

My best friend enthusiastically nods and steals a round of frosting with her outstretched finger and tries to smile. I watch in fascination. I'm reminded of Brock Wainwright doing the very same thing just six weeks ago.

For a moment, I let go of the hatred I have for him now, but then, it returns full force; I stagger back overwhelmed by its visceral force. I turn away from Ashleigh's probing gaze.

"Are you all right?"

"I'm just going to go change," I say. "Frosting everywhere."

"You're sure you're okay?"

"Geez, Ash. I'm fine."

I race down the hallway, gasping for air. I shut the bedroom door and sink down to the floor. In the sanctuary of my bedroom, I cajole myself to cry. Just cry for him. No one is watching. The heaviness is all around me. I close my eyes and welcome the blackness. I welcome it.

Dear God, let me cry. But, no tears fall.

⁓⊙⊱

Ashleigh has gone to pick up Max from preschool and deliver the cupcakes we've spent the afternoon decorating. Of course, I had to make them perfect, and after more than two hours of loving labor, little gray marshmallow replicas of sharks peak out of each one. I smile to myself knowing Max will be pleased. I'm doing everything I can to keep up the normalcy for him.

Ethan's last image flashes through my mind. Regret for the thousandth time for demanding to see him that way courses through me. I just had to see him in order to believe that he was really gone and then his face was so reminiscent of my father's. Now all these buried memories over the death of my parents resurface. *I feel the fear. I live with it.*

Days later, I am still reeling from the coincidental circumstances of all of it. The tragedy that pervades my life and the continual suffering of grief that presses down on me in all these inescapable ways.

Now that I'm alone, I unlock the desk drawer and open the box with all my teenage collections of memorabilia, including the police report and crime scene photos of my parents from Barcelona. My ability to read Spanish is rusty, but still better than my ability to speak it. I'm not sure what is worse, the description of my mother—sexual assault multiple times, facial lacerations, and throat slit—or the picture of her, where all I recognize is the color of her beautiful red hair. My mother. I stare at the grotesque picture of the beaten body of this woman labeled with my mother's name. The colors—purple, black, blue and red—make messy modern artwork of this once-beautiful woman. My mother. I flip through the rest of the crime scene pictures and see my father's face swim before my eyes. One green eye is open the other is a dark hole. His dark hair's matted with dried blood. It reminds me of Ethan.

With resolve, I finish the report as if I haven't read it all before. The banditos shot my father execution style, early on, from what the police surmised in the report. Then, they tortured, raped and killed my mother. The photos are gruesome. I cringe as I study them. My parents were beaten everywhere by their captors—these frenzied, out-of-control animals. Banditos. The police infer that it is only after the victims begged, that's when, mercifully, in the end, it *was* mercy that they killed them. First, my father. Then, my mother. At the time, I was assured by Officer Fernandez that they would find them. The Spaniards had been intent on catching the perpetrators, since dead Americans were bad for tourism. Famous, dead American actors, even more so. But, they never found them. The horrendous crime that took my parents from me was never solved. The flash of the hotel room the night of their murders returns full force. I envision myself as a young, scared teenage girl waiting for her parents' return. I remember the tears streaming down my face as I leaned against the wall. I'd left all the lights on in the hotel, somehow, believing that light would bring them back. After midnight, I'd called the front desk and told them that my parents hadn't returned. Officer Fernandez and the concierge, Annette Torres, arrived shortly after. Waiting the indeterminable five minutes after making that one phone call seemed like hours. When I heard Fernandez's rapid knock on my parent's hotel suite door, I remember going up to the door and swiftly realizing my life was changed with my first glance at the grim look on the police officer's face.

"You found my parents?" I'd asked, still naive and still hopeful in that moment.

"Yes." His answer would be the last word I heard for days after. The stark reality of being all alone engulfed me like a rogue ocean wave. The damage to my psyche had already begun and all the trust issues that arrived with it that I carry now. It's true. All the fairy-tales and happily-ever-afters deserted me with his utterance of that single word. Yes. Grief moved in on me so swiftly. I never did regain my balance. Then. Now.

I swallow and feel the familiar constriction in my throat. My eyes burn, but no tears fall.

I'm shaken from my reverie of those tragic moments, the old ones and the new ones, by the distinctive ring of my cell phone. Ashleigh has been screening all my phone calls for days, but now I feel compelled to take up the task on my own. I answer automatically without thinking of who might be on the other end.

"Hello?"

"Jordan, it's Brock Wainwright."

His voice seems so far away. I'm momentarily stunned to hear it.

In the next moment, it brings me back to Ethan and what has happened. Was it really only six weeks ago that we were all here doing tequila shots late into the night and laughing?

"Lieutenant." I hear the sadness in my own voice.

"Jordan, I just want to say how sorry I am. I was just told about Ethan last night. It's not enough to say I'm sorry, I know."

"Just told about him? What the hell are you talking about? You were *there*. What happened?"

"I don't know. I can't…I can't remember." His voice is barely above a whisper, but I press on.

"You promised me, Brock. You. Promised. Me." All the rage at my situation in losing Ethan culminates in that moment. "You promised me. You said you'd keep him safe. You promised. And, now? He's…gone. He's dead, Brock. He's dead!"

"Jordan, you have to believe me when I tell you how sorry I am. I…love…loved him like a brother."

"No! You don't get to tell me that! I *loved* him. And, you…promised me you'd keep him safe and bring him back to me. Well, he's back all right. I guess I just forgot to specify to bring him back alive." My pulse races as I unleash the fury at him that I've harbored deep inside for the past ten days, the past decade.

"I'm…sorry, Jordan. I'm so sorry."

I don't answer for a long time as I try to contain these competing emotions: this incredible rage and heartfelt remorse for my outburst. I gulp the air and finally say, "His funeral is tomorrow. Ashleigh came with me to D.C. and we flew his body home to Austin. The funeral will be in Austin. We leave tonight on a red-eye flight from L.A. You should come."

I hear him take in an audible breath and then he says, "I won't be able to make his funeral."

"Why? Why won't you be able to be there? He…he would have wanted you to be here. He would have done that for you."

"They won't release me." His voice is bleak when he says this.

I fight with feeling sympathy for him and the fury I have had for him at the same time. "What? Where are you?"

"I'm at Walter Reed in D.C."

"Walter Reed. Why? What's wrong with you? The officers wouldn't give me any information about what happened. Tell me, Brock."

"They're not sure what's wrong and I can't tell you what happened. I haven't been able…to remember what happened."

"You can't remember?" I struggle to breathe. "Ethan's dead! Oh God."

I stand up and begin to pace the floor unable to hang up the phone. Finally, I recover enough to say, "He would have wanted you at the funeral. He loved you. He would have wanted you to come."

"I can't."

He sounds so broken it momentarily gives me pause; I almost feel sorry for him, but then, the rage overtakes me.

"Find a way. Ethan would have. Look, I can't talk to you anymore. I'm sorry, but don't call me anymore, Brock. There's nothing left to say."

"Jordan, wait—"

"No!"

I power off the cell phone and undo the land line in case he tries to call me back on the house number. No more phone calls. Not one. Because there's nothing left to say to anyone, least of all, to Brock Wainwright.

❧❦

I've been here before, when at seventeen, I buried my famous parents, Davis and Laurel Breckenridge. Ten years later, I'm here, again, to bury Ethan. I'm alone. Once again. A punishment I've been expecting. *I am the tortured soul.* Brock Wainwright was right the entire time. The thought of Brock Wainwright brings about the powerful relentless emotion of pure hatred. Putting all my energies into hating Brock Wainwright has been rekindled in me at a soul level these past twelve hours.

I sit in obscurity at the side entrance to the church on these wretched cement steps and stare out at the long-forgotten garden. Withered stalks of Gladiolus, long dead and black with mold, keep me company. I breathe in the neglect and vegetative carnage and feel right at home. Maybe, I'll just sit here all day.

The smoldering cigarette in my left hand begins to singe my fingers. I throw it to the ground and smother it with the toe of my black Blahniks. Manolo isn't helping me out today. Being dressed to the nines in my favorite color from head to toe isn't working.

I light up another cigarette thirty seconds after putting out the last one and inhale deeply. I smother the cough that rises in my throat, determined to suffer in silence in any way I can. My eyes begin to water and I blow the smoke out in desperation and cough, anyway, despite my self-determination. I stare at the cigarette and inhale again. The nicotine rushes through me and I start to smile at the weird heady feeling. I'm not a smoker. The politically correct rules would say the widow shouldn't be smoking. But today? I do. I don't care. I don't give a damn. Not today. Not the day, I'm burying Ethan.

"Hey," Ashleigh says from behind me.

She takes the cigarette from my hand, takes a few puffs, and hands it back.

"I should be saying you shouldn't be smoking," she says.

"I should be saying, fuck you, but I don't," I answer back. She laughs; I make a concerted effort to laugh as well.

We share in this conspiracy together. It reminds me of the time we tried cigarettes at seventeen—the end of summer between our junior and senior year. My parents had been dead a couple of months and I remember thinking that there was no longer anyone around to truly tell me what to do or watch over me. My grandfather didn't count. He wasn't too enthused about taking care of a grandchild he barely knew. He and my mother had a falling out, about what, I never really knew. My guess was it had something to do with my father. Davis Breckenridge was not my grandfather's favorite, my mother had once told me.

Now, I half-laugh, remembering how Ashleigh and I decided that no matter how cool we looked, cigarettes probably weren't going to be in our future, except when we really needed to fulfill a desire for social deviancy. Obviously, that day has arrived. Earlier, we had a shot of tequila in the limo on the way here. Ashleigh knows what I need before I do. This morning, we both agreed that all the rules should be broken on this day.

I don't care. She knows this, too.

❧❦

I stand at the front of the church and stare at the dark wooden casket that holds Ethan. Cremation. I wanted cremation. Ethan said once that would be his preference, too. Maybe, he had a premonition that he would die a violent death. Maybe, the thought of rotting in the ground bothered him as much as it bothers me. But, Ellen Holloway couldn't bear it. If I had an ounce of love for Ethan's mother, it has been annihilated in the last eleven days. Ethan will rot in the ground in Austin because of his mother. The process has already begun with his face. Despite the best efforts of Igor Dasher to make him as presentable as possible—his face is still missing. Ethan wears his finest suit, the charcoal one by Armani that I loved on him so much. He wears the silk boxers, the black ones, I bought him for his twenty-sixth birthday, two years ago. He wears his gold wedding ring and his Rolex. But, neither vows nor time nor his favorite things will bring him back to me. No.

I finger the key to his casket. I bury it deep into the palm of my hand. It's tied by a thin red ribbon around my left wrist. The sharp edges dig in. I close my eyes and ride the small waves of pain it provides. Pain of any kind, physical or mental, I welcome. I just want to feel something before the numbness asphyxiates me completely.

The good news out of all of the bad is this: I have caved on every major decision with Ethan's funeral, except one. Max is *not* within a twelve-hundred and thirty-five mile radius of this spectacle. If five hundred people in Austin need to pay respects to Ethan at his funeral, his only son will not be among them. Ashleigh backed me up on this and Max's preschool teacher was more than willing to take him for the week. In fact, she'd insisted that he stay with them and Max was enthralled with the idea of spending time with his best friend, Davey.

Max. I have tried to explain to him that Daddy went to Heaven and that makes Mommy really sad. My son just nods and gives me a bewildered look. He seems to comprehend that we won't be able to see Daddy, again, until we meet him again in Heaven, but that is as far as the tragic event that has transpired with us registers with my son. I'm grateful that Max is doing all right, but feel this constant agony and struggle to hide it from him.

I'm unable to compartmentalize my own grief in the same way as my child. I have no faith in Heaven. No faith in God. No faith in seeing Ethan again. He's gone. He's just gone.

"Brock's here," Ashleigh whispers to me.

I look over. He's in his full white dress uniform coming in from the back of the church with a blonde woman dressed in a navy dress, holding on to his arm.

"Not alone. A beautiful blonde at his side, how typical." My sarcastic tone causes Ashleigh to give me the once-over.

"Are you all right?" Ashleigh whispers.

I give her a stony look and try to nod.

In the next few seconds while the crowd settles, I covertly glance beyond Ashleigh at Brock Wainwright. He grasps the blonde woman's arm and then slides in at the end of the pew, right next to the aisle across from us. He looks, well, awful. His right arm is in a sling, so his uniform jacket is slung over his shoulder on one side. His face is drawn as if he hasn't slept in days and he is wearing dark glasses. He looks straight ahead and the blonde whispers something to him and he just nods. I tear my gaze away and try to concentrate on the beginning of the service.

Ashleigh has planned most of this thing, so I watch in a daze as the funeral unfolds. The music she's chosen is poignant and beautiful and I get lost in its sad melody. The priest starts to talk about life coming full circle and I judiciously tune him out after a while. *Fuck the full circle.* I paste a serene look upon my face and try to ignore the priest's imploring predictions that life goes on and it's God's will and all that slick stuff that must bolster all the rest of the mourners here.

I want to shout: What do you *fucking know* about it, Father? But I don't. No. I giggle inappropriately at my silent wicked rant. Ashleigh gives me a crooked smile and squeezes my right hand.

It's my turn to go up and speak. I debated about this, of course, but now, I rise as if Ashleigh has implanted puppeteer strings within me and make my way to the lectern.

"Thank you all for coming. He would be so touched by all of you for being here today."

I stand up taller and summon courage. I hold my prepared speech in my hand, but the words are out of focus. I look over at Ashleigh and she just nods with encouragement for me. I try to smile.

"Ethan always liked a party, especially if it was for him." I smile out at the crowd and hear the faint rustle of hushed laughter from the large crowd. My smile disappears. I falter and clutch the sides of the lectern still tighter. "I don't know all of you well. He was always more outgoing than me. One of those the cup of life is half full people, while I was forever pointing out the empty part. My parents. My parents would have loved him." The onlookers snicker again and I draw a breath before going on. "I guess that's how it goes. Opposites attract. He was the sunshine to my rain. He could find the best in an ordinary day of clouds and I gravitated towards his rays. He taught me how wonderful life could be and he gave me so much. And for that, I am truly grateful."

All these people are crying. I'm disconcerted at hearing it and pause again. "But, we always want more. I always wanted more. It was simple really. I wanted more time." I'm transfixed and stare out at the crowd and single out Brock Wainwright and his all white uniform. "We always want more." My mind drifts. I break away from staring at Brock and glance around the room. The minutes tick by. The crowd gets a little restless, a little uncomfortable. *The widow is over-sharing. The widow is me.*

I smile with a great deal of effort.

"I wrote a poem. That seemed the best way to…remember him." I smooth out the piece of paper before me and begin to recite what I've written.

"The world seems to have stopped spinning on its axis,
Now, that you're gone.
I look to the sky for a sign
A sign of you
And there you are.
The sparkle in the sun's ray
The gleam in Max's eyes
The gentle breeze that blows in from the ocean
The splendor of you is everywhere,
And, in me.
I miss you.
In loving you,
Ethan,
I've found—
so many wonderful gifts.
Your magic is everywhere
Inside of me.
You are the promise in each new day
And the beauty in the stars at night.
You are life's perfection.
And, in loving you, to have had you touch my life, I feel truly blessed.
And now, I carry you inside my soul."

I hear all these people crying now. There's a concerted creaking sound through the crowd as mourners scramble for fresh tissues.

I concentrate on navigating the four steps that lead away from the podium and past Ethan's casket. I grasp Ashleigh's outstretched hand and slide in beside her. Then, I glance over and I'm taken aback when I see Brock stand. He holds on to the blonde woman's arm and she leads him forward to the platform talking into his ear as they go.

What am I seeing? What am I missing?

Six weeks ago, this guy was so full of life, and today, I see nothing, but a broken man before me. I watch him grip the lectern and the blonde woman continues to talk only to him. She finally moves a few feet away, but keeps vigilance.

"He's a better fisherman than me. We met in third grade at Quake Elementary. We liked the same girl, and it would seem we would come to blows over this, but the girl changed her mind and chose my first cousin, Tate, over the two of us. Ethan and I made up and forged our friendship at Logan's Pond, where I taught him how to properly rig a fishing rod, and we've been friends ever since. When I eschewed law school with only a semester left and signed up for Navy SEAL training, Ethan did the same. I taught him how to shoot a rifle at twelve and he became better at that than me at sniper school. The only thing he did without me was marry Jordan." He pauses, having captivated the entire church with the low timbre of his southern drawl and his amazing story. I hold my breath to keep from crying out as his pain of losing Ethan reaches for me.

"Ethan and I served in Afghanistan for the past three years. We are… were on our last tour together. He promised Jordan he was coming home. But I have to be honest; I'd grudgingly agreed to it being our last one, but I didn't really want it to end. We had this amazing friendship and we got to spend a lot of time together. As Jordan has just told you, Ethan was a special guy to be around. One of a kind." Brock stops talking.

He seems to have lost his place and I watch this incredible sadness come over him. He grimaces as if he's in deep pain. There's a peculiar thaw of the hatred I feel for him. It gives way, just a little, in witnessing his own devastation in losing Ethan. Then, the blonde leans in and whispers to him. My hatred of him returns full force. I watch him nod. He grips the lectern and starts again.

"Sorry. It's hard to put into words what he's meant to me. Jordan asked me to be here and I'd told her I wouldn't be able to come, but then, I realized she's right; Ethan would have done the same for me. He was the bravest man I knew. His ability to stay in one place, not moving for hours, was amazing, in and of itself. He made me want to be a better soldier. A better man. Ethan loved his life—his wife, his family, his friends, his country. He touched everyone and I believe he made all of us better people for having known him and loved him. He touched my life in so many ways and I'm sure he's done…he did the same for all of you in some way. The world is a harsh place, but Ethan reminded most of us here, I would think, how truly wonderful it can be and, for that, I am so grateful for having known him, for having loved him." Brock's voice seems to falter at this point and he stops speaking.

There are tears running down everyone's face again, including Brock's. But, I sit dry eyed; watching him in this distant cold detachment. The anger begins to fill me up and work its way outward.

The blonde takes his left arm and he grimaces, again, as if in tremendous pain. It dawns on me that he hasn't removed his sunglasses and I feel this intense resentment that he's wearing them, apparently afraid that people might see him cry. The gall of the man. I'm in a rage all at once. I abruptly stand as he moves past me.

"Brock, thank you for coming," I say with barely contained anger.

He turns his head toward me, but keeps moving.

"I'm so sorry, Jordan."

"You should be," I say. The Austin crowd all around us gasps at my outburst, but I'm undeterred. "I think you should go."

He nods, turns away from me, and doesn't say anything more. The blonde woman keeps her arm around him, glares back at me, and then leads him back up the aisle and out of the church.

I glance at Ashleigh. She moves in close and holds me by the shoulders.

I shake my head, back and forth. "He promised me."

Ashleigh whispers, "Promised you what?"

But now, I'm too distraught to answer. The inconsolable tears of grief I've been calling upon for days finally fall.

CHAPTER

SEVEN

Brock – I'll see you soon

BLINDNESS TESTS ALL OF ME. My ability to depend on others has always been suspect. The only person I ever fully trusted was Ethan. Now, I'm among strangers all the time. My unit still fights in Afghanistan and other than a quick visit from my commanding officer, Captain Thomas Stein, telling me how sorry he was, I've got no one. Not all true. I sent my parents packing after their two-week vigilance at my bedside after my foolhardy return from Ethan's funeral, which led to a collapsed lung because of a wayward bullet fragment and almost cost me my life a second time. After another fourteen days in the continual darkness, my mother's lyrical reassurance that everything was going to be fine and my father's stoic silence was more than I could handle.

I'm on my own.

Still alone. Still blind.

Fully immersed in the company and care of strangers, I've become close to Major Kate Richards. I live for her voice, her perfume, the familiar click of her shoes as she taps her way across my hospital room floor, and her seductive voice when she asks me how I'm feeling every day. It's part of her nature, part of her job. I never would have given a psychiatrist a second look in my former life. But, in this one? Kate Richards has misted her way into my psyche, both professionally and personally. Maybe, it's the vulnerability of my situation. I can't see, so I'm more dependent upon the only person who seems to understand me these days. Never mind the incessant and endless questions she has asked me from my personal life to my time served in Afghanistan. The woman has left nothing to chance as she tries to undo my mind's prison that holds onto my sight.

"Will I ever see?" I finally asked her a few weeks ago.

"I don't know. There's no physical reason that you can't see. It's something psychological. Perhaps, something you've put on yourself that keeps you from seeing. But, Lieutenant, the longer it goes on…there will be permanent damage to the nerves." I detected the worry in her voice. I felt the acquiescence in her demeanor, even though I couldn't physically reach out and touch her right then.

"Who wants to be with a blind guy like me?"

She didn't answer for a long time and then, when she did, it changed everything between us. "I do."

❧✦☙

The door to my hospital room opens and I automatically look up toward the direction the sound came from. I sigh at my own reaction. *Will I ever get used to this darkness?*

"Lieutenant Wainwright," Kate says to me.

"Major," I say in my most seductive voice.

"They're releasing you. Your wounds are healed enough…"

I grimace at her sudden hesitation. "Go on. Get it over with."

"The blindness appears permanent. As you know, we haven't made any more progress in prompting your memory."

She stops again and clears her throat.

I wait.

"I've made arrangements for you to attend the Criss Cole Rehabilitation Center in Austin. It's out of process, but I've convinced them to take you. That way you'll be near your family there." Her tone takes on this consoling bedside manner. I frown in her general direction as she sits down beside me. "You'll learn to better cope with the blindness," she says. "They'll teach you Braille, how to use a walking cane, help set up your permanent residence, assist you with your career choices, get you a guide dog—"

"So, you're giving up on me," I say with a sardonic tone. Her body shifts next to mine.

"No," she says in a low controlled voice. "It's the best way, Lieutenant."

"Major, don't tell me you're about to break protocol."

Her breath comes faster. I smile.

We have been playing around with this growing thing between us for a couple of months and I am suddenly more than ready to take it to the next level, desperate to take it to the next level, even.

"Stop flirting with me, Lieutenant," she says. "I'll come visit." Her tone gets more serious. A hint of caution seems to play in her tone. She sighs before saying, "I can't…be your psychiatrist anymore, Brock."

She lightly touches my hand with hers and then she moves off the bed and away from me.

"Kate, wait. Don't go."

"Have to." Her silky voice is farther away and I wave my hand through the air hoping to reach for her somehow.

"Kate."

The sound of the door clicking closed is my only answer. Another door, like so many in my life, seems to have closed.

⧂⧁

With the voice command feature on my cell phone, I place my sixty-fifth phone call to Jordan Holloway's home number. It's been just over four months since Ethan's death, but Jordan has yet to take or return any of my phone calls to her. I'm prepared to leave another message when she answers on the third ring.

"This is Jordan."

I'm taken aback at just hearing her voice. Her breathing comes in a rush as if she's been running or doing stairs.

"Uh, it's Brock Wainwright. Don't hang up! I *really* need to talk to you. I wouldn't be calling you if it wasn't important."

"I have nothing to say to you, Brock."

I wince at hearing her barely contained anger. *She hates me. She blames me. And, why not? I blame myself.* I hang my head.

"What is it? What do you need to tell me?"

"Look, I'm the executor of his estate. Like it or not," I say gently. "We need to talk about some things."

"When? Where?"

Panic sets in. I wasn't planning on meeting her in person. She still doesn't know I'm blind and I want to keep it that way.

77

"We don't have to meet in person," I say quickly. "I just wanted to ensure we set up a time to talk in the next couple of days or so. I've sent the documents to you. If you could look them over and then we could talk. Does that work?"

"Okay, I'll look around for them and then we can talk in the next couple of days and I might even answer your call." Her attempt at humor should make me laugh, but I hesitate too long and it comes out as a forced tittering sound.

"Is there something you're not telling me?" Jordan asks.

"There are some things with the estate that we need to talk about. You haven't returned my calls."

She laughs at my accusation. This soft laugh that causes my heart rate to speed up. "Don't feel bad. I haven't returned anyone's calls, except Ashleigh's. I've been pretty pissed off at the world, at Ethan, at you."

"I'm sorry, Jordan."

I hear her take a deep breath. "I know. Me, too," she says after a minute.

Closing my eyes, I imagine her standing right in front of me. My free hand reaches out as if to touch her face. I smile despite the circumstances. The irony of it all. My being attracted to her is probably the reason Ethan is dead. Guilt attacks me with a full frontal assault with this thought.

"Jordan." I speak her name with this unbelievable reverence. I shake my head in an attempt to get a grip on the emotions she stirs up in me in just talking to her. "If we could just be friends," I say with diffidence.

Another silence. A long one. I shift my weight, trying to maintain my balance as I wait for her answer.

Her exasperated sigh says it all.

"Truthfully?" Her voice trembles. "I'm not ready to be friends with you." There's another long pause. "Brock, I've really got to go. I'm picking up Max from preschool. I can't be late."

"Sorry," I say without attempting to mask my disappointment with her answer. I shake my head and silently curse the darkness. "Okay. I'm flying home to Austin, tomorrow. I'll call you in a few days."

"I thought you'd be back in Afghanistan by now."

"Yeah. Me, too." Bitterness seeps into my voice and she must hear it.

I need to end this call before she starts asking me too many questions. Instead, I'm hanging on to every word she utters.

"Why aren't you in Afghanistan?"

"I'll talk to you soon," I say. "Take care of yourself, Jordan."

"Why aren't you in Afghanistan?"

"It's a long story," I say. "They can't use me right now." I wince at my excuse, hoping she doesn't pick up on its faulty reasoning.

"That doesn't make any sense. You have to finish your tour."

This is spoken like a true military wife. Tours, obligations, contracts. I'd underestimated Jordan's familiarity with all of it. *Shit. Hang up the phone, Wainwright.*

"None of it makes any sense," I say.

"Where *exactly* are you?"

"I'm still at Walter Reed. They'll be releasing me in the next day or so. Then, I'll be in Austin for a while."

"What? Why? You were at Ethan's funeral. How can you still be in the hospital?"

"There were complications. I had a few more surgeries."

She takes a shaky breath. I strain to hear her and discern the tapping of her shoes, and, finally, the start of a car's engine.

"What's going on, Brock? What aren't you telling me?"

There's a hint of worry in her voice and, like a fool, I savor it. "The flight back from Austin to D.C. with the cabin pressurization dislodged a bullet fragment and entered my lung. That took some time to recover from…" My voice trails off. *I'm telling her too much.*

"A bullet fragment? Were you *shot* that day, too?"

"A few places." I hold my breath as I crave her sympathy while at the same time I cajole myself to reject it. "I'll call you, Jordan."

"What happened that day? If you could just tell me."

I close my eyes at hearing her desolation, realizing she just wants to make sense of it all, too. So do I. But I don't have any answers for her. "I wish I could, but I don't remember anything about that day." I breathe deep and let it out slowly, feeling light-headed by the action. "Take care of yourself, Jordan. I'll call you in a few days. Give Max a hug for me."

I end the call before she can respond, berating myself for saying too much. I don't want Jordan to know I'm blind because the last thing I want from her is sympathy. *What do I want from her?* I don't allow my mind to answer. Being blind is one thing, but having Jordan Holloway know about it is quite another.

⋛⋚

Awash in conflicting thoughts about Jordan Holloway, I fail to hear the opening and closing of my hospital room door, until Kate's seductive voice stirs me from my reverie.

"I've got your final paperwork to sign that essentially makes you an out-patient at Criss Cole. Did they tell you that you're being awarded the Medal of Honor?"

I grimace, while pushing myself away from the window ledge, unseeing. "Doesn't matter."

"Oh it does," she says, touching my hand and placing a writing pen in it. "Sign here, just like we practiced."

"How do I know what I'm signing?"

"You can trust me."

I nod. Right now, Major Kate Richards, famed psychiatrist, is the only one I trust. She touches my hand, the signal we worked on a few days ago, indicating where I should be signing. I hear the shuffle of papers and wait for her next move. *I could be signing my life away. But then, what is my life these days?* Blackness swims at me.

"There. All done. You're officially no longer a patient of this hospital. You are officially an out-patient with Criss Cole in Austin, Texas. It's all arranged."

"I'm packed, ready to go. I guess my mom will be here soon enough to cart me home."

"There's been a change of plans," Kate says softly.

"What do you mean?"

"Well, it's your last night in town. I thought I would cook you dinner. At my place. Your mom is meeting you in Austin tomorrow morning."

I swallow hard, knowing we may have just crossed over to a different threshold in defining our relationship. There are a lot of things to consider about this. I'm not looking for anything long term. I'm not looking for anything short-term. I'm not looking for anything because I can't fucking *see.*

My mind races with all these competing thoughts, but I remain silent, even as she takes one of my hands and clasps it between both of hers.

"Kate," I say with a sigh. "I don't. We can't..."

"Hey," she says. "We can just be friends. Okay?"

"Okay."

I close my eyes and just nod.

"I just thought, maybe, you'd like a home-cooked meal and I was going to take you to Criss Cole, myself, in the capacity as your friend, your companion for this road trip. Nothing more." The tremble in her voice betrays the casualness of her words. Her body shakes next to mine.

"Friends," I say to another woman for the second time today. "We can be friends."

I force myself to smile.

⚜

A friendship with Kate lasts through the car ride to her apartment in Georgetown, through a home-cooked meal of Le Cordon Bleu, which I suspect she's gotten from a take-out restaurant. Even the Tiramisu for dessert is suspect. She finally admits she bought it at a famous deli just down the street. The woman is mixing French cuisine with Italian, but her secret is safe with me.

Ironically, she has a love of jazz music like one of my former girlfriends and I find myself wanting her even more by the time we start in on the second bottle of wine.

I'm out of practice, out of shape, out of options, even. I long to ask her what she looks like and in lieu of actually posing this question, I begin to explore her hair, her face, and her body with my hands. This brazen touching in search of answers leads to more.

I'm selfish. Alone. Blind. Vulnerable. Pick one. Part of me wants to have sex and just get it over with. All my insecurities about being blind and being able to still perform will finally be answered. Maybe, I'll resume my old life and fuck my way through it.

Kate is the perfect conquest. I know her. Somewhat. I trust her. Somewhat. She's the only one in the room I do trust. Because. Right now? I don't trust myself.

The blackness swirls. I get up, unsteady, and grip the furniture, only stumbling once as I feel my way over and reach out to a large glass window. I spread my hand across the glass. It feels cool to the touch even for June in D.C.

I wonder what the weather's like in Malibu? A memory of Jordan running along the beach reaches for me.

Kate laughs lightly behind me and I feel her spread her fingers across mine. She kisses the side of my neck. I drain my wine glass in a single gulp. I turn around as she takes it from my outstretched hand and sets it down. Her fingers explore the inside of my jeans. Her boldness surprises me as she takes hold of me. I discard the thoughts about the weather in California and even the woman, I covet, who lives there.

Once the proverbial role-play of seduction begins, it's only a matter of minutes before we're both undressed. Kate explores my naked body as much as I explore hers. No words are actually exchanged between us. We acknowledge the taboo restrictions that the military imposes upon us—no fraternization between officers— in a shared silence. It slowly comes to me that unless I can see I will no longer be an officer serving and that this may be what Kate's been waiting for all these months. *Three months. Almost four?*

I swim in the blackness while a part of me registers this building frustration at not being able to see her. Yet, another part of me feels liberated when I experience these unique sensations with her that are arousing and exquisitely different. I savor her touch, her scent, even the sounds she makes. Things I've never paid attention to before. I jettison the feelings of intimidation and vulnerability and become bold and more assured in my movements. If this is some kind of sick experiment with Dr. Kate Richards in fucking me, I don't care.

All my reservations about doing this are extinguished by the time we make it to her bedroom with the euphoria of foreplay.

"All the lights are off. It's pitch black," Kate assures me with a soft laugh. "I can't see anything more than you can."

"Come here," I say, harboring a need for control.

I hold out my arms. She slides into them and reaches up and touches my face. I bend my head and kiss her. Her hair falls to her shoulders. I run my fingers through it. I wish I knew what she looked like. An image of Jordan comes to me. I push my nose into Kate's hair and breathe deep. Her scent is a mixture of apple blossoms and garlic. When I kiss her, I taste red wine and Tiramisu. Involuntarily, my mind sifts through the comparisons to Jordan Holloway from food preparations to physical attributes. Jordan's hair is longer. I remember how it reaches the middle of her back. Jordan's signature scent is this mesmerizing lavender combined with the sweet sugary smell of cake batter and frosting. I barely stop myself from uttering her name as Kate's lips find mine.

"Kate," I say, feeling unsteady.

"Lieutenant."

"Hey, I'm practically a civilian."

"Almost," she says softly. "That's what I like about you."

We both laugh awkwardly at this juncture.

"We're way out of protocol," she says now.

I nod. With clear intention, I stroke her inner thigh and explore her further. She moans at my touch. *Some things never change.*

Her hands stroke my chest, she blows on my stomach and her lips travel further down. My breathing gets unsteady. I try to clear my mind of all other women before her with one exception. *Jordan Holloway.* Our phone conversation from earlier plays through my mind. I lose my concentration. I try to focus back on Kate. But, now, there's nothing. I have no physical response to her ministrations.

At this point, the blackness seems to swallow me whole.

"Maybe, this wasn't such a good idea," she says quietly.

We lay back side-by-side on her bed, not touching. Me, cloaked in blackness. Kate, reassuring me in that psych way of hers that it's okay and these things happen.

Not to me. At least, never before.

"I could lose everything, you know. My job, my entire military career," she says with a shaky laugh. "But *you.* You'd definitely be worth it."

I'm slow to answer, dismayed by her profound honesty, while persistent thoughts of Jordan Holloway invade the rest of me.

I slide off her bed and reach out into the blackness to balance myself.

"Don't fuck up your career over me," I finally say. "I'm not worth it."

This strange sensation of guilt and undeniable fear threaten to take over. I shake my head slowly and hear Kate's movements from the other side of the bed.

"Take your time. I'll go clean up the kitchen," she says.

I listen as she slides on her jeans. I hear the sound of her distant footsteps in the hall. By the determined tap of her high heels, I imagine she's pissed that we didn't finish what we started, while I feel this profound, inexplicable relief. I breathe deep. Maybe, my body is trying to tell me something. I dress more slowly, then spend an inordinate amount of time in search of my cell phone and eventually make a few phone calls.

✥

Pots and pans clatter together as I enter the kitchen.

I ignore Kate's anger as she continues to clang dishes and silverware with conspiring silence. I'm reminded of my father. I wince. Henry Wainwright's attitude for anything out of the ordinary, including my mother's temper, is to ignore it completely. *When did I become like him?* I fumble in the blackness into a tall kitchen chair and slide onto it.

"This was a bad idea," Kate says after a few moments.

"Yeah," I say. "For what it's worth; I'm sorry."

"Sorry for what? This is my fault. I took an oath. I have a job to do and you're a patient."

"*Former* patient." I lift my head in defiance in the general direction of her voice and curse the darkness and the sudden silence.

"It never should have happened," she finally whispers.

"Nothing happened. That's the fucking problem," I say with a harsh laugh. "I guess I'm not ready for all of this." I extend my arms around and then attempt nonchalance with a shrug, while inside I shake in real fear at my nonperformance status. "I changed my flight to tonight. I can go it alone."

She audibly sighs. With disappointment and frustration. I smile toward the sound.

"I'll take you to the airport," she finally says.

"I was hoping you would."

We leave everything else unsaid.

I swim in the darkness and allow her to guide me out to her car.

✥

On the way to Dulles, I begin to feel the familiar sensation as if I'm drowning, while Kate seems to stew in the protracted silence between us.

"I thought I'd be able to help you," she says as we park the car.

"Is that what we were doing at your apartment? You were *helping* me?"

"No," she says. "That was career suicide."

She sounds lost, confused. I reach out to her, trace her jaw and trail my fingers along her collar bone. She moans and climbs into my lap. This fear takes hold. Am I going to have the same non-reaction as before?

"I really like you, Brock," she says. I hear the uncertainty in her voice.

She kisses me slowly and I kiss her back. My mind is a blank slate for once. Kissing Kate is like a passing glimpse at my old life—a free pass.

I smile beneath her lips and luxuriate within her quest for seduction. My mouth explores hers and my body starts to respond. I breathe a sigh of extreme relief. I feel her smile beneath my lips. The sound of a car door being slammed closed right next to us brings us back. We pull apart. Guilty.

"Maybe, next time," she says, sliding off of me.

"I think you *did* help me, just not in the way we thought you would." I reach across and trace her lips. "Thank you, Kate.

I take a moment to control my breathing, leave the thoughts of the failed seduction of Kate behind, and begin to focus upon getting onto the airplane and not making a fool of myself on the way there.

We walk in companionable silence, side-by-side. I'm reminded of Ethan's funeral. Kate Richards has been my lifeline for the past several months. I owe her a great deal; yet, I struggle to put it all into words. My lack of performance, from earlier at her place, looms again. I'm reminded of my failures. There's too many of them now.

"Here. We can sit here until your flight is called."

I grip the edge of a chair she puts my hand onto and slide down into it. Then, I fumble around for her hand. I bring it to my lips and kiss it. She sighs. "Kate," I say. "Thank you for everything you've done for me."

"I wish I could have done *more*." Her emphasis on the word more makes me cringe, but I force myself to smile.

"You did *plenty*. Write to me. Call me. Maybe, everything will be different in a few months." I reach out awkwardly and touch her hair, running a few strands of it through my fingers. It's shorter than Jordan's by a good eight inches. *Why do I always compare Kate to Jordan?* I slip my hands in my pockets.

Kate guides me to the security line and stays with me until I reach the front. She talks with authority to the TSA officials. One of them grabs my arm, prepared to escort me to the plane. *My humiliation for this day is complete.*

"I'll call you in a few days after you're settled," Kate says.

"I'll see you soon." My sarcasm fails like everything else has this day.

CHAPTER

EIGHT

Jordan - Gravity

HIS EMAILS HAD STOPPED COMING. IT was the one and only sign. The man wrote me without fail, regardless of circumstances. He'd written to me every day for over three years. And, the emails had stopped coming. He'd written to me for more than a thousand days, whenever we were apart. Without fail.

And, then? Nothing. For more than two days. *Nothing.*

Ethan's silence signaled his death, long before the Navy graced my doorstep to tell me he was gone.

Months later, and I am still pretending that everything is okay, that nothing has changed. I go on with my life and perform the most ordinary of tasks, as if, somehow, by doing so, I can change the outcome of what I already know: he's gone. *Ethan's gone.* And, I carry my darkest thought, deep inside, the one I've kept secret all these years: I knew he would die someday. *Who thinks that way?* At this juncture, it doesn't matter that I abided this incalculable foreboding and saw this outcome for him. In the end, it doesn't matter whether I ever overcame my fear of losing him or not.

In the end, it didn't save him.

He isn't here.

I am.

Aren't I?

For more than five months, almost six, and counting, I pretend that everything is okay and that nothing has changed. But, we all know it has.

Friday. The first Friday in August. My mind automatically performs the calculations. Ethan has been dead for one hundred and fifty-nine days. My obsession with time persists. I shudder, thinking of what the day, not too far in the future, will be like, when I mark the number of days he's been dead and connect it with the number of days we spent together in total.

"Momma?"

I glance up at the rear-view mirror and take in the startling blue eyes of my son that mirror Ethan's. We're on our way to a play date with his friend, Davey. As always, my precocious son vies for my attention which is still vaguely absent so much of the time most days. I wanly smile as I negotiate the route to his friend's house and mechanically answer his questions.

"Yes, the clouds looked like marshmallows today. Yes, I see the elephant's trunk. No, I'm not sure why elephants are grey. Yes, I can see that some of the leaves are yellow. Yes, summer is almost over and then it will be fall."

"Can Daddy see the leaves turning?" Max asks, during a lull in our conversation.

I hesitate, debating how to answer. "I don't know," I finally say in a faraway voice. "I hope so."

He nods with an enthusiastic dip of his chin and I force myself to smile, while this overwhelming sadness tries to smother me. *What should I be telling Max? What should I be telling myself?* I swipe away a tear and try to focus on the road.

Minutes later, I catch his intense gaze at me in the car's rearview mirror. His forehead is wrinkled as if he's in deep thought.

"Will we ever see him again?"

"I don't know."

My throat closes up. I glance at the traffic up ahead and then focus back on him via the rearview mirror again. He leans back in his car seat and closes his eyes.

"Sometimes, I can see him when I close my eyes. Like this," Max says softly.

I blink back tears and smile at the same time at his thoughtful words. His simple outlook buoys my spirit just a little.

"That's when I see him, too," I finally say. The car is silent, except for the purr of the engine. Then, I accelerate with the green light.

"Momma," he says. "You'll always be here; won't you?"

I look at him intently in the rearview mirror. "I'll always be here, Max. Always."

He nods, seemingly reassured by my answer. He takes a deep breath. Then, he's looking out the window and up at the blue sky, while I'm quaking deep inside with a memory of my mother telling me the same thing when I was about six. *Why do we make these promises we can't keep?*

A flash of Brock Wainwright comes to mind. Guilt stabs at me. Why did I expect him to keep his promise to keep Ethan safe when I cannot even believe in the one I just uttered to Max?

A car honks. I reconnect to the drive ahead of me, shudder, and take an unsteady breath.

"Why do elephants mostly live in Africa instead of here?"

I wanly smile at my Max's ability to switch from the heart-wrenching questions to the easy ones. Then, I launch into a long dissertation about Africa and elephants as much for Max's benefit as my own.

⊰⊱

At the restaurant, I consult with Louis and spend an inordinate amount of time with the maitre d', Monica Lee. I laser in on the importance of tonight's private event for the Mastons' anniversary. Everything needs to be perfect I reiterate to the entire staff more than once. Louis and Monica exchange looks of concern, but I choose to ignore them. I don't normally tell any of the staff how to do their jobs. As head chef, I believe in their capabilities and allow them the freedom to execute the religious experience of dining at Le Reve all on their own. I trust them. *Normally.*

"Everything, okay, Jordan?" Louis finally asks.

He absently touches his suit lapel as he speaks, belying his frustration with my continuous speech in detailing the finer points about the Mastons' party. It's something I would normally leave to the staff's discretion, but my unfulfilled need to control something, *anything*, countermands it.

"Everything's fine." I contrive a bright smile, but it lacks true sentiment. Louis seems to notice.

"Max. He's good?" His French accent gets more distinct.

"Max is great."

I shrug my shoulders and start to turn away. He grabs my arm.

"And you, Jordan? You are okay, too?" His friendly tone is etched with concern and leaves little room for me to argue his point. I hang my head a little and reluctantly follow him to the private office we share. The place is littered with paperwork—piles of it—that I have neglected for months. Delivery orders, bills, even Max's scattered artwork seems to indict me from all corners of this small space.

Louis's constant soliloquy about looking at the documents that have piled up, a foot high, physically confronts me as we enter. As his head chef, he lets me run things my own way, but I have a feeling that is about to change.

I feel a twinge of guilt because I have put off the estate document discussion with Brock for the past month or so, too. We never did have that promised conversation about Ethan's estate. Like a petulant child, I have again ignored his phone calls and messages for the past six weeks even though I promised him I wouldn't.

Promises are made to be broken. The bitter thought pulls at me, even as I cajole myself to push thoughts of Brock Wainwright to the back of my mind. Instead, I bleakly stare at the mess in front of me and blink back tears for the third time this afternoon.

Louis pushes the largest pile to one side of the desk and sits on the edge of it. More alert to his actions, I watch as he takes a deep breath and shakes his head side-to-side.

I cringe inward, knowing this particular discussion has been building for months. We both know it. I'm somewhat relieved that this showdown is finally taking place and watch in fascination as he retraces his steps, shuts the door with a decisive click, and closes the blinds. This action effectively shuts out the curious onlookers of the kitchen staff much to their recognizable disappointment.

Louis retakes his perch on the edge of my desk. His black mustache twitches as he prepares himself for what he, apparently, has to say. I lift my head and defiantly glare at him, though my insides tremble a little. Louis treats me like a daughter; it is rare that he loses his temper with me.

Am I getting fired? Is my blowup last week at the truck driver for delivering the wrong order with our herb supplier finally going to be addressed? Is the time I locked myself in the cooler, where Monica found me two hours later, crying going to be discussed?

My life is fucked up. I'm fucked up. Is he finally going to notice?

"You are not fine." His French accent thickens with these simple words.

"Every day, you come here. Every day, you oversee the finer details of this restaurant, but I see the way you hide your suffering and carry on as if everything is normal, as if, nothing has changed, when everything has." He gets this sympathetic look. I cringe when I see it. "And, your temper is getting the best of you now."

He heard about the delivery guy. I hang my head.

"You're falling apart from the inside. And, I can't stand by and watch."

His sympathy is reflected by so many of the people I know in this town. I'm reminded of the pastor at church, the mother of one of Max's friends, the girl at Walgreens who rung up Max's antibiotic a few months before. Their looks are all the same. Louis has the same look that Beverley Maston did, when she held my hand a little too long when we first discussed her anniversary party a few months ago. The older woman had hugged me and told me how sorry she was about Ethan.

"Everyone is so fucking sorry, but it doesn't change anything for me. I just wish they would stop saying anything. I pride myself on how well I've coped with everything over these past months. I'm the poster child for how a widow should handle grief. The God-damn poster child for widowhood. Now, if everyone would just stop asking me how I feel, I'd be *fine*." My silent soliloquy has come to life and has been said aloud.

Louis looks at me with genuine surprise and growing dismay as if he suspected all along I was crazy. And now, that it's been confirmed; he's saddled with the unpleasant task of doing something about it.

I blink back tears and then look at him. Helpless. Wordless.

Silence fills the room and the two of us.

The man, with the most words, a lesson for everything, who is the most inventive culinary talent I've ever known, with the kindest heart, and the biggest smile, has no words for me.

I glare at him and he holds up his hand towards me as if to stop me from saying anything more.

"I'm not finished," he says. "Dr. Liz called here yesterday. She told me you missed your doctor's appointment with her."

I shrug. Indifferent. Undone. Liz Cantor can wait. She's a good friend, besides being my gynecologist, but I haven't even told her about what I now suspect was a miscarriage early on just after Ethan died.

"I got busy. I was going to go. It's just a physical; I'll reschedule."

I stand up.

"I'm not finished." His chest heaves up and down indicating he's just getting started.

"Everyone loves you, Madame Holloway. Everyone here. But this pretending that you are okay, that everything is fine, it doesn't fool any of us. We all know it's only a matter of time before the grief consumes all of you. You can't fool anyone. You have to *feel* it, ma chérie. In order to move on, you have to *feel* it."

Defeated, I sit back down in one of the executive chairs, lean back, and close my eyes. I open my eyes, allowing him a glimpse of the devastation that losing Ethan has done to me.

"What would you like me to do?"

Louis gasps. Then, he grabs both my hands and kneels down in front of me. His face contorts with concern and remorse for his outburst.

"Take a break from all of this." He sweeps his arm around the office as he stands up. "I'll take care of it. Go somewhere, *anywhere,* for a few weeks or a month or two. Deal with the grief, because if you don't, it *will* win."

His grip loosens, and then, he hugs me tight. I'm taken aback by his display of emotion. Louis is normally all business. His concern reaches at me. He lets go first and seems momentarily flustered by our unexpected closeness.

"I'm sorry I got so upset with you. We're all just so worried about you."

"Are you trying to tell me that my continual search for the best kind of thyme is a waste of time?" I ask with a little laugh.

It effectively breaks up the seriousness of the moment. This is an inside joke between us. When I first came to work for Louis, we had a fascinating discussion about the best preparation of Lemon Thyme Chicken. We both agreed that it would be our mission in life to find the most organic process for growing this fantastic herb. We smile at each other now, sharing in this memory of our first meeting.

"Go find the thyme," he says. "Yes, that's what you need to do." He claps his hands together, then proceeds to open the blinds, and sheepishly shuffles to the office doorway. But then, he turns back and just stares at me. "Go home, Jordan. The Mastons' party will be fine. See you in a month or so."

"Is that an order?" I ask in a low voice.

"Oui, it is an order," Louis says with satisfaction.

He dons his chef hat and coat from the shelf and adjusts the red neck-erchief at his throat. Then, he leaves without another word. I stare at his retreating figure with my mouth half-open.

Have I just been summarily suspended as head chef? The idea is both frightening and liberating at the same time.

I actually smile.

∾∾

I hold the estate paperwork in my left hand, absently fingering it, and thinking about its contents. *Why is Brock selling the Lazy J, and what does it have to do with me?* I glance down at the 'sign here' sticky notes. How is it possible that Ethan is part of a place that's worth ten million dollars? How is it that I don't know anything about it? And, where did he get that kind of money? So many questions, and the only one with answers, besides Brock Wainwright, is dead and buried in Austin, Texas.

"What's that?" Ashleigh asks, plowing through the side kitchen door. She carries two cardboard boxes of stuff. I attempt to sing the lyrics to Alice Cooper's song, "School's Out," now that she's just finished up summer school and officially has three weeks off before the fall semester starts up. She grins at me and plops the boxes down on the kitchen table. "What is that?" She snatches the paperwork out of my hand.

"I own a ranch. In Texas. Ethan does. Did. With Brock. Now, it's mine. Ours. Brock wants to sell it."

"Why?"

"I don't know. Because he wants to pay me back Ethan's share? I guess. I don't know. I haven't talked to him."

"Where did Ethan get the money to invest in a ranch?" Ashleigh glances at the real estate paperwork. "It's worth ten million?" she asks.

"Yeah. Something Ethan forgot to mention, I guess."

"Austin, huh?"

"Austin," I say it like it's a bad word. Ashleigh smiles at me.

"Austin could be fun. Cowboys. Jazz music. Dell."

"Four things I never thought I'd hear you say in the same sentence," I say with a little laugh, then frown. "I should take Max to see the Holloways. If I do it now, I might be able to escape the obligatory Christmas visit."

My best friend rolls her eyes.

"Christmas in Austin doesn't sound all that inviting," she says.

93

"Would you come with me this weekend? We could stay downtown in a hotel, or at this place, the Lazy J? I own half of it. Brock probably won't mind."

I sigh with exasperation. The thought of seeing Brock sends me in a new way. I'm still angry with him, unforgiving.

"I just want my life back," I say.

Ashleigh gives me an appraising look. "Are you okay?"

"I'm fine."

"What are you doing *home* anyway? It's only four o'clock. I thought the Mastons' party was tonight?"

"Louis is handling it." I keep to my simple explanation, despite her quizzical glance. I shrug for effect.

"Louis is handling it," she echoes. "Okay. That makes sense. It's only the biggest party of the year for Le Reve, but, as head chef, you're not there?" Her eyes narrow as she scrutinizes me more closely.

I get up abruptly and seek solace with Viking refrigeration, attempt to focus on dinner, and generally ignore her probing stare.

"What about Coq au Vin?" I ask.

"Sure. And, Pouilly Fuisse and Baked Alaska for dessert."

"Okay," I answer automatically.

"*See?* I knew something was wrong because you aren't drinking white wine these days, and you never make Baked Alaska because you said it's too much work with too little payoff. That's what you say, anyway. So, what the hell is going on?"

In defiance, I set out two wine glasses and pour the white wine into both of them, while Ashleigh just watches in fascination. I hand her one of the glasses. "Nothing's wrong."

"That's not true either," she says slowly.

I load up my arms with all the ingredients for Coq Au Vin while she looks on.

"Where's Max?"

"Play date." I glance over at her and force myself to smile. "What about you? Big Date? Big plans with Michael?"

Michael Carswell has been Ashleigh's latest conquest, an up and coming actor, normally a taboo for Ashleigh, but this guy has been completely different. He's British. Ashleigh seems taken with his wonderful accent and his blonde, princely looks. They've been hot and heavy for more than six months. Even Max likes Michael, but that's probably because he brings my child a gift every time he comes by the house for Ashleigh.

"No. I'm beat. School's out. What's left of summer lies in front of me. No plans." She sips at the wine. "I've got all night." She gets this guilty look. "Louis called me two hours ago and told me he told you to take at least a month off. I think it's a great idea."

"Louis called you?" I ask, irritated. "I was going to tell you."

"Uh-huh. When? A month from now? So. Okay. You have some time off. So, what are you going to do?

"Go to Austin. Settle this thing. Whatever it is. See the Holloways. Get my head together and decide what to do next."

"I'm coming," Ashleigh says.

"I was hoping you would. I should call Brock."

"You should."

"But, I can't talk to him." I chop at the raw chicken with newfound zeal and refuse to look at her.

"I *get* that to a certain degree. But, baby, at some point, you're going to have to stop blaming Brock Wainwright for what happened to Ethan. Whatever happened out there in that God-forsaken land was—" Ashleigh stops talking when I look over at her.

I don't attempt to hide my grief. She must see it. The silence stretches forever. Me, wielding the chopping knife mid-air, while Ashleigh just stands there looking at me, as if debating what her next word should actually be. "It was…an *accident*, Jordan. That's what I believe. And you know it, too. Brock *loved* Ethan. He would never do anything to jeopardize his life. You have to believe that."

"Do I?" I ask in a low voice.

Heartbreak takes over. I put down the knife, move over to the sink, turn on the hot water, and begin washing my hands, like a cardiac surgeon, over and over. I can feel Ashleigh studying me from behind.

"I just want my life back. I just want Ethan back."

"I know." Ashleigh takes a deep breath and rushes on. "I went to see Brock. In D.C., when I was there for that teacher's conference four months ago."

I turn around and look at her, stunned into silence.

"He refused to see me. *Refused.* I know it was just a fling, nothing serious, but his refusal to see me—" Ashleigh waves her hand through the air. "Well, I was surprised. His doctor came out to meet with me. The blonde? She was the one with him at Ethan's funeral. She said he was weak and still recovering from a second emergency surgery and didn't want to see anyone. She told me he barely allowed his parents to see him when they were there. She said he was so broken up over Ethan's death that he refused to see anyone. That doesn't sound like a man who would jeopardize Ethan's life; does it?" Ashleigh asks me quietly.

"He promised me," I say simply.

"I know. But he shouldn't have." She shakes her head slowly. "It was an impossible promise. And, you *know* it."

She hands me a kitchen towel, and then the untouched glass of wine I left on the counter. I take a tentative sip, and then another.

"So, let's go to Austin." I hold up the paperwork. "And finish this thing."

"Austin," she says.

Her words from earlier echo back to me. *Whatever happened in that God-forsaken land; it was an accident.* I shiver, hoping she's right.

❧⊙❧

When Ashleigh goes off to take a shower, I make a call to the phone number Brock has been leaving on his messages. Ashleigh has penned it across the white message board with a red dry erase marker with the words 'Call Brock!' It's underlined.

"Janie Wainwright," says a lyrical voice. The woman sounds like a mother. Her voice is soft and unhurried, as if to say everything is all right without actually ever having to say those words. I fumble for a response.

"Mrs. Wainwright? This is Jordan Holloway. Ethan's wife. Your son and my…husband were sniper partners. I was just calling to confirm—"

"Oh, Jordan. You're coming," she says with a little sigh. "I'm so glad. This is going to be so special. We're doing a tribute to Ethan. I was so hoping you would come. I'm so happy you are."

She's so disarming; I rush on to explain myself.

"Yes, Ashleigh. She's my friend. And my son. Max. We'll all be coming, if that's okay."

I'm tongue-tied and undone by her enthusiasm and my lack of it.

"I'm remembering Ethan's face. His casket. Lying in it with him, when everyone else had gone to the cemetery for the graveside service. Igor

Dasher had to rescue me." I gasp, realizing I'm telling this story out loud.

Janie Wainwright is crying. Now, so am I.

"I'm sorry," I say. "I don't know why I would tell you all of that."

"I'm glad you did. I want you to know how sorry we all are. We loved Ethan. The funeral was so beautiful. I know how hard it was for you. Ethan spent a great deal of his childhood at the ranch with us. He was like a son to me. Then, he and Brock went off to sniper school." She sighs. "And then, Ethan married you. After that, it seemed like they were always in Afghanistan." Her heavy sigh matches mine. "Anyway, you're coming. I'm thrilled, beyond the moon, as they say. Come stay with us. Brock's staying here on the weekends after spending his weekdays at Criss Cole. Can you be here as soon as Friday? That would give us the whole weekend together."

"I don't know. I need to see the Holloways. Max needs to see them. I should talk to Brock about the Lazy J."

"Weren't there some papers you needed to sign? He's been so worried about that. Blind or not, he remains adamant about selling the ranch. Henry and I keep telling him to give it a little more time, but he wants to do the right thing and get you out from underneath the obligation of it."

"What ranch?" I ask, and then gasp as I register what else she's just said. *"Blind?* Brock is *blind?"*

I hear her gasp. "He didn't *tell* you?"

"No."

My breath leaves me all at once. My mind races back to the scene of the funeral when I accused him of breaking his promise and how he didn't actually look at me. I remember how lost and sad he seemed to be. Memories return of his constant grip on that blonde woman's arm.

"He's blind," I say slowly. "I don't understand."

"He'll be given an honorable discharge by the Navy in the next month or so, if his sight isn't restored. Right now, he's attending Criss Cole, here in Austin, to learn how to live on his own. They don't know what caused it. Even this psychiatrist, Kate Richards, he's been seeing, can't figure it out. He's blind, honey. I thought he told you. He *should* have told you."

There's a lot of unspoken sentiment in her tone. My face feels hot as I recall the way I've been acting toward Brock.

"You didn't know," Janie Wainwright says with this uncanny clairvoyance. Somehow, she knows how badly I've been treating her son.

My eyes sting. The way I've been acting is unforgiveable.

Brock's own pain reaches for me. Remorse sets in as a moan escapes my lips.

"Seems like you both have been suffering in silence," she says. "Come to Austin. Brock can pick you up at the airport on Friday."

I'm unable to talk for moment. How can Brock pick us up, if he's blind?

"I can't wait to meet you in person," Janie says.

"I can't wait to meet you," I manage to say back.

Guilt takes hold of me as I hang up the phone. *Brock is blind.*

Shock and fear swirl all around me. Blind. Brock is blind. Intense sadness takes the place of all the anger I've felt towards him.

Brock is blind and he never told me.

I don't have time to explore that aspect because Ashleigh waltzes through the living room, sporting a large white bath towel and little else.

"What?" she asks intuitively.

"I've been blaming him for everything. And now, his mother just told me he's blind. *Blind*, Ashleigh. Brock." Her face registers with shock. "He can't see. He's to be honorably discharged by the Navy soon if his sight doesn't return. He's blind."

"That's why he wouldn't see me," she says slowly.

I turn away from her sudden close scrutiny of my face as this incredible anguish washes over me, but apparently not before she sees it.

"What?" Ashleigh asks softly.

"I don't know. I just have this feeling. It just seems like Austin might change everything."

"It might," she says in an ominous voice.

Nine

Jordan – Violet walk

Y GYNECOLOGIST'S OFFICE IS IN DOWNTOWN Los Angeles. I wait in Dr. Liz Cantor's office, impatient, while she writes in her chart. She looks up from her notes every once in a while and studies me.

"Tell me about the missed period in February."

"It was probably nothing. I was late; that's all, but there were a million things going on at the time," I say for the umpteenth time.

"But when it came, it was normal."

I begin to squirm under her scrutiny. I clasp my arms about me and glare at her for a moment. We were college roommates, so her doctor status is secondary to her good friend status in my life.

"Not exactly," I say in defiance. "It was heavy. You know, unbearable. I couldn't leave the house for a day or so because it was hard to keep up." I try to shrug, but she catches my trembling.

"You had a miscarriage," she says.

"I guess so, but I'm feeling great."

She grabs my wrist and takes my pulse with her stethoscope. "You should have told me, called me, made an appointment."

"You were in Hawaii at the time with Adrian."

Adrian Saines is Liz's long-term boyfriend. Ashleigh and I have been waiting for more than five years for the two of them to get married. But no. Liz just continues to date him and lead a separate life from him.

Adrian is a touchy subject. It's usually one we save for a girls' night out, involving plenty of wine. Her eyes narrow. *A typical Liz warning.*

"We're not talking about Adrian or Hawaii. We're talking about you."

"Ethan died. I wasn't myself."

"I'm sorry I wasn't there for his funeral." She gets this guilty look as she tucks a tendril of my hair behind my ear and then hugs me.

"S'okay," I say.

"Not really. I haven't been a very good friend. Things have been chaotic." She glances at my face. "But that doesn't excuse not being close by and calling you and seeing you more often."

"You've been busy. So have I. I mean, between Max and the restaurant, I stay busy. Ashleigh's staying at the house. She gave up her apartment, months ago."

"Yeah, but she's busy with Michael."

"True."

I look away in an attempt to avoid Liz's clairvoyant-like gaze. It tends to work like an x-ray, making it hard to keep things from her.

The truth is grief has occupied my waking moments whenever I'm alone, so I try not to be alone too much. And, there's this whole other preoccupation with pretending that everything's fine whenever Max or Ashleigh or Louis are around. It's a full time job, portraying normal. And, I'm not as good at it for some reason. The proof of that is clear, ever since I lost it with the delivery driver and with the freezer incident a few weeks ago. And now, I'm dealing with this renewed, incredible sadness over Ethan, and this intense anguish over Brock's condition. *He's blind.* All these thoughts rage through me.

"Jordan? Where did you go?" Liz asks, looking anxious.

"Sorry," I say. "What did you ask me?"

"I asked how you were doing with everything."

I practically wilt under her penetrating gaze. "It's hard."

"Hard. How?" Liz asks.

I never should have said anything. Liz is not one to let things go. I bite my lower lip.

"Putting one foot in front of the other, some days, is hard enough."

I give her a little smile, but she's not fooled.

She gets up from her chair, comes around the desk, and sits directly in front of me on the edge of it. I wither under her intense stare and try to focus upon her haphazard ponytail and the trendy black glasses that tend to slip down her too straight nose. Liz Cantor is gorgeous in this stunning Angelina Jolie as Lara Croft kind of way. Ashleigh and I have known her since our first days at USC just before she entered medical school. We hold the honor of being her best friends as well as her first patients when she set up her practice. There are few, if any, secrets between the three of us.

"It's been almost six months." She stares at my face as if she's getting a psychic reading. "Though everyone's different. It's a different process, this grief thing, for everyone." She reaches out and takes my hand. "Are you pissed off at him, yet?" She half-smiles at me. I try to return it, but fail.

"No," I finally say. "I think I'm going to skip that stage."

"Saint status already?"

"Something like that."

"And, who's in Austin, besides the Holloways?"

"Ethan's best friend, Brock Wainwright. That's who Ethan was serving with in Afghanistan. I've been blaming him for Ethan's death, and I just learned that, well—" I swallow hard, struggling for the words. "Brock is *blind*. Somehow, in the ambush when Ethan was killed, Brock was injured, too, I guess." I move my head side-to-side in bewilderment. "I knew he couldn't remember, but I had no idea that he was hurt, and I've been blaming him for everything, for Ethan's death."

Liz still holds my hand, and she's squeezing it now. My tears land on her hand.

"Jordan, you cannot carry all this grief and guilt around by yourself. It's not good for you."

"Don't you *see*? I blamed Brock. I made him promise me he would bring Ethan back safe. I blamed him for Ethan's death. I did that. I'm a horrible person."

"No. You're not. You're a grieving widow, who has suffered a tremendous loss. *Again*. Just like your parents. You're a strong person, Jordan, but you're only human. And, sweetie, Ethan was only human, too. And, this Brock Wainwright? He's only human, too. No one is to blame for what happened to any of you, except the bad guy who pulled the trigger and killed him."

I wince at her truthful words. Liz looks at me more closely.

"Everyone lost something on that day. Ethan lost his life. You lost your husband. This Brock lost his best friend and his sight. Max lost his daddy. It's all terribly sad for all of you. And, Jordan, you're only human, which makes you wonderful, quirky, lovable, and deserving." Liz sighs. "Someday, you're going to find happiness again."

"I'm happy. Relatively." I lift my head in defiance. Tears come unexpectedly. "I really wanted that baby; you know? Somehow, losing that baby, in just a few short weeks after losing Ethan, just made everything impossible."

"How did you hide that loss from Ashleigh all these months? From me?"

"I'm a professional when it comes to grief; you know that," I say with an unsteady laugh.

Liz hands me a tissue and I dab at my face. She goes back behind her desk.

"Sex would be good for you," Liz says slowly. She rewards me with an expectant appraising glance.

"*Please*. I'm not going to have sex with Brock Wainwright."

"Who said anything about Brock Wainwright? I'm sure there are plenty of cowboys in Austin."

Liz looks at me intently while I just stare at her in astonishment.

"Sex would be great for you—liberating, a freeing of the soul and the guilt and the grief and the agony. Here's your get-out-of-jail-free card."

She taps the needle and, in the next second, jabs me with a shot of Depo-Provera. We'd discussed this, but I'm still surprised by her covert ways of handling my fear of needles by utilizing the sly technique of surprise and speed.

"You could have warned me."

"No. You hate needles. It's better if you don't see them coming. Now, use other contraception for the next week or so."

I roll my eyes as she hands me one of her appointment cards. She's scrawled her cell on the back as if I don't already know it by heart.

"Call me if there's anything that gives you pause. Don't wait. Don't think about it. Just do it."

"Right."

She gives me a meaningful, all-knowing look. I take the card and put it inside my purse.

"Do you know what I'm saying?" Liz asks.

Her insistence makes me smile.

"Yes. Day or night. Call you, if there's anything," I say. "Don't wait. Don't think. Just do it."

"That's right."

She hugs me and then steps back.

I feel like I'm a college freshman being sent off for first semester. Don't do this. Don't do that. Have fun. Have sex, but only if it feels right. Or, better yet, because you're liberated. Don't wait. Don't think. Just do it.

Her strange speech from minutes ago reverberates with me like a meditation mantra as I make my way to the waiting room door. A memory of Liz and Ashleigh's fantastic dating line-up while they were at USC comes back to me. I smile wider, turn back, and wave at her. Liz gives me the thumbs-up as I leave.

Once outside, I'm engulfed in the late summer heat of L.A. I check my watch and begin the race against time and traffic in getting to Rivera where I'm meeting Ashleigh for dinner. Max has a baby-sitter, who has already assured me she'll have him in bed on time.

Incongruent thoughts flash at me as I make my way to the parking garage. *Sex. Brock Wainwright. Ethan.* The words reach at me one at a time with every step I take. *Don't wait. Don't think. Just do it.*

⁂

"Sorry, sorry. God, it's been the worst day." Ashleigh sidles up beside me at the bar at Rivera.

I give her a sideways glance. "The worst?"

"Well, relative to what *normal* people experience, Jordan, yes," she says. "Sorry. I know how you hate to wait, and well, we probably should have picked a different place."

"No, it's fine. Peter's already been by to say hello and offer me employment again."

"He did? Wow, that would be fabulous. We could get a place together and be right in the center of L.A. again. Perfect."

"Slow down, Ash. What about Le Reve? Louis? Your teaching job? I thought you loved Malibu." I brush my hand across my eyes. "I can't even begin to think about that right now. I've got Max to think of and Louis has been so good to me."

I glance over at her and detect her disappointment. "You don't have to stay with me, you know. I'm fine. *Really.*"

"Sure you are," she says with detectable sarcasm. "I just think a change might be good for you. For me. For us."

Then, she gets this miserable look and her eyes fill with tears. I'm shocked. Ashleigh doesn't cry. Neither of us are criers.

Well, I used to be that way. Now, I seem to be crying in secret all the time.

"You broke up with Michael," I say intuitively.

She plays with the menu, effectively hiding from me. "Yes," she says in a weepy voice.

"What happened?"

"We wanted different things." Ashleigh looks away toward the darkened window of the restaurant. I swear I see her swipe away at a tear.

"What kind of *things*? I thought you guys were perfect for each other. You're both afraid of commitment," I say with a wan smile. "I *like* Michael. He's good for you."

"He is good for me," she says with a grimace. "But he wanted more. He wanted to be exclusive."

"The cardinal sin."

"Exactly! Why did he have to go and ruin everything by asking me?"

"Asking you what?"

She doesn't answer. Instead, she opens her purse and carefully unwraps a flashy diamond ring from white tissue paper.

"He proposed? Oh, Ash. And you turned him down?"

"He told me to think about it and that we'd take a break for a few weeks, while he's filming in London, but he wants me to wear the ring. You know I won't do that."

She looks so sad. I squeeze her hand and take the ring from her and hold it up to the light. It sparkles from every angle.

"Maybe, you should give it a try. It's beautiful."

"No." With a heavy sigh, she leans back in the bar chair. "The thing is I *really* like him," she says with a little laugh.

"And that's a bad thing?"

"He thinks he really loves me." She turns her head and stares across the room, garnering a few interested glances from the male patrons at the other end of the bar and nods in their general direction. "But I don't even know what it's like to be in love," she says, looking back at me.

I struggle to concentrate on Ashleigh as a distant memory of Brock Wainwright returns. "I was engaged once. It didn't work out," he'd said. Now I wonder what he meant by 'it didn't work out.'

"Where are you?" Ashleigh asks. "I'm pouring my heart out here and you're not even listening."

"I'm sorry. What did you say?"

"I said I want to be in love like that. I do. But, I'm not."

"You don't want to be in love. Look what happens when you love them? They leave," I say softly. "And, they never come back."

"I'm sorry. I wasn't thinking. I didn't mean to make you feel bad. Listen to me go on. I'm fine. I'm okay. Michael and I—we just want different things. I want fun and carefree. Michael wants all the other stuff."

"You just said you want to be in love," I say, exasperated. I get up from the table. "I'm going to call and check on Max. I'll be right back."

"Jordan, I'm sorry. I shouldn't have said anything. I wasn't thinking. I'm just all mixed up about everything."

I shrug and sit back down with a heavy sigh. "You say you don't know what you want. But what you are is scared." She looks at me in surprise. "Scared of being in love."

"How did you know? With Ethan?" Ashleigh finally asks.

I close my eyes, remembering. When I open them, Ashleigh is staring at me, waiting for my answer. I take a deep breath.

"See that table right there?" I extend my hand over to our left. "That's where we met. I came racing out of the kitchen, demanding to know which jerk it was that kept sending his food back. Ethan raised his hand. God, I don't even think I got to sit down before I knew he was the one."

I look at Ashleigh and smile, remembering the first time I saw Ethan. "Wait for him, for the one. When the right guy comes along, you'll know. You'll just know. And, even with all the heartbreak, it's worth it," I say gently. "Because he gave me so much in return."

I stand up again, pretend to toss my hair and covertly swipe at my face. A few of the guys from the bar seem to notice.

"Maybe, you need this trip to Austin to figure things out for yourself. You know. Take a break from it all." I sweep up my purse. "Right now, I just want to check on Max. We'll be out a little late and he'll be asleep soon." I glance at my watch and start to back away from the table.

"You need the break, too," Ashleigh says. "You're the one that needs to figure things out. I mean, it's been almost six months and I worry about you. I know you have Max, but what are you going to do? I think you need a change. You're just wallowing in things out in Malibu."

I study her face for a moment. "I'll be right back."

"Fine. Check on Max, but we're not finished talking about this," she says, giving me this determined look.

❧❦

Ashleigh has decided to make it her mission to sell me hard on the merits of living in Los Angeles again. Her face is flushed. She attracts even more interested looks from the male patrons at the bar as we pass and the hostess seats us at a table for dinner. It isn't long before the waiter comes by with two complimentary glasses of wine for both of us from one of them.

Ashleigh seems bored by the attention. She just sits there and looks amazing in her red silk blouse and her white linen pants. Only Ashleigh can wear linen without a single wrinkle. I pull subconsciously at my conservative navy sweater dress that swims on me. I've been working long hours and running too much. Liz lectured me about that, too.

"I'll think about it," I say. "But, I really don't want to have this conversation right now. I know I need to contemplate making some changes. *Maybe.* But, not tonight. I saw Liz today. She said to tell you hi."

"I bet she told you that sex would be good for you." Ashleigh laughs.

"How did you *know* that?" I ask. "She wouldn't let up about it. I got a shot of Depo-Provera just to get her off my back."

"Because Liz thinks sex is good for a lot of things," Ashleigh says with a giggle.

"I wish I could let go of all these social mores and feel like that. It would be liberating."

"Yeah, sex with Michael was supposed to be with no strings attached and look where we are." Ashleigh gets this serious look. "Did you tell her about the miscarriage?"

"I didn't even tell you; did I?"

"Not outright, but you mentioned something before his funeral about missing your period and writing to him about it." She gives me this once-over-intense-Liz-Cantor-look. "I thought you'd want to talk about it, at some point. I knew Liz would eventually talk to you about it. I'm so sorry. I tried to be there for you."

"It was early. I was barely pregnant. Six weeks, at the most."

"Yeah, but you'd just lost Ethan. Louis is right. You can't keep going along like everything is fine and nothing has changed." She gets this decisive look. "And, I'm with Liz; sex would be good for you."

I toy with my wine glass and try to ignore her words. I shake my head.

"This is *Liz* we're talking about. This advice comes from a woman who has dated the *same guy* for five years and refuses to talk about marriage with him or the two of us." I flip my hand in the air in frustration. "And then, there's you. You refuse to consider a heartfelt proposal from a truly sensational guy? By all means, let's worry about whether Jordan is getting *any*."

I glare at her. She starts to laugh.

"Come on," I say in a pleading voice. "Let's talk about Michael."

"No. Let's talk about Brock," she counters.

"What about him?" I flush as she scrutinizes me closely. "You and Liz."

"What did Liz say?"

I sigh. "When she told me that sex would be good for me, I told her I had no intention of having sex with Brock Wainwright. She said it didn't have to be Brock; any cowboy would do." I make a face.

"It would be good for you. I've been telling you that for *weeks*. You should have taken an interest in Damon."

I roll my eyes at her. A few weeks ago, I made the mistake of agreeing to see a movie with Ashleigh, only to be set up on a blind date with one of Michael's friends, Damon something or other.

"He took one look at me and my kid, but was too polite to run the other way right then," I say with a grimace.

"Damon liked you. Loved you, in fact. He just asked about you the other day when I saw him at Michael's place." She shakes her head side-to-side and then looks at me more closely. "Let's not get sidetracked talking about Damon. Let's talk about Brock. He asked about you. In Malibu, while he was with me? All the time, asking questions *about you*."

"Like what?" I gulp my wine and look away from her.

"Different stuff. What you were like in high school, at USC. How you met Ethan. What you did when he was gone." I look at her in surprise and she starts to smile. "Don't worry; I told him you barely went out and that you spent all your time at the restaurant or with Max."

"You make it sound like I have no life at all," I say, deflated.

"Of course, you have a life," she says. "Look, I just find it curious that he asked so much about you. Before, all of this." She sweeps her hand across the room and gets this thoughtful look.

"I mean there were never really any sparks between us, besides the sex," she says with her usual candor. "Maybe, he had a thing for you all along."

I take another sip of my wine. "Do I want to hear this?" I finally ask.

"I think you should. Things are different now."

"How are they different?" I ask with growing irritation.

"You're single. He's single. I'm practically engaged." Ashleigh holds up her left hand. She slipped Michael's ring on during dinner.

"Your ability to twist things around is stunning. I don't consider myself single." I twist my wedding ring and glare at her. "Why are we talking about Brock?" I shake my head in disgust. "You and Liz."

"She's right. Sex would be *good* for you."

"No. There's nothing to talk about."

"I think there is." Ashleigh takes a sip of her Chardonnay and then toys with her drink napkin. "I've moved on. I'm seeing Michael, *have been* seeing Michael. I'm wearing his ring." She holds up her hand to the light and gazes at the brilliant diamond again. "Brock's not interested in me. I think he's interested in *you*."

"His mother is the one who told me what had happened to him." I get this unsettled feeling in the pit of my stomach. "Maybe, he didn't even want me to know he's blind. But, why wouldn't he want me to know?" I remember his uncanny ability to read me. I shiver and discover Ashleigh giving me this weird look. "I mean I'm sure it's difficult for him," I say. "He was so active. It must be incredibly hard on him."

"Brock can take care of himself," she says. "It's *you*; I'm worried about."

"No need to worry about me." I blush under her penetrating gaze.

"Brock Wainwright was a great guy, but—."

"Still is," I say with surprising vehemence. *Why am I defending him?*

"He's interesting, Jordan, but he's *blind*. He's handicapped."

The apprehension in her voice is obvious. Fear of the unknown? Fear of blindness? Who knows? Ashleigh has always been squeamish around medical issues, imperfections, or anything that has to do with feeling something deeply beyond lust. I pulse with sudden irritation at her and something else. "Nobody says that anymore. He's visually challenged. And, it may not even be permanent."

"Really?" Ashleigh finishes the last of her wine and gives me an appraising look.

"But I don't think you should get involved with Brock Wainwright," I say slowly, hoping to put an end to this conversation.

She gazes at her sparkling left hand and then back at me. "I'm not talking about *me* getting involved with Brock Wainwright."

I sit silent, refusing to take the bait as to what she is getting at.

"I have to take some time to figure out what to do about Michael," she says with a sigh. "Maybe, Austin will provide answers for both of us."

Wisdom and experience force me to shake my head. I smile at the irony of this entire conversation.

"It's never that simple."

I look around the restaurant at this magical place where Ethan and I first met.

"If it was just about a diamond ring and saying you're committed to one another, everyone would get married and live happily ever after," I say quietly.

Ashleigh reaches for my left hand and fingers my wedding ring. "It's never that simple. Is it?"

"No," I say. "That's just the fairytale we like to believe."

Chapter

Ten

Brock – It will come

I'VE BECOME THE PIED PIPER OF Criss Cole Rehabilitation Center. The adolescent high school students, all blind, seem to hang on to my every utterance. How the word got around about my being part of a famous sniper team; I'll never know. The reputation has brought with it, hero status. No matter if it's unwelcome. No matter that my resentment at my situation has made me become somewhat surly and definitely unlovable. Attributes both my father and my mother will willingly attest to now.

The students of Criss Cole don't care. Our shared lot in life, in combating blindness, binds us together like the magical Gorilla Glue I used to pack in my rucksack, which proved so useful in the deserts and mountainous terrain of Afghanistan. That special glue and baby wipes made us believe we lived in a God's paradise, at least, for Ethan and me at the time. And now, my followers, here in this new foreign place of Criss Cole Rehabilitation Center, refuse to leave me alone and function like the Gorilla Glue from my past, sticking to me no matter what I do or say.

My new combat field is littered with misplaced chairs and tables, unfamiliar hallways, and the constant barrage of strangers and their voices. The noise of a black world and everyday objects I no longer see are unsympathetic to my sightless plight in every way.

Kate was right. I've managed to learn Braille. The raised dots rule my life at the Center and my parent's ranch house, now. My mother has enlisted the Center's help with the service of labeling everything I could possibly touch with the language of the Blind. My refusal to accept my fate, of never being able to see again, seems to have only spurred everyone onward. Those that surround me from the director of the school to my family and, most unexpectedly, the adolescents of Criss Cole, do everything possible to accommodate me and my blindness.

Blind, like me, my groupies swarm me whenever there's a free moment at the Center. Now, I sit on top of one of the lunch tables reluctantly entertaining my brood—my newfound world of blind worshippers.

"Lieutenant Wainwright, what was it like to be under fire?" Ruben Lowenstein asks from somewhere near my right.

"It didn't happen often," I say.

My mind flashes to our last mission, and I try to remember anything about that day, but nothing comes to me. I conjure up Ethan's face in my mind and can feel the sweat begin to form on my upper lip as I do so. My breathing accelerates.

"But, you made it right? You're here. Was it the shrapnel that blinded you?" asks another boy. His voice is now familiar, but his name escapes me.

I'm beginning to hyperventilate in attempting to call up any memories of that last day with Ethan and our last mission.

"I made it. I can't explain the blindness. No one can." My words come out harsher than I intended, and my breathing becomes even more labored.

"Children, I think that's enough for one day. It's time for class, anyway." The voice of Lucille Gestner breaks through the rising volume of excited students hurling questions at me. "Come. Come back to class."

I hear the kids shuffle off with the rhythmic tap taps of their white canes, also known as mobility tools for the visually impaired. I turn away from the direction Lucille Gestner's voice came from, trying to recover from my near panic attack before the director of Criss Cole Rehabilitation Center sees it.

"Have you given thought to being a teacher?" Lucille Gestner asks when the room becomes quiet again.

The very fine, vivacious director at Criss Cole and my personal champion, whether I like it or not, will not be deterred. Every day she asks me about my vocation plans.

Her enthusiasm for the blind grates directly on my soul, at this point.

"I'd like to be a sniper again."

I position my hands around an invisible rifle and pull the trigger in a generalized direction away from the sound of her voice.

"Okay," she says patiently. She reminds me of Glenda the Good Witch from the Wizard of Oz. "Your second choice, then. Teaching?"

The woman will not give up on me. I have tried to convince her so many times that I am not worth the effort. The more difficult I make her life, with my lack of enthusiasm and cooperation for her benevolent work, the more steadfast and determined she becomes. Like now. I sigh in exasperation.

"No." I sound so resolute; I've convinced myself. I give her a fake smile.

"I've got all day," she says in this cheerful voice.

"Lawyer," I supply without thinking. "I'll finish my last semester of law school. It will make my father happy."

"Okay. Lawyer. Hmmm…I'm kind of surprised at that choice, but we can arrange it. Special software. Computer. Audio aids, a tutor—" Her sweet voice trails off and I turn my face in her general direction, feeling this sudden despair and profound loss.

"I don't know. Let me think about it."

I've given her the pat answer of lawyer to get her off my back for the day and yet feel this rising panic as my life continues to spin out of control as I realize, once again, I'm helpless to stop it.

"Walk with me," Lucille says in her brisk business-like way.

I automatically stand and grasp the collapsible white cane that was bestowed upon me three months before when I first arrived here. I feel for her presence and grasp her outstretched arm and instinctively tap my way out the door to the campus grounds with Lucille Gestner. Arm-in-arm. It's fucking pathetic.

Lucille encircles her arm with my left one and we move along at an easy pace in the warmth of a summer day in Austin. I lift my head up toward where the sky should be and take a deep cleansing breath, faltering with my step in doing so, and feel her grasp my arm more tightly.

"You're doing well."

"No. I'm not."

"You are. One of these days, Lieutenant, it will come."

"What will come?"

"The peace. The tranquility. The acceptance. It will come. I've seen it happen."

"Well, you're lucky to be able to *see*, Ms. Gestner. So lucky." My tone is bleak and bitter. I do nothing to hide it.

"You have some decisions to make. Where you plan to make your permanent residence, for one. Then, we can go through the place and prepare it for you. Where and what you want to do your vocational training in. Life awaits, Lieutenant Wainwright. You really must get on with it."

"Is that so?" My sardonic tone does not dissuade her.

"It is."

We walk in absolute silence for the next fifteen minutes. If she hadn't been holding on to me, I would have thought I was walking alone. Maybe, that was her intention. I don't know.

"You know, Brock, it's okay to be scared," she finally says with a heavy sigh.

"I've never been more scared in my life and I've been to Afghanistan for Christ's sake."

"I know."

"I just want—I just want my life back. I just want my best friend back." I falter and am overcome with emotion that invades me every time I consciously think of Ethan. "I just…want to go home."

"I thought you were home?"

"Afghanistan," I finally say.

"Something or someone brought you back here, Brock. One day it will come to you. One day, you'll embrace your future. One day, you'll know what it is."

"Yeah, but will I be able to *see* it?"

"Yes. You will," Lucille says.

Her voice holds such conviction that I stop walking and search in vain, in the blackness of it all, for her face. For some sign.

"I need you to be right."

"I will be," she promises.

⁂

I stand at the Center's curb, testing the edge with my white cane. I'm almost thirty years old, and I'm standing here, waiting for my mother to pick me up. The perversion of it all is not lost on me in this moment.

A few dark minutes pass, and then, I hear the whir of a V-8 engine and recognize the familiar drumming of my mother's Buick sedan.

"You need to get your oil changed," I say.

The electronic hum of her window rolling down gets closer, and she calls out a hello in her lyrical voice. "How do you know?"

I slide into the passenger seat. Chanel No. 5 assails my nostrils, and I grimace once again at the improved olfactory talent I now possess.

"I can hear it, Janie."

"Don't be cheeky, Brock."

"I'm not. It's true. You practically run the engine out of oil every time, and Dad's warned you about it, too. I can hear the cylinders practically freezing up."

"Fine. I'll get the oil changed," Janie concedes with an exaggerated sigh. "How was your week?"

"Great. I have to pick a vocation and a place to stay so they can get me all fixed up. I'm done in a couple of weeks. Then, I'll be out on my own."

"You're going to be fine," she says in her soothing voice. "What vocation are you going to choose?"

Nothing is lost on my mother, and I sigh heavily at the realization.

"Well, I still want to be a sniper." I hear my mother's soft laugh, and it buoys me up in some way. I grin in the general direction of her voice.

"You need to stop giving Lucille Gestner such a hard time, Brock. She's a good friend of mine." Her reprimand is soft. My mother has been one of my biggest fans my entire life, much to the dismay of my twin sister, Diana, who still complains that she favors me too much. "Come on; tell me what you're going to do."

"Lucille Gestner thinks I would be a good teacher. I suggested a lawyer. That way I could work on my own; wherever. The truth is—I don't know what I want to be. It wasn't supposed to work out like this." She pats my hand where it rests on the console between us.

"Okay, just know that no one is more overjoyed than me to have you back home. You can stay with us as long as you want."

"I realize how thrilled you are that I'm back, mother," I say with a wry smile. "But, just once, I wish you would take the time to appreciate all that I've lost."

"Oh Brock, I know it seems impossible right now, but I just know that everything is going to sort itself out."

We lapse into silence. I try and quell the frustration that lurks inside of me, just below the surface most of the time these days.

I can't even drive. My Porsche 911 sits, unused, in the garage at the ranch. My mother drives me everywhere, as if I'm eight-years-old again.

I've come to know all the various sounds of the drive from the Center to my parent's ranch. There's the buzz of the highway, and then, the soft feel of asphalt, and finally, the lurch of the car as it traverses onto an uneven surface and the familiar ping of pitched gravel against the tires and the car's underbody that leads straight to my parent's ranch house ten miles out of Austin.

"I almost forgot," my mother says in her best teasing, singsong voice as she pulls the car to a decided stop. "You have two new emails. I printed them off for you."

"What? So, I can *read* them? From who?" I ask as I slide out of the car.

"Kate and Jordan."

"What? Kate? Jordan?"

My heart rate beats faster, and I hold my breath to maintain some kind of semblance of coolness with my mother. She grabs my arm and leads the way as I tap into the house with my walking cane.

"Nice try, Cowboy. I've read them both. And now, I'll read them to you."

"You're not making this easy, mother."

"It's never meant to be easy, Brock," she says with a little sigh.

❧❦❧

My mother rushes out the door to go deliver something to my father in the farthest corner of our ten thousand acres while I sit here waiting.

Waiting. Waiting. Just waiting.

I become impatient, accompanied by equal doses of frustration and resentment. All those hours spent on the battle field with Ethan, where we had to stay absolutely still and look for the enemy, don't help me, now. For the thousandth time, I censure myself for not allowing the Center to install the proper audible software on my parent's desktop computer or better yet, for not buying my own laptop, so I'm no longer dependent upon my mother reading my email to me like a school boy.

After an interminable half hour, she returns, calling out an airy hello that echoes to me from the front hallway. I listen intently as she finally settles herself down next to me to read my email to me. I give her a perturbed look in the direction of her melodic chatter, but she just laughs softly. She rattles the pages with such drama that I almost laugh, but this uneasiness rushes at me. I may have missed Kate, but that doesn't even begin to cover the scope of feelings I've experienced for Ethan's widow.

With one last clearing of her throat, she begins:

To: Lieutenant Brock Wainwright

From: Major Kate Richards M.D.

"She *outranks* you?" My darling mother asks.

"Yes," I say in irritation. "Get on with it. What does it say?"

Brock,

How is Criss Cole? I figure they have you set up with your computer by now, so I thought I would drop you a line. I've been doing some additional research about your condition and have contacted Dr. Tethers about some new methods to try to reactivate your memory. There's some new research being done in Europe on conditions such as yours and some new medications that we might be able to try. Anyway, I miss you. I hope you're doing well and enjoying your family.

"She knows about us?" My mother stops to ask.

"She knows my life story, for the most part," I concede. "She's met Diana, a few times, when she's come to town.

"She sounds lovely."

This is a rhetorical response. Lovely is a term my mother uses for things she doesn't necessarily care for: bridge, democrats, promiscuity. She makes an exception for me on the last one, but that's about it. I frown upon hearing her use the word, lovely.

"Well, if you ever get the chance to *see* her, you'll have to let me know," I say.

"Do you want me to finish or not?"

"Finish it."

I hope to consult with Dr. Tethers in the next couple of days. Would you be up for some company in Austin, then? I believe we have some unfinished business to conduct, Lieutenant.

Kate

I hear the familiar clucking of disapproval over Kate's suggestive words from my mother and grimace.

"That's it?" I ask in a noncommittal tone.

I'm not sure exactly what to make of Kate's email. Well, maybe I am, but there's this invading image of Jordan Holloway that has annihilated all my good common sense, and I'm fighting for this semblance of control before my mother discovers it.

"Sounds pretty suggestive to me," my mother says with a dainty laugh. "Okay, here's the other message from Jordan Holloway."

She begins to read word for word.

> *To: Brock*
>
> *From: Jordan Holloway*
>
> *Brock,*
>
> *Hello. It's been a while and I am remiss in getting in touch with you sooner for a myriad of reasons that seem selfish at best. Let's just say; I haven't been myself, although I've gotten very good at decorating cupcakes.*

"What does that mean?" My mother asks in her most persistent voice that will not be denied an explanation. "About decorating cupcakes?"

"I gave her a hard time about perfecting the art of cupcakes once," I mutter. This inner ache begins to throb inside of me as I realize how much I miss Jordan's emails to Ethan in Afghanistan. It's just another one of those things that I've been missing all these months. The loss of Ethan reverberates in so many ways for me; it's astounding.

My mother is still beside me. "Go on. What does she say?"

> *I've been going through the documents you sent and I have more questions than answers. I know I've been remiss in get-ting back to you. I'm sorry. In any case, we're making a trip to Austin. Max needs to see his grandparents; and you and I should probably meet in person and make the final decisions about the estate. You can fill me in about the Lazy J. "It'll be nothing, but fun and games" as Ethan would say.*

"He would say that," I say, when my mother pauses again.

I grimace, remembering Ethan's famous sayings and experience this deep heartache again. I miss him. My mother clears her throat, pulling me back again, and continues on in her cheeriest voice:

> *Here's the thing, Brock. I don't like to fly, but I will. I've got some time off and I'd like to bring Max and Ashleigh, too. A change of scenery for all of us would be good, at least for a week or so.*
>
> *Call me when you can, so we can determine the best way to meet up in Austin while I'm there.*
>
> *Take care, Brock.*
>
> *Jordan*

"She wrote her phone number at the bottom," my mother says softly.

"I know her number."

I've tripped my way across my parent's living room, and stare out, unseeing, at what must be in the direction of their large living room window. I tap the dial on my watch, and the mechanical voice states the time 'five zero six p.m.'

"L.A. is two hours behind," my mother says.

I grimace in learning she's already calculated the time difference. "Yes." My voice is low, and I can barely utter the word.

"Are you all right, Brock?"

"No."

I turn toward the sound of my mother's voice. My face must say it all. My mother gasps as this unbearable pain, this never-ending suffering and the enormous loss of all of it washes over me now. Grief over Ethan. Grief over her. She haunts me. I have endless nightmares where she screams at me for breaking my promise to her in not keeping Ethan safe. And, on the nights I actually get some sleep, I dream of her, but the guilt of lusting for her makes me weak. Jordan Holloway serves as my own personal tormenter. And, to even be in the same room with her, again, as a blind man? No. I won't accept her pity.

"I don't think I can do it," I finally say.

"Oh Brock, you have to," my mother says. "You've been moping around for months about all of this, about what happened. We all loved Ethan, but his wife is reaching out to you. You have to help her. Be there for her." She sighs. "You have to call her. You should call her, now."

"Mom, it's not that simple." My voice rises, and I try to control the racing emotions as best I can. "Can you just give me a minute here? She doesn't—she doesn't know I'm blind. I don't want her to know."

My mother makes this clucking sound. "What? I don't understand why you wouldn't have told her," she says, uncertain.

I sense her hesitation. If there's a sound for hand-wringing, my mother is making it now. She's building up to something, and I'm suddenly on high alert.

"What did you *do*, mother?"

"Well, Jordan called here, earlier, for you." She sighs. "And, I told her what's been going on with you."

"You did *what?*"

"She was completely taken aback at your situation. She had no idea. I'm not even going to begin the lecture about you holding back on the truth of your condition from the people you care about, Brock. Anyway, I invited her to Austin. You've been trying to work on the estate paper-work with her. It seemed like a good idea."

My body has gone completely lax. *Jordan knows I'm blind.* The one thing I didn't ever want her to find out, and my mother has told her. And, now she's coming to Austin.

I try to summon righteous anger at the woman who brought me into this world, but I have this uncanny sense of relief. I've been absolved of the burden of telling Jordan.

My mother responds to my silence with a quickening in her speech. "I'm sorry, Brock. I betrayed your trust and I'm sorry about that, but don't think I won't do anything in my power to try and help you."

My mother takes my hand, while I begin shaking my head side-to-side and finally start to laugh. It's an inappropriate response to what she has just done to me. I think my body is as confused as my mind, which wavers with only mild annoyance at Janie Wainwright's meddling.

"This isn't going to be like my senior prom; is it, mother?"

My senior prom was a comedy of sorts where I went with two different girls to the same function, entirely due to my mother's interference. One girl was the one that I'd actually asked, and the other was a distant cousin from a small town who had never been to such a fancy event, and my mother had promised I would take her. We are on familiar footing here. I should have known that she would take it upon herself to tell Jordan one day. I didn't expect Jordan to ever call, let alone agree to come to Austin.

"Did you call Kate, too?"

"No. I'm going to leave that one up to you," she says with an impish laugh. "Jordan's flying in on Friday. She's taking care of some loose ends with the house and the restaurant."

"Le Reve," I say quietly.

My mind is busy trying to process all of these events. *Jordan's coming. She knows I'm blind.*

"Maybe you should call her."

"I will," I mutter.

"See? It's all working out just fine."

My mother is doing what she always does, putting a positive spin on things and ignoring reality that might be incongruent to her way of thinking.

"Can't *see*," I retort.

"Sorry slip of the tongue," my mother airily calls out.

Her voice drifts farther away from me. She must be going back down the stairs, but I can only surmise. The only truth I really know is this: I can't see anything.

Chapter

Eleven

Jordan – Hope you're happy

I'M PACING BACK AND FORTH BETWEEN the kitchen and the dining room, wondering what I have done in committing myself to a trip to Austin, while my inquisitive child watches me in gleeful fascination. I've finally told him we're going to Texas this weekend. Now, Max is busy looking at the atlas and the state of Texas that I've gotten out for him.

"Is everything pink in Texas?"

Max is staring at the road atlas. I start to giggle, realizing how the world must look to an almost four-year-old.

"No. I don't know why they do the states in different colors like that."

He holds the atlas closer and scrutinizes the map with various shades of pale yellow, blue, and pink. I kiss the top of his head and outline the borders of Texas with my finger and then, point back to the state of California.

"This is our state. This is where Brock lives, now. Far away. So, we'll go on a big airplane to Austin. Where your daddy used to live. Where Grandpa and Grandma Holloway still live. Brock's parents live on a ranch there. His mom sounds very nice."

"A ranch?" Max crinkles up his nose. "What's a ranch?"

"A ranch is a place where people live in big states like Texas. The people have lots of land, and they might raise cattle or horses. I don't know what they have on Brock's ranch." For the millionth time I reflect how little I really know about Brock and his life in Austin.

"Do you think they have horses on his ranch?"

"I don't know. Maybe. Would you like to go see?" His enthusiastic nod is barely contained. I start to laugh. "Okay. Good. So, we'll finish up Mommy's work at the restaurant and take a vacation. We'll pack our clothes and go visit your grandparents and Brock and his family. Ashleigh's coming, too."

"Can I take my picture of the elephant so Brock can see it?"

My son's question elevates my anxiety about Brock's condition. I couldn't believe it when his mother told me he was blind. How could I have not seen it? My behavior at Ethan's funeral comes rushing back. I was horrible to Brock. And, he was blind and injured; and I was awful. The guilt rushes at me from all sides. The reprieve from Liz and even Ashleigh has worn off.

"Max," I say. "We can take the picture, but Mommy will have to describe it to him. Brock's eyes got injured while he was in Afghanistan and he can't see."

"He can't see anymore? He's hurt?"

"I think he's all right, now. His mother said he's going to a special school where they teach blind people how to get along in the world."

"How do they do that?" Max asks.

Why did I bring this up? The questions are endless now. Max rushes over to the computer and is asking me how to spell Braille as soon as I begin describing how blind people read.

"B-R-A-I-L-L-E," I answer.

Within thirty minutes, we are engulfed in everything to do with learning Braille, and I have already promised Max that we will stop by the library tomorrow to pick out more books on the subject and to see if we can get our own book in Braille. It takes another fifteen minutes to get him into his pajamas and into bed for the night. His excitement about seeing Brock and learning Braille makes it almost impossible to get him settled down.

Finally, out of pure exhaustion, he closes his eyes and falls asleep. I sit with him a little longer, stroking his hair. He insists on wearing it in a crew-cut style just like his dad. I sweep my hand across his blonde head and feel the familiar boar bristle brush. The action stirs to life this incredible grief deep inside. I'm transported back, remembering the last time I touched Ethan's hair like this. I close my eyes and allow the memory to take me to him. I'm startled awake by the sudden movement of Max's right arm flopping onto my chest. I check the clock and calculate I've dozed off for a good hour.

Weary from these unsettling dreams of Ethan, I get up and find my way back to the living room and sink into one of the chairs there. I have just begun to unwind in the absolute solitude, when the phone rings. My heart rate speeds up as soon as I see the area code for Texas. What is wrong with me?

His voice is the same, but his southern drawl is more pronounced. I imagine being around his family makes it more prominent. I tease him about it during the first few minutes of conversation.

"So, I hear you're coming to Texas," Brock says haltingly.

"Well, that's the plan. We'll fly in Friday. Max. Ashleigh. Me. You and I can finally go over the paperwork for the estate. Max needs to visit his grandparents. They haven't seen him since last Christmas." I swallow hard and feel the pulse at my neck beat uncontrollably. "Do you mind us staying with you at the ranch? I guess we could stay at the Holloways', but since they still refer to me as the girl from L.A., you'd really be helping me out." I sigh and start to fidget, somewhat disconcerted by his long silence.

"You can stay with us," he finally says. "My parents would love to have you."

"Your parents."

"Me. Them. We'd love to have you stay. You. Max. Ashleigh." He sighs. "I'm living with my parents," he says in a conciliatory tone.

I almost laugh, but realize he must be sensitive about that and catch myself in time.

"We're not putting you out, are we?"

"No. It's just things are different." He seems to hesitate. I remain silent, intent on hearing what he has to say. "They really referred to you as 'the girl from L.A.?'" he asks, sounding puzzled.

"Yes. I told you this already." I find myself smiling. "I don't know. I married their only child, their only son. My parents were the essence of Hollywood. I guess that's a lot to handle. Our elopement to Vegas probably didn't help. My getting pregnant right away probably didn't endear them to me, either. A lot of things."

I'm telling him too much, exposing my long-held resentment and hurt feelings about the treatment of me by my in-laws to this almost stranger.

I just need to stop talking.

"Yeah, but you're so great," he says slowly. "I'm sorry they treated you that way."

"Still do," I say softly. I hear him gasp, and I rush on. "Look, the last six months have been a kind of personal hell for me, on so many levels. But now? I'm trying to get my life in order. I *need* to get my life in order. I guess that starts with Austin. The Holloways. The estate. And, you." I take an unsteady breath. "I'm sorry for the way I've treated you. I blamed you for everything. I shouldn't have done that. I just hope you'll accept my apology now. I'm so sorry, Brock."

My throat gets tight. Tears well up. There's a long silence. I finally hear him sigh.

"Don't worry about me," he says. "I just want you to know that I will *never* call you 'the girl from L.A.'"

I start to laugh, and so does he. It breaks up the seriousness of the moment.

"Well, thank you for that," I say. "I should have met you sooner, and then, you could have vouched for me to the Holloways. Maybe, everything would have been different."

Our conversation seems to have reached this strange crossroads. It's as if Ethan is right there on the phone listening in. Brock seems as uncomfortable as I suddenly feel. I can hear his unsteady breathing on the other end of the line. I shiver as this weird sense of Déjà vu comes over me. I half-smile, remembering how silent he could be, at times, when he was here.

"No need to apologize. I know how hard it's been for you," he says gently. "I think I know how you feel. I miss him, too. It's weird. One day, I'll be fine, and the next, I'm remembering something he would have said or would have done. I can't shake the incredible sadness. I mean, the blindness practically engulfs me, making it hard to even breathe, but missing Ethan is so much worse."

I'm stunned by what he's just said. Somehow, I know he's just told me more than he's told anyone else. I can feel it.

"You're probably the only person on earth who understands. I mean, you spent more time with him than I did, and you're combating blindness, too." I close my eyes, imagining the darkness that Brock must combat every day. Tears prick my eyelids as I think of Ethan.

"It's not so bad," he says.

"Liar."

"It's made me more self aware," he says with a slight laugh.

"Well, there's that."

My mind races as I search for a less sensitive topic.

"I made the mistake of telling Max about your parents' ranch, and well, I hope you have at least one horse."

"We have several. Cattle, too."

"Great. I'll tell you what; I'm going to let you explain cattle to him. I tried, but started laughing too hard when he said, 'What's a cattle, Mommy?'"

"Sounds like he's doing all right," Brock says.

"Yeah, he's holding his own. I think he still thinks Ethan will just show up one day."

Brock sighs. I silently chastise myself for initiating this part of the conversation about Ethan again.

"So, how are you really doing, Brock? Like I said earlier, I'm so sorry for the way I treated you at the funeral and all the unreturned phones calls and emails. I had no idea that you were—"

"Blind? Come on, Jordan, you can say the word," Brock says softly. "It's not going to break me. It might not be permanent. I have dedicated doctors working on it around the clock."

"Oh. Great. That's great news. I'm glad. And, your family's there. Your mom sounds wonderful, just like you described her when you were here."

I brush at a tear and cannot begin to fathom why I'm crying. I cover the receiver, so he won't know.

"Everything okay?" Brock asks.

I don't answer right away. "Fine. Everything's fine."

"So, about the Lazy J—"

"Brock, would you mind if we just talk about it when we get there? Well, it's late here, and I'm really tired."

"Sure. Sorry to have called you so late." He sounds irritated that I've cut him off.

I feel guilty for doing so, but my own emotions are getting the best of me. "I'm glad you called," I say.

"I'm glad you answered."

"I'll email you the final itinerary."

"Sure. Great. Take care."

"You too, Brock."

I manage to hang up the receiver before these mournful sobs overtake me. I cannot explain my sadness, but there is something—something in Brock's voice. Loss. There's so much loss between us. Me with Ethan; him with Ethan and his sight.

All these months, I've battled the grief, but, tonight, I can't find my way out of it. After turning out all the lights and sitting in the darkness for close to an hour, I finally stumble to bed. I'm grateful Ashleigh isn't here to witness this. She's busy celebrating Michael's last night in town before he leaves for London.

I stumble in the dark to bed, lie down in the blackness with my eyes wide open, and think of Brock Wainwright.

We share loss. This incredible loss. His and mine.

And, it must be a loss so deep, a canyon so wide, we may never cross it to one another. Where we used to have Ethan between us, there is now, nothing but the loss of him within us both that we must inevitably share.

❧ ❧

"You want to tell me what's going on?" Ashleigh asks the next morning.

She looks officially tumbled and still wears the clothes she wore the night before. I absently sip my coffee and stare at the clock and silently note that it's almost ten, making it nearly noon in Texas.

Why, oh, why am I thinking about Texas?

"Nothing's going on," I say.

"Uh-huh. Sure." She stands there with her hands on her hips as if I'm one of her wayward students. "Are you *packed*?"

"No."

"Are you going to be? The plane leaves in four hours. We should actually be thinking about leaving for the airport."

"I was going to call a cab," I say, staring at my fingernails, while making no other outward sign at getting ready. *I should have gotten a manicure instead of the bikini wax.*

Undone. I sit, half-dressed, on a kitchen chair, while Ashleigh leans against the counter, sips at her coffee and watches me. Eventually, she makes her way to the master bedroom. I cringe.

My bedroom is in complete shambles. I hear Ashleigh gasp when she must see it. With growing trepidation, I get up from the chair and make my way down the hall.

Here's what I know so far about today. I don't have anything to wear in Texas. I should have gotten a manicure instead of the bikini wax. I came to these conclusions about an hour ago.

And now? I don't even want to go. I can't explain it to myself, so I'm definitely unable to explain it to Ashleigh.

"Do you want to tell me what's going on? Or, do you just want me to guess?" Ashleigh calls out from the closet.

I hesitate at the bedroom doorway. "Nothing's going on."

"Like hell!"

I wanly watch as she pulls a bunch of clothes from my closet and throws them on the bed. I'm too helpless and too distraught over everything to begin to even articulate my problem. She stops and looks at me.

"What?"

"You're scared." She nods as if she's just discovered a new wonder drug. "That's it. You're scared."

Scared of what?" I ask with disdain. "I'm a *mother* of a four-year-old. His birthday is in ten days, you know." Ashleigh just nods. "We're doing a shark theme. I'm a *widow*. Exactly what do I have to be afraid of?"

"We don't have to go," she says in her best teacher voice.

"Okay, let's *not go*."

"Okay, we're not going," she says.

Helpless. Undone. I watch her shove a variety of my clothes and hers into the open suitcase on the bed. I don't say a word the entire time.

Within the hour, we're packed and loading ourselves into the waiting taxi and on the way to the airport, Ashleigh looks over at me.

"You want to tell me what that was all about back there?"

She points her finger in the direction of the Pacific Coast Highway and home. I shake my head side-to-side.

"I should have gotten a manicure, but no, I went for the bikini wax because they had a special."

"Holy shit!" She gets this supreme satisfied smile.

At the airport, she gives me the once-over and seems to approve of my white blouse and skinny black jeans that she helped me with, two hours earlier. "You look amazing," she says. "I *mean* it. I don't think you've ever looked more beautiful."

I pull at the blouse, suddenly self-conscious, but try to smile.
"Thanks."

"I *mean* it; you look incredible."

"Who paid you to say such nice things to me?"

"The manicurist where I get my nails done," she says, bestowing me with a sly smile.

We both laugh.

PART TWO

Give In To Me

"I'VE NEVER BEEN WONDERFUL OR HOPEFUL a single day of my entire adult life. Never the entire day, anyway. And, you *know* this about me, better than anyone else."

Jordan Holloway

CHAPTER

TWELVE

Brock – The space between

ANXIETY, TREPIDATION, AND THIS INEXPLICABLE ANTICIPA-
TION overtake me. I see nothing, but blackness. My heart
pounds at this bizarre rapid pace, while we wait at baggage
claim. Me, unseeing. My sister, Diana, beside me, grasps my arm, being
my eyes.

"This might be them," Diana says next to me. "There's a blonde little
boy holding on to a dark redhead's hand. She has really long hair like you
described."

"That's Jordan and her son, Max.

"There's a blonde bombshell with them."

"That would be Ashleigh."

"You *know* her?"

"She's Jordan's best friend. We're acquainted." I wince as I admit this.

"Geez, Brock. It's going to be hard to keep all your conquests straight,"
Diana teases.

"How's Jordan look? What's she wearing?"

"She's wearing a white blouse and skinny black jeans. She's gorgeous.
God, she looks just like that actress, the one who was killed. God, what
was her name?"

"Laurel Breckinridge. That was her mom," I say with hesitation. "I
didn't count on you recognizing Jordan."

"She won an Oscar. She was married to Davis Breckinridge. Who hasn't
seen their films? What was it ten years ago they were killed in Europe?"

"Spain."

"Wow. She looks just like her. She's so beautiful," Diana murmurs, sounding impressed. "Didn't Mom go to school with Laurel?"

"Di, she doesn't talk about her parents. Don't bring them up to her."

"I won't."

Out of nowhere, I'm assailed by an intense headache that comes on just like that. I close my eyes and stretch my neck. The blackness greets me as I open my eyes. I start to shake. "Not today," I say.

"Are you all right?" Diana's voice gets closer to my face. "Here, come on, Brock." I feel her pull me along, and she gently pushes me down into a hard-backed chair. "Wait here. I'll get them."

My sister's voice gets farther away. I concentrate on taking deep breaths, while an excruciating headache throbs at my temples. I rub my forehead, trying to massage it away.

"Brock!" Small hands rush at my chest and close around me.

"Max, is that you?"

I feel him reach up and touch my face, then my sunglasses. I can picture this cherub little boy running around in his backyard so clearly. I remember the pure joy displayed across his features that day. I reach for him and scruff his hair. It feels like bristles under my fingers.

"You cut your hair," I murmur.

"Like Daddy's," Max says. "Can you see it?"

"No," I say with a shaky laugh. "But, I can feel it."

"Neat." He gives me a hug. "I miss you, Brock."

His little arms go around my neck again, and I hug him back. Max smells of cookies, shampoo, and crayons.

"I missed you, too, buddy." I land a kiss somewhere on his forehead. "Missed you, too." I bury my chin in his shoulder for a minute. He giggles as I pull back. "What?"

"Can I see your scar?"

"Sure, but later. Okay, Max?"

"Max, you shouldn't ask Lieutenant Wainwright things like that." Jordan's voice trembles from above me. I'm overcome by her amazing perfume as she must slide into the chair next to mine.

"It's *Brock*, Momma. He told me last time it was okay to call him that."

Max is impatient with her, and I hear Jordan openly sigh beside me.

"Right."

"It's okay, Jordan." I turn my head in the direction of where she must be. "You look great. My sister, Diana, here, she told me you look great."

"Brock, I…thank you," she finally whispers.

"Well, Lieutenant Brock Wainwright, you sure know how to keep a girl guessing."

There is no mistaking the provocative intonation in Ashleigh Blondell's voice. I'm stunned to hear it—the attractive sex appeal for me. I'm laughing and flirting back with her before I can stop myself. She plants a kiss on my cheek, taking me by surprise.

Jordan gasps beside me. Her body shifts, and, eventually, she moves away. There's only a faint trace of her perfume as evidence that she was even there. Ashleigh takes her place. Her fingers trail up and down my arm in a familiar pattern. I smile because Ashleigh is so easy to entertain and to read, unlike Jordan Holloway, whose very presence is already achingly evocative.

My headache worsens. This unbelievable pain cuts across my forehead. I have days like this. I was just hoping today wouldn't be one of them. I really wanted to show Jordan that I can be independent. Self sufficient. I'm not sure why this is so important to me, to establish this on day one, but it is. But now, I feel awful. This continual shaking takes over, and I can't stop it.

Diana does her own introductions. Then, my twin sister gets busy discussing the logistics of baggage with Jordan and Ashleigh.

I listen for Max. He's close by, and, after a few minutes, he puts his hand in mine. It's amazing how this little gesture from him affects me. With casual ease, I wipe at my eyes from underneath my dark glasses with my free hand and have to hope that no one sees me do this.

The scent of Jordan's perfume returns. She sits down next to me again and loops her arm through mine.

"Diana and Ashleigh went to go get the luggage. Somebody has to watch Max. Sorry, I didn't mean anything by that. God, I just keep saying the wrong things, doing the wrong things."

"I know you didn't mean anything by it. You never do anything wrong. Ever. Whereas, I?"

I sigh heavily as memories of Ethan rush at me, and then, images of Jordan follow, but the blackness infiltrates. I can't see anything or anyone.

"I'm sorry I ignored your phone calls. I haven't been myself." She sighs.

"The funeral was bad enough, but I had a miscarriage shortly after that, and, well, that kind of took its toll."

"You were pregnant? I'm so sorry. I didn't know."

"I'd just written him an email the day before—the day before to tell him. Didn't he talk to you about it?"

I sense her looking at me, searching for answers, and grimace both from the headache and her obvious disappointment when I don't answer right away.

"I don't remember anything about that day," I say slowly. "I didn't know. I'm sorry you lost the baby."

"I wasn't that far along," she says in a low voice. "But, somehow, losing that baby was like losing him all over again. I've spent a lot of time these past months pretending everything was okay, but—"

She stops talking, and I lean toward her, waiting for her to say more.

"But what?" I finally ask.

"I don't know. I guess seeing you makes it all too real. I can't pretend he's in Afghanistan any longer."

The wistfulness in her tone is so strong that I reach out until I find her hand. "I'm sorry." Pain shoots across my forehead.

"Are you okay?" Jordan asks.

"I'm okay. It's just a headache. I get them sometimes."

"Oh. Let me see if I have some Ibuprofen. Can you take that?"

"Yeah, sure. I'm blind, Jordan, not an invalid." My face feels hot. "I'm sorry. My head's pounding. I'm not myself."

Max climbs up on my lap again. His little hand pats at my face.

"Brock, are you going to be okay? Mommy said you could take me around to show me the cattle and horses and stuff."

"Sure, buddy. I'm okay."

Jordan's hand closes over my left one. She opens it up and presses three pills into it one at a time. Somehow, I thank her and swallow them down with the bottled water she gives me next. I've reached invalid status in a matter of sixty seconds.

"Jordan, thanks. You don't have to fuss over me."

"You sound like Max," she says with a laugh.

She pats my hand and takes the bottled water from me. I'm helpless and enthralled all at the same time. All the while, my head throbs out of control, but there's this big smile spreading across my face.

"You look good," she says.

Her fingers brush across my arm. It's fleeting; it's there one second and gone in the next. Max leans against my chest, and I stroke his hair. Jordan rests her hand on my arm again. I relish the companionship of both of them, mother and son, for a few minutes. Then, Ashleigh and Diana's distinct voices rise above the chatter of baggage claimants. For once, I take solace in the suspended blackness of it all because I'm not sure I would actually survive seeing Jordan's face right now. My body and mind react to her like a tuning fork. I'm on edge.

Unsettled by this self-revelation that Jordan has this strong of effect on me, even after all this time, I try to conjure up an image of Kate's face, but having never seen it, I'm left with envisioning nothing more than shadows. We've carried on a long-distance relationship, since I returned to Austin. Kate's been to see me a few times, though we have yet to take things further in our relationship, since she, literally and figuratively, straddles the fine line of once being my psychiatrist and still being my superior officer, until I'm officially discharged from the Navy. And, I've been reluctant to sign that paperwork. The documents for my honorable discharge remain in an envelope hidden in my father's desk drawer, while I hold out secret hope that I'll soon see again and be able to return to my unit in Afghanistan.

Jordan's face flashes through my mind. Her amazing smile. The way her silky, dark mahogany hair blew in the wind that day. The way the sunlight lit up her amazing face and made her look like a goddess. I shake my head, trying to clear it, suddenly feeling troubled and conflicted about these two women. Kate and Jordan. Jordan and Kate. In a matter of minutes, I've convinced myself that Jordan's visit is a bad idea. Kate will be here in a few days. I can't see. All these factors add up to a very bad idea. I clench my jaw, frustrated by the easy banter all around me between my sister and these two women that I'm not really a part of. Their chatter makes the dark world I inhabit even more potent.

"You okay?" Diana asks, gripping my elbow and apparently steering me toward the airport entrance.

"Not exactly."

I don't hide my angst from Diana. I might be six minutes younger than her, but we share the common twin bond of knowing what the other is thinking and even feeling.

"They're taking Max to the restroom," Diana says. "It's just you and me for a few minutes." I hear her sigh. "She's beautiful," Diana finally says. "I'm talking about Jordan. Her friend is, too, of course, as you well know." Her sarcasm is fresh and biting; I flinch when she says this. "But Jordan, she takes your breath away. Yet, she hardly seems aware of it, which makes her even more so."

"She is," I manage to say.

My sister must glimpse the torture that I carry at a soul level for Jordan. She gasps beside me.

"God, Brock. She's Ethan's wife. Talk about *complicated.*"

I wince at Diana's blunt words. She squeezes my arm tighter in hers.

"There's nothing between Jordan and me," I say evenly. "And, Kate will be here in a day or so." I force myself to smile, though the incongruence of Kate and Jordan meeting one another starts to worry me.

"Kate Richards isn't going to be able to save you from Jordan Holloway, little brother."

My sister's clairvoyance into my predicament is unexplainable. I shake my head in the direction of her voice and almost smile. Diana has made it clear during a few of Kate's brief secret visits over the past three months to Austin that she is less than impressed with my psychiatrist. "Whatever *this Kate* is to you," Diana had said once, "she's not good for you."

Only Diana has met Kate, since I have yet to actually do more than make reference to her with my parents. 'This Kate' is how Diana refers to my supposed girlfriend. I've tried to talk to Diana about Kate, tried to explain my base attraction and need of her, but my sister isn't buying it.

"I really need your help with all of this," I say to her now.

I extend my free arm in a general wave of the surroundings and beseech her to understand my uncertain, complicated version of the world, but Diana just laughs.

"Yeah, I'm sure you do," Diana says with sisterly affection. "Look, we can't talk about any of it right now. Here they come. Where's Tate meeting us?"

"Just out at the curb."

"Well, I'll be out Monday night." She pats my right arm and pulls me to my feet. "Mom's putting on dinner and such. You're on your own until then, Cowboy, so try and keep it together; shall we? Here they come."

Jordan laughs at something Max has said. I stop to hear it.

"Leave it to my almost four-year-old to find magic even at the airport," Jordan says. "Restroom entertainment."

"Brock!" Max grabs my hand. "They have this giant hand dryer. You stick your hands in. It dries them real fast."

"That sounds like fun," I say.

Diana's voice drifts away from me. I hear her telling Ashleigh and Jordan about the travel plans to the ranch.

Jordan's perfume drifts closer. In the next moment, she takes my arm. Her soft breath caresses my cheek as she nears my face. "We're just walking through the entryway, following Diana. She told us we're meeting Tate curb side." She hesitates. "Who's Tate?"

"Our first cousin. My best friend, besides Ethan." I shake my head. "Sorry, I shouldn't have mentioned him."

"It's okay to talk about Ethan. We *need* to talk about him."

I can only wonder what she thinks we still need to say.

"You think so?" I finally ask.

"I do."

Jordan squeezes my arm near my elbow. I startle at the swishing sound of metal against metal; the only signal the electronic doors have opened. We pass through them together. I greet the openness and gasp a little for fresh air while she guides me to the curb.

I curse the darkness and do battle with the intrinsic urge to be able to see, to see *her*. But, my eyes fail me. I swim in the blackness with only this pounding headache to shadow me. I suddenly feel undone by Jordan's very presence, both by her amazing touch and her auspicious prediction that there are still things that need to be said about Ethan.

God, I hope so. Don't I?

Chapter Thirteen

Jordan – Spell

Brock informs us his parents live about ten miles out of town, as Diana, his twin sister, makes a hasty exit with an airy wave of her hand.

"Tate will drive you out to the ranch," Diana calls out as she leaves us.

Tate turns out to be an outright cowboy that both Max and Ashleigh seem to have become enamored with the moment we meet him at curb side. He leans up against a shiny, black pick-up truck and begins loading our baggage with no more than a shy hello and a quizzical raised-eyebrow look in Ashleigh's general direction while my son watches Tate load our luggage in awed fascination. "A real cowboy," Max says, at one point. I bite my lip to keep from laughing out loud, also intrigued by this tall, dark, handsome cowboy, who does look like he is directly related to Brock Wainwright. I'm somewhat dismayed at Ashleigh's behavior in showing interest in him, when five minutes earlier she was flirting with Brock at baggage claim. Only Ashleigh.

She's already started twisting Michael's engagement ring on her left hand, back and forth. She bestows me with an I-can't-help-it forlorn look while I shake my head at her in warning and roll my eyes at her.

A secret part of me, buried deep, is elated with this turn of events, but another part feels sorry for Brock. He can't even see what's transpiring between Ashleigh and his tall, dark-haired cousin. Their attraction to each other began within seconds of their first meeting at curbside.

Five minutes later, Diana waves from her navy blue sedan as she passes us, calling out through the open passenger that she promises to catch up with us tomorrow at the ranch. Brock, somehow, acknowledges his sister's departure with a casual wave of his hand. Then, Max is there, holding Brock's hand and chatting ninety words a minute. Their close interaction and easy laughter captivates me, until Tate touches my arm and introduces himself.

"Mrs. Holloway? I'm Tate Matthews, Brock and Ethan's best friend from way back. Brock and I are first cousins, actually." He grins, revealing a too-white smile. In the next few seconds, it disappears, and he removes his cowboy hat. "Anyway, I knew Ethan from way back. Here in Austin. I was a few years younger than Brock and him, but we hung out. We did some fishing and such. I just want you to know how sorry I am about everything. He was a good guy. I'm just so sorry for your loss, ma'am."

He puts his black cowboy hat back on his head, tips it at me, and reaches for my right hand. I'm taken aback at his words. I think the man before me is, too. My first impression of Tate Matthews that he was quiet and introspective, the polar opposite of Ashleigh, seems to be true.

"Thank you, Tate. Please call me Jordan."

I reach out and shake his hand. I'm astounded at his firm grip and become dazzled when he smiles at me again. A hand at my lower back causes me to look over. It's Brock. Somehow, he's planted himself between Tate and me.

"Why don't you help Miss Blondell with her luggage, Tate? I can't exactly *see* how much she has, but, knowing Ashleigh, I'm sure it's more than enough."

I glance over at him, taken aback at the edge I hear in his tone. Tate gives me a curious look and then studies his cousin for a long moment.

"Everything okay?" Tate asks Brock.

"Fine," Brock says in a clipped voice.

"You sure? Because you're acting kind of edgy. I was just telling the lady how sorry I was about Ethan."

"We're all sorry about Ethan."

"Brock, it's fine. He was just saying that he'd known Ethan. That's all. I'm not upset or anything. It's okay. Like I said before, it's okay to talk about him. I'm not going to fall apart." I watch Brock's face contort. "Are you all right? You do seem kind of on edge."

"I've got a headache. That's all. Like I said before, I get them."

Max comes over to us and starts jumping up and down. I spend the next few minutes fiddling with his car seat and cajoling him to climb up into the truck cab. Ashleigh claims the front passenger seat, and I give her a dirty look, while I climb in to the middle of the backseat. Brock gets in next to me. The truck is roomy, but our thighs practically touch. Brock insists he has more than enough room. I give up trying to convince Ashleigh to do the right thing by sitting in the back with me. The girl is captivated by Tate Matthews, and there is no point in trying to get her attention when she's like this. I hear snippets of their conversation as Tate gives her the tourist rundown on Austin as the scenery whizzes past us. I'm fascinated by their instant attraction to each other, amazed, and a little uncomfortable all at the same time.

"Is he married?" I ask in a low voice.

"No. Came close. A friend of ours lost his fiancée, Annie. She was killed in a car accident our last year in school. It left a lasting impression on all of us about marriage. Well, except for Ethan."

This sad look crosses Brock's face.

"Please tell me he dates a lot. Gets around."

"He holds his own." Brock's face flushes and he half-smiles. "He can handle Ashleigh, if that's what you're worried about."

"I'm sorry. I know you and Ashleigh have been close." I sound like a woman from the Victorian age. Brock laughs and I blush, thankful he can't see my face.

"I've moved on."

He turns to look out the window, and I try not to feel like I've been stung by his abruptness, effectively ending our conversation. Now, I'm on edge. These mixed feelings about how I've behaved these past months and the enviable ability that Tate and Ashleigh are allowed in being attracted to each other assails me now. I lean back against the headrest and close my eyes.

Breathe. Concentrate on breathing. Ignore your best friend's sexual innuendos. Forget you've gotten a bikini wax and been shot up with Depo-Provera. Concentrate on Max.

I open my eyes and look over at my son. He's sleeping. The plane ride wore him out. I smile and take a deep breath. Brock must hear it. His head turns in my direction. Expectant? Vulnerable? It's hard to tell. He's wearing dark glasses. I can't see his eyes.

I look past him out the window, surprised, once again, at the greenness of the landscape and the terrain's rolling hills. "Somehow, I had the impression that all of Texas was flat and dusty. I always forget how green it really is."

"You don't come here often enough," he chides. "It's not Malibu, but Austin is beautiful in its own way."

"It is."

I'm somewhat confused by his underlying critical tone. I blush under his unseeing gaze. My breath quickens as I breathe him in; he's a mixture of mint, a hint of Armani cologne and this distinctive woodsy smell. *Have we been this close before?* He should remind me of Ethan, but I'm more reminded of my dad. Brock has the same dark hair, the chiseled features, and the incredible good looks of a Greek god. I glimpse his dark chest hair through the opening of his polo shirt and my insides shift a little. *He's not a soldier anymore. I'm not married anymore. We shared Ethan. Now, what do we share?* Somehow, I'm comforted and terrified at the same time by these thoughts. We're in uncharted territory.

The movement of the truck sways me into him. I lean in to his face so he can hear me.

"Thank you for picking us up. I'm sure it was a hassle. I'll have to call the Holloways and let them know we're here."

"I've already called them. I told them you were staying with us."

I take in this latest development with cool silence.

"Thank you," I finally say. "You have no idea how much you've saved me."

He nods. "I told her Max wanted to stay at the ranch. I hope you're okay with that." Brock winces as he says this and looks anxious.

"Max will be excited to stay at the ranch. He's already worn out, though. He fell asleep five minutes ago." I start to smile, but then, it fades. "I'm so sorry about your...sight. You mentioned on the phone that they're working on it. What are they trying to do?"

"There's no physical reason for why I can't see. At least, that's what they tell me." He gets this tight smile. "So, I'm hopeful that with some help, my memory will return and so will my sight." He looks uncertain and then his forehead creases as if he's in pain.

"The headaches. Do you get those often? I mean, I can tell you're in a lot of pain, right now."

"Not often." He turns away. "I just need to lie down for awhile."

Sympathy invades every part of me. It's strange to be able to observe someone, a stranger, in such an obvious way and not be detected. I loosen his seat belt and in a commanding way force his head down onto my lap.

"One thing I am good at is head massages," I say, removing his sunglasses. Brock looks disconcerted.

"Close your eyes. Just relax. Let's see if we can get rid of this headache before we reach the ranch."

I surprise myself as much as him with such a bold move.

Ashleigh glances at me from the front seat and silently mouths, "What are you doing?"

I just shrug and begin running my fingers, back and forth, along Brock's forehead. His eyes are closed and I enjoy the proximity of his handsome face near mine. His head rests somewhat awkwardly in my lap, but I solely focus upon smoothing away the sharp edges of his pain.

Eventually, I look up into the rearview mirror to find Tate studying me. He nods and then turns his attention back to Ashleigh to quiz her further about her life in Los Angeles.

For some reason, I revel in the surrealistic feeling to it all. The unexplainable closeness. The shared silence between Brock and me, and even the blessed escape from heartbreak that normally follows me everywhere. There's an inexplicable peacefulness present in Tate's truck that I haven't felt in a long while.

I may never leave. I smile to myself, imagining myself firmly entrenched in Tate's black truck for days to come.

⁂

I'm ill-prepared for the Wainwrights' expansive ranch. When we come up over another rolling hill, Tate calls out, "Welcome to the Wainwrights' version of paradise, J's Paradise Ranch, in fact."

Brock sits up, breaking our close contact of the last twenty minutes. He feels his way to the truck's passenger window with outstretched hands.

"Where are we exactly, Tate?" Brock asks.

He looks a little dazed and out of sorts as he runs his hands through his dark hair. I grimace at the thought of his blindness and start to turn away, foolishly afraid he can somehow sense my pity.

"What do you see?" Brock asks, leaning over my way.

"I see this great line of trees, bordering this incredibly green pasture, a few cows—"

"Cattle," Brock says with a laugh. "We call them *cattle* in Texas. Cows are—never mind." He smiles. "What else?"

"There's a dirt road on the right with a wooden arch above it."

"That's our drive, well, my father and mother's drive. Welcome to J's Paradise." He pauses and gets this anxious look. "You'll see the Lazy J in a day or so. Maybe, tomorrow, if you're up for it." His face gets flushed. "You know what I mean."

"I know what you mean. I'm up for it." Now, I'm blushing. Brock smiles as if he knows this.

"What else do you see?"

"All I see is *you*. You're blocking my view out the window."

I start to laugh and catch Tate's quizzical stare in the rearview mirror again. He slowly nods at me, then smiles, as if he's figured out the answer to a question that hasn't even been asked yet.

"How long did you say you're going to be here for?" Tate asks.

Before I can answer, Ashleigh chimes in, "A week, maybe longer."

She shoots me one of her don't-argue-with-me looks and I keep my protests to myself. This is supposed to be a quick trip. We agreed to four days, maximum, and she knows it.

"Great. A week, maybe longer," Brock says beside me. "That will give us time to go through Ethan's paperwork, see the ranch, see everything."

My eyes start to sting, missing Ethan comes in waves and always unexpected, like sudden nausea or the flu. I shake my head and lean against Max, who is still asleep in his car seat. I try to regain the happy feeling from minutes before, when I was massaging Brock's head as if I was holding time back and nothing had changed. The truth is this: everything has changed and it's moments like these that cause me to realize that I'm all but breaking apart.

"Are you okay?"

Brock touches my arm. I tremble uncontrollably at his touch and know he can feel it. I shake my head side-to-side, and then belatedly realize he can't even see me. Tears return.

"Define okay for me." I swipe at a stray tear, just as he reaches out and touches my face.

"I miss him, too," he finally says.

With his fingertips, he traces the trail of my tear down my face, and then strays toward my collar bone. It's the most intimate touch I've experienced in six months, nine days, and two hours. The last time I saw Ethan alive. It's the recognition of that moment that must cause this unexpected pain to course through me like a freshly opened wound. I take an unsteady breath.

Notably, this close proximity is interrupted by the first glimpse of the Wainwrights' ranch house which seems to be at least a city block long, New York style, with a paved circular drive, a humongous bronze statue with Greek-like figurines of a man and woman sharing a pitcher of water, complete with a working fountain below, and most notably, an American-made navy sedan graces the driveway. All of it just seems to welcome us.

"Welcome, to J's Paradise," Brock says.

He sweeps his arm across the landscape as he alights from the car and helps me to my feet as I hold on to his free arm.

"It's amazing."

I gaze around in wonder. I had no idea that Brock came from any sort of money, but the wealth is apparent all around me.

"It is," Brock says back to me. "It kept me going, many a day, while I was in Afghanistan, in just wanting to get back to this place, so I could feel the breeze, hear the wind whistle through the grass, and see the blanket of stars at night. There's nothing like it, anywhere. The peace and quiet. It keeps me going, even now, knowing it's still there. Even though I can't see it, I can *feel* it."

I close my eyes, and smile, when I hear the wind whistle and the rustling of the long golden grass.

"I hear it, too," I say unsteadily.

Brock traces my eyelids, seeming to instinctively know my eyes are closed.

"I'm glad you came," he says slowly. "Ethan—well, he loved the ranch. He practically lived here when we were growing up. Did he tell you about it? "

"No, he didn't—"

Max breaks the moment, stirring awake from his nap. "Momma, is this where Daddy lives?"

I pull out of Brock's grasp, suddenly undone by his closeness and notice Tate and Ashleigh openly staring at our friendly embrace with keen interest. I lean back into the car and undo the straps of Max's car seat.

"No, Baby. Daddy's in Heaven; remember? This is where Brock lives. We're in Texas, though. Soon, you'll see Grandpa and Grandma Holloway."

"Oh."

Max looks so disappointed. I'm not sure where the idea that we would be seeing Ethan has come from. Max hasn't talked about Ethan for a few weeks.

Brock leans in next to me. "Come on, buddy. I want you to meet my mom and dad," he says.

Max scrambles into Brock's outstretched arms and puts his little arms around his neck. I watch Brock trail his hand along the bed of the truck while holding onto Max. This little modicum of happiness comes over me in just watching the two of them interact. Max's confusion in seeing Ethan seems to have been forgotten. I breathe a sigh of relief, grateful to Brock.

"My mom makes the best chocolate chip cookies in Texas and my dad is a big-time rancher and oilman. They really want to meet you. Show you around and stuff," Brock says.

"I love cookies. Can we see horses? And cows? What's an oilman?"

"Yep, we're going to see it all," Brock says. "Oil is black gold. It makes the world go round."

"Oil, huh?" I ask with a little smile.

"Oil," Brock says to me.

I watch him hoist Max up on his shoulders with relative ease. I'm surprised when he flips out a white walking stick that I've seen blind people use and taps his ways to the front door with Max chattering all the while. Ashleigh grabs two of our bags, gives me a surreptitious look, and then exchanges a knowing, seductive look with Tate Matthews before following Brock and Max.

"So, how long have you and Brock known each other?" Tate asks as he openly watches Ashleigh strut across the drive and into the house.

"We met for the first time this past February, just before he and Ethan returned to Afghanistan for their final tour."

"Really?" Tate asks in surprise. "It looked like…It seemed like you two have known each other for a long time. It looked intimate to me."

I'm surprised at his word choice. It must show on my face.

"Intimate. Really? We're just friends," I say, laughing nervously.

Tate studies my face for an endless moment. Then, he shakes his head.

"Brock Wainwright isn't friends with any woman that I know of," he says slowly. "Not ever. Not even, now."

"Oh really? You know this for a fact?" My breath gets uneven at his insinuation and I know I'm blushing. "Because he seems pretty broken, so different, from the last time I saw him when we first met. Back then, he acted as if he owned the world. Now, he doesn't seem to own anything."

"He'll snap out of it. He has to, for Ethan, for himself. He can't waste his life just because he can't see it."

I step back, surprised by this handsome cowboy's sudden discordant tone. His duty to protect Brock is admirable and disconcerting at the same time. I shade my eyes with my hand and look at him more closely. He seems to be sizing me up, too. His eyes narrow as he studies my face.

"He's like a brother to me. So was Ethan. It's hard to see him like this. You're right; he's broken in some ways." Tate gets this disconcerted look as if he's said more than he should have. "I've got this. Go on. Aunt Janie is going to love you. A week under her care, and you'll be a new woman." He finally smiles.

I silently nod and start to leave, still smarting from his insinuation that my actions with Brock were somehow intimate. *What is going on with me today? Why did I touch Brock like that on the way here? Intimate. Inappropriate. We're just friends; aren't we?*

"Jordan," Tate calls out to me. His tone, all at once, is conciliatory.

I turn back, looking at him, still uncertain, and give way to the strange confusion his words have conjured up inside of me.

"I love him like a brother, like he loved Ethan," Tate says. "I love them both. I just don't want to see him get hurt anymore than he has been already. Sorry. I shouldn't have jumped all over you like that."

I nod, trying to understand where he's coming from, but still undone by what he's said.

"I was married to Ethan. I loved him. I'm still in love with him," I say with a helpless shrug. "I have no intention of getting involved with anyone. I have my child to think of. And, I can't lose anyone else. I don't know." I look up at him. "I don't know if I'll even survive this loss, let alone be able to love anyone else again. Not with the possibility of losing them." My voice trembles. I know he hears it.

I haven't admitted these fears to anyone. I'm embarrassed to be admitting them, now, to a perfect stranger.

"Just so you know," I say in a low voice. "Ashleigh goes through men like a pair of pajamas. You best stay clear."

I gaze at him in defiance.

At first, he looks disappointed that I would say this, but then he says, "Yeah, I got that."

Thirty seconds later, his face dissolves into this wide dazzling white smile. I catch my breath, awestruck by his stunning beauty, so like his cousin's.

"But just so you know, I'm going to marry that girl."

He gazes at me with such confidence that I'm too taken aback by his audacious comment to even respond. I turn around and walk away from him, trembling with a mixture of anger and embarrassment at his insinuation about Brock and me and his incredible self-assurance about Ashleigh.

Eventually, I turn back. "I think you just met your match, Tate Matthews. You best prepare yourself," I call out to him and finally laugh.

He shakes his head and starts to laugh, too. Then, he turns his attention back to the luggage. Mystified, I watch him for a few minutes as he deftly unloads more of our luggage. Then, I turn away, too confused by his revelations about Ashleigh and even myself.

I cross the vast threshold into the Wainwrights incredible ranch house. My eyes are just becoming adjusted to the dim light of the stunning dark granite foyer in comparison to the bright light of the outdoors when I'm engulfed into the outstretched arms of a beautiful older woman, who can only be Brock's mother.

The faint perfume scent of Coco Chanel's No. 5 assails my nostrils. I breathe in deep and am instantly reminded of my mother.

"Oh, Jordan," the dark-haired woman says.

She has a young Jackie Kennedy thing going on with this amazing shoulder-length hair, the color of espresso, and golden brown eyes that sparkle and just take you in and make you feel welcome. I like her immediately.

"My God. Look at you! You're gorgeous. Just like her," she says, fingering a strand of my hair.

I'm confused by the *her* reference, but before I can ask what she means by that she's stroking my hand.

"You look fantastic. Oh honey, let me hold you for a moment."

I can't say anything.

And, all at once, the sorrow of the past six months takes all control. I start crying in this woman's arms without further provocation.

⋄

A tall glass of lemonade, a guest suite made up to welcome someone of royal status, and a much needed nap have restored my sensibilities into their proper place of outward decorum.

Janie Wainwright is a human dynamo. She runs her household like a cruise ship captain, ensuring all of us have what we need. Ashleigh has already stolen away to catch up with Tate, who is apparently on the Back Forty, wherever that might be, with Brock's father, Henry.

In discerning how much work there is to do on the ranch, since I first arrived a mere six hours before, I'm now indebted to Tate for taking the time to pick us up at the airport, especially since he had to dash off with Henry Wainwright as soon he unloaded all the bags. Of course, this was after my untimely emotional outburst over Ethan and Janie's motherly ministrations. Seeming to realize I didn't want Max to see me upset, Tate was quick to take Max's little hand and hurry him off toward the barn a fair distance from the main house. I'm just trying not to worry too much, since I haven't seen Max since we got here. Janie has assured me that my son is in good hands with her husband, her son, and her nephew Tate.

"Ashleigh's there, too," she says to me now.

I watch her settle in to a cozy chair directly across from me. The furniture in this room is upholstered in silken material with a bright white background and patterned with huge red exotic-looking flowers. Janie Wainwright's sense of decor is on the same scale as my late mother's. I have flashbacks of our mansion in L.A.

"Ashleigh isn't exactly clued in to the details of motherhood."

I have this vision of Max falling off a fence or a horse or something in a faraway field and envision Ashleigh just standing by, unable to determine what to do next other than to reach for her cell phone and call for help. I force myself not to openly shudder.

"I shouldn't have slept so long. I was just so tired. I don't know why."

"Of course you're tired. You've been traveling all day with a small child," she says with a laugh. "Tate said he would bring Max back with him. He'll check in around five, so there's really nothing to worry about."

I clear my throat, hesitant to ask my next question, but somehow, I need to know. I tossed and turned during my nap, restless, by Janie Wainwright's strange reference to her. The words, *you look just like her* kept spinning through my mind.

"Did you know her?" I finally ask. "My mother, Laurel Breckenridge." My mother's name seems strange to say, but easily rolls off my tongue. I rarely speak of her; and yet, with Janie Wainwright, here I am talking about her.

"Yes. We attended high school together here in Austin. She moved with her mom, your grandmother, after her senior year. She attended UCLA. I stayed here and went to the University of Texas. Then, she met Davis. She had her dreams of being an actor and she'd fallen in love with one. I met Henry. We got married and stayed in Texas. We tried to keep in touch." She shakes her head and tries to smile. "But Texas is a lot different from Hollywood. You were about two when she flew in to Austin, her last visit here. Brock and Diana were about Max's age. I remember the three of you playing in the back yard near the old Oak tree. Brock was pushing you on a swing." She laughs softly, remembering. "It was lovely to see you and your mom. She was so happy, so in love with your dad. And, she loved you. That's how I like to remember her."

Janie gets this haunted look. "I'm sorry I wasn't there for you, when they were killed. I read about their murders in the paper. I couldn't believe it. There wasn't any information about you. I was hoping you'd be with your grandmother, but then I learned she'd passed away a few months before their deaths."

I'm assailed by the memories of that terrible time after their deaths. I take an unsteady breath. She grips my hand even tighter. I just nod, unable to speak for a few minutes.

Finally I say, "I went to stay with my grandfather, my dad's father, in Northern California, until I was eighteen. Then, I went back to L.A. to live with Ashleigh. I sold the mansion in L.A., kept the beach house in Malibu, and started over. I went to USC and then culinary school. Ashleigh and I lived in Manhattan for a while, spent a summer in Paris, but we missed L.A. and, soon after, we moved back. I became head chef at Rivera. Then, I met Ethan. I got pregnant; we got married. He left for Afghanistan. I stayed in Malibu." I stop talking and swallow hard. I try to smile and brush away a stray tear.

"Soon, he'll have been dead longer than the number of days we were together. Can you believe I keep track of stuff like that?"

"I would, too," Janie says in a consoling tone.

A tapping sound along the hallway's wood floor interrupts us. Brock appears in the doorway. He's changed into a black Polo shirt and fresh blue jeans. His hair appears damp. I'm surprised that he's apparently taken a shower in the middle of the afternoon. Janie gives me a little smile and studies me intently as she continues to hold my hand.

"Brock, Jordan and I were just talking about Max. He's with Tate; right? They should be back soon."

"Right." Brock cocks his head to one side and seems to hesitate. "Jordan," he says softly. "There was a little mishap with the water trough at the far side of the barn, but he's fine."

"What do you mean?" I ask, trying to mask my sudden alarm.

"Max was climbing the coral fence and almost fell into the trough. I caught him in time, but I got soaking wet." He grins. "But, he's fine."

"Is that why you've taken a shower in the middle of the afternoon?" I can't quite keep the worry out of my voice. My heart rate has sped up at just visualizing Max almost falling into the water.

"He did great. A little surprised is all," Brock says, shaking his head.

I'm stunned by wondrous beauty of his amazing grey-blue eyes and reminded of the Pacific in winter once again from not so long ago. My reverie is interrupted by Janie who jumps up all at once and announces she needs to attend to dinner.

Brock and I are left alone. He stands at the living room doorway and seems as uncertain as I suddenly feel.

"Your mom is amazing."

Brock half-smiles. "Amazing, the human form of magic, meddlesome," he says with a slight frown. "Sometimes, all three at the same time."

"You're lucky."

"I know I am."

He's still standing there, kind of half-leaning against the doorway for support with his white cane in his left hand. He runs a hand through his hair and eventually sighs.

"Could you describe the room a bit? They haven't been in here to mark this one. I guess they're coming tomorrow."

"Oh. I'm sorry." I jump up and race toward him. "Let me help you."

I slide my arm though his. He gives me an exasperated look.

"Jordan, you don't have to escort me in here. Just describe the room. Where things are."

"Oh, well, I'm here now," I say, trying to mollify his obvious irritation.

I sympathize with his sudden pitch into a world where he has to depend upon others so much. I feel somewhat self-conscious, standing next to him, holding on to him. It stirs up all these uneasy feelings.

Our friendly companionship on the ride from the airport has since evaporated and been replaced by this total awareness of the other. It seems to permeate from both of us and offers little protection.

"I'm sorry about falling apart. Earlier. I don't." I pause for a moment. "I don't usually do that. I haven't. I don't know what's going on with me."

"It's okay to be human, Jordan. We all are."

"You sound like your mom."

"My mom is mother nature, herself," he says with a laugh. "Didn't you know?"

We're still standing at the doorway, arms locked together, as if we're a bride and groom about to descend down the aisle toward the altar and just awaiting a blessing. The incongruence of this image unsettles me. I hold my breath, trying to chase it away. I flashback to what Tate said about marrying Ashleigh one day. I have yet to get my best friend alone for a minute to even discuss the audacity of that prediction. Ashleigh actually getting married is such a foreign thought, such a remote possibility, even with Michael, let alone Tate Matthews. I start to laugh a little. Ashleigh marrying Tate is about as remote as Ethan coming back from the dead. A flash of Igor Dasher in his green velvet suit comes to mind and I grip Brock's arm tighter in response to thinking these thoughts.

"You okay?" Brock asks.

"I don't know. I think so."

I wipe away a tear that has managed to find its way down my face and am suddenly glad that Brock can't see it. I realize at the same time how incredibly painful that would be, to never know what people were really feeling around you because you couldn't see them. I take an unsteady breath and sigh.

"Jordan," he says, breaking my reverie. "Describe the room."

"Oh sorry," I groan. "I got distracted. There was this guy Igor Dasher and he was—"

"I don't really want to hear about your love life, even about a guy named Igor," Brock says with a grimace. Can you help me get to the sofa?"

I start to laugh, however, inappropriate with the idea of Igor in any way serving in the role as my lover. Brock frowns, extricates himself from my groping arm, and starts making his way across the living room by himself.

"Igor Dasher was the director at the funeral. He let me see Ethan one last time. I don't know why I was thinking about it."

Brock stands stock-still halfway across the living room. He turns back toward my voice. "You saw him? You saw Ethan?" There's so much pain in his voice and face; I have to look away for a moment.

"Yes. I told you that. Months ago. I saw him." I look back at Brock. He's shaking and I go over to him and take his arm again. "I had to say goodbye. I had to know it was real. That he was really gone. Forever."

"You saw him," Brock says more to himself.

I sense the sadness in him and it reaches at my own.

"What do you remember?" I ask. I'm unsure I even want to know anymore, but feel compelled to ask him.

"That's the thing. Like I said before. I don't remember anything about that day." Brock touches his forehead. "Kate says it's locked up here. And, until I do remember, I won't be able to see anything. She thinks it's why I can't see. She thinks whatever I can't remember is the key to being able to see again."

"Kate." I'm unable to hide my uncertainty in his mentioning this Kate.

"She's my psychiatrist. Well, she was while I was in D.C. at Walter Reed. We've been—"

"Friends," I say with sarcasm. I step away from him. His hand drops to his side.

"It's not like that." His voice doesn't hold much conviction though.

"Friends," I say softly. "Like we're friends? Or something different?"

He looks away. I half-smile that my probing question has made him uncomfortable. I don't do more than a cursory calculation as to why I would be pursuing this line of questioning about being more than friends with this Kate.

"She'll be here in the next couple of days. She's coming down from D.C. with some new idea for my therapy." His voice trails off, and he looks back in my general direction.

I sense his helplessness in the situation with my intended silent treatment and in not being able to see me. There's no outward indication from me about how I feel about what he's said. This incredible feeling of jealousy comes out of nowhere. I hold my breath a moment and attempt to get my bearings. Guilt for feeling this way pushes at me from all sides. I gasp for air and try to pace my breathing after that.

"You're so different," I finally whisper. "I hated your playboy ways before. I wanted Ashleigh to dump you on your ass back then. But now? I don't know. You're so sad. It's hard to see you like this, so broken."

"It's hard not to see," he says with a trace of irritation. "Look, I don't need your sympathy, Jordan. I wanted you to come here so we could go over Ethan's estate and settle a few things. You should see the ranch, the Lazy J. We'll have to figure out what to do with it now. I was hoping—" He stops and starts again. "I was hoping it wouldn't come to that, having to do something with the ranch, but Kate's told me that the blindness may be permanent. And the truth is, I need to get on with my life."

"Kate says! How does she know?" I ask. "Can't the people at Criss Cole help you? Maybe, it's as simple as going on a grassy hill and putting yourself back there. Maybe then, you'll remember and your sight will return."

"I can't keep hoping for miracles, Jordan. I have to get on with my life. If this is it, so be it."

"Why? I don't understand why you would just give up."

"Don't you see? I can't have a life in Austin anymore. I can't *see* the ranch to run it. I'm going back to D.C. to—"

"To Kate," I whisper. All at once, I understand what he's really saying to me.

"Yes."

"Does your *mother* know?"

He looks taken aback, then shakes his head, and bitterly laughs.

"No."

He moves the white cane out in front of him, blindly taps his way toward the sofa. I just watch, angry and unmoved.

"Ten feet," I finally say. "There's a chair. On the right. Sofa is about two feet in front of you. There's a lamp to your nine o-clock. Perfect. Okay. Turn around. Feel the sofa at the back of your knees. You're golden."

I watch him slide down to the sofa and collapse his walking stick and place it along the coffee table. A sigh escapes his lips. "Come sit by me."

Somehow, I'm drawn in with a need to connect with him again in the same way we did on the way here. I walk over and slide in beside him. He pats my knee, and I move a little closer, as if we're old friends.

"How can I help you, Brock?" I ask.

"Want to go to Afghanistan with me? Lie on that hill one last time and see what comes back to me?" He looks sad. "Sometimes, that's what I think I need to do."

I shiver and let go of him. "I could never go there, just like I can never go back to Spain again." I glance over at him. "Your mom knew them. Did you know that? My parents, Davis and Laurel Breckenridge. Your mom went to high school with my mom. Here in Austin. How weird is that?"

"Pretty weird," Brock says. "I didn't know. I wasn't sure. I guess I knew it was possible. They're about the same age. Austin isn't exactly L.A. People know each other, here. But I never talked to her about your mom."

"I know. She says I look just like her. Not many people remember my parents anymore," I say slowly. "However famous they were, people move on, but it's nice to know someone who knew them. I guess I came to visit once, when I was two, here in Austin, with my mom. You and Diana were almost four. You pushed me on a swing. That's what your mom said."

Brock gets this thoughtful look. "I might remember that. This cute little girl with long dark red hair came to play once." He smiles. "I guess that was you."

"Maybe."

"So." He reaches out with his hand and trails it along my jaw line and traces my collar bone. "We'll be friends," Brock says in an uneven voice. "Ethan would want that. *Us.* To be friends."

We settle back against the sofa in an uncomfortable silence. Me, disappointed, somehow, by his pronouncement. He, distant, all at once, probably thinking of this Kate.

"Tell me about the light," he finally says, effectively breaking our shared silence.

I glance at the large bay window where the last rays of sunshine pour into the room and quickly surmise this room was solely designed to capture that miraculous light every day.

"It's majestic. The light in here," I say. "It's been a beautiful day, and now, with the setting sun, the light pours through the window and touches everything with this filmy gold. I can see why your mother did everything in white and red. It's like living in a garden of flowers, being in this room. The reds turn orange and even yellow. It's amazing the light." My voice trails off at the look of peace that crosses Brock's face. He smiles. I smile back even though he can't see it.

"That's how I remember it. Thank you. I just wanted to make sure it's still there and that it has that effect on someone else, besides me. When I was a kid, whenever I was scared or felt alone, this is where I would come, to this room, with that incredible light coming through the window pretty much any time of day."

"Uh-huh."

I'm staring at him, taking advantage of being able to look at him without being judged by anyone else for doing so. I take a deep breath.

"You okay?" Brock asks.

"Think so. It's been a long day."

I continue to stare at him, taking in the way his hair, now longer, falls across his forehead. I clasp my hands together to keep from reaching out and playing with his hair.

"So," I say. "You come in here a lot?"

"All the time," Brock says with a forced laugh. "I keep hoping I'll see something, *anything*, but I never do."

"How's your headache?"

"You want the truth or you want me to lie?"

"I always want the truth."

"I feel worse than I did at the airport."

"Fine. Let's get you to bed. I'll help your mom with dinner and bring you some tea and something to eat."

"You don't have to wait on me."

"I'm not." I stand up and pull Brock to his feet. He seems surprised by my actions. "Lean into me a little bit. We'll get you to bed. We can talk about the estate stuff tomorrow."

"I guess one more day isn't going to hurt," he says. "But, Jordan, we really do need to talk about all of it." He looks anxious. I'm not sure if it's from his headache or something else, but when I ask him about it, he tells me it's nothing.

CHAPTER

FOURTEEN

Brock – Satellite

INFLUENZA PREVENTS THE ESTATE DISCUSSION FROM taking place. I've been bed-ridden for the past day, quarantined, actually. Max and Jordan are off-limits from me because of youth and guest status. But separation doesn't do any good because eventually, both mother and son come down with the same symptoms as me: high fever, headache, nausea—the works—influenza.

Max shuffles in first. The little boy sniffles as he crawls into bed with me. My mother rushes in, clucking in her familiar, motherly tone, yet, once, she ascertains he's running a fever; she lets him stay.

Then, an hour later, Jordan arrives. She sounds weak and just as sick as me, cajoling Max to leave and come back to her bed.

"It's late. You can see Brock in the morning."

"No. I want to stay with Brock. And you, mommy."

"Max, please. Mommy doesn't feel well, either."

"Let's stay here with Brock. I *never* get to see him."

I think she puts on a brave front, but she finally succumbs with an exasperated sigh. I feel her crawl in next to me in this king-size bed in my bedroom.

"I'll just stay a few minutes until he falls asleep," Jordan murmurs. "Is it all right with you if he stays?"

"It's all right," I say.

My heart races with her unexpected presence in my bed, but I keep my breathing shallow and steady. It's ironic. This special kind of torture God plans just for me. The woman who haunts me—this goddess in all of my dreams now—is finally next to me. Only, I can't see her.

After a long while, I hear her slip away. I turn my head toward her sound.

"Good night, Brock," she says softly. "I'll come get him in the morning."

I don't say anything. I'm incapable of saying anything. I listen in the swollen blackness for her, but there's nothing more. My reverie, in imagining Jordan still standing there in the doorway, is interrupted, when Max rolls over my way. His arm lands hard at my chest. I catch my breath, reach out for the blankets he's thrown off in his sleep, and cover us both back up again, and curse the forever darkness.

⋘⋙

Early Sunday morning, I get up with Max. He's vomiting up the last of dinner from the night before and Candy Corn, he informs me. His little voice echoes up from the toilet rim along with regular intervals of his retching. I feel around for a wash cloth and wet it at the sink. Fumbling. Fumbling in the dark.

"It's okay, Max. It's just the flu. You'll feel better after this. I promise."

In my black world, I wave my hand through air until I feel his head and then wipe his face and neck with the wash cloth. My hands run over the tile countertop until I reach the cool porcelain sink. In ransacking the drawers, I come across a plastic wrapped toothbrush, swab it with toothpaste and hand it to my patient.

"Mommy brushes my teeth for me."

He's crying softly now. I take it back from him, feel around for his lips, and gently swish it through his little mouth. The Navy's spent thousands of dollars on rehabilitation for me at Criss Cole Rehabilitation Center, and just look at me now. Mr. Independent. I hold tighter onto Max and put my free hand under his chin and work the toothbrush around in his mouth with the other a little longer.

"It's kinda spicy," he says after a minute.

"Yeah. Sorry about that. We'll get you something else in the morning. Okay, buddy?"

He nods into my hand. I actually smile. Max makes me feel normal. He's the only one. I help him rinse his mouth by showing him how to cup his hands together and rinse with the tap water. He seems to cheer up a bit. He slips his wet hand into mine and hugs me at the waist.

"So," I say. "Do you need fresh pajamas?"

"Can't I sleep in my underwear like you?"

"Sure, I suppose for tonight you can."

I help him strip off his soiled clothing and gently wipe his hands one more time.

"Now, tell me about this mess. I think there's some towels here I can wipe it up with. Wouldn't want your mom to step into it."

"Aren't those the good towels?" Max whispers.

I feel the embroidered "W" logo under my fingertips and start to laugh. "You're right. Okay."

Properly chastised by a four-year-old, I grab a rustic towel from under the sink and feel around for some kind of cleaning spray. For once, I guess I'm glad that my mother had them label everything in here in Braille. I hold out the bottle, point out the special label to Max and take his hand and run it along the raised dots.

"That's says cleaning solution for the bathroom. Pretty neat, huh?"

"Really neat," he says.

I hear his tired yawn, wait for him to go to the bathroom one last time, and help him wash his hands. Then, I quietly direct him back to bed and tuck him in.

Within a few minutes, I have the bathroom reasonably cleaned, I think. I turn at the sound of the door opening, expecting to hear Max's voice.

"What are you doing in the dark?" Jordan asks.

"Max got sick. I'm just cleaning up."

"Here, let me help." She kneels beside me.

"No. I've got it. You should get your rest. This flu is pretty bad; it's going to knock you out for a while."

"Let me help you," she says. Jordan grabs my arm and takes the cleaning solution away from me.

"Jordan, I've got this."

"Brock, try not to be so stubborn. You've got to let people help you."

"That's not what the Criss Cole people say."

"Well, maybe they don't know everything." Her tone is teasing, not as guarded as she's been since her arrival just yesterday.

I start to smile. "Maybe not."

I stand up, suddenly self-conscious. I'm in nothing more than boxers and a t-shirt. I move to the sink and wash my hands. When I finish, she's pressing a fresh towel in my hands.

"Thanks," I say.

I fumble my way in the blackness, giving up on the idea of looking cool as I try to find my way back to the bed. I start to slide in, but discover a sleeping Max has completely taken over my side.

"Can you carry him to my room?" Jordan asks from just behind me.

I gently pick him up and lay him across my shoulder. "Where to?"

She's there, pushing me forward. "Let's just take the short cut back through the bathroom. I left the door open at the other end."

"Lead the way," I say.

Max moans in my arms, but he's out for the most part. I know Jordan gave him some medicine earlier. After a long twenty steps, I feel the edge of the mattress at my knees, lay Max down, and hear the rustle of bed sheets as Jordan must cover him.

"Thanks," she whispers.

"No problem. How are you feeling?"

"Better. I don't usually get sick. So, after a twelve-hour bout where I'm sure I'm going to die, I recover," she says with a soft laugh.

"Are you hungry?" I ask.

"Starving."

"Janie was trying to sell me on some chocolate cake earlier. I refused at the time, but now, that sounds good."

"It does."

She takes my hand and pulls me along to the hallway where the coolness of the wood floor hits my bare feet while the warmth of her touch courses through the rest of me. With her guidance, I follow her down the stairs. Me, swimming in the blackness; she, serving as my eyes.

I slide onto one of the bar stools at the kitchen counter and try to appear nonchalant as if raiding the kitchen with Jordan Holloway was something I do every night.

"What about pancakes?" she asks.

I detect a hint of a smile from her. "Pancakes would be great."

"Good."

The muted sound of her movements as she must sift through a series of pots and pans proves entertaining. She seems comfortable at making herself at home in my mother's kitchen. I'm a little surprised, but don't say anything. I'm reminded of Ethan and all those hours we spent together side-by-side in companionable silence. Being with Jordan has a similar effect on me. The minutes slide by. Time is still indeterminable, just like it was in Afghanistan with Ethan, but, at least, there, I could see it. I could see it all.

I listen to her as she whisks the batter in a metal bowl. The swishing sound eerily comforts me on some level.

"Do you miss the restaurant?" I ask, wincing at the sudden realization that I've been remiss in asking her about Le Reve at all, since her arrival. "How did you get away, anyway?"

She sighs. "Louis. The owner? He made me take a break. He said I couldn't go on pretending everything was all right and that nothing had changed. He said I needed to deal with the grief. Take a break. I probably shouldn't have lost it with one of the suppliers about a mixed-up delivery, and I'm pretty sure that locking myself away in the walk-in freezer and staying there for a few hours didn't help." She sighs. "That's why we came to Austin."

"Louis is a good guy. He's right. You need to take a break. You're an awesome chef. You'll be back at Le Reve in no time."

"You think so?"

"I spent some time with him the night we ate there. He said you were an amazing talent and he was lucky to have you."

"*Louis* said that?"

"Yes." I decide to change topics. "You mean you're not here for the surprise party?"

"You're not supposed to know about that."

I start to laugh. "My mother is the worst at keeping secrets. I used to find the presents from Santa every year. The woman has the RSVP calls ringing at the house. Who does she think is answering the phone?"

"It's a big deal getting the Medal of Honor. It's this coming Wednesday, right? Do you feel well enough?"

"Yes, Wednesday. It's fine. I'm fine. My mother always makes a big deal out of stuff like that." I shake my head.

"It *is* a big deal."

"I just want to *see*, so I can go back to Afghanistan."

The whisking stops.

"You'd go back?" Jordan whispers. She sounds distressed. I automatically look up.

"Sometimes," I say slowly. "I think that's the only thing that will bring my sight back."

"What about this Kate? What does she think?"

I frown at her *this Kate* reference; it's too reminiscent of Diana's open disdain for dear Kate as well. "Kate's not my psychiatrist any longer."

"Right," Jordan says with an air of disbelief. "She's your *friend*."

"Right."

I don't say more as this peculiar frustration and downright irritation with Jordan surfaces for so many indefinable reasons.

Why is she asking about Kate? What the hell does she care for?

We exist in the waning silence. Only the sizzle of pancake batter on a hot pan invades the space and the two of us.

"It's none of my business," she finally says. Her tone is the model for politeness. "Here are your pancakes. I should really go check on Max."

She places a fork in my hand, guides my other one to the edge of the plate, and then apparently walks off. Disappointment with her abrupt departure is as visceral as the blackness. I feel as if I've been struck.

Disconcerted, I cut through the hotcakes with the fork and take a large bite. Within seconds, I have to admit, these are the best pancakes I've ever tasted. I spend the rest of the time, savoring the ingredients, trying to identify the elusive spice she's used to give them this incredible flavor, and not dwelling on the apparent fact that she's suddenly pissed off at me.

I don't hear her return. There's just this sudden increase in the noise level with the fresh sizzle of pancakes. It's the only indication that she's back and, apparently, making more pancakes because she's certainly not talking, at least, not to me. I decide to indulge her in this endeavor and remain silent.

The chimes from the grandfather clock in the living room sound off four times. I put down my fork, steeple my hands together and just wait for her to speak.

"He's fine. He's sleeping," she says after a few minutes.

"Good," I say and resume my ritual of eating her pancakes. "These are amazing." I hold up my fork.

I listen for her, but still jump when she touches my right hand.

"Sorry, I didn't mean to startle you. Here's more," she says.

"You're not going to tell me what you put in these; are you?"

"Not today," she says.

I hear her movements get farther away. There's the sound of running water from the faucet and then the sizzle of the pan as it meets up with the water. The identifiable routine of washing dishes emerges. She hums a little as she works. Maybe she's not pissed at me over Kate anymore. I finish the last of the pancakes, somewhat content with the familiarity of sounds and the simple domesticity of the situation.

"You're so different than Ethan," she says in a low voice, jarring me from my reverie. "You can live with the silences forever; can't you?"

I'm immediately confused by her hot and cold ways and my apparent inability to understand her or read her signals. It takes me a minute longer to answer. *I wish I could see.* Part of me wants to tell her that, but I resist.

"I guess so. What do you want me to say?" I ask.

She doesn't answer my question. Instead, she asks one of her own. "How long? How long before your tour is officially over?"

"I have the paperwork. I haven't looked at it."

"You haven't *signed* it."

"I can't fucking *see* it."

"Show it to me."

"Why?"

"Because I can read it to you. You've wanted to go over the estate paperwork. Let's do both now. Let's read your paperwork from the Navy, and I'll look at the estate documents you sent me, and you can explain them. We're awake. We need to talk about it."

"I don't know."

I run my hand through my hair, frustrated that I can't see, frustrated by her blatant interest in my release paperwork, and even more frustrated by her sudden enthusiasm for having the estate discussion. *Where the fuck has she been all these months? Why do we have to do this in the middle of the night? Why now?*

"You're not going to like everything I have to say," I say with an edge to my voice.

"I know," she says with disquiet. "Where's the paperwork?"

"My dad's office."

This sense of foreboding comes over me. I allow her to guide me down the hall, though I could have done this by myself. Still, my free right hand reaches out automatically and follows the subtle Braille markings along the walls. A part of me savors the touch of her, this one last time. The truth is this: she most certainly is not going to like everything I have to say about the Lazy J or even about Ethan, himself.

And somehow, she'll blame me. That much I do know.

CHAPTER

FIFTEEN

Jordan – Catalyst

APRIL 28TH. THE DAY TAUNTS ME from the page. We spent a lot of time planning for that day. Ethan and me. It was the day he was supposed to return home from Afghanistan. For good. Now? It doesn't matter. He's home all right, buried in the cemetery, here in Austin. The loss of him weighs me down. I didn't think it would be so hard to see the date on the page, but it is. My hands begin to shake, and I put Brock's release papers down on the desk and clasp my hands together to keep them from trembling.

"So, it looks like you're approaching a kind of deadline, within a three-week range, where they won't recall you back to serve your term, unless you're medically fit to return." My voice has this lyrical quality to it. I sound like his mother. I catch my lip between my teeth and have to hope he didn't notice the catch in my voice.

"Unless I can *see,*" he says.

"Yes."

"A few more weeks then, hoping for a fucking miracle," he mutters.

"Yes."

"Do you have any in mind?"

Brock's attempt to be flippant doesn't quite work. His distress is still palpable. He has this stoic, proud look as he sits across the desk from me, but, I notice his hands shake just before he clasps them behind his head. He leans back in the chair and sighs.

"I'm sorry," I say.

"I know."

I sink back against the chair across from him and nervously tap its leather surface in a regular rhythm.

The room is cold, and so are we.

He leans forward, rubs his eyes for a moment, and then holds his face in his hands. I'm overwhelmed with sympathy and something else.

"I just want to *see*."

"I know," I say. "But then, you'd have to go back."

"I want to go back. My whole team is there. They need me."

With irritation, I grab the sheaf of papers, lean across the massive desk, and shove the documents his way. He looks disconcerted by my sudden action and fumbles with a key, and after a few unsuccessful attempts, unlocks one of the desk drawers and throws the paperwork inside. He barely misses his fingers when he slams it shut and turns the lock with the key.

"God damn it," he says in a low voice. He looks so unhappy.

I experience this unexpected urge to reach out to him. I blink rapidly and attempt to get a handle on my emotions. I press my body back further into the chair as physical distance from this man becomes paramount. *What the hell is wrong with me?* I touch my forehead and feel the instant heat. What do I want him to do? Why do I have this inexplicable need to beg him not to return to Afghanistan? These confusing thoughts race through me as this out of control heat surges. With rapid clarity, I realize that I'm scared for him. For me. *I care about him.* The revelation rushes through me like adrenalin. I get even more light-headed and feel undone all at once. This incalculable fear and profound guilt arrive together. I gasp with the recognition and struggle to breathe. He lifts his head from his hands upon hearing me.

"Are you okay?" Brock asks.

"Yes. I'm fine."

"No, you're not," he says. "What's wrong?"

I move my head side-to-side. What's wrong with me? I look over at him, helpless, while this rising crescendo of emotions overwhelms me. *I care about him. I want him to stay. For me.*

"Before. Why did you ask me if I was happy? If Ethan saw me," I say in a low, unsteady voice. "Why did you ask me that?"

"What?" He looks disconcerted by my questions. He hesitates and gets this dismal grim expression and clasps his hands together.

"Just tell me. Tell me why you asked me that," I say.

"He loved you. You love him."

"Yes. So, why did you think I was unhappy?"

"He loved you, but I did wonder, especially after meeting you, if he really saw you. Your fear of losing him was off the charts." Brock shakes his head. "And, it was, as if, he didn't see it or acknowledge it in any way." He shrugs, indifferent, looks away for a moment, and then, seems to look directly at me. "So, I did wonder if he ever saw you. If you were happy. Really happy." He gets this haunted look. "I didn't get the impression you ever trusted yourself or him enough to be truly happy."

He lifts his head in defiance and seemingly stares straight at me as if daring me to argue.

I'm too shaken by what he's said to respond right away. I stand up, trembling from head to toe, combating fear, anger, and this incredible heat. My head aches. My stomach churns. And yet, there's this overwhelming attraction for him, even after everything he's just said. Guilt for feeling this way washes over me. I step back.

"Why are you doing this?" I whisper.

"Because the one thing you'll get from me is honesty, Mrs. Holloway." He sounds so detached. It feels like an invisible shield has just been put up between us. I can barely hear him. My head buzzes with pain, and I have trouble focusing on him. *What's happening to me?*

"We're partners, you and I, in the Lazy J. You're in debt up to your ears, lady. He made sure of that. He had a plan. He set it in motion, while we were in Malibu. Ethan, always at the ready, with a big idea no matter what it costs or what the consequences were or who it hurts. His grand plan. The one that would bring you here. To Austin."

"What are you talking about? Why would we come here?"

"Because he wanted to come home. He wanted to bring you home, his girl from L.A., to be close to his family. To me. All of us." He sighs. "And, I made you a promise that I would keep him safe. A promise I knew I might not be able to keep, but it was already too late. For a lot of things. Everything was set in motion, far beyond me. And you."

"I don't understand."

"I know. When you see the Lazy J, you will. He spent a fortune. A fortune he didn't have or, rather, a fortune that wasn't his to spend."

This sick feeling overtakes me. I grip the desk and try to steady myself. The flu-like symptoms surge again at full force.

"I think I'm—"

"You should go, Jordan," he says with sudden impatience. "Go now."

"What's wrong?"

"Everything's wrong. Don't you *see*? All of this." Brock extends his arm across the space between us, shaking the estate documents at me. "All of *this* is *wrong*. It wasn't supposed to be this way. And now? It can't be undone."

I start to sway. "I don't feel so well."

I'm overwhelmed with nausea and feel too weak to stand. I reach out for the chair arm to support myself. Brock feels his way around the desk and grasps my arm.

"What is it?" Brock asks in alarm.

"I don't know. I'm burning up."

He reaches out and trails his fingers across my throat and works his way up to my forehead. "You're burning up."

"I told you I was," I say dully.

"So you did."

He half-carries me up the stairs with his arm around my waist and the other around my shoulders. I grasp the stair rail and pull myself upward, while he stumbles alongside me. He curses the blindness, while I try to control my breathing and the sudden urge to throw up. A minute later, he pushes me through the bathroom door and I vomit, barely reaching the toilet in time. He holds back my hair and lightly strokes my back. I'm too overcome by sickness to be embarrassed. When I'm through, I sink to the floor and rest my back against the wall and stare up at him. I close my eyes.

Minutes later, I open them at the sound of running water. And then, he's there, wiping my face and tendrils of my hair. I urgently move away from him and vomit once more. He holds my hair back away from my face again until I'm finished.

I sink to the floor and gaze up at him, helpless. I watch him move easily through the semi-darkness of the bathroom as he leaves. Weary, I rest my head against the cool bathroom tile for a moment.

He materializes again, minutes later, sporting two white pills in the palm of his left hand and a bottle of water. He kneels next to me while I swallow the pills and cautiously sip the water. I stare at him through this sick-induced haze and attempt to recall our conversation from before.

"I'm so sorry," I finally say.

"You have the flu. There's nothing to be sorry about. How do you feel?"

He reaches out and puts the palm of his hand against my forehead.

"Seriously? Like I've been run over by a truck or I should be."

"That's the flu," he stands up, grabs my hand, pulls me up to him, and puts his arm around me. "Come on. Let's get you back into bed."

He pulls me along through the bathroom and into the adjoining guest room. I weakly smile at seeing Max sleeping in the middle of my bed. Surprisingly, Brock seems to find his way to it without any trouble. He gently pushes me into the bed, leans over me, and pulls the covers back up to my neck. About the same time, Max turns over and snuggles into me with a sleepy sigh.

"I'll stay for a few minutes, until you fall asleep," Brock says.

"You don't have to."

I'm almost asleep, when I hear him say, "I want to."

⋙⋘

Unceremoniously, I'm awakened by an exuberant Max. Sunlight streams through the windows, and I'm fully awake as Max climbs on top of me.

"See? I told you it would be okay," Max scolds, turning back toward the doorway.

I look over and discover Brock standing there. He looks a little out of sorts. I glance at the bedside clock and groan. It's half past eleven. I've slept through the entire morning which can only mean Brock has been handling Max, who seems to have fully recovered from his own bout with the flu.

"Have you been good for Brock? Mommy overslept."

"You sure did." Max grins at me. "Brock wouldn't let me wake you up any sooner."

"He's been great. He ate breakfast. Pancakes. The works," Brock says with a defiant lift of his head. "Not as good as yours, I'm afraid."

I'm caught up in the man's beguiling smile. The lack of sleep seems to have had little effect on him as he stands there in a crisp white shirt with the sleeves rolled up and his blue jeans hugging his hips just so. He folds his arms across his chest and leans in the doorway looking cool, sexy,

171

and together. I run my hand through my wild hair. For a moment, I've forgotten he's blind as I openly gaze at him and recall only remnants of an intense conversation right before I threw up all over the place. My face reddens at the last memory of him, where he was holding my hair back while I was sick.

"Jordan, how do you feel?" Apparently, Brock's asked this question more than once. He sounds impatient.

Max gives me this quizzical look, too. My lips part, but I don't answer, too embarrassed in getting caught by my child in the open appraisal of the man in the bedroom doorway. I blush.

"I'm fine. Shoo. Both of you. Let me take a shower and get dressed."

"I called the Holloways. I told them that you both were under the weather."

"We're not exactly *dying* here."

Brock looks guilty for a moment. It matches my own guilt. I haven't exactly been fair to Ethan's parents, since our arrival, even before that.

Brock smiles now. "We can see them tomorrow."

"You'll come with us?" I ask, seeking reassurance. Max looks over at him, too.

"Sure," Brock says, a little disconcerted. I smile at him, but then, my smile fades because he can't see it. Max walks over and hugs him around the legs. "Whoa, Buddy, what's up?"

"I'm just glad you're better, Brock."

"And you, too. No more Corn Candy for today, though. Okay?"

"Okay," Max says.

I'm confused by the Corn Candy reference, but apparently they have this deal between them all worked out.

Brock raises his head and seemingly looks my way. "If you're up for it, I thought I'd take you to the Lazy J. Well, I'll direct you to it."

"Okay." I slide out of bed, clad in only a t-shirt and panties, and smile a little, since he can't see me half-undressed. There are some advantages to this not seeing thing. *I'm thoughtless.* I silently scold myself for thinking this way.

"Momma, where you'd get that cool t-shirt?" Max asks.

I look down at the 'Go Navy' black t-shirt I'm wearing and try to recall when I put it on. *Is this Brock's?* I bite my lip and feel my face go aflame.

"I let her borrow it," Brock says quietly.

When did he change my clothes? I remember him holding my hair back, but the recollection of changing my clothes escapes me.

"You woke up later on and got sick again. I changed your clothes. You were a mess. Don't worry; I didn't see anything." He wanly smiles.

Max is looking curiously at both of us. Brock saunters further into the room.

"You changed my clothes." I try to keep my tone neutral, but sound accusing.

"Someone had to take care of you, Jordan." He gets this innocent look and casually shrugs.

"Thank you, I think," I say with a touch of petulance.

"So. Do you want to go to Lazy J? Do you feel well enough?"

"Yes. I do."

"Henry said I could ride Lucy if I feel better. And, I *do*," Max says, running over to me and fingering my hair and face as I sit on the edge of the bed. "I feel great!"

I put my hand across his forehead. It's cool to the touch.

"I guess you can go, but I want you to behave. No accidental mishaps with the coral trough today. You listen to Henry and Tate and anyone else who is nearby, while Brock and I go check out The Lazy J. Got it?"

"Got it, Momma. I'm glad you're better." He wrinkles his nose and looks worried. "Brock couldn't read me *Cat In The Hat*. We couldn't *find* it."

"It's in my suitcase. We'll read it tonight before bed." I glance up at Brock. "Thank you for taking care of him and me," I say, uncertain.

"No problem."

He looks a little unsettled, too, and I wonder why. I feel guilty that I can't remember much about last night other than the pancakes I made for him.

"I'll just get ready and then we can go. Has anyone seen Ashleigh?"

Brock gets this mischievous smile. "She and Tate are going to meet us out at the Lazy J around four. They went into town. That gives us a couple of hours to explore the place and sign the paperwork." He gets a thoughtful look, but I'm drawing a blank. "What do you remember about last night?" Brock asks.

All at once, he's clairvoyant. My face gets hot.

"Pancakes," I say with a shrug. "After that, it's all kind of a blur."

"Okay, I'll fill you in on the way there."

He picks up Max, who puts his chubby little arm around Brock's neck. The two of them make their way out of my bedroom. Max is giggling while Brock looks troubled. I watch his retreating back and wonder what we actually talked about last night, but I don't really remember any of it now.

❧∙❧

After a hot shower and a change of clothes, I feel normal. I've decided to put the whole Brock-Wainwright-heard-you-vomit-and-changed-your-clothes-and-put-you-to-bed into the farthest recesses of my mind that it will go. The man is blind. I'm sure with my vomiting, alone, the idea of touching me beyond the necessity didn't even cross his mind. At least, this is what I tell myself to believe even as I get this uncanny, unexplainable thrill in just thinking about his touch.

Seriously? What is wrong with me?

The house is surprisingly quiet. Janie has left a note saying she's run into town and that Max is with Henry. No word about where Brock or Tate or Ashleigh might be.

I relish the idea that I've been left on my own. Max seems to have attached himself to Brock's father, Henry, as if he's his first mate or Brock, himself, since our arrival. I have to admit, I've felt ill at ease with Brock since the one-on-one conversation with his friend Tate and the mystery of what transpired between us last night beyond pancakes. I'm thankful to have a few minutes to myself to sort things out in my mind. Alone.

There is this underlying sense of awkwardness in acknowledging that I probably shouldn't have come. Ashleigh has moved on to a new conquest in Tate Matthews. Brock is coping with his blindness and a woman named Kate. And me? I'm a widow and Max's mother. These are the roles we play. Ethan isn't here to set the tone, to provide the social ease that always came in being around him.

I've reinvented the memories from my first encounter with Brock Wainwright when I disliked him so much of the time and created all these new ones which do nothing more than confuse me. I return to these memories, thinking only of how we all got along and laughed as we emptied a bottle of tequila among the four of us. I remember making love to Ethan that night, one of our last together, but thoughts of sex with Ethan fill me with sadness and put me further on the edge.

I'm alone. My worst fear has been realized.

Did I bring it upon myself?

Liz would have a theory about that. Or, at the very least, an action plan.

I text her, "All is well in Austin."

She quickly sends back a message: "Liar. Otherwise, you wouldn't be 'texting' me. Met any cowboys, yet?"

"A few. Ashleigh is on the case."

She texts back: "Not worried about Ashleigh, just you! Don't wait. Don't think about it. Just do it!"

"No way," I text back.

"Why do you have to be so difficult? Just go with it."

"So bossy. Talk later," I text back.

I shudder, because, at times, I find myself struggling to remember Ethan. His face and body and even his smile elude me more and more often. Oppression presses down on me. I wander outdoors to escape it and immediately spy Max and Henry in the far distance, tending to some fence line. My son's animated movements indicate his happiness level. It appears Max is thrilled to have found someone to listen to his chatter and share in his fascination of the world. *Why can't I be a better mother?*

I gaze in their general direction, but can't make my body move there. Henry leans back and seems to laugh, though I can't hear it. I smile, knowing Max works his special brand of innocent magic on Henry Wainwright. *So like Ethan.*

Grief twists its way through me like a serrated knife. I fight for breath for a few minutes as I absently trail my hand along the wooden coral fence as if to tempt fate with a splinter. Maybe, inflicting physical pain on purpose will transport me back to somewhere else. Maybe, this action, alone, will wake me up from the nightmare that is my life—this life without Ethan and a future that no longer includes him.

Melancholy settles in on me. I take another deep breath and hold it. Maybe, this is leftover flu symptoms that have me feeling this way. I lean heavily against the top of the fence line and attempt to find my equilibrium. It seems I've been out of sorts, since I stepped off the plane and onto the tarmac of what is Austin.

Why do I feel this way? Why?

Because Ethan is really gone.

I close my eyes and acknowledge that I've been carrying around this warped idea that somehow Ethan wasn't dead. It's true. On the surface, I seem fine. God knows I've dealt with my share of death and tragedy, but, maybe, the only truth is I'm a really good actor like both my parents were. It's true; Ethan is dead, but I've managed to stay far enough away from that reality for the past six months. I just kept on pretending that nothing had changed. But seeing Brock changed all of that. No more pretending. Ethan is dead. It's true. And, nothing is going to bring him back.

Everything's changed. Have I?

My eyes sting. I close them and see the redness from the warm sunlight. I can *feel* the darkness. I just can't *see* it like Brock can. I open my eyes.

I ponder what I revealed to Tate about my fears in loving anyone else again because of the possibility of losing them. I start to shake when I think of the cowboy's uncanny ability to perceive my feelings so clearly.

With all of my fears, I hold myself back; don't I? I always have. Even with Ethan.

I am seriously fucked up.

Liz would say exactly that if she heard me tell it, so would Ashleigh. I should be the one to say it. "I'm seriously fucked up."

Somehow, voicing this truth out loud comforts me. My body physically relaxes. There's nothing more that can happen to me. I've suffered the worst kinds of loss, and I'm still here. A shell, but here, nonetheless. *Seriously fucked up, but here.*

I half-smile and shake my head side-to-side to clear these pervasive thoughts.

The familiar plod of cowboy boots causes me to stir from my reverie. I look back and there's Brock Wainwright stirring up the road dust as he makes his way towards the coral, unaided by his walking stick. He blithely carries it beneath one arm as if taunting fate in not using it.

"Over here," I say.

He sighs. I assume he's frustrated with not being able to see, but he half-smiles at me. "I knew you were there, Jordan," he says softly, tweaking the side of his nose. "Your perfume." He comes up beside me and casually leans both arms against the rail. "Max is having a good time."

I close my eyes and listen intently and hear Max's tinkling laughter alongside the wind that stirs the land all around us.

"Hmmm," I say, opening my eyes again.

Brock rests his head against his hands and seems to stare intently into the coral. After a few quiet minutes between us, he turns towards me.

"There are some things we should talk about. Now, that you're feeling better. I know you've been pretty pissed at me, but there's some things with the estate that you need to know. I just want—"

"I'm not pissed at you," I say, blushing. "Well, not anymore. I suppose I was because it made the heartbreak easier to bear. You promised."

"I know I did."

"It was wrong of me to ask you for that kind of promise. It was unrealistic at best. You both were in a war zone. What happened to Ethan could have just as easily happened to you. It's just fate. The way things are."

I'm overcome by too much sadness again. I hastily wipe away a stray tear and experience profound relief that he can't see me breaking down.

His hand moves to my face and catches a tear. *How does he know?*

"I'm sorry. I want you to know that. Ethan had everything to live for. He loved you and Max so much. Know that. I'm sorry I didn't save him." Brock takes his hand away and looks back toward the coral again, unseeing. He casually wipes his eyes with his forearm. "Anyway, we should—"

"Talk," I say.

"Yes, we should talk. There are things he didn't tell you." Brock sighs. "He wanted to keep it a surprise for when he returned, but you should know about the Lazy J. *Everything*. I've been trying to tell you that for months, but you kept sending all the paperwork back, unopened. You might not like me. You might hate me for all I know, but we're going to have to work together and figure things out."

"I don't hate you, Brock."

I lay a hand on his arm. He looks surprised by my touch.

"Sorry, I shouldn't have done that," I say with hesitation. "And, let's be honest, for a little while, I did hate you."

He looks taken aback. I start to laugh.

"No one has ever hated you before?"

"No," he says and gets this wounded look.

"The great Brock Wainwright loved and revered by all."

"Something like that," he says evenly. "Come along, Mrs. Holloway; let's talk about the estate and this paperwork you've refused to look at." He undoes his walking stick and accompanies me back toward the main house. "There might be a few surprises." He looks uneasy.

I force myself to look away from him and concentrate on the uneven path of the road for both of us as we make our way inside. I fight the sudden foreboding feeling that I'm not going to like everything Brock has to tell me about this curious surprise of Ethan's.

⁂

Growing apprehension beats a steady rhythm in the pit of my stomach as I study the paperwork that Brock has handed to me. We sit opposite each other in his father's study again, though I don't recall much from the night before.

"Where is the Lazy J?" I finally ask.

"It's a property about five miles from here. Ethan, Tate, and I bought the land years ago. We worked on the plans for the main house, the two guest houses. It's only been in the last eighteen months that we began construction. We bought the land before he met you." Brock frowns and begins to look even more uneasy. "He didn't tell you about the land?"

"No."

My one word response doesn't hide my distress in learning about this property now. This building anger at Ethan begins to work its way through me. Why did Ethan withhold this vital piece of information?

"What?" I ask with derision. "We were just supposed to pick up our life in L.A. and move to *Austin*?" I say Austin like I would a swear word.

Brock winces when he hears me say it. "I *told* you all of this last night." He runs his hands through his hair in notable frustration.

"I had the flu. I didn't *hear* you."

His fingertips move over the paperwork which is covered in raised dots. Braille, I presume. He's obviously intent on finding something specific. I sit in silence, seething inside, while he sifts through the documents and finally hands one of them to me.

It's a deed of some kind. My eyes scan the pages. It's a deed for the land

and a business contract for a company called WHM Oil Productions.

"Oil?" I ask, getting even more confused.

"There are a couple of rigs on the site. We incorporated years ago. Tate. Ethan. Me." He looks uncertain.

"Any luck?" I ask in a low voice.

He won't look at me now.

"No. That's the problem. We aren't having very much luck in discovering oil. I just can't believe that the land is no more than sand and gravel and clay. You know? My father has had an abundance of luck. I was hoping. We were hoping to have the same thing, oil, just five miles away." He winces and tries to smile. "But, like everything else, nothing turns out according to plan."

"WHM?" I ask slowly, looking down at the document again.

"Wainwright. Holloway. Matthews," Brock whispers.

"So what's with the paperwork you've been nagging me to sign?"

"We need to sell it. To make you whole, we need to sell it."

"Sell your dream? Tate's too?" I ask, incredulous. "

Brock nods. "Tate understands. He knows we need to make this right."

"What exactly is wrong?"

"It's hard to explain. You really need to see it first."

"Okay. Show it to me."

We look at each other. Me, all seeing but not understanding. Brock, unseeing, but understanding everything. A part of me doesn't want to know what he's really trying to say. Somehow, I know I won't like it. I start to shake and try to focus on getting enough air to breathe.

"What's really going on?" I ask.

"I'll tell you after you see the place."

"Momma," Max calls out as he races toward me down the hallway. His borrowed cowboy boots are a size too big, and he's scattering clops of mud wherever he steps.

"Max, you're traipsing mud through Miss Janie's hallway," I say, suddenly weary. "Stop where you are. Go back outside and take off those boots and leave them on the back porch."

"Okay," he says with an impish smirk, which turns to worry as he sees me wipe at my face. "Momma, are you okay? You look sad. Are you sad?"

"I'm not sad," I say with an airy wave and force myself to smile. I push at the tendrils of my hair that have fallen and try to compose myself.

"Brock and I are just talking about some plans Daddy made. Run along back outside and take off those boots."

"Okay," Max says. "I'll take them off, and then, I'm going to tell you about the cattle and the horses!"

His boots make a faint echo along the wood floor in a regular thumping pattern as he leaves. I follow my son's retreat for a moment and then go in search of a broom and dustpan to clean up his dirt trail now littering the hallway. I leave Brock standing there, looking unsure of what to do or say next. I take solace in his confusion, knowing that because he can't see me he doesn't know what I'm thinking about the whole situation or how to respond. I decide to let him stew in my silence while I go to clean up the mess.

A few minutes later, he's right behind me. "We'll talk later," Brock says softly. "You need to see the Lazy J."

"Let's go as soon as I get Max settled. I want to see it."

"I want you to see it, too," Brock says quietly.

He looks more and more uneasy. His face is etched with sadness, and I can only wonder why.

"What's wrong?" I ask putting my hand on his forearm.

"You'll know soon enough. Come on; let's get some lunch, and then, we'll take a drive out to the Lazy J."

His hand touches the small of my back as I straighten up from sweeping the last of the mud from the parquet floor. I set aside the broom and dustpan and fold my arms across my chest and step back from him.

"I'm sorry he didn't tell you. About the land. Everything," he says.

"Yeah. Me, too." I nod and start to turn away and then turn back to him. "I was just beginning to think I was moving on with my life; now, it feels like I'm just starting all over again." My tone sounds bleak. He must hear it because he reaches out and trails his fingertip along my jaw line. His tender touch brings unwanted tears, and I blink rapidly to hold them back.

"I know that feeling," he says gently. "It's going to all work out. We'll figure it out. I promise."

Unseeing, he doesn't discern my doubtful expression as he pulls me in close for a hug. His arms are long. He folds me into them as if I am no more than a child. He's taller than Ethan; wider, bigger. My body longs for his comforting embrace while my mind rejects this kind of closeness from an almost stranger—someone I've practically hated these past months, someone who is not Ethan. I step back away from him and hear him catch his breath.

I'm too vulnerable. I shouldn't be doing this. I steel myself from giving in and going into his arms again and fight the sudden urgent need to be held and told everything is going to be all right, even if it is exactly what I want him to do.

Max saves me. He's skipping through the hallway in only his socks, looking triumphant.

"See, Momma?" He grins. "I took my boots off like you said. I *love* it here."

I kneel down and gather him into my arms for a hug. "I know you do, baby, but we're going home in a few days."

"I don't want to."

"I know. But, we are." I hold him close and sniff his hair. A mixture of sweat and dirt and baby shampoo greets me. "You need a bath, bud. Now. Before Mommy leaves with Brock to go take a look at some land."

"Land?" Max wrinkles his nose in disgust. "That sounds boring. I want to stay here and ride Lucy. Henry promised to take me fishing, too, at the pond."

"I don't think you can get that all done in one day." I stand up and hold him close in my arms. "You're getting too big. Almost four, Max."

"I want to spend my birthday *here*. Can I, Brock?"

I glance over at the silent man beside me. He half-smiles and inclines his head.

"It's up to your mom. We'll see."

"We'll see means *no*," Max says unhappily.

"It means we'll see," I say. "Mommy needs to get back to work. I can't play all the time, like you."

"I don't want you to work. I *never* see you."

Brock gets a curious look when Max says this.

"That's not true. I see you all the time." I sweep my hand through his hair. "Right now, it's bath time."

"It's lunch time," Max whines. "I'm starving."

"I'll get your lunch while your mom gets your bath," Brock says.

I watch Brock's retreat as he makes his way down the hallway. He touches the wall markers along the wall so he knows where he's at.

Max pulls at my arm, vying for my attention. I glance down and smile. "Momma, can we stay? Can we stay forever?" Max asks.

"We'll see," I say with a laugh. I glance back at Brock, just before he disappears through the kitchen doorway. "We'll see."

Chapter

Sixteen

Jordan – Chasing cars

"Can you drive a stick?" Brock asks me an hour later.

"Sure. It's been a while, but my dad taught me when I turned sixteen. He said driving a stick could come in handy."

Curious, I follow Brock out to the huge garage. He punches in a code and the wide doors open, revealing a sporty metallic grey 911 Porsche.

"My dad drove one of these. We still have it. Ethan always wanted to drive it, but we rarely took it out." My throat constricts in remembering one of our fights about my father's car. "I'd always been so protective of my parents' things, trying to preserve the mementos of my childhood, my time with them. Ethan didn't always understand that about me," I say quietly. "Is this *yours?*"

"Yes," Brock drawls. "It needs to be driven. It's been sitting too long. My father hasn't been able to get to it. Tate's been busy, too."

Brock tosses me the keys. I catch them one-handed. It's unlocked and we slide in from either side. I adjust the seat and he turns to me with this expectant look. *He trusts me with his car.* I'm surprised and honored at the same time.

"We could wait for your mom. Or, take the truck." I glance at the other vehicles in the humongous garage. It must be able to hold ten cars.

"Nah. This is mine. Let's take it. I want to ride in it, at least."

"You know, when you get that wistful look, I almost feel sorry for you." I smile wide. He laughs and turns his head toward me.

"Don't feel sorry for me, Mrs. Holloway. I might take advantage of your sympathy." He raises a quizzical eyebrow and gives me a leering glance before donning his sunglasses.

"And, here I'd thought you'd changed," I say with a nervous laugh.

"Nobody changes that much." His hand reaches for mine and he guides it to the stick shift. "Put in the clutch. Down and out for first. Let's see what you've got, woman," he says softly.

I do as he says and start up the car. The power of the engine roars right away. This surge of excitement travels through me. *I'm driving a Porsche 911.* It's been years.

I let out the clutch and we sail out of the garage and into the blinding light. I circle the fountain and head out the drive. Brock rattles off directions for the main road and I try to keep up with all the gears as we race along.

"You got it," he says as we edge out onto the highway. "Slip it into the 6th gear. No grinding. Pretty good, Holloway."

"Thank you, sir. It's a pleasure to drive. I'd forgotten that. My dad and I used to drive up the 101, sometimes, all the way to Mendocino to see my grandfather. We'd call my mom and tell her we were going to be late for dinner." I laugh at the memory and look over at Brock in time to see him smile. "I'd forgotten about those road trips with my dad. I've buried those memories for so long; I never allow myself to think of them."

My heart feels a little lighter just sharing them with Brock. I glance over at him again. He looks peaceful, completely relaxed, for once, and rests his head back against the seat.

I refocus on the open road and accelerate the car. It zips along the road at a fast clip.

"Slow down to thirty-five for a moment," he says a little while later.

When I do, he presses a button on the center console and the roof folds back and disappears into a compartment in the back.

"Nice!" I speed up again.

"Let me know when we reach milepost 29," he says.

"Got it."

The open road and the continual wind feed the building exhilaration inside. I can't help, but smile. It's freeing. It's the best I've felt in months.

Maybe, Louis was right. I need to *feel* it, feel *something* anyway. I think of Ethan and, for the first time in a long while, I'm not sad when I do. I'm happy. Maybe, it's the car. Maybe, it's my passenger. The whole thing is liberating at a soul level. "When are Tate and Ashleigh coming again?"

"Four this afternoon."

I glance at the car's clock. It's just a little half past one. "Are you hungry?"

"Starving. I can always eat. The Lazy J is fully stocked. Tate made sure of that. We can rustle up something for lunch. I thought we might grill steaks while we're there, after they arrive. Is that all right?"

"What about Kate?" I ask.

Why do I ruin the moment by bringing her up?

"Kate's spending a few more days in D.C."

"Oh."

"Don't worry. You'll get to meet her. I just wanted to spend a few more days with you and Max. On our own. Get everything settled."

"Oh."

I'm a task on a to-do list.

My mood swings in the complete opposite direction from euphoria to disappointment. I sigh. He must hear it.

"It's not like that. She's coming to consult with Dr. Tethers. I told you that."

"It's none of my business."

I reach out and downshift to fifth, then fourth gear. Brock looks a little disconcerted.

"Milepost 29. Where to, now?" I ask with indifference.

"There's a gravel road about a quarter of a mile from here. Take that right." He hesitates. "She's my psychiatrist. A friend," he says softly.

"Uh-huh. Like Ashleigh's your friend? Or, something different?"

"Ashleigh is a friend. And, Kate's just trying to help me out."

"And, how's that going for you?"

"You're impossible," he says. "Kind of cranky."

"Maybe, it's the flu."

"Please don't throw up in my car," he says.

"Are you *begging* me, Mr. Wainwright?"

"No. But I will," he says with a wan smile.

Truce.

Kate appears to be a touchy subject for both of us. I don't stop to examine why.

I, again, revel in the amazing exhilaration of driving his car. As we approach the turnoff, I automatically slow way down, careful not to pitch up too much gravel on his beautiful car. He gets this satisfied grin as if he knows I'm taking care with his precious Porsche.

"What are you thinking?" Brock shouts above the dense road noise.

"I'm thinking that all men love their cars more than anything else."

"More than anything else? That's what you *think*?" Brock asks. He seems somewhat disappointed with what I've said.

"That's what I *know*."

"It's just a car," he says. It's easy to detect the wistfulness in his tone. Even unseeing, he shifts his gaze toward the passenger window. *He wants to drive.*

I slow to a stop. We're in the middle of nowhere. The road is about fifteen feet wide. The wind grazes across it and stirs up the dust. I climb out of the car, walk around, and open up the passenger door, and greet a bewildered Brock from the other side.

"What are you *doing*?"

"It's *your* car. *You drive.*"

He leans further back into the seat and looks dejected. "I *can't*."

"Says who? It's *your* car. You drive," I say again.

I pull hard on his arm, effectively drag him out of the car, and lead him around to the other side. I put out my hand and protect his head from the car frame as he reluctantly gets into the driver's seat. A minute later, I slide in on the passenger side and close the door with a decisive thud. He looks over at me, unseeing, with uncertainty.

"You *trust* me?" Brock asks.

"I do. I think you know this car better than anyone else. I think you know this road better than anyone else. We're about a hundred feet from the main highway. Just keep it straight and I'll correct your course. Go as fast as you feel comfortable going."

"Why are you doing this for me?"

A loaded question. I'm uncertain as to why I'm doing this. I don't answer.

And, he waits. He just waits.

I smile a little and shake my head side-to-side, still in awe of his ability to embrace silence as he just waits for me to say something. "Because everyone deserves to have their dreams come true. Driving this car feels like a dream come true to me; I'm sure you feel that way, too. It's something unexpected that you really want to do. Now. *Drive your car.*"

He gets this silly grin. I'm reminded of Max when it comes to surprises.

Brock exhibits that same uncontainable excitement. I settle back into the passenger seat and watch as he runs his fingers along the steering wheel and the gear shift in some kind of spiritual ritual.

After a few seconds, he puts in the clutch, moves the stick a few times through neutral, and then shifts into first and then second. We sail forward. He races through the gears and we're traveling at a steady clip of thirty miles per hour along the gravel road, stirring up copious amounts of dust behind us as we go.

For the first couple of minutes, I try to relax, but that proves impossible as he begins to veer off course.

"Whoa, Cowboy. Let me help you there." I straighten up and grip the steering wheel and guide us back onto the center of the road.

"Sorry," he says, inclining his head in my direction. "It's seems like I'm going straight."

I sense his frustration and try to put him at ease. "Don't worry about it. I'm not scared," I say airily.

"Are you *ever*?"

"All the time. Normally. All the time."

☙ ❧

"Stop the car!"

I scare the hell out of Brock. He slams on the brakes. We're both pitched forward and then back hard in our seats.

"Jesus Christ, Jordan!"

"Holy shit," I mutter.

There is a cluster consisting of three houses just ahead of us. All grand in build and structure. Modern. Architecturally beautiful in line and stature with just the right amount of glass, wood, and stone. Very un-Austin-like. More Malibu style. More Hollywood glamour than Texas prairie. More Frank Lloyd Wright with linear lines and impossible grades and angles. It's breath-taking. All three, but the one in the center is the grandest of them all.

Brock parts his lips to say something and then stops. Without another word, he shuts off the car's engine and carelessly throws the keys in the console.

Who's going to steal it out here in the middle of fucking nowhere, anyway?

"I take it we're here," he says with a touch of sarcasm.

I just gaze at him in stony silence, then turn away to stare back at the monolith house directly in front of us.

"About fifty feet out," I finally say.

I bite at my lower lip to stop its trembling. I'm going to cry again, but I don't want to. Not here. Not in front of him. My throat gets tight. I can't talk. I take an unsteady breath.

He shoves a document into my hands. "Here," he says. "Start here." "Read it. Ask questions, but all I'm going to say is you need to *see* it first."

"I can *see* it."

"I wish I could," he mutters.

"Don't go down that feel-sorry-for-me-now path, Wainwright. It doesn't suit you."

"Read the paperwork." He hands me the document. His fingertips work over the Braille. "Start here. Then we'll go inside."

"It probably wasn't such a good idea to do this now," I say, in a mopey, feel-sorry-for-me tone.

"Probably not," he says, as if he's talking to Max instead of me. "But I did a spreadsheet. *Read it.* It outlines your assets and debts from what I was able to put together. Have you received the life insurance payment?"

"Not yet. I think it will be another four weeks. They were waiting for the final report from the Navy before issuing the check."

"Stalling."

"Maybe."

"I took that into account. It should be about a hundred thousand, assuming the standard policy."

"I think he told me about that once. We talked about getting more coverage, but then we had Max. I took the head chef position at Le Reve."

I glance over at Brock. He looks miserable, staring out the car window and seeing nothing.

The exhilaration and joy of driving his Porsche has left him as much as it's left me.

"The house in Malibu is paid for," I say, automatically filling in the silence. "The taxes and upkeep are all we pay on it." I glance down at the spreadsheet he's done. Under property taxes, he's put in $55,000. "That's about right. A little over $55,000 in property taxes."

He remains silent. I look more closely at the figures. There are a few zeroes and even negative numbers in red within the line items. Ethan's income is zero. That makes sense. He's gone. I swallow hard.

Brock has listed my income at $130,000.

"My income is about right plus $20,000 or so. Louis pays me a bonus every year, depending on how the restaurant does."

All Brock does is nod. It's as if he's willing me to figure it out for myself as if he's afraid to say anything more. The hair on the back of my neck rises up.

"Where did he get the money to build this place with you and Tate anyway?" I ask quietly. "Our money was all tied up in stocks and bonds—money I earned from when I was working at L'Ecole and the trust fund from my parents' estate that came through when I was twenty-five." This disconcerted look crosses Brock's features as he looks in my general direction. "No!" I say with sudden understanding. "He used our life savings to build a house on this ranch with you?"

Brock hangs his head. Seeing or not seeing, he won't look at me.

"Yes."

My body and mind can't sit still any longer. I push open the car door and climb out. Brock noisily follows suit. We seemingly gaze at each other across the roof of the car for a moment.

"No," I say again. Backing away, I start toward the biggest house. "There's more than eight hundred thousand dollars in that account. He took it all? You're sure?"

"We each put in eight hundred thousand. And, there's a mortgage for twice that on the property. It's quite a place," Brock says, following behind me at a slower pace. "And, for the record, I told him to tell you about it. He wanted it to be a surprise. The plan was to finish the tour in Afghanistan, return home, surprise you, and move you all down here. He had it all worked out; said you'd be thrilled. That it would be the best place for Max to grow up and that you would love it."

I stop walking. "Just give up the beach house and a magnificent view of the Pacific and move to God's country? To Texas!"

I flail my arms about. Even though he can't see my frustration, I'm pretty sure he senses it.

"I'm sorry. He said you'd be thrilled. I tried to tell him it was a crazy idea, a big change for a city girl like you."

"You don't even know me!" I clench my fists at my sides ready to pummel him if he comes any closer to me as fury surges through me.

"How could Ethan have done this? To us? Without asking me?"

"I'm sorry," Brock says slowly, shaking his head. "I tried to tell him based upon what I knew of you that you weren't going to exactly be thrilled with the idea of moving to Austin, but he wouldn't listen. He said you'd come around."

"Come around," I repeat his words.

My breathing becomes more jagged. I struggle to maintain what little composure I have left.

"What about my dream of opening my restaurant? My own place? What did he say about that?"

"You need to see it first before jumping to too many conclusions."

"See it? He tramples over my dream and just supplants everything in our life with his vision without telling me! What does that say about us? Our marriage? God damn him! And now you're telling me I need to *see* it?"

Brock grabs hold of my hand and pulls me along. He holds his white cane with the other and taps along the driveway. I flush with embarrassment at my temper and the way I've spoken to him.

"I'm going to take a wild guess that buying me out, right now, is out of the question, given your current circumstances."

He gives me a sideways glance. He looks grim.

"I tried to tell you," Brock says quietly. "All these months you ignored me."

"Yeah, I did." I shake my head side-to-side in disbelief. "Well, now, I know."

We stop walking. His breath stirs my hair. I look at his face and see a mixture of remorse and sadness.

"Did he tell you *anything* about the Lazy J?" Brock asks. He sounds despondent. I begin to wonder why.

"No."

I look down at the paperwork I'm still holding. The numbers swim at me now. These hot tears streak down my face making it hard to see. The bottom number is the scary one. It shows a negative $600,000 dollars in red. "I don't understand," I manage to say. "What's the minus $600,000 listed here?"

"Debt on the Lazy J," Brock says quietly. "Ethan's share."

"Holy shit," I say with a gasp. I put my hand over my mouth and try to control this sudden urge to start screaming.

"I've been trying to tell you about it for months. Like I said, we owned the land outright. We bought it years ago when the owner died. It was right after high school, I guess. We've been drilling for oil on various parts of the property, but so far not much is there. Then, we started making plans about eighteen months ago and began construction on the houses. The plan was to finish the main house and have you and Max move here this summer and wait for him, until he was done with this last tour."

"Just pick up and move to Austin."

He looks surprised by my soft tone. It belies my absolute total fury.

"He wanted to move home. He wanted to have a place *here* with you and Max. I told you all of this last night," Brock says, exasperated now. "That was the plan."

"The plan," I echo. "But, what about Malibu? Le Reve? My life there?"

"He wanted to move home," Brock says.

"Home."

"Austin."

"What day is it?"

"It's Sunday."

I slip out of Brock's grasp and begin walking up the long drive. I absently admire the fine stonework, while traversing the surface. We're about thirty feet from the biggest house. The main one, I assume.

I don't care. I don't want to be any closer. I stop and gaze at the landscape. The full sun overhead lights up the hills and the world. The bright light touches my face and I close my eyes and attempt to garner some of its warmth, but the world has suddenly gone cold and my body is fast discovering this. I shiver and open my eyes and view the world—the Lazy J—Ethan's version of paradise. Brock's, too.

At least, I can *see* it.

Brock catches up to me. I brazenly stare at him.

Me, all seeing. He, blind and unseeing, but, somehow, seeing it all so clearly. I envy him.

I blatantly regard his handsome face and allow my eyes to travel downward and openly admire his physique. The way his waist tapers into his jeans. The outline of his body beneath his shirt is easy enough to discern. His six-pack abdominal muscles rival Ethan's. I retrace my seeing path and note each of these assets on my return to his amazing face. *Handsome.* The word comes to mind so easily. I shiver.

His lips slightly part as if he has something he wants to say, but he remains silent. He basks in the stoic silence, as usual.

I shake my head as if to clear it of these wayward thoughts and almost smile, but the confusion over Ethan and the man in front of me takes hold.

"We were married almost four years," I say. "Two days short of four years. One thousand, four hundred and fifty-eight days."

"Jordan, I don't—"

"And, out of that, we spent two hundred and ninety-eight days together. One thousand, four hundred, and fifty-eight days we were married. And, he wrote and told me that he loved me. *A lot.*" I openly gaze at Brock. "But out of all those days, there was never one day, where he wrote me and said, 'Baby, let's move to Austin, build a ranch house there, and hang out with my buddy, Brock.' Not one of those days did he say that." I start to laugh. It has a maniacal quality. "He said he loved me."

"He did."

"Maybe, he did," I say. "But, you were right. He could never *see* me."

"That's not true. He saw you. I never should have said that."

Brock's remorse reaches for me. My breath gets more and more uneven. I just stand there, looking at him, and trying to put this all together.

I'm broke. These innocuous words keep coming back at me. *I'm broke.* I take a deep breath.

"I'm broke. I'm alone. I'm a widow. I'm a mother. I have Max. I have everything, except money and Ethan." The tears fall freely now. "I don't have a marriage. I don't have a life; I'm broke, but other than that I'm fine."

I start to breathe as if I've just run a ten-mile race. Jagged breaths escape me. I feel like I'm going to hyperventilate. And, Brock just stands there. He gets this disturbed, sickened look. Yet, he just stands there.

"There's more," I say, accusingly, after a long five minutes.

He just moves his head up and down. I watch in this fascinated way. *He's just the messenger. Where the fuck is Ethan?*

"I told him to tell you while I was there. He'd run short on his share of the money for the construction. He was playing with some investments. We were out in the field for too long and he couldn't get online." Brock shakes his head back and forth. "But by then, he'd lost a lot of the money, but we wanted to keep going on the construction and—"

"My mother's jewelry," I whisper. "I'd shown it to Ethan once. I kept her jewels in a safe at the house, probably because that's where I felt the safest, so I assumed her jewels would be safe there, too. I'd given Ethan the combination right after we were married, after we'd only known each other for fifty-six days."

I frown and look over at Brock. He has this grim expression.

"It was an old safe, the twist-and-turn-the-knob kind of safe. A locksmith once assured me it was very good. The man told us no one could break that code, unless they *knew* it. I remember looking over at Ethan and smiling and him smiling back at me, like we shared this amazing secret. And, we did. We shared a nest egg of over two million dollars for a rainy day." I stop, and try to catch my breath. "I guess it rained; I just didn't know it had."

"I'm sorry," Brock says into the stillness. I glance over at him. He looks even more ill at ease.

"Are you okay?" I ask.

"Are you?"

I start to laugh. "No." I sigh. "He knew what those jewels meant to me. She wore them the night she won the Oscar. My dad gave them to her." I shake my head and then shiver, remembering as the words tumble forth. "She looked so beautiful with this amazing diamond necklace and these long silver earrings with a teardrop diamond suspended at the end of each one. I helped him pick them out. He spent a fortune, but he told me she was worth every penny. Can you imagine loving someone like that? Believing in them so much? The extravagance of their love is something I will never forget. It's what I try to remember and what I hold on to even now."

I brush at my hair and wipe at my face. I'm suddenly grateful he can't see me cry. "It's silly; I know."

"It's not. It's amazing and beautiful," he says. "Just like you."

My breath catches in my throat at the intense look on his face. I ignore what he's said. I'm too moved by it, too confused by it. It's too much to acknowledge. I'm in emotional turmoil over Ethan. Did he ever see me? Did he even love me? And, if he did, was it enough? *Does it matter?*

"He sold my mother's jewelry for a house," I say in a low voice. "Who does that without telling their spouse?"

"He wanted it to be a surprise," Brock says.

"Well, I'm surprised," I say with a bitter laugh.

"Come see inside."

His three little words seem to bring me back. He holds out his hand, and I grasp it tight. He taps his walking stick and leads us forward.

"What a pair," I say.

"Yeah."

I lean my head on his shoulder. He snakes his arm around my waist.

"You're going to have to trust me on this. You're going to love this place."

I stare up at him.

"I hope so."

"I know so."

He flashes me a white smile. He hugs my shoulders tighter, and I allow myself to be led along to the Lazy J. All the while, I fight the urge to run in the complete opposite direction away from this house, even away from this man, because my mind already knows that everything's about to change even more.

CHAPTER

SEVENTEEN

Brock – Crazy about this girl

EVEN MAD I KNOW SHE'S BEAUTIFUL. I can't fucking see her, but I know this. Beneath my arm, her shoulders tremble. It's the only signal that tells me we're getting close to the massive front doors. I breathe deep of the hot air, realizing how crucial the next part is. I've gone through the tour of this house with her in my mind so many times. Do I show her the backyard with the herb garden, first? Or last? Do I show her the gourmet kitchen or the commercial one, first? There's so much to show her, and more than anything, I want her to love it all. I don't examine too closely why her reaction means so much to me. She might hate it. She has every right to hate it.

There are a lot of unanswered questions between us already.

I'm blind. That matters. Instinctively, I already know it doesn't matter to Jordan, and, that, alone, scares the hell out of me.

She was Ethan's wife. I was his best friend. We can't be together. And, yet, I'm the one she's holding hands with as we enter the doors of this grand house.

I listen for her and hear her gasp as we enter into the main foyer.

"There's a skylight overhead with a prism. It casts this amazing light in this foyer all day long. The black and white stone is like old Hollywood."

"Yes," she says. I hear a hint of amazement in her voice. "Two staircases?"

"It's pretty big," I say. "There are three distinct wings and two other houses. We kind of planned it around the idea of the three of us being here. Ethan. Tate. Me."

"Tate, too?"

"There's a guest house. Tate's to be the foreman, running the cattle side of the business. Ethan and I planned to run the oil company. That way, we'd share in all the profits all together. Equally."

"Like your father's place."

"Yes. But it was to be *our* place." I stop. "It would have been ours."

"Still could be," she says softly.

"Maybe. I have to *see* first," he says with a heavy sigh.

"You will. I told you that." She sounds impatient. I'm surprised.

"But that's not why I brought you here. I just thought you should see it. See it all. Before, we sell it." In an instant, I make up my mind about what to show her first. "Let's eat," I say, pulling her along to the right.

Now, I'm thankful that I had the service put Braille marks throughout the house. I know the place like the back of my hand. I built most of it in my spare time with Tate before my injuries.

"Wow. Commercial grade," she murmurs as we enter the kitchen.

I imagine her hands trailing along the granite countertop and the Viking stove.

"All the stuff you like."

"Uh-huh."

I move toward the middle of the room, reaching out with my hands to get my bearings. I pace off to the refrigerator and open the door, feeling emboldened as my fingertips travel over all the food items. They are all marked in Braille. "What are you hungry for?"

"Stop showing off. This, I can do. Go sit down some place." She pulls me out of the way. I smile in the general direction of her voice and go sit at one of the tall kitchen chairs at the counter.

"We wanted it to have that restaurant feel, of being able to sidle up to a counter and casually drinking a glass of wine while conversing with the cook. Sorry. The chef of the house. True entertainment value. Ethan said that's what you'd like."

"I do."

She takes my hand and puts it around the stem of a glass. "Pouilly Fuisse. Drink up."

I hear the steady slicing of a knife through an apple. Then, she's back again, placing my hand on the edge of a plate. I feel the soft sponge of what must be cheese and the apple slices and begin to eat. But then, the sizzle of butter or oil in a pan distracts me. "You're cooking?"

"It relaxes me. Be glad," she says. "Be *very* glad."

The minutes drone by. She moves around in this magnificent gourmet space, while I'm cloaked in the blackness. But, strangely, it's not as daunting today. *Because she's here.* My mind silently bellows.

The plate is empty. I gulp at the wine, nervous, captivated by her sounds. Then, Jordan's there again. She touches my hand and tells me she's poured more wine into my glass.

"Thanks," I say.

"It's a fabulous kitchen. Who designed it?" Her voice has an edge to it.

I start to say Ethan, but realize she's too in tune to actually believe that. She knows Ethan, just like I do. She knows Ethan can handle the fluff of the project, but not the details. "I did."

"How did you *know?*" She sounds breathless, all at once.

I lean closer. "I checked out the kitchens where you worked. The restaurant designs that you liked and frequented according to Ethan. I spoke with some of the architects who designed them. We hired one and we worked it out together. He had a different design in mind for this kitchen, but I thought I knew what you'd want." I pause, listening for her. "I take it you like it."

"I like it," she says.

I detect her indifference. It affects me as if the temperature in the room has dropped twenty degrees. The kitchen grows quiet. She works in silence. I assume that's what she needs. It's a lot for her to take in.

I move my head side-to-side in quiet exasperation over Ethan and what he did.

"What is it?" Jordan asks softly.

"I told him to tell you of the plans. In Malibu. We had a few heated arguments about it. He was so stubborn. I feel guilty for not talking him out of the idea of taking the loan out against your mother's jewels. That's on me. I should have talked him out of it. I didn't. I'm sorry."

"That's on *him,*" she says evenly.

"I know you're pissed. Just see the whole place first."

"Let's eat." She touches my hand again and places it on a different plate, a bigger one. "Chicken Caesar salad. Easy. No mess. No fuss. Goes with the wine."

"Great," I say. Now, I wallow in frustration. If I could just see her, maybe, I could better explain all of this. Maybe.

She slides in next to me. Our elbows briefly touch. She moves her chair farther away. "The wine's good," she says.

That's all she says for the next ten minutes.

My spirits wane further. I listen for her, willing her to say something, *anything*. My normal ability to cope with silence leaves me. I finish off the salad and start in on the wine again, finishing it in a long single swallow. It feels like the walls are closing in on me. The blackness shimmers.

The only sound in the room comes from the scraping of her chair against the hard wood. She clears the plates without a word. In the next few minutes, I hear only the sound of running water. She's doing the dishes and not talking. It's so unlike her. This much I do know about her.

"Say something," I finally say.

"*You* say something. God. You and your silences. You can live with them forever. I really hate that."

"You do?" I say in surprise. "It's the training. We always had to be silent on patrol. For hours at a time."

"Well, we're not on patrol, *now.*"

"Do you want to see the rest of the house, or not?"

"I don't know," she says. "What if I *love* it?"

Her question catches me off guard. Is the wine wreaking havoc on my system? Have all those dry months in Afghanistan caught up to me, finally? Besides being impotent, I'm a lightweight when it comes to alcohol on top of everything else?

"Do we have more wine?" I ask.

"We do, if we open another bottle," she says with petulance.

"Open it." I shrug. "And, so what, if you love it?"

"If I love it, how will we sell it?"

"Maybe, we won't. Maybe, we'll discover oil before you leave and we'll all have enough money to do whatever we want."

"You're very optimistic," she says, touching my hand as she pours more wine into my glass. "I like that about you. You're so," she pauses and giggles a little bit. "You're so God-damn *hopeful.*"

"I'm glad I entertain you," I say with irritation. *Where is she going with all of this?*

"And you look like Henry Cavill. Not bad. Not a bad imitation of Henry's sidekick at all."

"Do you want to see the house, or not?" I ask.

"I do. Show it to me. I want to see what an Oscar winner's jewels can buy these days."

Oh shit. She's pissed.

⊰❦⊱

"The colors are amazing. The dark wood. I love that."

"He said you would."

"I don't want to talk about him. Okay?"

"Okay."

I swallow hard. Ethan has always served as a barrier between us. Now, she's asked me not to mention his name. Exactly how am I going to do that and still resist her? If only I could see her, then, I could better gauge what she's really thinking.

We move slowly from room to room. The Braille markings help me keep on track. She remains silent and stays a few steps behind me, but still holds on to my hand. Every once in a while she seems to sway. I can't tell if it's the effects of the wine or how she's feeling about everything else. I long to ask her what's she's thinking, but I remain ever silent, beholden, in this strange way, to this thing between us. I'm too afraid to upset the equilibrium that seems to run through both of us right now.

I touch the markings on the door and open it and allow her to step inside first.

"This could be Max's room." I force myself to smile, still trying to sense where she is in relation to the doorway. I recall the blue walls and the boyish elements we added to this room. "Tate built the ship bed."

She lets go of my hand. I feel a little lost without her touch. I shake my head side-to-side, disconcerted. *Get it together, Wainwright.*

"It perfect," she says quietly.

This isn't going as well as I had thought it would. Somehow, I thought the house would win her over, but then, the images of her home in Malibu flash. The ocean view. The way you can hear the waves from every room, late at night. The Old Hollywood style of that house. Nothing compares to that place, not even this one.

And, I know this.

The darkness swelters around me, closing in even more. I'm sure Jordan must feel like that in this house. Ethan's betrayal emanates from her like an all encompassing heat. Even I, can see it, *sense it*, anyway. I grimace at my naiveté and at Ethan for assuming that she could so easily give up her Malibu life for this place. As hard as we tried to emulate what Ethan said she would like, it dawns on me that he never shared with either of us, Tate or me, what the Malibu house was like. *Her life.* He never told us what we were trying to replicate. It's so like Ethan. He was never one for details.

"Your room," I say with awkwardness, then flush, remembering the gold and crème colors of the room. The king size bed. The dark wood. The amazing view of the valley and the hills beyond through the floor-to-ceiling windows that cover one entire wall.

"It's got a Scarlet O'Hara feel," she says with diffidence. "Canopy bed. I always wanted one of those." She takes an unsteady breath.

I hear the clink of her wine glass. She must be pouring more wine. A minute later, she nudges my hand with the bottle.

"Want some?"

"Sure," I say. "How much have you had?"

"Enough."

She clinks her glass with mine. I listen as she drinks it down and swallows.

I'm getting uneasy. My palms are sweaty. I hold onto the stem of the wine glass with a firm grip. She grabs my free hand.

"More?" Her voice is silky and seductive.

I close my eyes and shake my head. "No."

I grab her hand and pull her along to the hallway. Being in what was to be her and Ethan's bedroom leaves me unsettled.

"We didn't see the bathroom," she says with genuine protest.

"We'll see it later."

"But I have to *go.*" Her whining makes me laugh. It releases the building tension for a second. She puts the wine bottle in my hand. "I'll be right back."

I experience the solitude of the hallway and attempt to relax. The wine has made me unsteady. We shouldn't be doing this. She's upset. I'm uneasy. I touch my watch. 'Three zero five p.m.' goes the audio.

"Tate and Ashleigh will be here in an hour," she says in a husky voice as she returns. "Nice bathroom."

"Yeah. There's only one more thing to show you."

"Okay. Show me. Your place?"

"No."

"Two things, then," she says.

I set down the wine bottle at the end of the hallway and retrieve a key from my pocket. "This part isn't done. He wanted to finish it, but I thought we should wait and see what you wanted."

"We agreed not to mention him," she scolds. "Wait and see what I wanted." She laughs bitterly, and then, sighs. "You wanted to wait and see what I wanted," she murmurs, sounding surprised.

I struggle with the lock and get more frustrated the longer it takes to undo it.

"Let me help you. Please?"

In frustration, I step back and hand her the key with some reluctance. "I can't even open a God-damn door."

"Don't worry about it," she says. Out of nowhere, her hand strokes my cheekbone and then it's gone.

I try to smile in the general direction of her voice, but I'm getting more and more uneasy. I'm not sure how long I'm going to be able to resist her touch, and this strange sense of foreboding overtakes me. This is not going well or the way I planned it. *What I want from her, I cannot have.*

"Fine." I strive for nonchalance and swallow hard. "Go in."

She sucks in her breath. How I wish I could see her face as she first glimpses the restaurant. Her place. Because Ethan loved her and thought of just about everything, except for asking her what she truly wanted and spending her inheritance without her permission.

"Out in the middle of nowhere?" she asks.

"It's a twenty minute drive from town." I shrug. "People would come. Believe it or not, we're pretty civilized here," I say wryly. "There's a lot of wealth here. With oil. Dell. Cattle. Austinites like the finer things, just like everyone else. They would come. Here."

"Did he name it?"

"No."

I listen as she steps over the paper still covering the slate floors. I sense her hands as they must trail along the bar's granite countertop. The thought of her fingers turns me on.

"The lighting is great. Eight tables would be perfect, manageable. Wow. Nice bar. The design of the place is stunning. Subtle. Intimate."

My heart rate speeds up. I can sense her as she steps closer to me.

"Why didn't you finish it?" she asks. "You have the money."

"I'm giving you the money back. We're selling it, as is, so we can pay you back," I say.

"You're selling your dream for me?" Jordan asks, incredulous.

"It's not fair to burden you with something you don't want. A life you didn't ask for."

I extend my arm around the room. "In Austin," I say it with the same disdain she used just an hour or so ago.

She ignores what I've said. "The walls should be crème. That will bring out the candlelight at night. You don't want it too dark. People need to see their food, the people they've come with." She starts to laugh. "I'd call it *Laissez Faire.*"

"What does that mean?"

"Let be. It's French. It means: let be. Something along those lines, anyway."

Her perfume fades. She's stepped away.

"Who bought the appliances?"

"I did."

"How did you *know*?"

"I told you I researched the places you worked. The places you liked."

"Oh yes, you said that."

The room fills with sound.

"Nice stereo equipment."

"Ambiance," I say, uneasy. *What is she doing?*

"Dance floor?" Jordan asks. Her voice is sensuous, mesmerizing. I nod. She takes my hand and places it at her waist. "Dance with me."

"I can't."

"You *can.*"

Her arms slink up my shoulders. Her hands clasp around my neck and she draws me closer. I attempt to focus solely on the music. The sound seems to infiltrate us both. Our bodies move of their own volition.

"I'm going to make you see," Jordan sings. "I'm gonna make you give in to me."

"This is a bad idea," I murmur.

"Stop talking," she says with a low laugh.

We sway with the music and the seductive lyrics of the song. I lean in closer and catch her amazing lavender scent. My hands comb through her long hair. I groan and pull her to me. I sense her face is raised to mine and her breath catches at the same time mine does. Her lips explore mine. My body seems to awaken from its long mysterious sexual slumber of the past six months. I kiss her back and our bodies seem to form an alliance. The heat between us rages like the sudden attack of a lightning bolt. It's all powerful and consuming.

I think it's a full five minutes before we come up for air and realize the song has ended.

End it. An errant voice goes off inside my head, sounding just like Ethan.

I shudder and pull back from her.

"You think too much," she says softly.

"I suppose I do."

"You think he loved me?"

"He loved you very much. I know he did."

"He loved me?"

"He did."

She sighs. "Show me your place," she says.

CHAPTER

EIGHTEEN

Jordan – Give in to me

NEITHER ONE OF US ACKNOWLEDGES WHAT just transpired with that kiss. I hold onto his arm as he leads the way to his place and try to remain outwardly calm while inside I tremble. We descend down some back stairs at the far side of the restaurant and through a door, and then, we're outside in the waning afternoon hours, traversing a gravel path that leads to his house. I strive to appear nonchalant, while inside, I start to break apart emotionally. The culmination of what Ethan has done starts to work its way through me. My mother's jewelry. He sold my mother's jewelry and used my inheritance to finance a house. This house. I look back at the magnificent place behind us and feel bitter disappointment. He knew what it meant to me. That's the worst part. *Ethan knew.*

Deep down, I recognize the urgent need to fill this vast void. *Brock.*

I glance over at him and see the determined set of his jaw line. *Is he angry with me or beholden to the inexplicable connection between us?*

We shared Ethan. Now, what do we share? Each other?

Desire for him roars through me like a raging inferno through a bone-dry forest as we approach his front door. I want him. He wants me.

We can make this work. I need to make this work, at least, for now.

I take the key from his outstretched hand and work the lock. I push the door open and pull him along inside, exuding an air of false confidence.

"I got it, Jordan." Brock moves past me at lightning speed, turns back to face me from the center of his living room, and looks uneasy.

A part of me wonders why. The other part knows.

"What's wrong?" I ask.

"Nothing."

He shrugs his shoulders like he has nothing to do with this outcome and gives me this let's-just-get-this-over-with look. "We can't stay. We should get going. We can't stay."

"Worried about Tate and Ashleigh? Or, worried about me?"

"You."

I smile when he says this. He can't see mine, but he smiles, too.

There's that inexplicable connection between us again. It roars through both of us like a tangible electric current.

Seeking distraction, I glance around the room. The darkest colors—navy, brown, grey, and black—dominate the space. He's included enough variations with whites from light yellows to crèmes to make it work. Touches of red displayed in some of his artwork, in the pillows scattered about, and the fresh flower arrangements help balance the space and enhance the look of the subtle richness and understated elegance he's going for.

I'm enchanted to discover he's a fan of Impressionism. So am I. The walls are adorned with a vast collection of Monet and Seurat and even some post-impressionist work of Van Gogh's.

"You designed all of this?"

"Yes."

His one-word answers prove tiresome. I sigh, sensing his reluctance to show me around.

"It's beautiful. Truly. I love what you've done."

He shrugs with indifference. I decide to ignore him and perform my own self-guided tour of his place.

He trails behind me a good twenty feet, while I peruse his home with a brazen you-invited-me-here attitude. *So far so good.*

I've counted three bedrooms and admired his gourmet kitchen which has a similar set-up to what would be mine, but on a smaller, more functional scale. There's a media room, four bathrooms.

I hesitate in the open doorway of his master bedroom, the fourth bedroom, it seems, but the room all but beckons me inside. His modern, dark wood furniture indicates a guy's signature wish for the massive, but it fits easily into this giant space of a room. My eyes slowly adjust to the muted track lighting he's so carefully placed along the high ceilings. I pause to admire the ornate pure white crown molding, the gold silk duvet, and the black silk sheets that peek out from underneath one edge.

Then, I'm captivated by the single piece of artwork he's hung—a giant reproduction of Klimt's *The Kiss*. He's incorporated the colors from Klimt's painting of yellows, golds, and oranges throughout the space.

The room's warm, inviting, and sensual. This amazing space has been designed by a man who's spent the last five years of his life in a God-forsaken land, like Afghanistan.

Elegance permeates and envelops.

Fresh white Calla Lilies adorn a crystal vase on his night stand and I can only wonder who put them there. *When was he here last? And with whom? Dear Kate? Was he here with her? Fucking Kate?* This visceral jealousy circles through me and works its way outward.

What is going on with me?

I listen to him as he slowly makes his way down the hallway. His now familiar tap tap sound announces his presence, long before he appears in the doorway. He looks unsettled.

He knows where this is going.

I walk back toward the center of the room.

"I love Klimt, especially this piece."

"Thanks."

"I could spend hours here," I say without thinking.

"Not today," he says firmly.

He sounds out of breath, but saunters in to the room as if time has stopped for him. His movements are so deliberate and painstakingly slow, I grow impatient. I roll my eyes and sway with the effects of all that wine, the emotions of the last hour, and the man, himself.

I'm turned on by all of it, now, and pissed off at the same time. At him. At Ethan. At *her*, 'this Kate.'

An exhilarating combination of lust and rage courses through me now. I hold my breath and try to get my racing emotions under better control, but Liz's words come to mind.

Don't wait. Don't think about it. Just do it.

"I have a get-out-of-jail-free card."

"Those don't really work," he says gently, but looks mildly amused.

"Oh, yes they do."

"I know this looks like a fantastic way to get back at Ethan, but it won't be."

"It would be fantastic."

I walk over to him and put my arms around his waist. I gasp when I feel the hardness of him through his jeans, pushing at my midsection. I take in air, hold it for a moment, and will myself to keep it together.

"It's not that I don't want you," he says softly. "I do. Obviously. But this is a very bad idea."

His reluctance is palpable. I think of Ashleigh and our discussion about the word, *palpable*. Yet, I can still feel his physical response to me against my thigh. Let's talk about *palpable*. I laugh a little.

"My friend, Liz? She told me that sex with a cowboy is just what I need."

"Let me call Tate," he drawls. "In fact, he should be here in the next ten minutes."

"Funny," I say with notable disappointment.

He touches his watch and we both listen as the mechanical voice, a woman's, calls out the time of three fifty-four.

"You think you're ready," he admonishes. "But, you're not. We could do this and it would feel great, in the moment, but then, there would be all these other moments afterward."

"Are you turning me down?" I ask, incredulous.

"I am."

"Because of Kate." I hang my head, refusing to look at him.

He moves closer and brushes his fingers up against my neck, and feels for my racing pulse. Then, he lifts my chin with his index finger.

"No," he says. "Kate has nothing to do with this."

"Liz said: don't wait, don't think about it, just do it."

"We should wait. We should think about it. We can't do this."

"Stop talking. Where's that silent guy persona you always convey, huh?"

"Does my talking *bother* you?"

"Not exactly, but I prefer you do something else with your mouth."

He groans and finally laughs. "There is nothing I want more in this world than you, but I can't do this. Not like this."

He gently pushes me away. And, I stand there, a few feet away from him, and struggle with this raging turmoil as I try not to feel rejection or guilt about my desire in wanting him so much in the first place.

"Friends," he says after long while.

"You use that word like a shield," I chide, shaking my head.

He doesn't say anything. He just waits, and appears so calm, cool, and collected, that I hate him for it for a few seconds. Then, my mind begins to race with too many revelations about Ethan, about myself, and about him.

My chest rises and falls with each breath I take. It feels like I'm going to hyperventilate. He just stands there, while I try and catch my breath.

"When?" I finally ask.

"When what?"

"When did you know we could never be friends?"

He looks amazed as if I've guessed his most cherished secret.

"Can't say."

He looks unhappy, but his eyes glint with anger. I decide to test it.

"Won't say."

He gets this defiant look and shakes his head side-to-side. "Won't say," he whispers.

I watch him closely. He forces himself to smile, but I can see him struggling with a myriad of emotions I cannot begin to understand. He runs his left hand through his hair and gets this inconsolable look.

"We can't do this," he says.

I recognize the sudden air of desperation in his tone and manner and start to feel uncertain. I've breached our unspoken contract—this thing between us, whatever it is—has just been violated, in some way, *by me.*

Distress over his rejection of me begins to filter through and I react with anger.

"You'll fuck Kate, but you won't fuck me. Why?"

"I didn't—it didn't work out with Kate. We tried, but it didn't work out."

"You tried, but it didn't work out?" I try for nonchalance, but utterly fail. I'm jealous and now he knows it.

"I'm blind," he says. "Why can't you *see* that? Accept it?"

"What does that have to do with anything? It didn't matter with Kate, but it matters with *me?* My God! She's your psychiatrist. Where are the ethics and the military protocol you all so religiously follow?" I sigh, and, in the next instant, I lash out. "You're willing to fuck her. But me? I'm off limits?"

"She's not married."

"*I'm not married.*"

"You were. To my best friend. I can't forget that and neither can you." He sighs. "Jordan, I'm blind. Why can't you see that? Accept it. Why do you have to be so fucking wonderful all the time? So hopeful?"

"Don't you put this on me," I say slowly. "I've never been wonderful or hopeful a single day of my entire adult life. Never the entire day, anyway." My voice breaks and tears sting my eyes. "And, you *know* this about me, better than anyone else." I push at his chest to make my point.

He staggers back away from me as if he's been burned by my touch. "Don't do this," he says.

I pause for a moment, surprised by the onset of inexplicable fury I feel as it continues to make its way out of me. "I asked you a simple question; I *deserve* an answer."

"It doesn't matter. Don't you *see* that? I can't be what you want."

"Oh really? What do you think I want you to *be*, Brock?"

He doesn't answer. His silence infuriates me further. I begin pacing the Persian rug. He inclines his head as if he's listening and counting my steps.

"I can't be Ethan," he says quietly. "I can't be what you want me to be."

"I don't want you to be Ethan."

"Yes, you do. He's right here between us. Can't you see that?"

"No. I can't. This thing between us has nothing to do with Ethan."

"It has *everything* to do with him."

He stalks over to me and grabs my arm. I've forced his hand. I can see that now.

"It will always be Ethan. You'll never *see* me. *Never.* You don't see me, now," he says.

"That's not true."

"You don't even see it. I'm *blind,*" he says. "And, you can't fix it." He stops. "But, maybe, Kate can."

His mention of Kate sets me off again. "Why? Why is she the only one allowed to try and fix you? Why?"

He hesitates for a moment, trying to decide what to do, how to handle me. Apparently, I need to be *handled.*

"She doesn't need anything from me," he says, defeated.

"I'm too *needy?*"

He doesn't answer me. It's another one of his God-damn silences. I'm in a foaming rage now. I take an unsteady breath and turn away from him in an attempt to maintain some sort of control, but fail. I turn back. "Fuck you, Wainwright."

He wanly smiles at my outburst, amused, I guess. "I'm not enough for you, Jordan. Accept it. Move on. Go back to Malibu," he says. "I'll buy you out. I'll figure it all out and buy you out. We'll get your mother's jewels back, somehow, too."

This profound despair takes over. *He hates me? He doesn't want me; he's made that perfectly clear.* I'm a *burden* to him. I'm *needy.* The one thing I've never wanted to be to anyone.

"When did you know we could never be friends?" I ask again.

"A long time ago."

Remorse thickens the air between us. Like a dense fog, it makes it impossible to see or feel anything, and, we're bound to its silence. Both of us are enveloped in this profound impenetrable sadness. Time passes. Our breathing becomes steady and synchronized. We face each other five feet apart, but it may as well be miles. He's as far away from me as I am from him. I close my eyes and try to combat the tangible despair that manifests itself between us and I'm plunged into the dark world that he sees. A tear makes its way down my face. I succumb to the blackness. It swallows me up. This is how he feels every waking minute of every day. I attempt to quell the panic as it rises. My breath gets uneven and the tears come faster. I hear him walk away from me.

How long has it been since we've spoken? Three minutes? Five?

I will myself to stay with his world and abide the agonizing darkness, but eventually, I can't take it anymore. I open my eyes, take a deep breath, and hold it.

He stands there, facing the largest windows, touching the glass with the palm of his hands, feeling everything, but seeing nothing.

"My mother's jewels or the Lazy J?" My question comes out of nowhere; even I'm surprised by it.

By the stunned look on his face as he turns to me, I can tell Brock is, too. "The jewels," he says. "Call me sentimental, but I've always had a thing for an Oscar winner's daughter."

"Okay, Sentimental, I'm going to go now. I'm going to go find Tate. Liz was very specific about cowboys."

I wipe at my tear-streaked face, grateful he can't see it. "Friends," I say with derision.

He shakes his head side-to-side and finally smiles.

I turn to go, then turn back, and rush back over to him. I reach up and pull his face towards mine and kiss him hard.

It takes a moment for him to respond, but he does.

"Thank you," I say against his lips after a while. "I think I mean that. Friends, you say. Okay. We're friends. I'll take whatever you're offering."

His arms come around me and he holds me against him for an amazing moment. Our hearts race in a strange synchronization beat for beat. His lips travel down my face, along my jaw line, and between my breasts. He lifts his head and seems to stare straight at me. I reach up and trace his lips. He leans down, kisses me long and hard, and then, lets me go. I stumble back from him, overcome by the powerful connection we just shared.

The world feels different. It's as if I've emerged from the depths of deep water and can finally breathe. Disoriented. Confused. Undone. I have trouble moving all of my body parts in the same direction. The very air, itself, feels raw and biting as it travels in and out of my lungs.

"Let's go find Tate and Ashleigh. They're probably looking for us," he says with a resigned sigh.

"Okay, Cowboy, lead the way." My voice trembles. He hears it. He seemingly studies my face for a moment.

"And, Jordan, if you ever kiss me like that again—" He takes an unsteady breath. "I won't stop."

He runs one of his hands through his dark wavy hair and gets this tormented look.

"I won't let you stop," I say.

The anger at him has mysteriously ebbed away with his kiss. Elation takes over; I brighten at my apparent power over him, however brief.

Still, the emotional turmoil from the last thirty minutes starts to rise up. My smile fades, and my eyes sting with fresh tears as my body all but betrays me again as soon as he reaches for my hand.

He brings it to his lips and kisses the inside of my wrist. My insides flare back to life again. Astonished by his action and my automatic response, I stagger back away from him again and almost trip. He reaches for me and puts his arm firmly around my waist. "Don't push it," he says.

"Who's pushing who?"

"Whom. I think it's whom. Christ," he says in irritation. "Let's go find Tate and Ashleigh. You're pushing me to the limit."

"Oh really? You have limits?"

He holds my hand and starts down the long hallway. We proceed through the various doors, and I barely glance at the yet unfinished restaurant as we pass it. As we retrace our steps back to the main house, right on schedule, I begin to feel the guilt for practically seducing him.

"You don't know how much—" His voice trails off and he turns away.

"What? Tell me."

He turns back towards me. "I can't. It'll freak you out."

"Freak me out? I don't think so."

"I do." His tone is bleak, and I wonder why.

He reaches out mid-air and makes his way past the brown leather sofa and toward the bar that dominates one side of the room. I watch him as he fills a crystal tumbler. His hands shake, betraying his semblance for outward calm. He touches the top of the glass with his index finger and pours himself a hefty amount of some amber-colored liquor. Then, he drinks it down in one swallow.

"You're not getting any. You have to drive us back," he says.

"I thought you could drive."

"Funny." He inclines his head. "They're here," he says in a flat tone.

Ashleigh's distinctive lyrical laugh comes from the direction of the foyer. It's hard to make out what she's saying, but she must have asked a question of Tate because it's easy to discern his low timbre response in answer. The intimacy between them is powerful. I shiver upon hearing it.

"Here comes your cowboy," Brock says with a wry smile.

"I already have one."

Brock practically chokes on his whiskey when I say this. I attempt to laugh, but it comes out more of strangled cry for help.

"Are you okay?" Brock asks.

"No. I'm just *needy*." My bitchy retort does not go unacknowledged.

"We'll talk about that later." He shakes his head in disapproval at me and moves farther away.

"No," I say in a low voice. "There's nothing left to say."

❧❦

"What did we miss?" Ashleigh asks as soon as she walks through the front door.

She's breathless and gorgeous and loved. I can see it. She shines like a beacon of light. Her blue eyes turn almost violet with uncontainable joy as she struts into the room. Tate saunters in after her, barely able to take his eyes off of her. He rewards me with a dazed, crooked smile. Tate Matthews is still the sexy, understated cowboy, but he seems slightly overwhelmed by his newfound companion.

Drinks are quickly dispersed. Brock plies me with seltzer water with a lemon twist and gives me a deal-with-it, defiant look. All unseeing.

The undertone of what has transpired between us minutes before leaves me speechless for the next half hour. My mind tries to sort through the various emotions he's evoked inside of me, but, after a while, I just acquiesce to this numbing state brought on by his outright rejection of me.

Oh yes. We can tease and laugh and dance all around it. And, we have. But nothing takes away from the reality that he turned me down. When I needed him, when I wanted him most, he told me no.

I damp down the competing emotions of guilt and sorrow that threaten to overtake me, but they keep fighting their way back up to the surface. I wallow in the misery of it all.

⁂

Tate seems to be studying our little social scene, while I covertly study him. He glances between Brock and me at regular intervals.

I play the subdued guest role, while Brock takes on the over solicitous host. My irritation with him grows almost exponentially with every charming word he utters. *He turned me down.* The thought reverberates through my mind like an endless taunt now. Truce over.

To distract myself, I continue to study Tate. Once again, I note that he's a very handsome cowboy with an ensemble complete with the casual red and white plaid shirt and the blue jeans and the signature dark wavy hair that could use a trimming, just like his cousin's. *Like Brock's.*

The smile I've been forcing myself to display for the past thirty minutes disappears. *What is wrong with me?*

I watch as Ashleigh reaches up and strokes Tate's hair. This loving possessive gesture is from a girl who normally dates bankers and lawyers and sometimes actors. She shoots me a can-you-believe-this-is-happening look. I subtly move my head in acknowledgement and force myself to smile at her in an attempt to share in her joy.

I'm happy for her. Scared for her. Sorry for me. All three.

Tate towers above her. Yet, he has his arm around her shoulders in this protective, manly way. My best friend seems to melt into his body as if she was made especially for him. They slide onto the sofa in one swift synchronized movement and sit next to each other, touching at every juncture. She languishes in the crook of his arm with her head pressed back against his cheek, apparently in need of all of his physical contact. There's this dreamy look upon her face and even his. I'm enchanted at the sight of the two of them, together, and have to blink rapidly as my eyes begin to tear up.

After a few more minutes of study, I conclude: they're definitely infatuated with each other. It's obvious that carnal knowledge has been breached. Yet, there's something else in the looks they exchange between them. *Love.* I've never seen it on Ashleigh's face, only mine, in photographs, when I used to gaze at Ethan that way, and someone would capture it on film.

And now? Why? Why is my life so damn complicated at every turn? Devastation for it all silently tears through me. Ethan sold my mother's jewels. *All of them?* I have to get to the safe in Malibu and see if there's anything left. And, Brock turned me down.

It's more than a single soul can handle in one day.

I glance away from Tate and Ashleigh because suddenly I'm too afraid I will burst into tears or too afraid I won't. In that single moment, I miss Ethan so much that I practically double over with the onslaught of pain in the form of guilt over my attraction to Brock and the ever-present grief.

Brock settles next to me and reaches for my hand. He wears this apologetic look like a scout badge.

"Are you all right?"

"I'm fine." I strive for a neutral tone, but it comes out bitchy. To make up for it I sweetly say, "I'm going to go start the steaks. Check in with your mom and talk to Max. You should take Ash around. She'll want to see it all."

"I've already seen it," Ashleigh says with a secret smile. "Tate brought me by yesterday. We stayed at his place across the way last night."

She reddens at this admission. *Ashleigh blushing?* Now *I've* seen it all.

"I'm down with the flu, and you're having a sleepover?" I ask.

"Brock took care of you; didn't he?"

"Yes. Yes. He did." Now, it's my turn to blush.

This stricken feeling comes over me for so many things. My memory flashes with my untimely vomiting right in front of him the night before and my disastrous almost seduction of him less than an hour ago. I catch my lower lip to stop it from trembling. Tears sting.

Ashleigh must see them. She studies me for a few seconds and then jumps up from the sofa and out of Tate's arms.

"Let's go work on dinner," she says, taking both Tate and me by surprise. He looks as disconcerted by her sudden reaction as I am.

The girl doesn't know how to do more than lift a fork. She doesn't even boil water as far as anyone knows. Yet, I follow her through the swinging doors to the kitchen because I'm so grateful she's here, grateful she's rescued me from the onset of an emotional breakdown that I couldn't possibly begin to explain to her or anyone else for that matter.

In a daze, I turn back and admire the swinging doors. It's just one more thing that I love about this place. Swinging doors just like ones you find in a restaurant. It's something Ethan should have thought of, but didn't. I know this is another designer touch that Brock came up with. I start to smile, but then the emotional roller coaster of this afternoon with him completely catches up to me. My head starts to pound. Too much wine. Too much angst. Too much unbridled passion. There hasn't been a release for any of it. I covertly wipe at a stray tear, force myself to smile, and turn back toward Ashleigh.

"Spill it," she says with irritation. "What's going on? You look—" Her voice trails off as she looks at me. "You look scared, freaked out, like you're about to cry. What the hell is going on?"

⊷⊶

Ashleigh has beautiful eyes. Blue-violet. She could have been an actress with her flair for drama and her golden looks. But no. She chose to be a teacher. An honorable vocation. It's in sharp contrast to her voracious appetite for sex without commitment. Yet, as I stare at her now, I can tell those days are already far behind her.

I tell her what Ethan has done in the most dispassionate voice I've used all day. She reacts with predictable vehemence and shock when I tell her that Ethan sold my mother's jewels for the house, but then, looks anxious and undone. I absently wonder why, but I'm too focused upon putting the food together to stop and ask. I whip through the chores of dinner preparation. I slice bread, chop lettuce, sauté vegetables, and season the steaks, while Ashleigh just watches with her usual, helpless stance.

"Why should I help when you can do it so much better and faster than I ever could, Jordan?" she asks with a laugh.

After a half hour, I look over at her and sigh in exasperation. Ashleigh has always been able to control her feelings, compartmentalize her life. She's so unlike me. I have to *feel* everything. And, I'm, apparently, *needy*.

"What are you going to do?" Ashleigh asks in a low voice.

"What do you mean?"

"About this." She extends her arm around the grand kitchen.

"I'm going to call Liz and Adrian. They can look in the safe and determine what all Ethan sold," I say bitterly. "They're staying at the house all week. Adrian's a lawyer. He can at least look over the sales documentation that Brock wants me to sign in order to sell this place."

"You'd *sell* it?" Ashleigh asks. "It belongs to Tate and Brock, too, you know."

"I *know*. I don't know what I'm going to do. Maybe, the Lazy J will produce oil soon," I say with a nervous laugh. "Maybe, I don't have to decide about anything right now."

"Tate thinks they're close to discovering oil." She gets this mysterious smile. "You could move here."

"That's not such a good idea." I wince, recalling Brock's rejection and the fact that he thinks I'm needy.

"Why not? It's a fabulous place. It's your dream home. You could finish and open the restaurant. Ethan did that for you."

"Exactly what did he *do* for me? I paid for it with my mom's Oscar jewels and my inheritance, Ash," I say, as the anger at Ethan burns through. "Who does that? And, what does that say about us? Our marriage; huh?"

"I think Ethan loved you. I think he just wanted it to be a surprise."

"I'm *surprised*."

"Austin's not so bad," she says, trailing her fingers along the shiny surface of the countertop. She gets this dreamy look.

"It's not that simple. I have Max to think of. We have a life. In Malibu."

"His grandparents are here. He's three," Ashleigh says in protest.

"He'll be four in five days. And, I don't want to make any permanent changes. Not yet."

"*When* will you? Do you *ever*?" Ashleigh asks.

"Are we talking about me? Or *you*?"

"Tate's the one," she says in this kind of amazed wonder.

"What do you mean?"

I brush my hands down the side of the chef's apron I found hanging in the pantry to stop their sudden trembling. I know what she wants to tell me, but I'm not ready to hear it.

"I mean, I love him. I *know* it. Like you said, you just know. Well, I *know*."

As if on cue, Tate pokes his head through the kitchen door and informs us the grill is ready. He smiles wide at Ashleigh, while I hand him the plate of seasoned steaks to cook. I glance over. Brock lurks in the hallway right behind him, but I guess he's too afraid to actually enter the kitchen because *I'm too needy*. I turn away from both of them in irritation and the door swings shut.

"What's going on with him?" Ashleigh asks with clairvoyance.

"He turned me down." I try to sound casual as I take off the apron, but my hands shake.

"What?"

"I guess he's with Kate. He says he's not, but he must be." I shrug, affecting nonchalance. "She's not *needy*, like I am."

"He said you were needy?" Ashleigh gets this wan smile.

"He said Kate didn't need anything from him. Like I do."

"I don't think that's it," Ashleigh says slowly. "There was this girl. Annie. They were supposed to get married, but she was killed in a car accident, almost six years ago."

"No," I say. "Brock told me that happened to one of their friends."

"No. It wasn't a friend of theirs. It was Brock. Tate told me the whole story. That's why Brock quit law school. Tate and Ethan were both so worried about him that Ethan followed him when he joined the Navy SEALS and went on with him to sniper school."

"You're sure? Why wouldn't Ethan have told me this a long time ago? And, why wouldn't Brock tell me now?"

"He doesn't talk about it. He doesn't allow *anyone* to talk about it, including his family. Janie. Henry. Diana. They haven't known how to reach him. No one has." She gets this thoughtful look. "Tate doesn't think he ever got over Annie's death, until he met you. Tate sees a change in Brock because of his connection to *you*."

"Me? No. I think Brock hates me." My voice breaks. "I'm too fucking needy."

She gets this sympathetic look and puts her arm around me. "I'm sure you scare the hell out of him, Jordan. You two have more in common than most; you've both lost people you cared about. That's why it's so hard for you to trust or love anyone else. Even Ethan." She catches one of my tears. "You held yourself back. You *know* it's true."

"I know."

I sink to the floor and hide my face in my hands. Ashleigh slides in right next to me.

"That's why Brock doesn't commit to anyone for long because he doesn't trust himself in love. And, he doesn't want to fall in love, take the risk, and lose someone all over again," she says softly.

I glance up at her. "Tate told you," I accuse.

"Yes. He told me that you admitted to him, quite openly, I might add, what your biggest fear is." She strokes my hair, tucking strands of it behind my left ear. "Sweetie, you can't live like this. You have to trust that things will work out. You have to give yourself a chance at happiness."

I get up and start across the kitchen. "I need to call Janie and check in on Max. I left my cell in Brock's car. I'll be right back. Keep an eye on the steaks, not the guys," I say darkly.

Before I reach the door, she says in her sweetest voice, "I said yes."

"He proposed to you? Already?" I ask, incredulous. "This is all moving way too fast." I lean against the wall for support.

"Move to Austin. With me. We'd be right next door. Neighbors. How cool is that?"

"You make it sound so easy. But my life has never been easy."

My eyes fill with tears. I reach toward her happiness, but all that I can find is this overriding devastating feeling. *Ashleigh is leaving me, too.*

"Don't cry. We're not eloping. You'll be here."

She squeezes my hand. "Max will be the ring bearer. It's going to be simple and lovely. Even my mom is coming."

She gets this anxious look, seeking my approval. Her mother has never been really involved with Ashleigh's life. The woman's too caught up in portraying herself as younger, single, and worthy. Laina Blondell has always been preoccupied with landing a man, a rich life, and never actually pays much attention to her only child. We haven't seen her for a few years. Since New York.

"When?" I ask, breathless.

"Valentine's Day. Kind of cliché, I know, but you know how much I love holidays, especially that one." She laughs.

I throw my arms around her. "Ash, I'm so happy for you."

"Then, why are you crying?"

"I don't know. Give me a minute." I wipe at my face and try to smile.

Ashleigh gets this pensive look. Maybe, it's all a bit much for both of us.

"Are you okay?" I ask.

"I think so," she says. "Are you?"

"My best friend is getting married. She's leaving me behind in L.A., for a new life, here, in Texas. I deserve at least a minute to get used to the idea."

"Take your time," she says. "You've got a whole sixty seconds. Where's the champagne?" She opens the refrigerator door and looks around.

"Maybe, there's some in the walk-in cooler of the restaurant. I'll go look."

Ashleigh grins over at me, and then, follows me out to the hallway. We laugh a little and hug and begin to talk about her plans for a wedding in February.

"We have plenty of time," she says naively.

I smile, but, deep down, this profound sense of loss comes over me, even as I say, "I'm so happy for you. I am. *Really.* It's going to be great."

CHAPTER

NINETEEN

Brock – Your eyes open

DINNER BECOMES AN EVENT. TATE AND Ashleigh share their big news about getting married, while Jordan and I share in the facade of being happy about it. I sense she's just as upset as I am that these two can so easily plan for the rest of their lives. I'm in awe and experience anguish at the same time. Now, I think both Jordan and I struggle to keep up gallant appearances. Her enthusiasm seems as forced as mine when we toast the happy couple.

Remorse for rejecting her and hurting her feelings works its way through me, too. Jordan's quiet, only answering the happy couple's questions when they're directed at her. I take solace in the fine champagne that Ashleigh's opened and make an extra effort to ensure my glass stays topped off. I've made a rapid descent into the darkness. It's bleak down here all alone. *You can't have her. You can't want her. But, I do.*

Halfway through dinner, my cell phone rings.

"Kate," I say, self-conscious with this particular audience. "Hold on a minute." I get up from the table. "Excuse me. I need to take this."

One-handed, I touch the top of the leather furniture while clutching the cell phone with the other. It's slow progress, and from behind me, the dinner conversation has all but stopped. I reach out, until I feel the coolness of the glass windows at the far side of the living room and finally stop.

"I'm in town. I came early. What's up?" Kate asks. She sounds both curious and seductive. "I called your parents and they said you were out?"

"Yeah, we're having dinner at the Lazy J. Jordan Holloway, her friend Ashleigh, Tate, and me. I wanted to show her the house."

"The house. *Your* house?"

"Her house. Mine. Tate's."

"All together? That's interesting," she says with a laugh. "Ethan's idea? Moving to Austin after a life in L.A.? Did he even *ask* her?"

Kate's ability to quickly guess at the situation is stunning. "No," I say in a low voice. *How much did I tell her during our sessions?*

"Wow. Is she pissed? I would be. I imagine she's a lot of things."

"A lot of things." I wince because I'm not hiding my exasperation with Jordan over the past few hours very well.

Kate picks up on it immediately. "Everything okay?"

"Sure. I'm blind. He spent her inheritance on a house, *here*, not L.A. Things are great. Pretty fucking grand."

Kate laughs.

Why did I ever think she was some brilliant psychotherapist that was going to save me? She's a bigger psyche job than I am.

"You like her," Kate says with an edge to her voice.

"Doesn't matter."

"It certainly does matter. She could be the whole key to this mind fuck you're experiencing."

"Do we have to do this particular diagnosis over the phone?"

"No," she says. "In fact, we need to get you started on a new drug. Have you been taking the one Tethers prescribed?

"I started it a few days ago."

"Well, there's this eye drop medication we want you to try. It will relax the eye muscles. Tethers wants to see you tomorrow. He called it in and I picked it up on my way from the airport. I'm at the Renaissance on Arboretum Boulevard. Come by, so we can put some in. That will give it time to start working before tomorrow's session."

"Why isn't Tethers calling me?"

"I told him I'd take care of it. I was hoping you'd come by, so we could talk or something," she says with a seductive laugh. Kate is so uncomplicated in comparison to Jordan that I laugh, too.

"Jordan's driving."

"Okay. Bring her by. I'd love to meet her. I *want* to meet her."

"All right. Give us an hour or so. We'll swing by," I say. "I need to go. I have guests to entertain."

"I'd love to see that," she says. "You, as the entertainment."

"Behave, Major Richards, I mean that, especially if I bring Jordan by."

"Fine. I'll be on my best behavior for Mrs. Holloway." I wince at her sarcasm.

"See you soon."

I retrace my steps back to the dinner table.

"We need to stop by Kate's hotel for some eye drug Dr. Tethers has recommended," I say. "I'm supposed to use them before our session tomorrow morning. Jordan, would you mind taking me by there before we head back to my parents'?"

"To Kate's hotel?" Jordan asks.

"Yes."

"You have a session with Dr. Tethers and Kate tomorrow?"

"Yes. A session," I say firmly. I detect the doubt in her tone. "She's trying to help me *see*."

"Right. And, she isn't needy or anything," Jordan says. "Excuse me. I'll get dessert. We'll need to get going then. Max is getting anxious for me to get back. Wouldn't want you to miss your session with Kate in the morning because you didn't get your medication."

She's pissed. I wince at her sharp tone. Ashleigh and Tate actually stop talking, suddenly in tune to the heated exchange going on between Jordan and me. "It's not like that," I say.

"It's not like what?"

Her anger is easy to discern. Not answering her question directly is probably the only way to handle her.

"I'll help you clear," I say.

"No. I don't want anything from you," Jordan says.

❧✦❧

At one point, while Jordan and Ashleigh make a point of disappearing together with the excuse of getting dessert, Tate takes me aside.

"Just *tell* her," he said. "Tell her about Annie."

"You know I don't talk about Annie."

"Well, maybe, you should. Because frankly, Brock, you're being a jerk and you know it."

"I'm blind. Why can't you people see that?"

"What does being blind have to do with Jordan?" Tate asks.

"Everything."

"Jordan can take care of herself."

"How can you be so sure?"

"Because she's suffered from loss just like you. I don't think it's asking for too much for you to be nice to her."

"I *am* nice to her. It's too much. All of it."

"What's going on with you?"

"We have a connection."

"I can see that. Everyone can. But, why are you so miserable about that?"

"She was Ethan's *wife*."

"Ethan—isn't coming back." Tate sighs. "Do you know you incline your head towards her whenever she's in the room? The connection between you two is pretty obvious for anyone to see."

"Well, aren't you lucky that you can *see*," I say.

The two women's voices filter through to us. Tate mutters something about behaving myself and moves away from me. He compliments Jordan for putting together such a magnificent dessert, while I'm left in the dark as to what it is.

"Here," she says, touching my right shoulder and placing a fork in my hand. "Chocolate cake with whipped cream and raspberries."

"Thanks." I have reached helpless status again.

After that exchange, the only other sound from her is the scraping of her chair against the wood floor to my right. I spend the next ten minutes struggling to eat every bite of the cake, but I'm too stressed out by her veiled anger at me and her very presence at this point.

Tate and Ashleigh make a point of leaving us alone, feigning a sudden interest in locking up Tate's place, but that only makes it worse. We're alone now and definitely not talking.

My ability to fix the situation reaches an all-time low. No matter what I say, I get only one-word responses from Jordan.

Are you all right?"

"Fine."

"Can I help you clean up?"

"No."

She leaves me sitting at the dining room table. The effort to blindly find my way to the kitchen is insurmountable, so I just sit there and swim with the blackness.

Everything is fucked up. Me, most of all.

Fifteen minutes later, she calls out. "Let's go. I want to be back on time so I can tuck Max in. He's getting cranky. He wants a bedtime story."

"Fine," I say with an edge. I get out my cell phone and call Tate to let him know we're taking off.

"Talk to her," he says just before I hang up.

We make the long walk to the car without saying anything. The drive back into town is the polar opposite from the one we shared on the way to the Lazy J as we both stew in the stony silence and attend to the emotional wounds we've managed to inflict upon each other over the long afternoon and into the evening.

I give her directions to the Renaissance. I hear her key them into the car's GPS. The mechanical voice breaks the long silence with intermittent directions. It's the only sound during the car ride for the longest time.

"I just can't believe they're rushing into this," she says after twenty minutes.

"Tate and Ashleigh?"

"Yeah. They've known each for three days. Three days! Who does that?"

"I believe you and Ethan knew each other for a total of fifteen minutes before he asked you to marry him," I say quietly.

"That was different," she says with a catch in her voice.

"How was that different?"

I'm curious now. I flashback to the wide grin on Ethan's face, when we'd met up at the airport in Dulles for our first tour. 'I met someone,' Ethan had said. 'I married her. She's everything.' He'd gotten out a picture of the two of them in Vegas. And, there was Jordan in a white summer dress with her long mahogany hair in a French braid, looking like a Greek goddess. I remember her amazing smile and the way she stared up at Ethan. What I remember the most, when I first saw that picture, was the feeling that there was no one else in the world, but the two of them and how excluded I felt. Ethan had met and married a stranger. Where did that leave me? The answer became clear not long after we arrived in Afghanistan. Nothing had really changed. Ethan was married, but it was this whole separate life from Afghanistan, from Austin, from even me.

Until now.

"We were both young and crazy," she says now, breaking my reverie. "Too naive to know that nothing ever lasts."

"You really believe that? That nothing ever lasts?" I'm taken aback at her cynicism, even though I recognize it.

"What would you have me believe, Brock? Happily ever-afters?" She laughs bitterly. "That was Ethan's thing, not mine. You think I enjoy being right? No. I don't enjoy it. And, even though I don't believe in happily-ever-after, it doesn't stop it from hurting when it doesn't work out, when the people I love the most *die*. Not now. Not ever."

I want to answer her, to somehow convince her and myself that things can work out, but her cell phone rings, effectively ending our conversation.

"Max," she says with surprise. "Henry dialed the number for you, huh? No, you can't go fishing. It's late. It's getting dark. I'll be there soon and I'll read you a story. What? Well, Henry's right. It's getting dark. Just be good and listen to him; okay, baby? I love you. Okay, I've got to go. Mommy's driving Brock's car, right now. I'll see you soon. I love you, Max. I'll be there soon."

⊰⊱

Jordan parks the car with the valet at Kate's hotel. I whip out my walking stick, intent on showing my independence. This lasts a full two minutes, until we reach the lobby where I have to depend on Jordan to locate and lead the way on to the elevators.

"Room 2911," I say with nonchalance.

Only her perfume speaks to me. It's some amazing French scent that I remember a parade of forgotten women wearing before I met her. It's fading floral tones reach for me in this tight space we inevitably share. The snippets of complete strangers' conversations float all around us as we ride the elevator and get pressed closer together as more people get on then off. It's a slow, arduous ascent to the twenty-ninth floor. I count five different openings and closings of the doors in the space of three minutes. It's a busy place for a Sunday night. The crowd of people continues to push Jordan and me closer together. I take advantage of the close quarters by encircling her waist with my free arm while she holds onto my jacket sleeve. I breathe in the mesmerizing floral scent of her hair and enjoy the heady sensation of being right next to her.

"Floor 29," she says at the same time the elevator dings.

We move as one unit out of the elevator and on to what I surmise must be a long carpeted hallway. Behind us, the distinct sounds of the elevator ambiance quickly fade. Jordan stops and must be gauging the hallway signs. "This way," she says after a few seconds.

I'm pulled along in the direction of Kate's hotel room and revel in the irony of the situation. I'll be introducing Ethan's widow, my current sexual fantasy, to Kate, my former psychiatrist and past sexual fantasy. Fucked up doesn't begin to explain it.

The sound of a lock being unlatched and a door opening serves as my only cue that we've reached Kate's hotel room, because Jordan isn't talking.

"Dr. Major Kate Richards, this is Jordan Holloway."

"Wow. Come in. You look just like that actress, Laurel Breckinridge," Kate says with an uncertain laugh. I can practically feel her sizing up Jordan's fine attributes. "It's an amazing resemblance, in fact."

"She doesn't—"

"Laurel Breckinridge was my mother," Jordan says, cutting me off.

"Oh. Wow. That's incredible." Kate sighs. "Brock, you failed to mention that connection."

Her reprimand is real enough. I roll my eyes.

"I've never told you anything about Jordan," I say.

"Yes. Curious," Kate says slowly. "Come in. Both of you. Jordan, sit here. You look cold. Are you cold?"

"I'm not cold."

"Oh. Well, you look cold. Undone, perhaps. Is everything all right? I'm sure this is an emotional time for you, right now." She takes a deep breath and sighs. "Brock showed you the house, then? What was that like? How did you feel? And, Ethan spent your inheritance? Are you okay with that? I mean, if that's what you want, great. But is it what you want?"

Mortified that I told Kate so much on the phone and by the personal nature of the questions she's busy firing at Jordan, I move to intercede.

"Kate, she's not a patient," I say.

"Yes, but she's connected to you, Brock. In lots of ways, it seems. I'm sure her interests are as pure as mine in having you see again." Kate seems to pause for effect.

I close my eyes for a second. Tension seeps into me.

This is not going to go well. What was I thinking?

"Right, Jordan? You would help Brock in any way that you can," Kate says sweetly. "I'm sure of it."

"My intentions are as pure as yours," Jordan says.

"Drink?" Kate asks. Her high heels click across the bare floor.

"Love one."

"Wine? Champagne? Something stronger?" Kate asks.

"Champagne. Let's celebrate," Jordan says.

"What are we celebrating?" I ask, wary, all at once.

"Why, you, of course. And, our purest of intentions in having you see again." Jordan links her arm with mine and effectively leads me into the room. "Here, let me help you over to the sofa," she says, and then whispers, "Sit down, Brock. Let's get you a drink and get what we came for, so we can get the hell out of here."

She's pissed. She hates Kate. She makes that clear by the sharpness of her tone.

I gulp at the champagne, hoping to kill the bottle as fast as possible.

Kate makes a production out of administering the eye drops and spends an inordinate amount of time telling Jordan how to put them in three times a day, as if she's explaining this to Max instead of the grown woman sitting right next to me.

"Got it," Jordan says after Kate's five-minute dissertation. "I've got it, Kate. I can handle him."

"Great. So, tell me about growing up as a child of famous parents. Davis and Laurel Breckinridge. Wow." Kate sighs. "What was that like?"

"Magical. Amazing. Right up until the point they were murdered in Barcelona. After that, it was different," Jordan says with notable disquiet.

End of story. Yet, Kate ignores Jordan's reluctance to talk about her past and continues on with a litany of personal questions, which Jordan manages to deflect with clearly evasive answers. I listen in fascination as the two women spar.

"So," Jordan says in a rare opening, when Kate isn't plying her with another inappropriate question. "I hear you and Brock gave it a go, but it didn't work out."

Kate sputters her champagne.

"Yes. Well. I'm his psychiatrist. His superior officer."

"That's what I thought," Jordan says easily, like they're old friends.

"Those are two very good reasons for not fucking him." She stops for a moment. Then, she says in a low, hushed voice. "I take it you *like* what you do. That perhaps you're *good* at it."

"I am." The shrillness in Kate's voice gives her away. She's defensive.

"Great. Well that's just great. I would hate for your job, which you say you're very good at, to be put in any kind of jeopardy because you were inappropriately fucking a patient."

"Are you *threatening* me?" Kate asks, incredulous.

"Do I need to?" Jordan says with a little laugh. "No. I don't think I do."

Kate gasps and says nothing more.

I imagine she's silently berating herself for underestimating Jordan Holloway. I can't quite wipe the smile off my face after Jordan says this.

For another ten minutes, Jordan asks Kate perfunctory questions about the flight from D.C. and living on the east coast, while I listen in this fascinated stupor to their superficial banter.

As if choreographed, Jordan squeezes my hand. "Brock, we should get going. Max is going to be looking for me. For you."

"Who's Max?" Kate asks in bewilderment.

"My son. He's almost four. Brock's parents have been great about watching him, but we really should get back."

"So soon? I was hoping you'd be able to stay longer, Brock."

I get a little squeamish. I'm in the middle of a battlefield I can't even see. I'm not sure how to handle this.

"Well, it's getting—"

"He can't stay. Max will want to see him. Thanks for the medication. That was sweet of you to get it for him. Really," Jordan says. "You do go above and beyond the call of duty; don't you?"

"I suppose so," Kate says.

She's been outplayed, and she's just figured this out.

"Seems that you do," Jordan says. In one swift movement, she pulls me up from the sofa. "Let's go."

Another two minutes sail by, and we're going down in the elevator. I'm off balance over the battle that's just taken place in Kate's hotel room and the woman who grips my arm beside me. Like Kate, I've underestimated Jordan in every way. I sway with the elevator movements and the unexpectedness of what's just transpired.

"So, what did you think of Kate?" I finally ask.

"You really want me to answer that?"

"Are you going to be pissed for a long time?"

"Not long. I feel better already just being in the elevator."

I imagine her smiling and can't help but smile in the general direction of her voice.

"Why, Jordan Holloway, I do believe you enjoyed yourself in there," I drawl. "Just for humor's sake, can you tell me what she looks like?"

"She's got a blonde bombshell thing going on. She's trouble with a capital T. You'd be better off with Ashleigh. Safer, anyway." She laughs a little and links her arm with mine. I envision her smile again, and grin.

"What? And, you're here to rescue me? I need saving?"

"You know what would be nice, Lieutenant?"

"What?" I ask, uneasy by the sudden wistfulness I detect in her tone.

"If you would just trust me enough, to tell me, what's really going on with you."

I don't answer for a few minutes. She sighs and sounds impatient.

"I don't think that's a good idea," I finally say.

"Can I ask you something else?"

"Yes."

"When are you going to finally see me?"

I don't answer. After a few seconds, I hear her as she moves across to the other side of the elevator as far away from me as possible. It's as if the electric current between us has been shut off. I wave my hand in the air, attempting to feel for her presence, but she stays back away from me now. I hear her heavy sigh to my far left. Then, the elevator dings.

There's a rush of movement from the left again. A minute later, I grasp the sides of the doors and step out. This sense of vulnerability assails me. I'm lost for a few minutes. She's left me.

Then, I hear the tapping of her shoes against the pavement, but the sound of her retreats farther away from me.

"You're all I see," I whisper. Of course, she doesn't hear me. I can barely hear myself say it. *Coward.*

"I'll get the valet to bring the car around." Her voice echoes along the parking lot walls.

And, I don't answer.

❧❦❧

The drive back to the ranch is surprisingly pleasant, considering the tension of the past three hours.

Some sort of truce has been called between us again. Maybe, she feels sorry for me. This thought makes me feel uneasy again.

I listen intently to her as she hums along with the songs playing from the radio. Her earlier frustration with me all but forgotten, it seems.

I lean back against the headrest and close my eyes. The medication seems to make me relax as much as the way she's humming along to the song on the radio.

"I hate riding in cars ever since that first tour in Afghanistan when Humvees were getting blown up right and left by IEDs. And now, that I can't see, I really hate it. But with you driving, I'm actually okay."

She stops humming. "How much?"

"How much what?" I ask, automatically opening my eyes and turning my head towards her.

"How much did it just cost you to just admit to that? What you just said."

"Nothing," I say in surprise.

She pats my left hand. "See? We're making progress."

"Can't see."

"You will."

We bask in the warm essence of the latest peace offering between us.

"Cardamom," she says a little while later.

"Cardamom?"

"Just a little. In the pancakes. Sometimes, my French toast. Not hardly any. I don't know what it is about that, but people rave about them when I add it. So, now you know something that Ethan never knew." She sighs and begins humming the melody to another song.

I lean my head toward her, completely overwhelmed by the cloaking darkness, and what she's just said. How I wish I could see her. Just for a second. Just one glimpse of her.

I reach out and trace her lips. She's smiling. I smile back.

I don't think about it. I just say it.

"When you were frosting cupcakes. The "Nemo" ones? That's when I knew."

"Knew what?" Jordan asks.

"We could never be friends."

I turn my head back toward the window and fully embrace the blackness. She stops humming again and downshifts the gears as we must reach the ranch driveway.

"What did that cost you?" Jordan finally asks.

I detect the sudden fear in her voice. Unwittingly, I commit to the truth with the next breath and the next three words.

"My best friend," I finally say.

She draws an unsteady breath as if the air's been ripped from her lungs.

My memory of that fateful day with Ethan returns as if a light has been switched on. All the images come flooding back. The dust swirls. The unfamiliar dark boots I saw through the scope that day. The enemy. Calling out the coordinates. Ethan's anger. Mine. The chaos. The danger. The endless trek back to camp, carrying Ethan and all the gear. I was so sure I'd saved him. And then, I remember the absolute horror of seeing his bloodied face, half gone. The panic. The blood. The pain. The darkness descending upon me. Everything about that day rushes back.

"I remember," I finally say. The blackness moves in. I close my eyes and lean back against the head rest.

"He was distracted. So was I." I grimace as the memories assail me. "He got your letter where you told him you might be pregnant. He'd come to realize all he'd been missing. We were both distracted. In different ways. By you," I whisper. My voice breaks. "I saw the dust-up first. I warned Ethan, but he must have shifted from the coordinates I'd given him. That's why he missed. And, it's my fault."

I flinch as if I can, again, hear the fatal bullet that killed Ethan whiz past me. The eerie sound of metal meeting flesh and bone returns, as if it were happening all over again, making me shudder.

"Then, we were ambushed. There were bullets flying from everywhere. I tried to save him. Save him for you, Jordan. But I couldn't. And now you know. Now you know why we can never be friends."

My soliloquy ends. It's met with her absolute silence.

The Porsche comes to a stop. She turns off the engine and puts the keys in my hands. In the next second, her car door slams. I hear the furious click of her shoes against the garage floor, but the sound quickly fades.

I don't run after her. I hold my head in my hands and immerse myself with the blackness. It seems to have invaded my very soul. I can feel it.

And, she hates me now. I've made sure of that.

After a long while, I drag myself out of the car.

I glance up at the garage light, startled by the revelation that I can actually see it.

I can see.

The truth sets me free. Yes, but at what cost?

CHAPTER

TWENTY

Jordan – We fall down

IT'S TOO MUCH. I CAN'T PROCESS what Brock has just told me. I can't. I rush into the side entrance of the Wainwrights' house and race past the kitchen doorway in search of Max. I take the stairs two at a time up the grand staircase and sweep past Brock's bedroom door and mine.

This kind of desperation takes hold. I must see Max. I must see him. I have to get to him. I rush at his bedroom door, turning the handle at the same time.

"Max, Mommy's home. I'm here."

I make a whimpering sound as I stare in horror at the rumpled bed sheets. The blankets have been flipped back. But, no Max. In a daze, I walk out the door, down the hall, and traverse the stairs.

Janie is there. She's holding on to Brock and half-crying.

I stare in bewilderment, beginning to experience some kind of delayed shock.

"Max. Where's Max?"

"Brock can see," Janie's saying.

She's smiling, overcome with undeniable joy. I want to smile too, but I can't. This overriding sense of dread takes over.

I glance over at Brock. His eyes hold a mystical light, exhibiting both joy and pain. His revelation of a few minutes ago is already far away from me.

"Max. Where is he? He's not in his room," I say slowly. "He's not there."

"What?" Janie asks, finally connecting with my words. "We put Max to bed a half hour ago."

Somehow, I find relief in her reassurance, I dully watch as she races up the stairs two at a time and calls out "Max" at regular intervals. Her voice comforts me.

"Jordan, where would he go?" Brock asks. He looks worried. I reach up to smooth the worry lines on his face as if I can undo the terror that's begun to seep its way into me.

"I don't know," I say. My body begins to shake. I start pacing. *Think. Where would he go?*

"Where would he go? Think, Jordan. What was he talking about doing when you called him earlier? Where would he go?"

"I don't know. He wanted me to read him a bedtime story."

Henry walks in. He has this stricken, glazed look, as if he's having trouble breathing. Fear begins to claw its way in with more persistence. Janie sounds more panicked as she calls out for Max from upstairs.

"What did you do today?" I ask Henry.

"We were out by the back forty, repairing a fence. He helped me feed a baby calf. The only thing we didn't get done today was the fishing. He wanted to go to the pond where I told him his dad and Brock used to fish, but it was getting too dark. I told him we'd do it tomorrow," Henry says. "He wasn't happy. He said…I'd promised."

I'm looking at Henry, distracted by his strange contorted facial movements, but still trying to figure this all out. Then he makes this gasping sound as if he's struggling for air.

Where's Max?

I watch Henry as he falls to the floor. There's this long, helpless, wordless sound from him. A cry for help.

"Dad!" Brock rushes over to him, checks his pulse, and clears his airway in the next few precious seconds.

Shock descends upon me like a heavy cloak. I can't make myself move. I just stand there, but then, I stagger over to help Brock.

It takes a few minutes before Henry's last words begin to resonate with me. "The *pond*," I say in horror.

Brock leans over his dad while he yells for his mom. Fear takes firm hold. I can only watch as Brock picks up the phone and dials 911. Janie races back into the room and Brock spends a precious minute telling her how to do CPR, while he performs it on Henry at the same time.

Then, with this uncanny sense of dead calm, he takes my hand and pulls me along to the garage. He starts his father's truck, buckles me in, and guns the engine. We race toward the pond.

In a few miraculous minutes, we're there. Naively, I half expect to see Max just sitting there, waiting for us, but there's no one there.

There's nothing.

The harsh black night is partially softened by the white of the moon, but this eerie feeling settles upon me. It's hard to breathe.

Too late. The words chirp at me like a little foreign bird. *Too late.*

Brock calls out for Max, over and over. I try to speak, but no words come out. It's another five minutes before Tate and Ashleigh arrive, but it feels like an eternity already.

Brock tells them about Henry. I listen dully from this faraway place and try to summon up sympathy for Brock and his family. But there's this uncanny sense of foreboding, a foregone conclusion, taking over. Somehow, my mind already knows there's yet another tragedy in my life's path that I must endure.

And, I can't feel anything. Nothing. It's as if I've been shattered into a million pieces already.

Brock and Tate search the shoreline from the west side while Ashleigh and I take the east. The only sounds are our frantic footsteps along the dirt and gravel path and the rustle of the tall grasses as we plow through them in search of Max.

I stop for a minute to try and catch my breath. That's when I hear this strange sound coming from the middle of the pond. I glimpse a flailing white hand and the hint of a little boy's blonde head. *Max.*

"Momma. Momma."

It's a faint cry, a mixture of garbled words and gurgling water. Then, there's nothing but absolute silence.

"There!" I scream. "He's there. Max!"

I point to the middle of the pond. My arms shake violently as I maneuver out of my jacket and kick off my shoes. I plow through the shallow water and start to swim with frenzied strokes when the water deepens.

"I'm coming, baby. Mommy's coming."

The murky blackness of the water attacks me from all sides. I shudder and attempt to outrun my fear. *I hate the water.* Tate and Ashleigh join me in the search, while Brock hurries to the other side and dives in.

Over and over, the four of us dive to the bottom and only surface for much-needed air before quickly diving again. The water is gloomy, foreboding. It predicts my future with every jagged breath I take at its surface. But every time, the silt bottom just runs through my fingers as I ravage its murky depths, again and again, looking for Max. A hand. An arm. Anything of Max.

Desperation takes over all control of my limbs. The urgent need to find him, to save him, becomes paramount.

Time seems to hover, to almost stop.

The muffled sounds of everyone's voices from beneath the water's surface reach at me, but seem so far away. My body feels bogged down by the water and gravity. It's hard to move and I struggle to break free of it. The gasps for air dominate. The momentum of plunging ever downward in defiance of gravity's grasp by kicking through the water becomes frenetic. We share the desperation and fight the depths of pure terror in search of him. *Max.*

Max, where are you?

Max. Max, Baby, don't leave me. Please don't leave me.

Five minutes. *Too long.*

"I've got him," Brock calls out from some distance away.

I glance at my watch. It's been eight minutes since I first saw his hand. *Too long.*

I swim for the shore, stopping to help Ashleigh, who's coughing and choking, as she struggles to be free of the deep water. A strong swimmer she is not. Once onshore, we both gasp for air and hold onto each other, while we wait for Brock and Tate.

Ashleigh cries out when two tall shadows emerge from the murky dark water from the other side of the pond, while I just stare. They carry a small lifeless form between them.

Brock moves into action quickly, places Max on the ground, but shields him from my view with his body.

Resolute, I get up, walk over, and sink down on the other side of Max and grab his hand. In studied fascination, I watch Brock as he breathes into my baby's lungs and begins to do steady counts of compressions on his chest. "One. Two. Three. Four. Five."

Then, he breathes into Max's lungs. "Compression. Again," he says.

I silently mouth the same words. One. Two. Three. Four. Five. Compression. Again.

It's like a little prayer sent up to God each time we say it together.

On some far-removed level, I'm consoled by Brock's actions, by his continual count of five, by the way he breathes into my son, and does compressions upon Max's little chest. I take solace from these simple actions, these simple words and try to breathe.

Ashleigh sobs uncontrollably to my left. She grabs my arm and buries her face into my shoulder. I pat her head. My hair drips pond water onto Max's shirt. Some part of me registers that it doesn't matter because he's soaking wet already.

He needs a bath.

He needs more than that.

His cherub little face is streaked with mud. His eyes are closed. His hand is so cold in mine. I brush his hair with my free one. It bristles against my hand. *Like Ethan.*

"Don't leave me, Max. Stay with me."

Ashleigh cries harder. I don't do anything. Parts of me seem to be scattered across the very ground. Broken. A million pieces.

Too late chirps the little bird in my head. *Broken. A million pieces.*

Does it matter?

The ambulance arrives. The paramedics take over the scene. I wonder how they found their way out to Logan's Pond. It probably isn't on any map. Logan's Pond. Ethan used to talk about Logan's Pond. He used to tell Max how he and Brock used to fish there when they were a little older than Max is now. Brock spoke about it at Ethan's funeral. And Max wanted to go. To the pond. To catch a fish. Touch the water. *Be with Daddy?*

I should have read him *Cat In The Hat.* I promised I would read it to him and I haven't. *What kind of mother am I? I'll do better.*

Brock helps me climb up into the ambulance after the paramedics strap Max to a gurney and slide him in. The two paramedics hover over him from each side and burst into action. They put an oxygen mask on him and hook Max up to a bunch of machines.

They're going to save him. They're going to try.

There's this brief moment where they both exchange this surreptitious look with Brock, who just nods at them, as he slides in beside me.

Brock knows one of them. Steven. He served in Afghanistan.

"Sorry about Ethan," he says.

"This is his son, Max," Brock says. "This is Jordan. Max's mother."

"Jesus. Oh God." Steven looks at me in sympathy. He squeezes my hand before returning to help his partner with Max.

The third paramedic, the driver, slams the door shut. It feels like a tomb. I can barely breathe again. It registers with me that the red lights flash, but there's no sound.

I try to wave at Ashleigh through the little window of the ambulance as we start to drive away, but my hand doesn't cooperate. I stare at it. It seems disconnected from the rest of me. I get a glimpse of Ashleigh's tear-streaked face. She's a mess, in a very un-Ashleigh-like state. She tries to wave back, but seems to have trouble lifting her arm as much as I do.

There's another ambulance at the Wainwrights' as we pass, and I wonder if Henry is okay. I want to ask God to save both of them. Yes. It's a big wish. At least, one of them. Yes. A smaller wish. But I can't make myself utter the words to make either kind of wish. No, to put into words, to ask, and to receive some kind of trade for the other seems wrong.

Please God, I'll be a better mother. I'll try harder. I'll never get mad or yell or be sad ever again. I'll do better. Please God, let me have Max.

And, please God, save Henry. He's a good man, a good husband, a good father. Brock needs him.

Please God, save them both.

There. I've made my wish. I've asked for them both. Yes. It's a big wish.

I glance over at Brock. He can *see* me. I try to smile.

Thank you, God, for returning Brock's sight. Thank you, God.

But there are so many other wishes that we need. It's too much. There are too many miracles we need to pray for this night.

C H A P T E R

T W E N T Y - O N E

Brock – Never to know

EAR GOD, IF YOU GIVE US Max back and save my father you can have my sight. God, can you hear me? Are you listening? Please don't take Max. Please don't take my dad. Take my sight back. Please God. Please listen.

"Any word?" Tate asks as soon as he and Ashleigh appear in the doorway of the ER waiting room.

"No."

I stand up and shove my hands in the wet pockets of my jeans. I look at him with uncertainty.

"Wow. You can see."

"I know. I guess telling the truth helps, but at what cost?" I say in a low voice. "I can't tell that story, now."

Tate nods and glances over at Jordan. "How is she?"

I shake my head side-to-side.

He closely watches Ashleigh as she goes over to Jordan, who sits in the farthest corner of the waiting room and stares at the television. There's no sound on. It's just CNN running with the usual sensational headlines and she's been mindlessly watching it for the past thirty minutes.

"What do you think?" Tate asks in a low voice that only I can hear.

I stare at his solemn expression and can't help but feel thankful that I can see it. Guilt shoots down around me from all sides like a stray lightning bolt. I wince and silently acknowledge that I just said a prayer to God, exchanging my sight for Max and my dad.

I shudder and shake my head.

"I think they're going to come through that door any minute and tell her they did everything they could, but it wasn't enough to save him."

Tate's eyes get glassy. They mirror mine.

And your dad?"

"He's in the ICU. They'll only let Mom in right now. Diana said she'd text me when something changes."

Tate nods. We lean up against the wall side-by-side and wait.

Five minutes.

Jordan stands up as soon as the ER doctor in blue scrubs appears in the doorway. He comes over to her. He takes off his mask and holds it in his left hand and reaches for hers with the other.

I don't need to hear what he says. I know what he says. Jordan stumbles backward to a chair and resumes watching CNN while Ashleigh rushes over to her.

"Get my cell phone," Jordan says to her after a few minutes.

With shaking hands, Ashleigh digs through Jordan's purse for the phone.

Jordan waves us all off.

Helpless, I watch her as she walks down the hallway, alone, and makes a single phone call.

❧❧

Diana clutches the sides of the hospital walls every few feet as she makes her way down the hallway as if she's having trouble maintaining her balance.

No text message.

Whatever she has to tell us, she's saying in person. And, I already know what she has to say.

Tate makes a guttural sound beside me when he sees my sister. He pushes off the wall and walks unsteadily towards her.

I close my eyes and summon the blackness. It's not there. All I see are these swimming red blood vessels and the intrusive edgy lines of fluorescent lighting as it stabs its way through to me.

I can see. God didn't make that trade.

I open my eyes. I can see that I've lost so much, all in one single night, all within a few hours.

Diana collapses in Tate's arms and starts to cry. Loud mournful cries.

I didn't have time to even text her about Max. I was waiting for the shaking to stop in my hands and for Jordan's return. Neither has happened.

My first thoughts center on my mom and how she's going to handle this. My second thoughts are of my dad and all the things I left unsaid and his profound disappointment in me and all the wrong choices I've made since Annie's death.

And now, there's Jordan. And, the loss of Max. How is she going to handle it all? How am I?

I sense Jordan even before I see her.

She walks arm-in-arm with my mom. The devastation is apparent in both of their bodies with every step. My mother makes slow passage down the hallway, leaning heavily on Jordan. They meet up with Diana and encircle her. They encircle Diana. In a daze, I stare at the three women left in my life that I love more than anyone else. Tate reaches for Ashleigh and hugs her close.

And, I stand alone and can only watch.

❦

In some strange obligatory way, the hospital accommodates Janie Wainwright and Jordan Holloway by setting up a private room where the two women sit next to each other between the two gurneys next to their dead loved ones. Janie Wainwright requests this and the hospital makes it happen. Years of charitable giving has its privileges, I guess.

In a stupor, I watch my mother as she holds on to my dad's hand, while Jordan holds on to Max's.

They sit there for hours.

Hours.

At two in the morning. I can't take it anymore. I can't watch it anymore. I leave the room without either one of them noticing and go in search of Tate and Ashleigh. Diana has already gone home to her family—to David and the kids—to mourn, to plan, to cry.

"What's she doing?" I ask Ashleigh. I jerk my head toward the closed door.

"She's waiting for Igor Dasher."

"Who the *fuck* is that?"

Ashleigh gets this wan, sad smile.

"He's the mortician who took care of Ethan. He's coming from D.C. He caught a red-eye flight. That's the only one she trusts with—" Ashleigh starts to cry. Tate holds her close. "Your mom wants Igor, too," she says. "He's helping with both of them."

All I can do is nod. I've given up on understanding anything from here on out.

I whip out my cell phone and text Kate, "My dad died. Jordan's son drowned. We're at the hospital."

She texts back: "I'm so sorry. What can I do?"

I don't even think it through. No. I make another mistake to go along with all the other ones I've already made.

I text back: "I can see. Sign me off. Get me back to Afghanistan."

Kate texts back: "Done."

I text: "Don't come. I'll see you in D.C."

She texts back: "OK."

After a long while, I give in to the utter exhaustion and lie down on a couch in the ER waiting room.

Sunlight pierces the edges of my eyelids. I'm awakened by this sharp endless tapping on my left shoulder by someone's bony fingers.

"Lieutenant Wainwright? Igor Dasher here."

I open my eyes, confused and assailed at the unusual sight of this haunted-looking man in a green velvet suit and starched white shirt. He has dark eyes, a beak of a nose, and high sallow cheekbones all pasted against the pale white skin of a patrician face. The shock of black longish hair completes his ensemble. Igor is an apt name. He looks like a vampire unexpectedly caught in daylight.

"I'm looking for Jordan Holloway? For Mrs. Henry Wainwright, Janie?"

"Who are *you*?"

"Igor Dasher. Ms. Holloway called me. I'm so sorry to hear about little Max and your father." His tone is questionable of true sentiment.

I stare up at him for a full minute. What kind of insane connection does he have to Jordan? How is it even possible to be jealous of such a creepy little man?

I stand up. He's a good seven inches shorter than me.

I start to smile, momentarily relieved of the memory of the morbid circumstances in which we all find ourselves. He makes this clicking sound with his teeth and rolls his eyes at me.

"Jordan? You were going to take me to Jordan and your mother?"

Does he end all his sentences with a question?

I shrug, unwilling to pay any sort of homage to this guy. I incline my head toward the door.

"Mrs. Holloway and Mrs. Wainwright are in there. They're in there."

Waiting for the likes of you. This I don't say, but my sudden intense dislike of him must show on my face.

He gives me this superficial smile and turns on his heel toward the closed door—the makeshift tomb that contains my father and Max; and that, somehow, holds hostage both Jordan and my mother.

The memories of yesterday stir. I stand there, alone. There's nowhere to hide when grief catches up to me.

CHAPTER

Twenty-Two

Jordan - You're the storm

THE FIRST TIME MY MAGICAL WORLD fell apart, I was seventeen. Motherless, fatherless. I was the child left behind. Now, at almost twenty-eight, in the space of six months, I'm widowed and childless. It's all been taken from me.

Guilt arrives. It burdens me with unspoken questions.

Did I hold on too tight? Did I bring this on myself? Was I that bad of a mother that God would punish me this way?

Igor Dasher's long fingers press into my wrist, jarring me back.

"No service. Just cremation," I say in rote. "Take him with you, if you need to. I'll be in touch about the ashes. A silver urn. He liked elephants. Yes. He liked those. Winnie the Pooh. Cat In the Hat. Have some sort of engraving done. Put some saying on the front. Something Winnie The Pooh would say. That would be nice. Yes. Let's do that."

The words get harder to say. My hearing starts to go. It's as if Igor Dasher is speaking to me from under water. I look at him in some confusion, now, and attempt to smile, to move my lips, at least, but nothing happens. The effort is too great.

With trembling hands, I give Igor my credit card. He writes down the number and hands it back.

"Is there anything else I can do for you?" Igor asks in his quiet, breathy way.

I look over at Max. He looks like he's sleeping beneath that crisp white sheet. Not even a blanket for the dead. There's a little smudge of dirt one of the nurses missed in cleaning him up. I want to remove it, but I can't make myself move. Igor follows my gaze. Then, he gets up and, with the corner of the sheet, wipes at Max's face with delicate strokes.

"Thank you," I whisper. "You'd better help Janie, now. Her daughter, Diana, is here, too. Out in the hallway." I cast my eyes about the room, as if seeing it for the first time. "What time is it?"

"It's a little past noon."

"Have you seen Brock?"

"Mr. Wainwright is waiting for you down the hall." Igor sounds disapproving.

He gets this kind of greenish tint to his features. *How is that even possible?* It almost makes me laugh. I shake my head to clear my mind. The incongruence between Brock and this man is too much to assimilate. Too much.

"Thank you for coming."

The mortician squeezes my hand. Then, he brushes his lips against the inside of my wrist. And, I feel nothing. It doesn't faze me at all. My hand easily slips from his grasp, and I leave without looking back.

It's been fourteen hours.

The hospital has begun to lose its lustrous status for generosity. They need the beds. They need the room. They've made that clear to most of us.

I scan the hallway, move past the nurses' station and all the sorrowful looks bestowed upon me. I manage to avoid the gazes of all the fresh mourners that have arrived for the Wainwrights. I move past Janie and Diana, even Ashleigh and Tate. My eyes seek only Brock's.

"Let's go," I say as soon as I see him.

I grasp his hand and pull him to me. He's so close to me that his breath stirs my hair. I stare into his eyes and no longer care if the world watches and disapproves of the two of us being together. None of it matters any-more. Least of all, it seems, to the two of us.

❧ ⁂ ❧

The Porsche rockets along the highway. Brock seems to implicitly understand my urgent desire for acceleration, speed, and even danger. He's put the top down, and my hair whips at my face. Ten minutes into the drive, I look down at my white silk blouse and notice the mud and muck for the first time that's dried into the delicate fabric.

Ruined. Like so many things.

Brock looks over at me. His own hair blows every which way with the wind.

"Where do you want to go?"

"Your place," I say.

He looks momentarily surprised, and then, slowly nods.

❧⟡❧

Twenty minutes later, I stare at Klimt's painting and attempt to reconcile that it was, in fact, only yesterday when I stood here admiring it. So much has changed. Now, it feels as if a decade of time has passed.

"What do you want to do?" Brock asks from the doorway.

He looks out of sorts. He sounds unsure.

"Shower."

He pulls me along to the bathroom, turns on the water, and walks me under the spray. We stand there fully clothed, until our clothes are soaked through and the water begins to cascade off of us in sheets.

I lean back. The spray infiltrates my hair. I close my eyes and let the water envelop all of me.

I can't cry, even now, when he wouldn't know, I can't cry.

I hear the distant snap of a bottle cap and open my eyes. He's rubbing his hands together until there's foamy suds. He washes my hair by running his fingers down through the long strands of it in regular rhythm. It's sensual and soothing at the same time. I start to relax, to let go, to let him in. I close my eyes again.

After a long while, he stops. I open my eyes and discover him looking at me. Sorrow etches his features. Desire, too.

I trace his eyelids, his lashes and the straight ridge of his nose and jaw line. His pulse races beneath my fingertips. With decisiveness, I undo the buttons on his shirt and the belt of his jeans and remove them with blatant dexterity and certain purpose.

"We need this," I say.

He answers with only a sad smile. He doesn't argue. I sense he doesn't want to. We're both beholden to this thing between us.

With forged alliance, we're both stripped naked within ninety seconds. Emboldened, he fills his hands up with soap again and washes all of me with these transcendental strokes. I brush my hands across his and perform the same ritual. My attraction for him compels me. He catches his breath when I touch him there.

"It's good. This is good," I say.

His only answer is his usual studied silence. I embrace it and love him for it. I do. I love him. I want to tell him, but I don't. I balance myself within the realm of his silence and reach up and pull him to me.

Our kiss is sanguine. It restores us, commits us. When it gets deeper, more intense, our explorations of one another become bolder and more urgent.

There are wants and needs that must be fulfilled, must be met. Time doesn't matter. Circumstances don't matter. Nothing matters, but the two of us and this tangible connection between us. It's all we have left.

When the water runs cold, we make a production of toweling off as if we can somehow delay the inevitable that's already been ignited.

It doesn't last.

I'm impatient now and I want him inside of me. I need to *feel* something. Now.

Somewhere inside, I harbor this belief that I will be able to outrun the grief by doing this. Somehow, Brock will make me whole again. I've managed to hide the fractured pieces of myself from him and I'm convinced he can keep me from completely falling apart. For a while, at least.

Don't wait. Don't think. Just do it. Liz's words return to me.

The first time we come together is swift and powerful. It serves to ignite this covetous passion for him I've never experienced before. *How can this be?*

I crave his touch. I crave him. But the deeper we go, the farther away he feels from me. Desperation to reach him and possess him takes over. We christen every room, virtually, every horizontal surface as we come together. We make love in his dining room, the kitchen, the walk-in freezer, on his patio, on the stairway, on his piano, on the rug. He's insatiable and so am I.

Our hunger for each other drives out all rational thought, all judgment, until we're too physically and mentally exhausted to do it anymore.

And I begin to wonder if I'm losing him or losing myself.

We move as one, to his sumptuous bed, and climb in.

I glance over at him. He has this intense look. His lips part.

"Don't. Don't say anything."

He looks unhappy for a long moment, then nods, leans back against the pillows, and closes his eyes. I trace and kiss his lips. He smiles, but keeps his eyes closed. I smile, realizing he's too exhausted to argue with me.

"Tomorrow. I'm going to say it tomorrow," Brock murmurs.

I burrow into the crook of his right arm while our bodies become magically intertwined. Maybe, if we can believe in just one miracle long enough, if we can hold on to each other for a while, we'll be able undo the travesty that has descended upon us and all but taken over our very lives.

It's a reprieve, however brief. And, we take it.

✥

We wake up at the same time. Shy, disconnected, undone. I think it takes us both a full minute to reconnect to time and place and the events of yesterday that have transpired. A wave of grief threatens and I push the agonizing thoughts of Max far away from me. Instead, I sink back down into Brock's warm arms and allow myself to only concentrate on him.

I will not cry. I will not cry in front of him.

"I should have told my dad I loved him," Brock says.

There's so much remorse in his voice. I glance up in time to catch a glimpse of his face so etched with pain. Moved by his vulnerability, I attempt to smooth his pain away.

"I should have told him."

"He knew," I say. "We talked about you. The first night I was here? He told me how proud he was of you for serving in Afghanistan. How brave you are. Foolhardy, too, he said, but brave." I reach up and trace Brock's temple. "He loved you. He was proud of you. He told me."

"You're making that up."

"No," I say. "He wanted to tell me about Ethan, but we ended up talking about you. He said that the two of you didn't always communicate well. Imagine my surprise."

"What do you mean?"

"It's those silences of yours. You're just like your dad in that way."

"I told you; it's the training."

"I think it's genetic."

"I'll show you genetic," Brock says.

He moves with lightning speed and suddenly I'm underneath him and he's probing between my thighs with his hands. His erection explores the willing space between my legs and I let him in because, right now, he's the only connection I have left in this world. *And, I need this.*

He's an exquisite lover. And, I take the reprieve of being with him, once again. After we finish, Brock seems troubled. He gets this pensive look.

"What?" I finally ask.

"I don't know. Am I going to be enough for you?"

"Enough for me?"

"Yeah," Brock says slowly. "I know I'm not perfect, but, as long as we're clear."

"Clear about what?"

I sit up and the sheet falls off of me exposing my breasts. Brock bends and encircles one with his mouth. I momentarily lose my train of thought, but not for long.

"Clear about what?" I say again, trying to catch my breath.

"I want you. I need you in my life, Jordan."

"I live in L.A. How's that going to work?"

"I don't know, yet. There will be some changes to be dealt with because of the way my father set up his estate. We just went over his will, six months ago. He had it set up, so we'd share equally in the ranch, the oil company—Diana, Tate, and me. Mom will still live at the ranch house and we'll take care of her. That's the way he wanted it, ensuring Mom was taken care of, but he wanted us to have the money, the responsibility for everything else. I'll have to deal with all of it. It's a lot of money. It will take care of the Lazy J."

I don't need your help with my share."

"Jordan, you're not listening to me. I want you in my life."

I take an unsteady breath. "It's not that simple."

"What's not simple about it? I need you. You need me. I know you do."

"I don't want to talk about this, right now."

I throw back the covers and stalk away from him to the bathroom. I turn on the shower and stand under it.

I'm at the edge all of a sudden.

The abyss is right there.

Max. I've lost Max.

The aching sobs force their way out. I cannot hold them back any longer.

Seconds later, Brock is there. He holds me and wipes at my tears.

"Baby, it's going to be okay. It is. I know it's bad, but I'm here."

"Don't you ever leave me." I bury my face into his chest.

"I won't. I promise."

He kisses my face, my neck, and my tears. I wind my arms around him and pull him close. He hesitates and stares into my face for a few long seconds.

"Promise?" I ask again.

"Promise."

Chapter

Twenty-Three

Brock – Soul meets body

I PROMISE HER SOMETHING I CAN'T KEEP. Our time together is unceremoniously interrupted by the arrival of Tate and Ashleigh. They look like we do, as if they too spent the night fucking, in an attempt to put the tragic events of my father and Max farthest from their minds. Jordan rushes around, making coffee and breakfast, somehow insulated from reality. I watch her in fascination and with this strange sense of foreboding, wondering how long it will be before she crashes back to earth and actually begins to deal with the certainty of Max's death. Other than the crying jag in the shower, which lasted a mere five minutes, I haven't seen her cry. She chats on the phone with my mother and sister and fully immerses herself in the planning of my father's funeral.

I glance over at Ashleigh. She shrugs as we exchange concerned looks.

"This is what she does," Ashleigh whispers at one point when Jordan leaves the room.

The rest of us are all a little on edge. Who wouldn't be? But Jordan? Jordan doesn't even appear to actually be here any longer.

Within hours, the Lazy J quickly becomes the main gathering place for mourners. My mother easily falls into Jordan's plans to hold a reception for my dad here after his funeral.

Jordan cannot be talked into a service for Max. I have to admire the way she even stands up to Ethan's parents regarding this wish. Her reasons are simple enough, and I attempt to understand them and support her.

"All I want is a bottle of Jagermeister and a few quiet moments with my circle of friends where we talk about Max's favorite things and guzzle a few shots," she says. "I just did a funeral for a loved one. I'm tired of doing these events for everyone else's feelings, but my own. I don't want a service for Max. I want to remember him laughing and playing. I don't want to put on some morbid service where we talk about him in the past tense."

Even my mother gives up talking her out of these simple arrangements.

Jordan and Ashleigh's friend, Liz, and her boyfriend, Adrian, arrive. I like them both immediately. They have the whole L.A. success thing going on, but they're easy to talk to and forthright. They stay with us at the Lazy J as well. The house is large enough to accommodate all of us and still allow for privacy, just the way Ethan, Tate, and I envisioned.

Jordan seems to be in her element, doing all the planning and the cooking. During the day, she appears somewhat intent on avoiding me now. She's buried her grief over Max so deep down that it's hard to detect. But, late at night, when I hold her in my arms she still trembles in her sleep, and sometimes, she wakes up screaming his name. I know she's dealing with it all deep inside. I just wish she would let me in. She refuses to talk about our future, and I fail to mention my upcoming return to Afghanistan.

Guilt-ridden, I'm breaking my promise to her about never leaving her already. And, although I don't know her nearly well enough to accurately predict her reaction, I can already guess as to what she'll say.

⚘

It's been four days since Max's and my father's untimely deaths. The church is packed with mourners, and I marvel at my mother's ability to put it all together in such a short period of time. The tribute to my dad is incredible. We all take our turns, saying a few words. I reach down from this faraway place and deliver a nice speech about how great he was and how I aspired to be like him. Truthfully? I'm unaware of exactly what I've said.

After I finish, I slide in next to Jordan. She squeezes my hand and tells me it was good.

There are dark shadows under her eyes. I know she's not sleeping well because I'm right next to her, watching her silently suffer over the loss of Max in the dead calm of night.

The sense that our relationship is fragile and new terrifies me. It's only a matter of time before she knows that I'm leaving for Afghanistan.

A part of me feels somewhat relieved at this because the intensity of our relationship is beginning to wear me out. Maybe, time away will be a good thing for both of us. It will give us a chance to achieve some kind of balance and be completely separate from one another. Right now, we're so connected in sharing the grief over Max and my father that I can't remember how it feels to be away from her.

I've never felt like this before. I've never loved anyone this much, not even Annie. We were young, barely twenty, with our lives ahead of us. We were barely grown up. We hadn't explored the depths of love, yet.

Jordan is different in every way from Annie. I know I love her for it, but I do wonder if I can meet her expectations in the long term. I'm not Ethan. I'm not sure I can give her what she wants, what she needs. I love her so much, but at the same time, I've never felt more terrified and out of control in my life.

It's unfair that I haven't told her about my return to Afghanistan. Only Tate knows, and, he's been sworn to secrecy. He's already read me the riot act for agreeing to go back. I've been waiting for the final orders and the right time to tell Jordan. So far, the time has never been right.

⁂

Back at the Lazy J, the main house accommodates the staggering number of two hundred people who have all come to pay their respects to my father. Jordan is busy playing hostess, ensuring there's enough food and drink for everyone. I wallow on the sidelines, engulfed in misery and grief, unable to compartmentalize either one very well. I pour myself another whiskey and attempt to stay out of the general conversation all around me.

I reach in my pocket to check for my cell phone, only to discover it isn't there. I wander over to Jordan.

"Have you seen my cell phone?"

"No. Did you check the bedroom?" She blushes as she says this. I give her a knowing look and study her face intently.

"No. I guess I'd better. I can't believe I left it behind."

She reaches up and strokes my face. "You okay?"

"Yeah. It's hard. Harder than I thought it would be."

She nods. "See why I didn't want to do this with Max?"

She stutters on his name, shrugs her shoulders, and then tries to covertly wipe away a stray tear with the back of her hand. In the next second, Tate waves me over from the other side of the room. She follows my gaze.

"Go see what Tate wants. I've got to go get some more champagne. I'll check for your phone."

"Okay. Don't be long."

Our fingers linger, still touching, and then, she slips away from me.

There's so many things that I should tell her. I'm just not sure where to begin. I take another swig of the whiskey and feel it burn my throat all the way down. I saunter over to Tate and answer a few questions for the people from our high school days standing with him. The I'm-so-sorry-for-your-loss statements are getting old fast. I don't know how to deal with the grief on my own, let alone how to respond in social gatherings to these well-intended condolences.

I decide to go after Jordan, so I can finally tell her how I feel about her, about everything, because there are too many things that have been left unsaid between us the past four days. But the whiskey and the perfunctory conversation slow me down. I'm a good five minutes behind her now. I glance down the hall where Jordan's disappeared and resume my mission to get to her with a quick goodbye and a promise to keep in touch better to the guests Tate's entertaining.

Urgency starts to set in. *She's going to retrieve my phone.* Kate's supposed to let me know about the final orders for Afghanistan and text me my itinerary.

I race towards my place now, yank the door open, and run down the long hallway towards the bedroom.

She's standing there, holding my phone.

"You're going back?" There's recognizable terror in her voice.

I shudder. "Yes."

"It's says you're leaving Sunday. The day after tomorrow for Dulles, and then on to Afghanistan. The text is from Kate." She practically spits the words at me. "You promised. You promised you'd never leave me. And yet, you are," she whispers in disbelief. "You *will.*"

"It's not like that. I made those plans before we—right after my dad died. I asked Kate to get me back in."

"It can't be undone," she says dully.

"No."

I take a deep breath.

"I wanted to tell you, to tell you all of it, about Annie, about Afghanistan, about *you*. I want to tell you *why*."

"I know about Annie. Ashleigh told me what Tate told her."

"I want to tell you *why*. Tell you all of it."

"No. It doesn't matter." She holds her hands up out in front of her, as if to hold me off. "What's left to say? You're broken. *I get it.* I even understand it. You say you do it to serve, to be a hero, but, I know better. You taunt and play with death every day because you fucking *enjoy* it." She laughs bitterly. "Well, I don't fucking *care* why you're there, Brock."

Fear takes hold.

"Don't do this to us. Please, Jordan. Listen to me."

"Don't do this to *us*? *You* did this to *us*. You did this. I thought you understood. I put myself out there for you. I told you I loved you—"

"No! You didn't! You never have. And now, you want to put all of this on me? You never really told me how you feel."

"I *showed* you how I feel about you. No. This is on you. I've lost everyone. *Everyone!*" She begins pacing. "I can't lose anyone else. I can't. I can't do this, Brock. I can't wait for you to return from that God-forsaken place."

She stops.

"I can't wait for you. I *won't* wait for you."

"What are you saying?"

"I'm saying, I'm going back to L.A." She gets this sad smile. "Good luck with your tour, Lieutenant. Good luck with your life."

Dazed, I follow her out. I reach for her, but she angrily pulls out of my grasp and races up the hallway away from me.

I don't go after her.

What would I say? What would I promise her?

It's better this way. *She hates me now. And, that's better. That's easier.*

I stare at my phone.

The text is from Kate.

> "Good news. You leave Sun. Aust. to Dulles 0400 hrs. On to Afghan. 1400 hrs. You'll get your sniper partner upon arrival. Stein's ecstatic. 2 hours in Dulles. Let's make the most of it. xo Kate. Again, sorry about your dad."

Somehow, I have to make this right. Explain it to Jordan. Will she believe me? Would *I* believe me?

I've broken every promise I've ever made to her.

And, what do I promise her now?

CHAPTER

TWENTY-FOUR

Jordan – You lost me

THE LYRICS OF CHRISTINA AGUILERA'S, 'You lost me' reach for me, like tentacles tearing at my heart, breaking it wide open. I've lost too much. I pour myself a generous shot of Jagermeister and swallow quickly. Another. Another.

Ashleigh comes over to me. "What's going on?"

"I'm going home. L.A. Wanna come?" I mouth the words Christina sings, while Ashleigh takes control of the bottle, and pours us both a shot. Liz slides in next to me on the chaise lounge.

"What's going on?" Liz asks.

"Not sure," Ash says, studying my face.

"He's going back to Afghanistan. He leaves Sunday." I practically choke on the words.

Ashleigh hands me the shot glass, and I drink it down.

Prudence. Decorum. Manners. They all go out the window.

"Selfish son of a bitch. Sorry, Janie. Not you," I mutter.

I absently wave at Brock's mom, who's surrounded by a bunch of people near the fireplace in the living room. I raise my glass to Janie through the open patio door. She raises one back. *I love Brock's mom. I really do.*

"Are you talking about *me*?" Brock asks from directly behind my chair.

I turn and watch both, him and Tate, walk boldly around and up to our girls-only circle. Liz and Ashleigh physically block him from me. I stare at him with defiance and definable hostility.

"Can I talk to you?" Brock asks.

"No."

"Please?"

"No, Brock. You can't. Go pack or something. I'm spending time with the people I care about. The *only* people I care about. Tate, you can stay. Adrian, you too."

I wink at both men, who both now stand, uncertain, right behind Brock.

"Don't do this to us," Brock whispers.

"There is *no us*."

I stand up to prove my point, sway side-to-side, and attempt to look him in the eye. My balance is off. My head feels funny. Too many shots. No food. I helplessly look back at Ashleigh and Liz.

"I don't feel so good," I say.

Then, I promptly vomit all over the front of Brock's suit and shoes before he can jump back out of the way.

"Well, we're right back to where we started from," I say in despair, a few minutes later, while everyone rushes around to clean up the mess. Tate helps Brock take off his jacket and shoes, while Ashleigh makes an even bigger mess trying to clean it all up.

Liz takes control of the scene. Well, she orders everyone around, including Adrian, who carries me off to the master bath of the main house.

Once there, I look around in appreciation at all the gold fixtures, until I remember who probably designed them. I promptly turn away.

"Sorry, about this." I hang my head in embarrassment.

"No problem," Adrian says. "Brock got the worst of it. Maybe, that's not such a bad thing." He gets this wide grin, and I start to laugh a little.

"I don't want to see him," I say with sudden urgency.

"Okay. I'll tell him."

"Thanks, Adrian, you're a good guy. I like you. Liz should marry you. And, if she won't, I will."

"Nice. Hitting on the boyfriend, Jordan," Liz says as she comes through the doorway.

"Sorry. It's just that one of us should be happy. One of us. At least." I get teary. "Don't you think one of us should be *happy*?"

Liz links her arm with mine and puts me into the running shower with a knowing look. I'm still wearing the black silk dress I wore to Henry's funeral. *Ruined. Just one more thing that's ruined.*

"Sober up, sis. We're leaving in an hour. Back to L.A. I'd like you to be coherent enough to see us off."

"I'm coming with you."

"Are you sure?" Liz asks quietly. "Seems like you have some unfinished business here."

"It's finished. Definitely finished."

Ashleigh comes in, looking out of sorts.

At the same time, Liz and I say, "What's wrong?"

"Brock really wants to talk to you," she says.

I'm disappointed with her now. Disappointed with Brock for asking her to do his bidding for him.

"I can see you're anxious to fit into the family, but damn it, Ashleigh, whose side are you on?" I glare at her.

"There are no sides," she says emphatically. "He loves you. He told me."

"No." I shake my head emphatically. "Doesn't matter."

I wave a hand at her, begging for silence. I put my head under the shower spray, put my hands over my ears, and refuse to say anything more to anyone.

⌘

A half hour later, I feel slightly normal. With shaking hands, I put on lingerie and black jeans. I finger-fix my hair. I button up a fresh white blouse, slip on a black leather jacket, and shove my feet into black ankle boots.

Most of this get-up is Ashleigh's. She's looking at me with approval.

"You look really good," she says. "That's going to drive him crazy."

"I don't want to drive him crazy. I want him—to fuck off."

Ashleigh's lower lip quivers. Her eyes fill with tears.

"I really don't know what to say, what to do," she says. "About Tate. About Brock leaving you. About *Max*, most of all. I miss him. I love him. And, *I know* you don't like us to talk about them, but God damn it, Jordan, what are you going to do?"

"Please don't do this to me," I whisper. "Not now. I'm barely holding it together here."

Liz appears in the doorway. "If you're going with us, we really need to be taking off. Adrian wants to be early, so we can return the rental car."

263

Liz is worried about rental cars, while Ashleigh and I are caught up in a conversation about heartbreak and Max. The incongruence is so severe, I start to laugh, somewhat hysterically.

Get a grip. Keep it together. Don't let Ashleigh or Liz see your real pain.

With trembling hands, I hand her a note I managed to write to Brock ten minutes earlier. It's simple. *Sweet?* I'm not sure. I'm not sure he'll take it that way.

> *Brock,*
>
> *Thank you for everything. Best of luck in Afghanistan. I hope you find what you're looking for. I hope you see it, when you find it.*
>
> *Jordan*

"I'll be right there," I say to Liz's retreating back.

I look at Ashleigh. My eyes fill with tears, too.

"You don't have to do anything, you know. Stay a while," I say to Ashleigh. "Figure things out with Tate. Stay here." I sweep my arm around the room. "I *own* it *for now.* I just need some time to sort things out, to figure my life out from here on out. I need to get back to Le Reve. I'm sure Louis is buried with all of it. And, I'm going to be okay."

Someday.

Ashleigh wanly smiles at me. "You're sure?"

"Yeah. I'm sure. Liz and Adrian will help me out. I'll be fine."

"What about Brock?"

I take an unsteady breath and force myself to smile. "Tell him I said thank you for everything, for being there. Tell him I said goodbye."

"He's not going to let you go that easily."

"He doesn't have a choice." I feel defiant. I'm sure it shows.

Ashleigh shakes her head at me. "He's not going to like that."

"No, but he made a choice," I whisper.

"Afghanistan? Not you?"

I shrug and don't say anything. Ashleigh looks at me closely, but I hold firm, staying composed. We hug for a long while, and I fight the urge to break down.

"Be good. Find happiness. I figure you'll either be home in two weeks or get a teaching job, here in Austin," I say with wan smile. "Give it some time with Tate, okay? Just make sure it's what you really want."

"Good advice," Ashleigh says to me, watching me closely.

"Gotta go," Liz says from doorway.

She's oblivious, for once, to the serious nature that our conversation has taken.

I zip up my suitcase and look around. I've got just about everything. With reverence, I carry the intricately carved wooden box that Igor Dasher had delivered. The silver urn inside contains Max's ashes and is enfolded in a red velvet cloth. Igor had it engraved with one of my favorite Winnie The Pooh sayings. I already know it by heart.

PIGLET SIDLED UP TO POOH FROM behind. "Pooh!" he whispered. "Yes, Piglet?" "Nothing," said Piglet, taking Pooh's paw. "I just wanted to be sure of you."
~A.A. Milne

I hold onto the box as tight as I can. I don't cry, and I don't say goodbye to anyone else.

PART THREE

To be sure of you

PIGLET SIDLED UP TO POOH FROM behind. "Pooh!" he whispered. "Yes, Piglet?" "Nothing," said Piglet, taking Pooh's paw. "I just wanted to be sure of you."
~A.A. Milne

CHAPTER

TWENTY-FIVE

Brock – A falling through

AFGHANISTAN HASN'T CHANGED ALL THAT MUCH. Only me. I've changed. My sniper partner has changed. The reason I'm here has changed. I guess everything has changed.

The dust infiltrates at a soul level. I inhale deeply of the air-less, lifeless land. I remain oblivious to the harsh conditions, oblivious to the danger. And, if there's a risk to a mission, I'm the first one to volunteer. I don't hold anything back, least of all, myself. I'm too intent on self-destruction on some level, on any level I can find.

A breeze picks up and swiftly shakes me from my dark reverie. With a sigh, I recalculate the coordinates and reposition my scope. Sergeant Daniel Reed, my partner for the past three weeks, waits patiently beside me. A nice enough guy. An enlisted man, an officer, with three kids and a wife back home. He talks incessantly about all of them, all of the time. I listen with feigned interest, nodding at the appropriate times at the words and sounds he makes, but, in reality, I'm too far away to ever actually hear him.

I call out the newest coordinates and openly smile when his high-powered rifle goes off. I look through the scope just in time to see the bad guy fall. Another shot rings out. Another falls. Reed takes a final shot and the last one falls.

"Not bad for an honest day's work," I say after a few minutes as we quickly gather our gear. Reed looks at me as if I've lost my mind, while I slowly nod in the affirmative.

I start packing up the gear with solicitous interest and essentially ignore his studied look.

"You okay?" Reed asks for the hundredth time this day.

"Never better. It doesn't get any better than this."

He frowns with notable disapproval. "I don't quite see it that way."

"Look. I've got a hundred and sixty days left, and then, I'm out of this God-forsaken place. I'm going to Paris for a while, and I'll re-up after that."

"You're coming back?" Reed gets this incredulous look.

"I've got nothing else," I say.

∾∾∾

The ten-mile hike back to camp is treacherous. We keep low to the barren landscape and hide behind the outcropping of rocks and disparate pine trees and shrubs cascaded about. A forgotten land. God-forsaken. We uphold radio silence per the team's instructions, but Reed keeps glancing over at me. His continual scrutiny is laced with the usual are-you-sure-you're-okay rhetoric. It's getting old fast. At the six mile mark, I've had enough. I suddenly stop and face him.

"What the fuck do you want from me? Stop asking me if I'm okay. This is as good as it gets. If you don't like the way I call out the targets, then find somebody else."

"Do you *know* who I am?" Reed asks through clenched teeth.

I roll my eyes, knowing I've pissed him off for some reason. "I really don't give a shit. Like I said, I have seventy-five days left on this tour. I'm here to finish it."

"I know about Holloway," he says arrogantly.

"Oh, really? What do you think you know?"

"You guys went way back. You were the reason he was here."

"He made his own choices. He always did," I mutter.

"You're the best there is as far as spotters go," Reed says, shaking his head. "But, man, your attitude really sucks."

"What do you want me to say?"

"There's a meeting at twenty-one hundred hours. You better be there. Stein's office," Reed says. Then, he just walks off.

Somewhat bewildered by his open hostility, I follow him. We don't exchange another word for the next four miles. Fine by me. Dead silence is just the way I like it.

Reed and I split up as soon as we reach camp. He makes a point of saying he needs to meet with Stein. I look at him quizzically and then shrug. I think my sinister outlook has gotten to him. He's the third partner I've had in as many months. Although I'm not exactly keen on training yet another partner, I'm pretty sure he's going to ask for a different one.

Christ. I just want to get the hell out of here for a while. I want to drink until I'm completely shit-faced, can't even remember my name, and fuck someone. My intent in striving for the carefree days of over a year ago grow stronger the longer I'm away.

I push my way through to the equipment supply room and check in with the soldier managing the place. Then, I spend an interminable hour cleaning all my weaponry and finally head out. I plate up food from the mess hall that's left over from the dinner meal served two hours before. I nod at a few of the guys I know and let the door slam behind me when I move out. I don't want to talk about the next mission, the kill number, or the weather. My patience for this day and these people here has officially ended.

There's a full moon. I look up at the dark sky and glimpse a blanket of stars. I move in a haphazard stealth pattern between the makeshift barracks in an effort to avoid any errant enemy sniper fire just like we've been taught. And yet, as if magnetized, I stop and stare at the stars and allow myself a full five minutes to think of her.

Jordan.

She's somewhere out there in the world. She's all alone. This much I know. A part of me wants to find her, and another part, the dominant one, wants to forget I ever met her.

The pain rises up from deep inside. I meet it, head-on, while my mind prepares for the battle.

I close my eyes and embrace the blackness. I've been here before. These are the times when I miss it, because seeing it all has been so much worse.

The memories flash. Ashleigh's face, worried and anxious. "Where is she?" I'd asked.

Her first words when she finally confessed: "She's gone. She left." Ashleigh handed me Jordan's innocuous note. I still didn't get it. Not then. Tate and I made record time to the airport, but the flight bound for L.A. had already taken off.

"She said she just needed some time," Ashleigh said.

Ashleigh sounded so certain that I believed her. My second mistake.

So, we waited.

I gave Jordan six hours. Then, I called her cell phone and got her voice mail. Again and again.

No Jordan. *Anywhere.*

Liz called Ashleigh the next day. She was in a panic, out of sorts. They'd dropped Jordan off at the house in Malibu the night before with her insisting she was okay. Jordan told Liz she just wanted to get some rest, but when Liz went to check on her that next morning she was already gone. The safe emptied. The bills paid up for six months. She'd left a formal letter of resignation for Louis and taken her dad's Porsche.

Jordan was gone. And, she didn't want to be found. We couldn't find her anywhere. *Gone.*

We were unable to comprehend that she would walk out of our lives in the early morning hours of the fifth day in a life without Max and completely disappear.

⧼⧽

I can see. I can see it all. I can still see the exact moment when I lost them both. It was on the edge of Logan's Pond where I stood before her with Max's lifeless body.

She was broken into a million pieces already. I just didn't see it.

Guilt-stricken, uncertain, I returned to Afghanistan two weeks later per my service orders. Afghanistan. It's as if I've never left. Nothing has changed, but everything has changed. Me, most of all.

Who could have known that God would give me my sight back, only to take Max and my dad? And, that Jordan would just up and leave and disappear? The pain of losing all of them never leaves. This crushing sensation overtakes me. I first think of little Max. Five days from his fourth birthday, his life was taken away. I should have known what that was doing to Jordan. I should have seen that although she appeared to be fine; she was far from okay. I should have seen it.

Max. Jordan. My dad. I rub at my eyes and try to rub out the memory of all three of them. There are so many things I should have done, should have said, to my dad, but especially to Jordan. And, now I can't do or say any of them. *I just need to forget. Do my job. Serve my country and forget.*

A handwritten letter sits atop my bunk. I hold my breath for a second and allow myself to believe it's from her. But my working sense of sight begins to infiltrate my brain. It's my mother's handwriting, not Jordan's. With shaking hands, I open the letter. These have been frequent and unhelpful.

Dear Brock,

I continue to watch the news for any word on what is happening there, but, it seems this has become the forgotten war. Just know that I think of you each and every day. And, I miss you so much. We all do.

I went by the cemetery today and planted flowers at all of their graves. I commissioned a headstone next to Ethan's for Max when I ordered your father's. I know he's not there, but I think it makes us all feel closer to have some place to go and think of him, too. Anyway, it's finished. A beautiful granite one with an etching of Winnie The Pooh near his name. I put a stuffed Winnie The Pooh right next to it. So sweet. Just like Max. I left him a plate of cookies. I'm sure it just encourages field mice, but I like to think of Max, just sitting there and gulping them down as fast as his little hands can reach his mouth.

I wish you could be here for Christmas. Tate and Ashleigh are still getting married in February. I wish they would wait, but Ashleigh insists on going ahead with her Valentine's Day wedding plans. She thinks Jordan will come, but no one has heard from her.

Please don't sign up for another tour. Please Brock. I realize I should have said this long ago. I need you, Brock. I need you here. You need to be here with your family. And, I believe in my heart that Jordan just needs some time to work it all out. She's part of this family, too. And, you need to tell her how you feel. Yes, there's so much to say and, if we get the chance, we must say it. I love you, Brock. Be safe and come home.

Mom

I sink back further against the pillows and let the letter fall to the floor. My mother's sadness reaches me. I know she misses my dad. I know I let her down by returning to Afghanistan, but I hope she understands my reasons for being here.

I sigh. It's too sad. I try not to think about my dad too much and all the mistakes I made with him, with Jordan, even little Max. If I'd been paying better attention, maybe none of this would have happened. I close my eyes and try to keep my mind from thinking of them, but the memories return anyway. All the people I love. I reach out with an unsteady hand in mid-air as if to touch them, but there's no one there.

I glance at the clock. I have twenty minutes before I have to be in Stein's office. These perfunctory debriefing meetings suck. My mind drifts, and I begin to wonder what Reed meant by his do-you-know-who-I-am comment. In one swift motion, I swing up from the bunk, do a round of one hundred sit-ups to ensure I'm fully awake, then head out.

❧⊙☙

Kate's here. In Afghanistan. She's in full dress uniform, looking all brass and out of place, but she's still her usual Barbie-look-alike self.

Stein gives me a questioning look and then seductively regards Kate. We all glance over at the doorway at the same time when Reed appears. He looks glum, but, somehow, in charge.

My mind races with the possibilities. I get this sinking feeling in the pit of my stomach. There are way too many people in this room to be doing a debriefing on a mission that resulted in just three enemy kills. *Fuck.*

"Sit down, Lieutenant Wainwright," Kate says. "Please join us, Colonel Reed."

I glance over at Reed in surprise. He outranks me by two and one less than Kate. I thought he was an enlisted man. *Holy shit.* I sink further into the chair and realize that this meeting is all about me.

The softball questions begin right away. I'm inundated with the how-do-you-feel-about-this-Lieutenant questions. Kate starts off easy, but there's a sinister glint in her startling blue eyes. Within five minutes, I'm fielding questions about my personal life. She goes for the jugular on one of her first hardball questions. "Can you explain to us why you left out the part where your fiancée Annie Gilmore was killed in a car accident, just prior to you signing up for SEAL training?"

"She was dead. I didn't have anything to do, so I signed up." I shrug.

"You quit law school with just one semester left to join the SEALS; isn't that right?"

"Yes."

"And Lieutenant Holloway signed on at the same time?"

"Yes."

"And then, he met and married Jordan Breckinridge, just prior to leaving for his first tour with you here in Afghanistan?"

"Yes."

"Did you *know* her?" Kate asks. There's a perverse edge to her tone that is so evident that I clench my jaw tighter.

"Not exactly. Not at that time. We shipped out. First tour. Second tour. I met her for the first time last February, just before our third tour. Almost a year ago."

"And what did you think of her?" Kate's eyes narrow as she watches me closely.

"She was great. I met up with the two of them in L.A. at their place in Malibu for a long weekend." I shrug with indifference. "Then, Ethan and I returned to finish our tour. Here."

"How was Ethan when you returned for the third tour?"

"He was fine."

"Not distracted?"

"Not that I can remember."

Kate flips to her notes. "Let me refresh your memory. When we met on April 22nd of last year, during one of our sessions, you said, and I quote: 'Ethan had been distracted since our return to Afghanistan.'"

"I guess he was distracted. He wasn't as focused. Neither of us were."

"Why do you think that was?"

The loaded question. I thought I'd be ready for it.

Kate lifts her head and dispassionately looks at me and just waits for my answer. She's got an axe to grind and possibly a chance to save her job or get a promotion; I haven't determined which one yet.

"I'm not sure," I say with a defiant lift of my head. I stare straight at her.

"Surely, you must have a theory. You spent time with Lieutenant Holloway every single day. You knew him better than anyone else."

I flinch at the starkness of her words. She's pulling no punches now. Memories of Ethan come at me.

"Because of Jordan. She wrote him a letter and said she thought she might be pregnant, and he was upset."

"Why?"

"Because he had finally realized he was missing everything."

"And, how did that make you feel?"

"Unfocused. Guilty."

"Guilty about what?" Kate asks.

"I fell in love with his wife while I was with them in Malibu."

Kate sucks in her breath. I can tell she wasn't expecting my answer to be so forthcoming.

"Do you think your fiancée's death and Ethan's affected your service, your performance, Lieutenant Wainwright?" she asks with disquiet.

I take a deep breath before answering and silently debate the odds of telling a lie versus telling the truth. Either way, I'm out. That's why Kate's here. She's here to save her job. It's on her. She signed off on my psych evaluation for my full return to duty. Instinctively, I know Reed's involved as well. My gut tells me Reed set me up and blew the whistle.

"Annie was the reason I was here for tours one and two. Ethan is the reason I'm here for this one and the next. I avenge Ethan's death every day."

Kate makes a point of shaking her lovely blonde head side-to-side. Her hair is pinned to the nape of her neck and even now I long to undo it and fuck her properly.

She looks at me with detachment before saying, "I can't sign off on this, not with the information about your fiancée that's come to light and the fact that you've admitted to being in love with Ethan's wife." She even manages a little wispy smile as she says this. "I'm sorry, Lieutenant. You're going home. You're to be honorably discharged, effective immediately."

"I'll stay and serve and just finish my tour," I say.

"No. You jeopardize yourself and your team every second you're out in the field. You're here for the wrong reasons." She shrugs her slim shoulders. "You can pack your things and take the flight back with me. I've got authorization to sign your out papers."

I gasp for air, while she casually picks up a pen and starts signing my life away. Trying to recover, I glance over at my team leader. Stein shakes his head. He shoots me an I-can't-help-you-out-of-this look and gets up from his desk.

Reed has the audacity to shake my hand. "Good work, Lieutenant. Thank you for your service," he says.

Kate looks up from her paperwork long enough to say, "I'd like to speak to the lieutenant alone. You're both dismissed."

She outranks them both. They file out like good little soldiers, while I sit there and blaze in her seething silence.

"Why are you doing this to me?"

"I'm saving your God-damn life," she says. "Be *thankful.*"

"I don't need saving."

"Well, I think you do."

She gets this scornful look. I glare back at her.

"Go pack your things. We leave at twenty-two hundred. And, Lieutenant, don't keep me waiting."

We leave by helo, thirty-two minutes later. The woman has suddenly become a stickler for time. After take-off, she leans back against the seat headrest and closes her eyes and essentially ignores me, while I look out the window, dispassionate, and watch the dark abyss of Afghanistan disappear.

A mere twenty minutes later, we land at an unfamiliar airstrip where a private jet, with its engines running, waits. As we board the all but empty ten-passenger plane, we take seats together in what could be construed as first class. I start to wonder just how much pull this woman has.

"I have a new boyfriend," she says, watching me as I look around.

"Oh."

"You sound disappointed."

"I am. I thought we could have a little fun on the way back. Pick up where things were left off." I give her this brazen look and put Jordan out of my mind. I've lost all hope of finding Jordan. No one's heard from her in months. Three private detectives I've hired have turned up nothing. She's gone. Lost to me forever. Maybe, my bad boy persona is all I have left. And, Kate came to see me. Maybe, Kate is what I need. Maybe, if I say this often enough, I'll convince myself. "Like I said, a little fun."

"I'm in enough trouble already," Kate says.

I shrug and openly gaze at her. My fingers trail along her collar bone. She's wearing the full-dress navy whites. The ones they issue for female officers. My other hand slides up her skirt and lingers at her inner thigh. She moans at my touch, but stops me from exploring her further, and gives me this wan smile. "You are so fucked up, Lieutenant."

Her words and the way she says them pull me back to reality. My hands fall away and I slide back in my seat farther away from her.

She gives me a surreptitious look and disappears. Minutes later, she returns with a glass of water and two white pills, which she drops into the palm of my hand.

"Take these. You'll feel better. You really need to get some rest." I give her a scornful look. "Trust me. You're going to need to rest. Your body is in a completely separate time zone. I'll wake you up in a few hours. I've got a story for you."

She gets this contemplative look and half-smiles. I swallow the pills with a swig of the water, lean back in the seat, and close my eyes. I take solace in the blackness. I'm determined to play along with her unsolicited advice for sleep for a few minutes and then ply her with the hard questions about what she knows. Because, instinctively, I know Kate may have some answers for me about Jordan and what's been going on.

I fight to stay awake, but sleep overtakes me. I realize too late that what I assumed was Ibuprophen may have been something else. Before I can confront her about it, I lose the battle to darkness. Just like old times.

∗ ∗ ∗

I'm unceremoniously awakened with intense shaking at the shoulder level. Alert, at once, just like the training has taught me, I sit up from the leather sofa and throw off the blanket that someone has placed over me. I stare up at Kate. It seems so out of character for her to be hovering over me.

"Wake up, sleepyhead," she says softly.

Her eyes are this intense blue. She looks anxious, but subdued.

We stare at one another.

I begin to feel uneasy. Boyfriend or not, Kate isn't being completely honest or as selfless as to why she's helping me.

"We're in Dulles to refuel. We'll be here for an hour or so. And then, it's on to your final destination."

I look at her warily, then push up and out of my seat and step off the airplane. I'm assailed with the biting cold air that is Washington D. C. My first greeting stateside. Grogginess leaves with the first draw of breath and I rub my hands together to get warm. I make my way inside with

Kate following closely behind me.

"Next time, please tell me if you're going to drug me with something, besides Ibuprophen," I say dryly as I pull open the door and allow her to enter first.

"You needed your rest."

"I need to get to Austin. And then, I need to find Jordan."

"Let's talk back on the plane," she says, affecting this sad smile. "Like I said, I have a story for you." Before I can ask her what she means by that, she disappears into the ladies room.

I make a point of buying a toothbrush and then head to the restroom Kate so eloquently pointed out to me a few minutes earlier. I brush my teeth, splash cold water on my face, and spend a few minutes staring at myself in the mirror.

I recognize the permanent change. I love Jordan. There's no more or no less to it. I love Jordan. *I love Jordan.* The face in mirror nods back at me. In the next second, this rising panic takes over. What if I never find her? What if she's lost to me forever? But I push the fear way down because I can't deal with the thoughts of never finding her, of losing her forever. All I can do is try and find her. Kate's given me that chance and I'm taking it.

Dulles. It's the dead of night on a Tuesday in mid-December. I only know it's a Tuesday because I happen to glance at the television where CNN continually runs and happen to see the date and time in the lower right corner of the television set.

Kate waves me over and hands me a sandwich she was able to procure. The airport is all, but dead, at this hour. No one is around, but the cleaning crew and a few shop owners that, somehow, remain optimistic about staying open for the clandestine, early dawn travelers like Kate and me.

After less than an hour spent refueling the jet, the flight takes off from Dulles. I assume we'll be in Austin in a little over three hours. Kate and I sit across from each other, mesmerized by the familiar drone of the engines and surprising companionable silence. She undoes her seat belt and gets up from her seat once we reach thirty thousand feet at the pilot's announcement. She fills two highball glasses with Jack Daniels and hands me one with a seductive smile. My patience wears thin. I get this anxious feeling inside, while she affects this knowing look as she studies my face.

We are in a whole different place from those first few hours of traveling together. I'm determined to get home. To find Jordan. Everything with Kate is finished. She's a means to an end. I try to remain impassive under her watchful glance. The woman can still read me like no other. God knows she knows my history better than anyone else. I know that now.

I cajole myself to play nice. Kate has managed to fuck up my life and yet probably saved it in the past twenty-four hours.

"I believe you have a story to tell," I say with a tight smile.

"I do," she says. She gets this resigned look and then unlocks her briefcase and retrieves this file folder that must be an inch thick.

I get this sinking feeling in the pit of my stomach as I start to flip through it. There are various photos of Jordan. Recent employment history. A Social Security report for a Lisa Breckinridge. A driver's license in three different states. It reads like a felony record, but, upon closer inspection, it just reveals the life of a woman on the run. The photographs capture her devastation. There's one of Jordan walking alone along the banks of Lake Michigan. The grief, so evident, is etched across her face and captured in the photograph. It's been marked with red ink with a Chicago address dated from last month. There's a picture of her running in a marathon from there. She's looks haunted, like a ghost. If I had any doubt about what Jordan's been doing these past four months, it's been laid to rest with these photographs of her.

Kate waits patiently for me to peruse through the whole thing. I flip through the file quickly, pausing every few seconds as some small detail of Jordan's life momentarily captivates my attention. I hold a photograph up to the light, hoping for illumination or salvation, but all I can see is the tangible unhappiness and the true devastation of grief that must run through her at a soul level. I close my eyes and attempt to get a grip.

"Where did you get these? How did you get these?" I finally ask.

"She became—a project. I wanted to understand what you saw in her, so I started to think about what she would do, this woman, who had basically lost everyone she had ever cared about. If she disappeared, where would she go? I started with the four and five star restaurants, figuring she would do work in something she was good at and knew so well. It took a while, but then, we got a hit on a Lisa Breckinridge, five weeks ago. I knew I'd found her." Kate's voice trembles. "I didn't know, not right away, anyway." She stops. "I didn't realize that she was so broken."

"Couldn't you *see* it?" I hold up the photo to Kate, inches from her face. My hands shake with fury. "What kind of psychiatrist *are you?*"

"Not a very good one, I'm afraid," she says.

"Major, you better figure out something else to do with your life. Marry a senator or something."

"How did you *know?*" Kate bites her lower lip and actually blushes.

I look around the plane and realize the Virginia governor was recently widowed and that must be who dear Kate is involved with. She would need a replacement for me before she would officially admit defeat. This much I do now know about her.

I sigh and take a deep breath. "You could have helped her."

Then, I shrug and wanly smile at her. Kate is what she is and *isn't.*

"Never mind," I say. "Let's just focus on what you have done. *Thank you.* You found her for me. I've hired private detectives to no avail. And you? *You* found her. Thank you."

"Ironic; isn't it?" Kate asks with a wan smile. "I start researching her whereabouts with the intention of keeping you two as far apart from each other as possible and now I'm taking you to her."

"I'm not a senator, Kate."

"Well, you're plenty *more,* Lieutenant." I shake my head and give her a pleading look, but don't say anything more. "Anyway," she says, trying to smile. "She's back in L.A. Arrived a week ago. We're on our way to LAX. We'll be there within hours. She's working at Le Reve tonight. She'll be there late. We should be able to make it with plenty of time."

"Thank you, Kate." She gets this wan smile, and then, looks like she's about to cry. Something I realize I've never seen her do before.

Eventually, she pulls it together and so do I. We retreat to opposite ends of the cabin and leave everything else unsaid. The flight remains silent, until we land at LAX. We've gained three hours back. It'll be early afternoon. I reset my watch. All that matters to me is getting to Jordan.

There's a sedan waiting as we deplane. I look at Kate in surprise.

"What's this?"

"Just trying to make things right. Good luck, Lieutenant."

I take Kate's hand and bring it to my lips, sad that this is good-bye, but knowing I'll never see her again.

"Good luck, Doctor Major Kate Richards. You're quite something."

I wave one last time, then slide into the car, as she reboards the airplane.

I rest my head against the backseat as we traverse the streets of L.A. and head out on the 101 towards Malibu.

One thing holds true. I no longer feel guilty for loving Jordan. I don't feel guilty over Ethan anymore either. It's done. It's over. I'm here. Jordan's here. And, that's how it's supposed to be. And, I'll never leave her again. That's a promise I intend to keep.

CHAPTER

TWENTY-SIX

Jordan – What I've done

"ANY PLANS FOR YOUR DAY OFF?" Seth asks.

I glance up and over at him. The guy is nothing if not persistent. I nod my head at him and almost smile.

"Skydiving," I say.

He gives me a disconcerted look. "For real?" Seth asks. "In December?"

"Yes."

It's late, close to midnight. I finish scouring the Viking stove with a newfound zeal, belying my sudden nervousness at his personal questions. His constant inquiries into my private life, my love life, to be more specific, are playing havoc with me. In the past four months, it would have been a clear indication that it was time to move on, but living Jason Bourne's spy life took its own toll. I finally got tired of running, so I came home.

I glance up and discover Seth watching me. An accomplished sous chef. Louis has hired well. Seth can do wonders with a knife. He's incredibly gifted and creative when it comes to the culinary arts. He's cute, too, in a boyish kind of way. All of twenty-two. I am six years older and a hundred years beyond him at this point. His attractive golden-boy looks and lean build turn me on from this faraway place in the center core of my body that is not quite dead yet. He's handsome enough. He's six inches taller than me, but not as tall as the others I've known that I try not to remember.

"You should come," I say with a shrug. "Six o'clock out of Camarillo."

"Six a.m.?" Seth asks, incredulous.

A typical L.A. guy. I shake my head. Seth sounds as if he's never gotten up at six in the morning his entire life.

"Yes," I say somewhat bemused by him. "If you want to go. That's what time you need to be there. The flight's at six-thirty."

"I'm working awfully hard here," Seth says, running his hands through his shiny dark blonde hair.

He has this crooked, charming smile and brazenly stares at me, now. My heart lurches, as I study him for a few seconds, and allow my mind to travel backward. I'm assailed with vague images of Ethan and even clearer ones of Brock. Seth looks nothing like either one of them. *That's good.* I make a point of concentrating on the charming man standing so close to me and actually smile.

"Don't worry," I say thoughtfully. "You'll be rewarded. The jump doesn't take that long. We'll have plenty of time for other things. You could come back to my place. I think we can work something out."

For the first time in a long while, I actually find myself smiling as he reaches out and trails his hand along my neck with pretense of adjusting my red chef scarf.

Louis chooses that moment to pop his head in the kitchen doorway. He studies us for a moment as Seth and I self-consciously step back from each other. *Caught.*

"Can I talk to you, Jordan?" Louis asks.

I blush and step further back from Seth and smile over at Louis. "What are you still doing here? I thought you left an hour ago?" I ask.

"Just finishing up some paperwork. Swing by my office?" He scrutinizes Seth, for a moment, giving him the once-over. "Are you about finished Mr. Talisman? Jordan and I have some things to discuss. Go ahead and take off when you're through."

I almost roll my eyes, recognizing the upcoming conversation we're going to have about the non-fraternization with the staff policy. *Damn.* I just want to go home. Take a hot bath. Pretend I have a life, besides Le Reve. I've only been back for a week, and already, Louis is effectively play-ing the role of protector, even though I've begged him not to.

Seth gets this crestfallen look as Louis leaves. "I really need this job," he says.

"Well, I guess you won't be skydiving with me tomorrow, then."

"I guess not."

I stomp off in the direction of the office.

"Why are you doing this to me?" I ask Louis, as soon as the door closes.

I lean up against the door with my arms crossed and glare at him.

"It's not right. He's not right for you. Not good enough. Not old enough."

I scowl at him for the last comment.

"Sorry," Louis says with a sheepish grin. "Right now, it is perfectly clear that you're pissed off at the world, too pissed off to think clearly about the ramifications of getting involved with the likes of the young and oh-so-talented Seth Talisman. He's a great sous chef, but he will never *be right for you*, never as talented, as dedicated, or as exquisite." Louis flings both his hands in the general direction of the kitchen with a dismissive air.

"He's a *guy*. He's nice. He likes me. How could you possibly *know* what I need?"

"Because I *know* you." Louis shrugs his shoulders and gets this introspective look. "Perhaps, better than anyone else. How long did you expect me to keep it a secret that you've returned?"

"Liz called," I say in defeat.

"Liz. Ashleigh. Adrian. A woman named Janie Wainwright. It's been a regular parade of well-wishers, since the word got out that you're back in L.A."

"Please tell me that you didn't let them know I'm staying at the house."

"I was unaware of what was secret and what was not." He shrugs in that helpless French way of his that just infuriates me sometimes.

"Louis! God damn it! I just want some peace, to be left alone. And now? Now, they'll be dogging me *everywhere*." I moan and sink to the floor and cover my face with my hands. "Why did you tell them?"

"Because they love you. We all do, ma chérie. And, there's no skydiving in your future. I already cancelled the jump. You're not going."

"You're killing me," I mutter.

"No. No. I'm not. And, you're not killing yourself, either."

I gasp and look up at him in surprise. "What?" I ask.

"You know exactly what I'm talking about."

I hang my head again and refuse to answer.

"Well, what do you have to say for yourself?"

"It's not like that," I finally say. "It wasn't going to be like that."

I pause for a few seconds. "I just wanted to try another thing I've never done before. Skydiving was something I've always been afraid of doing. It was on my fear list. And now, you've ruined it." I sound like a child. Like Max. I quietly fight off the gut-wrenching feeling that begins to work its way through me before Louis sees it, but just barely.

I slowly get up and stare him down with my fists clenched at my sides ready to do battle. "Louis, I can't believe you did all of this. Why did you tell them? Why did you cancel my jump? How did you know about that anyway?"

He shakes his head at me, refusing to answer. "Go home, Jordan. Go. I'll finish up with Seth. Get some rest. Enjoy your day off. In fact, I don't want to see you before Monday." Louis wags his finger at me and gets this secretive smile.

"It's only *Tuesday*."

"You've been putting in too many hours already. We talked about this. I'll see you next Monday. Go home. Consider it a long weekend. Enjoy yourself. That's an order."

I yank off my chef's jacket and apron and rapidly fold them into a tight ball. I grab my jacket and jam the knit cap on my head and haphazardly tuck my hair inside. I grab the chef clothes and my purse and clear out with one final glance at my over-solicitous boss.

"See ya," I say, trying to be flippant.

"See you soon," Louis calls out. "Glad you're back. So glad."

I start to smile, despite my best efforts not to. Louis grins at me.

All is forgiven.

I half-wave at Seth and sail through the back door of the restaurant. Louis normally escorts me to the car this late at night, but tonight, he just lets me go. I slowly traverse the parking lot. *Why was he so willing to let me go, considering the overall nature of our conversation?* I stop and note the full moon. The white light of the moon bathes the parking lot. I'm reminded of another time, over three hundred nights ago, when Ethan and Brock stood on the beach below Point Dume. It's the same kind of white trick light on this night.

I retrieve my keys from my purse, shake them out. I'm prepared for an outright assault of any kind, as I hold the sharp jagged metal side of the car key firmly in one hand, and point it in the general direction of my dad's Porsche.

And, there he is. His arms are folded across his chest and he leans up against the Porsche and appears to be just waiting for me.

I swallow hard. A variety of emotions from outright joy to pure panic cascade through me in the thirty seconds it takes to reach the car.

Oh God. It's good to see him.

"I should have known," I say when I'm about five feet away.

"Known what?"

"That you were here. Louis doesn't let me go anywhere late at night without an escort of some kind."

"Is that what I am to you? An *escort?*"

He says *escort* like it's a swear word. It almost makes me laugh, but I sober quickly and move past him to avoid any kind of physical contact. One press of the key fob button unlocks the car, and I yank open the driver's door and slide in.

He bends down through the open door and studies my face for a few seconds. I hold my breath, hoping he doesn't detect my erratic pulse.

"Is that what I am? An escort?" he asks again.

"Right now? You just look like somebody who needs a ride."

He staggers back as if I've slapped him. I shrug, start the car, and attempt to breathe, while he goes around to the other side and gets in.

"Where to?" I ask softly.

"I think we're going home."

I shake my head. "You're a long way from home, soldier."

He gets this wan smile. My heart pounds faster when I see it, but I keep the rest of me as still as possible. *Breathe. Relax. Take control.*

"So," I say casually as the dome light goes out. "Where to?"

"It's late. Your place."

I put the car into first and start out toward the main entrance of the parking lot, but then spy Seth racing toward us. I stop the car and roll down the driver's window.

"About tomorrow morning? The jump?" Seth asks, gasping for breath. He peers into the car and immediately starts sizing up Brock. "I'll go."

"Okay. We're on. I'll pick you up at a five thirty. It'll take a half hour or so to get there." I reward him with my most benevolent smile.

With newfound courage, he leans further up against the car window and gets this big grin. "Okay," Seth says, nodding. "I'll see you tomorrow. It'll be fun. Louis will be okay with it, right?"

"Louis is fine. Let me handle Louis," I say with a laugh.

I sense this daggered look coming from Brock. It gives me a moment's pause, but only for a few seconds. *He's pissed. Good. So am I.* There's a lot to say, but I don't plan on saying any of it to him.

Seth becomes even braver, encouraged by my seductive look in his direction. He leans even farther into the car and kisses the side of my face.

"See you tomorrow," he says.

"Tomorrow. Today really, if one were getting technical," I say with a little laugh.

"Soon," he says, stepping back. He gives a slight wave as I put the Porsche into gear. And, for both illustrative as well as childish purposes, I gun the engine and race out of the parking lot, while Brock sighs heavily beside me.

"Nice," Brock says with recognizable disdain. "That's the closest to kissing you he's ever going to get."

"I'm not married. I can do whatever I want."

"You can make this as difficult as you want, Jordan," he says with a heavy sigh. "Believe me, you already have. We both have. But this? This is how it's going to be."

"How *what's* going to be?" I ask.

Brock just shakes his head side-to-side at me in disapproval. I shrug and attempt to concentrate on the road that leads back home. He gazes out the passenger window at the dark night and doesn't say anything more.

What else is new?

ॐ

I look around the Malibu house and note the counters are wiped clean from six days of Chinese takeout. Without too much fanfare, I open the refrigerator and discover it's fully stocked.

"You've been busy," I say.

"Just taking care of the things that need to be done around here," Brock says from the other side of the kitchen. "The cleaning lady let me in."

He takes a drink from the glass of brandy he's poured himself without taking his eyes off of me. Then, he walks over and hands me a cold bottle of Evian mineral water. "Here. I thought you might like this. I've got a bath running for you."

I try to not show my surprise. I try to remain calm and not linger too long on what he might know.

Instead, I walk down the hall to the linen closet, grab a pillow, a set of sheets and blankets and head toward the guest room. He follows.

"I can do this," he says from the doorway. "Your bath's ready."

"Okay. Thanks?"

I look at him suspiciously and manage to get by without touching him again and affect a nonchalant saunter down the hall toward the master bathroom, knowing he watches me take every step. I reflect that if I had touched him, I think I might have broken down. And, I definitely can't afford to do that.

I grab my cell phone off the dresser and text my skydiving instructor:

> "Rob, regardless of what you might have heard, we're still on for 6:30 a.m. tom."

My phone beeps, minutes later.

> His text reads: "Good. See you soon."

"Damn straight," I say to the walls.

I strip down and step into the bath water. It's just hot enough. Perfect. I actually smile and sink down under the water and allow my thoughts to drift. I've managed to take in ten whole seconds of peaceful bliss, when I remember the pregnancy test that I'd inadvertently left on the bathroom counter this morning. I push up out of the water and look over. The counter's bare. *Shit.* It's gone.

I swing out of the bathtub and go over and stare at the empty space where the test should be for a long time. My mind races. I bought it when I arrived in Malibu a week ago. Chinese take-out and a pregnancy test. Incompatible things. I bitterly smile and begin opening all the drawers, one by one. In the last drawer, I find the First Response box. I frown. Did I put it there? Or, did Brock? Or, the cleaning lady? Then, I remember the Evian water. *Brock.* Damn it.

I shiver, realizing the only thing I have control of right now is taking a bath. There's no sense wasting perfectly warm, scented bath water over a pregnancy test and who might know about it. I climb back in.

I'll have to come up with something. I just need to think. *Think. Perhaps, I should just take the test.*

I climb back out of the bathtub. Read through the directions with shaking hands and do the test. Then, I put everything away, including the test stick that may foretell my future. I push it all into the back of the cabinet behind the cleaning supplies. Thirty seconds later, I gratefully sink back into the tub and take a deep breath.

A quick knock at the door is followed by Brock's entrance.

"Are you decent? Oh, sorry," he says.

"You don't look sorry."

"I'm not." He smiles wide.

"Thanks for all the lit candles. The lavender bath salts. It's nice."

"You're welcome. I wish I could say I took the time to buy them somewhere like L'Occitane and not the gift shop at Dulles, but I can't." He gets this hopeful look.

"How did you get here? To the States? I thought your tour ended in April."

"Kate pulled the paperwork. She came all the way there and rescinded her sign-off."

"Kate."

"Kate," he says with a shrug. "I was having some trouble concentrating on the missions. I'd lost you and I was thinking about my dad and Max too much of the time. I wasn't focused." He frowns. "I had three sniper partners in as many months."

The intermittent sound of dripping water is all there is for a while.

"You lost your edge," I finally say.

"I lost my edge," he says with surprise.

I hesitate before saying, "I'm sorry."

"Are you?"

I invoke his propensity for silence and then finally answer, "No."

"I'm not either. I never should have gone back. I never should have left." He stops talking and gets this anguished look. "You. I never should have left *you*."

"Who left who?" I say with a wan smile. Then, I shake my head. "I'm not ready for this conversation." To prove my point, I sink down further in the tub and essentially ignore him. The water's cool now. I keep myself from shivering in front of him by clasping my arms across my chest and clenching my jaw to keep my teeth from chattering.

"Are you going to tell me about it?"

"Tell you about what?" I ask, testily.

"The pregnancy test."

I nod slowly, vying for time and a weak attempt at maintaining my composure. I've barely registered the existence of this baby to myself let alone to someone else. "There's not much to say about that," I say slowly. "I was careless. It happens." I give him this nonchalant shrug. "I'm not sure what I'm going to do."

This shadow crosses his features. He looks troubled, unhappy.

"I'll take care of you, regardless."

"I can take care of myself."

"I'm not leaving."

"Stay as long as you like." I flick my hand around. "Look. I've had a long day. I'm tired." I give him this pointed, please-leave-me-alone look.

"Did you tell him?"

"Tell who?"

"The baby's father?"

I nod slowly. "He knows."

I covertly watch his reaction. He looks even more despondent, now. The words, *it's yours,* almost escape my lips.

Instead, I say, "Bad timing."

Breathe.

He turns away from me. "I'm not leaving," he says again.

"Don't make promises you can't keep."

"I don't. Not anymore." He sounds so defeated that I sink further into the water to keep from reaching out to him. "Good night, Jordan," he says from the doorway.

"Night."

❧❦

I wait another fifteen minutes before I step out of the tub. Now, I'm freezing cold and shivering uncontrollably. I wrap myself in a towel and move quickly through the master bedroom, hoping he's asleep by now. I turn the clock radio on low, so my movements are muted by the sound.

Within a half hour, I've managed to dry my hair, reapply a bit of make-up, and get dressed again in jeans and a long white cable sweater. I spend a few minutes trying to style my hair, but it's hopeless, curling in impossible waves when I normally flat-iron it straight. But, I need to get going. Impatient now, I tuck most of it under the knitted cap from earlier and slip on my white winter coat from the living room's coat closet. I'm cold and hot at the same time from all the rushing around the past half hour.

I scramble around for pen and paper and write him a quick note:

Brock,

The timing's bad. You know this. I have some things I need to do. I'll see you later. I'll be back in the late afternoon. I suppose there are some things we should say, that need to be said, before you go.

Jordan

I stare at him for a long time in the semi-darkness. The long plane ride he must have taken from halfway around the world has caught up to him. Brock sleeps deep.

I'm reminded of Ethan when he first came home from his tours. He told me, once, that there's so much peace in being home that it always took him a couple of days to get used to it, to fully leave behind the stresses and constant terror that resided within him in Afghanistan. Ethan always said he constantly craved the sleep and peace of home. Brock is probably the same way.

Without thinking, I reach out and touch his face. He startles awake. In the next second, he grabs me by the arm and flips me down on the bed before I even have time to react.

"What? Who?" Brock shouts.

For a moment, I'm allowed a glimpse of his personal terror. He doesn't see me. He sees the darkness of a world I've only begun to comprehend.

"Get a grip, soldier." I breath heavy and can't help but be frightened by his crazed look. "It's me. It's Jordan."

The light of recognition returns to his eyes. "Oh. Jordan. Sorry. Forgot where I was," he says.

I'm still beneath him, and yet, I openly gaze up at his handsome face and try to breathe. *This is not good. Just go.* My body has other ideas and begins to respond. I'm so busy, trying to quell these sensual feelings, it takes a few seconds before I register that he's just grabbed the note from my outstretched hand.

"What's this?"

"Nothing. Give it back."

I slide to the right as he reaches over and turns on the bedside lamp.

We both blink with the sudden light. He glances down and begins reading my note.

"What do you think we'd do if the timing was actually ever good for us?" he asks quietly after he finishes.

"What would we do?" I ask in wonder.

I stare at his bare chest. My eyes stray down to his sexy boxer briefs. *I've slept with the man. I've grieved with him. But, have I ever stopped long enough to let myself really love him?*

My eyes begin to sting. He reaches out and traces my lips.

"Where are you going at almost three in the morning, Jordan?"

"Oh, the places we'll go, the places we'll see," I say in a lyrical voice, mimicking one of Max's favorite Dr. Seuss stories.

"Oh, the places we'll go," Brock says. He rereads the note and frowns. "I suppose there are some things we should say, that need to be said, before you *go*? That's kind of cold." He runs his hand through his hair and sighs.

"The timing's bad. You *know* this."

"Okay, if that's what you want me to believe, fine. But, where are you going at three in the morning?"

"I'm doing a jump at Camarillo Airport. Skydiving, remember? I have to pick up Seth. As you very well know, we have a date. Seth and I. We have a date. Me and Seth." I stare directly up at him with this try-and-stop-me look.

He runs a hand through his hair. I bite my lip to keep from physically reacting to the movement.

"It's a forty minute drive to Camarillo," he drawls. "There won't be any traffic this early in the morning. So, where are you *really* going?"

"I just need to go."

"What if I asked you to postpone your jump by a day or two?" Brock asks so softly that I strain to hear him. "I know I'm asking a lot, but if you just waited a day or two. For me. So I could say everything. Would you do it?"

He sounds so sincere. I want to believe him. I need to believe him.

"Have you been to Austin?" I ask in a low voice.

"No. I came to see you first." He hesitates. "I thought we could spend Christmas together. That we *should* spend Christmas together. Just you and me. Not Seth and you. You and me. The two of us. I haven't been home for Christmas in four years. And, I want to be home. *Here.* With you."

Tears spring up. He looks sad and lost and I'm still too close to him. It must be the damn, raging hormones making me feel this way. I nod slowly, still trying to decipher everything he's just said.

"Home."

"Wherever you are. That's home to me."

His words begin to undo all the complications. I emotionally soften with each word he utters. There's this shifting going on inside of me again. I wipe at my face with the back of my hand and try to stall for time. It seems to be slipping away from me the longer I gaze at him.

"Christmas, huh? That's two weeks away," I say slowly. "Isn't it?"

"Something like that."

"What would we do? That day? Christmas Day."

"Whatever you want. Whatever you need to do, we'll do it, together."

He gets this intense look and appears to be holding his breath, waiting for my answer.

I do the same and affect this nonchalance as I slide off the bed.

I grab my cell phone and turn away from him. With shaking fingers, I text an apology note to Rob that basically tells him I can't make it because something's come up. I send a similar text to Seth. Who, I imagine, will oversleep anyway.

Something's come up and he's lying in the bed over there. *He's alive. He's here. He came back.*

The shifting inside gives way completely. Joy surges. I believe him. In his promise. In what he's said.

"Okay," I finally say.

"Okay, what?"

"Okay, I won't do the jump for a day or two and I'll listen to what you have to say and you can stay. For Christmas."

"Okay," he says. "Come here, then." He pats the empty side of the bed and looks uncertain. "I promise I won't touch you. Frankly, I'm pretty tired, but I need you to be right next to me."

My body moves of its own volition. I slip out of my coat and jeans, pull off the knit cap, and toss it toward the chair. I walk over to the bed and slide underneath the covers and try to breathe.

For the next ten seconds, I shiver beneath the cold sheets. And then, he turns out the light and moves in next to me and wraps his legs around mine, effectively trapping me. I want to argue with him, don't I? But he's warm and I'm still cold, so I move further into his arms and chest.

"This I miss," he says, sniffing my hair from behind.

"You had what? Twelve hours with me?" I turn towards him in disbelief and stare at him. "Nobody can miss that with just twelve hours."

"Want to bet?"

"No," I say with a shaky laugh. I turn away, suddenly shy, and fully aware of him. And, deep inside, I'm flying high. *He's here. He's alive. He makes me feel alive, too. How did I end up here?* My mind races with all these unanswerable questions. He must feel me tremble. *I* can feel me trembling.

"Jordan, it's okay. I'm not going to touch you. I'm too tired. I just want to hold on to you. Is that okay?"

"Okay."

After a few more minutes, my body settles down. I tremble less. I slide further back into him and feel his length stretch alongside mine. His breathing becomes steady and shallower within minutes. He's asleep, for real, this time. His left hand encircles my abdomen. This kicking sensation stops my breath as the baby moves.

"Wow," he whispers. "My God. That's amazing."

"Go to sleep," I say.

"I am," he answers back.

"I haven't confirmed anything yet."

"What's to confirm? I just *felt* it. You're pregnant. You know it. I know it. It's mine. I know that, too."

"I never said that," I say softly.

"I think you did at one point."

"Go to sleep," I say.

"You first."

I turn to face him and wrap my legs around him. "I can't. I'm not tired now."

"Give it a try." I can see his lips curve into a smile even in the darkness, but he keeps his eyes closed. "Jordan. I'm really tired. I haven't really slept in thirty-six hours. If you could, just this once, give me a break. I'd really appreciate it."

"A free pass, huh?" I trail my fingers along his chest and down further. "Jordan, *please*."

"Okay. One free pass. But that's it, Mr. Wainwright. Tomorrow, you pay up."

CHAPTER

TWENTY-SEVEN

Brock – Chances

SUNLIGHT PIERCES MY EYELIDS. I WAKE up at once. A glance at the clock radio confirms we've missed the morning and part of the early afternoon. It's after one. Jordan moves more slowly beside me. She looks surprised and a little disoriented when she turns to me. She scowls in my general direction.

"Don't worry; all we did is sleep. No harm. No foul." I get up and begin rummaging through my rucksack.

"You don't have any civilian clothes," she says.

I glance up in time to watch her disappear out of the room and get this sick feeling in the pit of my stomach. I can't watch her twenty-four seven. If she leaves, she leaves. I'm going to have to accept it or get over it. Either way.

Five minutes later, she stands in the doorway and watches me. Her long legs are bare. All she's wearing is the white sweater and pair of lace white panties. *God. She looks hot. But if I tell her this, she might run.*

"What are you thinking about so hard?" Jordan asks with a little laugh.

"Honestly? How amazingly hot you look in that sweater and little else."

"Are you going to be like this all day? Should we just take care of that particular part of the discussion now, so we can get on with the rest of it?"

She's carrying a bundle of new clothes. She half tosses them onto a chair and saunters her way over to me. *Holy shit.*

"Can I brush my teeth first?" I ask, wary, all at once, and feeling completely out of control. My heart races at about a hundred beats a minute.

"No."

She kisses me hard and my body responds. Less than thirty seconds later, we're on the bed and I'm pushing my way inside of her. Just the sound of her shuddering breath turns me on. She takes me to a new place of wonder. This amazing place in my mind where there's only the two of us. The two of us and no one else.

I kiss her throat and nuzzle my chin into her neck. She laughs and moves beneath me in response. We're synchronized. Together.

I've been with so many women and sex has never been a weak point for me, yet Jordan takes me to this new level of euphoria and I feel powerless. I try to still my mind and concentrate on the physicality of it all, but she's deconstructing me. I don't know where she begins and I end anymore.

Sometime later, she traces a single tear that travels down the side of my face as we finish.

"Christ," I say, embarrassed.

"You're not leaving; are you?" She gets this solemn look as she gazes at me.

"No." I take a deep breath. "I can't. I can't leave you again. I don't think I can survive it. I'm not sure I'll survive, if I stay, either, though." I try to smile, but I'm overcome with too many unidentifiable emotions. "I love you. I've loved you for a long time."

She moves out from beneath me and straddles my waist. She strips off the sweater and drapes her long hair across my face.

"I've loved you for a long time, too." A shadow crosses her features. She looks troubled, guilty even. "Longer than you think." Her voice trembles.

I trace her lips. "You don't have to tell me when. It doesn't matter."

She looks relieved and settles down on my chest and buries her head into my neck. My pulse beats near her temple.

"I'm going to go see Liz. Get an ultrasound. Make sure everything's okay. Want to come?"

"Yes."

She slides off the bed and strolls to the doorway. I put my hands behind my head and watch her go. She turns back and stares at me for a long time.

"The beach that day," she says, uncertain. Then, she leaves.

I inhale deep as I begin to comprehend what she's just said.

I prepare my speech in the guest bathroom shower.

Jordan, marry me. Not because you need to, but because you want to. I need you, Jordan. I want us to be together. I repeat the words over and over.

I towel off and get dressed quickly after removing the tags from the jeans and dress shirt she's lent me. Everything fits. I wonder where she got the clothes and when she got them.

I wander down the hall. Before I can stop myself, I turn the handle to Max's bedroom. The twin bed's made. The toys are strewn across the floor the way he must have left them last. My throat gets tight. I miss Max. A silver urn rests on the dresser. *His ashes?* I go over and read the inscription:

*P*IGLET SIDLED UP TO POOH FROM behind. "Pooh!" he whispered. "Yes, Piglet?" "Nothing," said Piglet, taking Pooh's paw. "I just wanted to be sure of you."

~A.A. Milne

I leave everything undisturbed and close the door with a quiet click. Jordan's voice carries down the hallway to me. I head toward the direction of her voice, still somewhat amazed at being able to see her. She's making breakfast. The tantalizing smell of bacon and eggs and coffee greet me. She's talking on her cell phone, but studies my face for a few seconds, and then gets this wide grin.

"Okay, we'll be there within the hour. Thanks for fitting me in." She pauses and looks over at me. "I'll tell him. Okay. I said I would, and I will."

She hangs up the phone and continues to study my face. "So," she says with a shaky breath. "That was Liz. She said to tell you 'hi' and 'welcome home.' In the sense of welcome back to the States," she says quickly.

"I feel like we've taken three steps backward in terms of working everything out," I say with a dry laugh.

"Maybe, we have."

She gets this intense look as she flips the eggs. Five minutes later, she places a plate of food in front of me. Her hands shake as she pours coffee in a cup and slides it over to me.

"What's up?" I ask.

"She wants to do an ultrasound. I told her when, you know, it must have happened, but she wants to see me."

"She does."

"Yes. She does."

"And?"

"And, I guess I just want to be sure. You know. Of the due date. That everything's okay." Her eyes fill with tears. "I really *want* this. This baby. Our baby. It doesn't replace Max. It—*she*. I know it's a girl." Jordan gets this little smile, but then, it disappears. "She just makes it—"

"I know, baby," I say.

The moment's come. I slide off the chair and go around the counter to be right next to her. She stands there, just watching me.

"Jordan, I—"

My practice speech in the shower disappears. My mind draws a complete blank.

"What?"

"I just want to be sure of you," I finally say.

She stares at me with this kind of wonder. "*What* did you just say?"

"I said I just want to be sure of you. I *am* sure of you, actually. And, I think you are—sure of me, too."

"What does that mean to you?" Jordan asks, wary, all at once.

I take a deep breath and sigh. This is not going at all the way I planned or should have planned. "It means I love you. That I need you, here, next to me for always. It means: will you marry me and live with me for all time? Because I'll be wherever you are, for always. At least, that's what I think it means." I frown, getting more uncertain by her subdued reaction to everything I've just said because she's just standing there in a daze, looking amazed or confused or both. "Jordan, did you hear what I just said?"

"I heard you." She puts down the spatula and folds herself into my arms. After a few minutes, she looks up at me. "I'm sure of you, too, Brock."

"So that's a big yes to everything," I say slowly.

"That's a big yes to everything," she says.

Then, she laughs. It's the best sound I've ever heard.

CHAPTER

TWENTY-EIGHT

Jordan - Dream

THE PLANE DESCENDS INTO AUSTIN AND almost takes my stomach with it. I grip Brock's hand tighter, grazing up against the gold band on his left hand. He raises my hand to his lips and kisses it. It's been six weeks, since we said I do to each other at the L.A. County Courthouse, but I'm still adjusting to the idea of being Mrs. Brock Wainwright. It still feels weird. A good weird, but weird.

I glance over at Liz across the aisle. She gives me the thumbs up and smiles wide. I smile back at her. I'm giddy, joyous. I can barely contain myself. She and Adrian stood up for us. And now? They're both bound to our secret. Brock and I decided it was best to not announce our own nuptials. Well, *I decided* and begged him not to tell anybody, especially Tate.

"Let's just let it settle a bit before we say anything," I'd said. It's supposed to be Ashleigh's big day in a few months, not ours. He'd looked disappointed for a long while and then reluctantly agreed.

"Janie's not going to be happy," he said with disappointment.

I managed to placate him then, and he's been pretty good up until now.

"You need to take that off." I trace his gold wedding ring and slowly pull off my own.

"I don't want to. I meant it. It's for keeps," he says with a little smile.

"*Please.* You promised. Tomorrow's Ashleigh and Tate's big day."

"Tomorrow's Valentine's Day," he says. "I want the world to know you're mine." He gets this devilish, make-me grin.

"It's their wedding day. Let's just wait until they say I do and then we'll tell them. Right after the ceremony. Okay? One more day, basically."

"All right. Fine. One more day," he drawls and looks unhappy.

I kiss him and he kisses me back. Meanwhile, the rest of the passengers prepare for landing while we're making out. I smile beneath his lips.

"What?" Brock asks.

"I should probably stop kissing you. People are going to figure out we're involved. Just know, I want the world to know you're mine, too."

He lifts his head from mine and gets this secret smile. "You are going to have to tell everyone about the baby, though."

"True," I say with a frown.

I'm well into my second trimester, having denied my first. Brock and I will welcome a baby girl in mid-May. I've begun showing more, especially in the past two weeks. I can barely fit into my regular clothes. I resorted to a dress for the plane ride because all my jeans cut too tight across my mid-section.

"It happens like that," Liz said on the flight earlier. "One day, everything fits. The next, you finally feel and look pregnant."

"Thanks for that," I said. "Just what I need, to look pregnant in my Maid of Honor dress."

"Matron of Honor. It's *Matron* of Honor."

"You're killin' me."

"I have never seen you this happy," Liz said.

It's true. I've never been this happy. I've never let myself be this happy. No. The constant fear and worry about something happening to Ethan or Max that always followed me around is no more. Now. I've let it all go. I can't really determine why as of yet. Maybe, the morbid touchstone visits and confrontations with my past have put it all to rest. Maybe, it's Brock. Maybe, it's me. Maybe, it's both of us, together.

Brock breaks my reverie with a heavy sigh as he slips off his wedding ring and hands it to me. I carefully put it inside a zippered pocket inside my purse.

"Thanks," I say. "I love you."

He brightens up at this and kisses the side of my face. "I love you, too."

I absently note that the plane has arrived at the gate, but I'm too mesmerized by the wanting look in Brock's eyes. He's been busy making plans for us to be together at the Lazy J during our stay.

"We can tell them we're dating; right?" he asks now, looking worried.

"Sure. I guess so. Dating, huh? You're dating me? *This* I want to see."

He gets this thoughtful look. "We'll work something out. I guess we haven't really done that. The dating thing."

"I don't really need to *date* you. I already have the best parts about you figured out."

"Hey, lovebirds, they're deplaning," Liz says. "Join us?"

She and Adrian lean over our seats and affect these identical knowing smirks.

"God! Is anyone going to be able to keep a secret around here?" I ask.

Adrian laughs and shakes his head. He thinks the whole keep it a secret idea is flawed.

"We'll do our best. It might help if you two try to not look like you want to rip each other's clothes off right here in first class," Liz says with a laugh. "We'll go find Ashleigh and Tate in baggage claim. Join us; won't you?'"

With that, she and Adrian take off. I watch their retreating backs with a bit of angst. Brock and I haven't exactly talked about how the logistics are going to work here. We've spent the last two months together and have barely left the house. Other than me showing up for a few shifts a week at Le Reve, we've been together. And, I think even Louis has begun to suspect something is up with Brock and me. For his part, Brock has shown up at every shift and eaten dinner with me. I've begun preparing special dishes made especially for his nightly arrival. Louis has successfully parlayed these into nightly specials for the Le Reve menu on the nights I work.

We wait until the majority of passengers have deplaned. I smile over at him. He helps me up from the seat and kisses me one last time. His attentiveness is off the charts. In the back of my mind, I idly wonder how that's going to play out in front of his family and our friends. He retrieves our carry-on bags, and I follow him off the airplane in this kind of endless bliss. He glances back and smiles at me. My throat constricts with a myriad of emotions, ranging from joy to utter amazement. *He loves me.* I know it in the way he holds on to me late at night and, like now, when he reaches out and waits for me to grab hold of his hand. I love him, too.

"Come on, Mrs. Wainwright," he says. "This way."

❧•❦

Baggage claim is overrun with the entire extended Wainwright family. I'm overcome with handshakes and the warm hugs of virtual strangers. There must be at least twenty people here. I scan the crowd, looking for Ashleigh and Tate. Brock lets go of my hand to hug his mother.

Janie beams and holds on to Brock. I feel this twinge of guilt for keeping him from her the past few months, including Christmas, which we spent at the beach, wrapped in blankets and each other. I've been completely selfish.

Someone lightly squeezes my right arm in belated welcome. I glance over and take in the familiar face of Brock's sister, Diana.

"Diana," I say with a nervous laugh. "Hi! Oh, it's great to see you. How are you doing?" Unthinking, I go in for a hug, and she gasps a little bit when my bulging waistline hits at her midsection.

"Wow. Oh, wow," Diana says. She pulls me along to the edge of the familial crowd with her free hand. "*Please.* Tell me. I'm going to be an aunt. *Please.*"

"You are," I say quickly. "But it's kind of something we're attempting to keep under wraps, until after Tate and Ashleigh's wedding," I say slowly.

Feeling overwhelmed, I glance over at Brock and discover him talking animatedly to his mother. Now, Janie's looking at me in wonder. Then I can only watch as she bursts into tears. In the next ten seconds, she's making her way over to Diana and me with Brock trailing behind her.

"Oh, Jordan. Oh, Jordan. I'm so happy," Janie says, engulfing me in her amazing embrace. She wipes at her tears with a laugh as she pulls back from me and just studies my face intently. "This is everything I've wanted. I just can't believe it. I just can't believe it." She kisses each side of my face and hugs me once more.

I look over her shoulder straight at Brock. "What did you tell her, *exactly?*"

He gets this sheepish look. "Everything?"

"What happened to this being about Ashleigh and Tate's big moment? You agreed."

I successfully pull out of Janie's arms and take her hands in mine.

"We're not telling anyone else," I say in a panic. "Di knows most of it. You know all of it. That's it. I don't want to ruin Tate and Ashleigh's day. Okay?"

My mother-in-law nods enthusiastically. Diana steals up beside her.

"Okay," Diana says as she puts her arm around Janie. "Mom, this is going to be a first. You're going to keep this a secret." She waves her arm around. "Until Brock and Jordan are ready to announce it. Capiche?" Diana laughs. "Oh, my God, I finally have a sister!" She comes in for an official hug and practically crushes me.

"Get your hands off my Maid of Honor, Di!" Ashleigh says from behind her.

I delicately extract myself from my secret sister-in-law's grip, carefully hug Ashleigh, and manage to keep my protruding stomach far enough back from her normal clairvoyant detection. Nervous, I pull away from her within seconds.

Everyone gets this expectant look and gazes at me. Ashleigh looks from me to Brock.

"Hello stranger. Welcome back to Austin," Ashleigh drawls. "Looks like Malibu agrees with you, Brock."

"I like Malibu," he says easily. Brock gets this reckless, defiant look, puts his arm around me, and flashes Ashleigh this charming smile.

"The groom will be happy to see you," she says. "I have to admit, I've been a bit needy, since my best friend has effectively abandoned me and Liz insists on staying in L.A. with her."

I slide out from under the weight of Brock's arm and make an hasty escape. "Can I talk to you, Ash? We really need to catch up."

It's as if I've rewarded her or something. She beams at me. I wind my arm through hers, prepared to walk off with her, until I feel a child's hand pulling at my dress.

"Jordan. Jordan. I'm so glad you're back," says Diana's son, Robbie.

I stop and bend down to pick up the little boy. He's three, a year younger than Max. I bury my face in his neck and smell baby shampoo and graham crackers.

"Robbie, it's good to see you."

He cups my face with his little hands when I look up at him. Next, he plants a kiss on my cheek.

"Sorry," he says. "About Max."

"Me, too."

"Mommy says he went to Heaven to be with Ethan."

"That's true. He did. He's with his daddy."

My bravado starts to falter. Ashleigh sees it first.

"Robbie? Jordan's going to ride back to the ranch with me. She can catch up to you later; okay?"

I start to walk away with Ashleigh, reeling from the little boy's innocent reference to Max, but slowly turn back, remembering Brock.

He looks beside himself. I've been out of his reach for all of two minutes. Ashleigh sees his anxious face, too.

"What's gotten into him?" Ashleigh asks, as she propels us through the airport entryway. "Here. The car's this way. Brock can ride with Tate and Adrian. I want you and Liz all to myself." She stops and stares at me, for a second, while she unlocks the car with a press of a button on her key chain. "You look different," she says, lost in thought, but still scrutinizing me.

"I do?"

"Yeah," she says. "You look happy. Really happy." She looks over at Brock who is climbing up into Tate's big truck. He still looks out of sorts and scowls in our general direction. "What's going on with him?"

"Oh, you'd be surprised," Liz says as she slides into the backseat.

I give her a warning look as I get into the passenger seat.

"So, tell us everything. What's the plan? How can we help?" I ask.

It's the best tactic I can think of. Ask the bride what the plans are. Ashleigh is off and running within seconds, outlining the plans, beginning with the fitting of our dresses, which we're apparently going to do now. I cringe at the thought of fitting into a bridesmaid dress and anxiously look back at Liz. She just laughs.

"This is going to be such fun. Such fun," Liz says with a wicked laugh.

⁘

Two hours later, it's really stopped being fun. Ashleigh has turned into bridezilla because her own dress needs to be taken in one additional time.

"I don't believe this," she mutters as she preens in front of the mirror.

"I think it looks great," I say. "You look beautiful."

"Go try yours on. I'm sure we're going to have to take it in. You look like you've lost weight."

"I don't know. Maybe." I slink toward the dressing rooms, looking for one that is farthest away from her. Liz struts out, wearing the dark red satin version of the bridesmaid dress, rolling her eyes.

"It's tight-fitting. Let me model this for our lovely bride and then I'll come help you with yours," Liz whispers in passing.

"Perfect," I mutter.

The dress is this wonderful rich Bordeaux color. I was worried it would contrast with the red tones of my hair, but it's perfect. I even start to believe in miracles as the zipper goes up fairly easily in the back when Liz returns, but the bodice is a little tight. It shows a little bit more cleavage than I normally wear. It flounces out at the waistline, so no one will be able to really tell I'm pregnant. A little giddy at this unexpected revelation, I flounce back up to the front.

"It's too tight in the chest."

"I can see that," Ashleigh deadpans. She's changed into a bright red dress that reveals every curve of her perfect body. "For the rehearsal dinner tonight, I got you and Liz dresses, too."

"Where did you get the money?" Liz asks, swanking towards us in her regular street clothes.

"We struck oil at the Lazy J," Ashleigh says. "Tate took care of it. Well, Tate, Brock, and you, Jordan," she says with a wan smile. "Surely, he told you."

"I think he told me," I say. "I don't know; we've had a lot of other things to talk about."

"Really?" Ashleigh asks. "Do tell."

"Yes, do *tell*," Liz echoes.

I turn to my friend slash gyno and give her a warning look.

"I think it's about time to come clean with all of it," Liz says.

"Yeah, come clean with it. All of it. You can start with why you're sipping at that champagne and not actually drinking it and then you can tell me why your boobs are twice their normal size." She stops talking and gets this wondrous look. "Holy shit. Are—are you pregnant?"

"I don't want this to be about me," I say with a nervous laugh. I hang my head and refuse to actually look at her. "But, yeah. I am. I guess I'll be skipping the champagne at the wedding. Well, I'll do the toast. A half glass isn't going to kill me."

She sits down with a humph, much to the dismay of the dressmaker, who appears around the corner with straight pins ready to take in the bodice and re-sew the dress. I watch her scuttle away at Ashleigh's request. Our bride's satin dress billows around her like a cloud. I sink down right beside her on the sofa and lean my head against her shoulder.

"I've missed you so much, Ash" I say.

"I can see that," she says with a sigh. "What else aren't you telling me?"

Ashleigh looks over at Liz. "What else? Because everyone is acting weird. Ever since you all got off the plane. Weird, I tell you."

I shake my head side-to-side in warning at Liz.

"That's it. Come on. It's all about you. Let's go to the ranch and get ready for this fabulous rehearsal dinner of yours."

"Nice try," Ashleigh says. "It's Brock's, right?"

"Something like that."

"So, when's the big day?"

"No big day. We're just taking it one day at time for now."

Liz makes a strangled sound and mouths the words, "Tell her."

"Tell me, what?" Ashleigh asks.

"Nothing. There's nothing else to tell," I say with a laugh.

CHAPTER

TWENTY-NINE

Jordan – Looking for water

AT HALF PAST FOUR, I FINALLY escape Ashleigh's inquisition. Which is good because I was close to breaking down and just telling her everything, but I remain stubborn, scared, outside of myself, even at this point. I'm both physically and mentally exhausted, and my head is pounding. Weary, I climb the stairs at the Wainwrights' ranch, where Janie has now insisted we stay. I search the bedrooms, wondering where our luggage has ended up.

Per Janie's welcome note, she's at the hair salon, getting her hair styled for tonight's rehearsal dinner, since she's effectively Tate's aunt, mother, and father rolled into one. I feel this qualm of sadness and spend the next few minutes thinking of Henry.

My initial tour downstairs reveals that J's Paradise has been transformed. I can see what Janie Wainwright has spent the past several months doing. She's redecorated every square inch of space both downstairs as well as upstairs. I bite my lip in consternation, recognizing the frenzy of grief in all this extracurricular activity. What others will deem wasteful; I can only discern as heartbreak and grief. Pain. Inexplicable. Inescapable pain at the loss of a loved one.

I locate our luggage in what used to be Janie and Henry's master bedroom. Her personal things are down the hall in the guest room that Max and I once stayed in. The master bedroom is now a creamy off-white and adorned with fresh white flowers on each night stand. Everything is new. I recognize this kind of cleansing. I performed the same kind of ritual at the Malibu property six years ago and again almost a year ago. I might have to do that again I decide, recalling Max's bedroom, which remains untouched.

I finger the white lace duvet on the king-size bed and let my thoughts drift back to the present. The Paperwhites give off an amazing sweet scent. They're welcoming and exhibit that newlywed feel, just as my mother-in-law surely planned. I smile to myself, knowing Janie's ecstatic to have us here and her son home for good.

"For good?" I say to the empty space. *What am I committing myself to? Haven't I done that already?*

I take a quick shower and slip on the dress that Ashleigh's loaned me, since the one she originally picked out would not fit over my burgeoning waistline. This one's a black velvet mini dress. I gaze at myself in the mirror, dismayed at the skirt length, but I am out of options. I slip on a pair of only-in-L.A. black velvet pumps that Ashleigh insisted I borrow as well. I've left my hair down in its natural waves, and decide, I'm passable. I add a touch of dark red lipstick and turn to go.

Brock stands in the door frame, surveying me, wearing this amazing black Armani suit with a grey shirt and black silk tie.

"Hello, Mrs. Wainwright," he says softly.

"Don't. I've had the grand inquisition from Ashleigh, and I almost told her at least a half dozen times." My head pounds, but I hide it from him.

"Secrets are hard to keep," Brock says. "You look beautiful." He gets this weird look. "I don't tell you that enough." He shakes his head and looks uncertain.

"You tell me plenty. What's going on?"

"I want to give you something, but I'm not going to give it to you in the bathroom." He pushes away from the door frame and walks out.

Curious about his odd behavior, I follow him out to the bedroom. He stands there with his feet planted a foot apart with his hands behind his back. I pause to admire his fine looks.

"You're a very handsome man, Lieutenant Wainwright."

"Not Henry Cavill, I'm afraid," he says with a laugh.

"Better. Much better."

"Come here," he says.

I affect a sexy walk and saunter over to him, but get more nervous with each step I take. "What are you up to?" I ask.

"Turn around."

He touches the back of my neck for a second and, in the next, pushes my hair to one side. He connects some kind of clasp, kisses my neck, and rearranges my hair. In the next instant, he lets loose of a stone that dangles, and then, rests at my throat. It's cold and heavy.

"What is this?" I ask, turning back toward him.

"Go take a look," he says, pointing to a tall mirror on the opposite wall.

I walk toward the mirror and nervously clasp at the stone and the thin chain holding it. I raise my eyes to the mirror as I get closer.

"It's my mother's," I whisper. "How did you find it? When? I don't understand. I thought Ethan sold this?" Tears well up. "Brock, this must have cost a fortune."

"I told you I'd get it back," he says with a shrug. "I made you a promise. I intend to keep it."

"Brock, it's too much. Hundreds of thousands of dollars. I *know* this."

"I got a good deal." He puts his arms around me and kisses my neck. "The oil business has picked up exponentially for WHM Oil and my dad's company, too. We're doing all right, even if I'm running it all from L.A. But, most of all, Jordan, it's yours. It was your mother's. It was worth paying any price to get it back." He gets this secret smile. "So. I had to come up with something. Something else that would tell the world that you're mine and that you have my promise that I'll never leave you as long as I breathe. I'll be right here next to you."

I'm getting more unsteady. It's hard to stand, to even breathe. The headache worsens, but I don't say anything. I just lean further into him, and he holds me tighter.

"So," he says.

I pull away from him and turn back around. He gets down on one knee.

"When you tell the world we're married, they'll know I've made good on that promise."

He slips a ring on my left hand. I glance down at the platinum setting. It's a marquis-cut diamond that matches my mother's necklace.

"This is hard to find," I say.

"Yes."

"It's exquisite."

"Like you."

"Don't make me cry, Lieutenant." I dab at my eyes, trying not to mess up my mascara. "This is so over the top." I put my arms around his neck and pull him close. "Thank you. Thank you. Thank you." I kiss him.

"I love you, Jordan. For always," he says. "I'll always be here. That's my promise."

"That's a good promise," I say.

⊰৩৫⊱

Ashleigh left out one minor detail. The rehearsal dinner is taking place at *Laissez Faire*.

Yes. Every fine detail for the restaurant I listed off to Brock, months before, has been fulfilled. It's finished. *Laissez Faire*.

I stare in amazement at the intimate setting. The crème-colored walls and the Impressionist artwork hung throughout round out the ambiance. There's even a six-foot replica of Gustav Klimt's The Kiss that takes center stage near the front entrance. Lit votive candles glow from every table and shelf, completing the intimate feeling of the space. The place is staffed and ready to serve. I'm overwhelmed. I just stare at it. It feels like a dream come true. It feels like too much. I feel unsettled and my headache worsens.

Brock comes up behind me and holds me close. "Did I get it right?"

"Yes. Everything's perfect," I say softly, attempting to hide my sudden angst. I don't feel right for some reason.

"Am I selling it all too hard?"

I turn in his arms. "You don't have to sell me. You had me in Le Reve's parking lot, when you first said hello, two months ago."

"That seems like a long time ago."

"Sometimes," I say. "But, it's the first time I slept so well. In years." I force myself to smile as this jagged pain cuts across my forehead.

He fingers my hair, tucking tendrils behind my ear. Then, he glances past me, his hand drops to his side, and he moves away. "Show time. One more day, right?" he says with a sigh, looking frustrated, and then, he smiles. "Save me a dance?" His lips part as if he has something more to say.

"I'm all yours," I say, as I watch him go.

He makes his way over to Ashleigh and Tate. I can't help feeling disappointed that I didn't get to hear what he wanted to say.

My head pounds with this inexplicable pain again. In a haze, I watch Ashleigh dance her way over to me.

"Hey," she says, glowing in her sexy red dress. "How are you holding up? Whoa. Where did you get that necklace?"

She's staring at my neck. I look down and finger the diamond there, while the pain in my head suddenly worsens.

"That's your mother's. He found it?"

"How did you know?" I gasp for breath and feel more light-headed, now. I stagger over to a table and land in one of the chairs. "Can you get me a glass of water?" I ask her.

Ashleigh gets this weird look and then rushes over to one of the waiters. As she makes her way back to me, she sloshes over half the glass, as she returns with it.

Brock turns away from talking to Tate and gives me a quizzical look. I try to smile, but the effort is too great, now. I try to wave my hand in his general direction, but it's getting hard to even move.

"What is going on with you?" Ashleigh asks, looking more anxious.

I start to shake as I try to drink down some of the water, but I can barely hold the glass. She takes it from me.

"You're scaring me. What's wrong?"

"I don't know," I say, dully. "I feel weird. Really weird."

"What the hell? Where did the rock come from?' She lifts up my left hand and I stare at it as if it's the first time I've seen it. "Did Brock give you this?"

"I think so. Ash? I don't feel well. Something's wrong with me."

The sounds go first, and then, my vision dims. All I can really see are the flickering candles and the shadowy faces that suddenly hover over me.

I try and say, "I don't feel right," to anyone who will listen now.

Then, Brock's there. He's holding me, giving orders, breathing into me, and pounding on my chest.

"Don't break the necklace," I mumble. "Don't leave me. *Promise.*" *Promise.*

I think I hear him say it.

CHAPTER THIRTY

Brock – Keep breathing

ADRIAN SAINES, THE OFFICIAL ATTORNEY AMONG US, had it right. "Get your stuff in order. Prepare for the worst. Hope for the best," he'd said at our wedding when he and Liz stood up for us. My father used to say that, too. So, we did. We got everything in order. Name changes. Insurance. Wills. Finances. Checking accounts. Loans. Safe deposit boxes. Health directives. We just didn't tell anybody.

I scrutinize the wallpaper that covers the hospital waiting room walls and note the finer details of the blue fibrous weave that some designer has chosen. Blue is calming. I read that somewhere. Once. All it seems to give off to me is this sense of *false hope*.

Ashleigh's crying reaches for me. Tate comforts her in the opposite corner from mine, while Diana and my mother occupy the east end and Adrian and Liz take the west. I sit alone, waiting for some kind of word, some kind of sign that my life isn't over.

In the indeterminable silence, I resort to silent prayer. To God. He's let me down a number of times. I'm sure I've done the same.

Are we even now?

I wonder.

A guy in blue surgical scrubs approaches. The Déjà vu begins, as if, on cue.

"I'm looking for Jordan Wainwright's husband." Then, he studies his chart. "Brock. Brock Wainwright?"

"I'm Jordan's husband," I manage to say. "Brock Wainwright."

I stand up and vaguely watch Ashleigh lift her tear-streaked face from Tate's shoulder as she begins to comprehend what I've just said.

"You guys got *married*? Why didn't anyone *tell* me?"

Liz comes over, hugs her for a moment, and whispers something. Then, she comes to stand next to me. We're a united front for Jordan, all at once.

"I'm Dr. Sam Forrest. Head of emergency services," the doctor says.

We briefly shake hands, and I search for the right words. *Is she okay? When can I see her?* The questions constrict my throat. I'm too afraid to ask, too afraid of his answers. He has this grim, guarded look.

"I'm Jordan's OB/GYN, out of L.A., Dr. Elizabeth Cantor. Can you tell us what's going on here?" Liz asks.

"There's a swelling on her brain. We've brought in one of our best neurosurgeons for consult. He's looking at the MRI, now." Dr. Forrest pauses for a moment. "I believe he's going to recommend surgery tonight. We can't wait much longer. She's in trouble." He looks at me with this strange modicum of sympathy. "How old is she?" Forrest asks.

"Twenty-eight," Liz says, impatient. "As I told your staff earlier, she's twenty-seven weeks pregnant."

The doctor fumbles with his hands. "Complicated," he says with a heavy sigh. "Mr. Wainwright, you'd better come with me. I want to introduce you to Dr. Stephen Anders. He can explain what they're going to do."

"The surgery," I say, and then, swallow hard. "Is it necessary?"

He looks mildly surprised. "She'll die without it."

I turn to Liz, and fail to hide the sudden terror that takes a firm hold.

"Can you come with me? Maybe, explain the stuff to me in layman's terms."

She nods and links my arm with hers.

We follow the good doctor down the hallway, moving at a fast clip that reminds me of the missions we used to take in Afghanistan. From this faraway place, I remind myself to prepare for battle. 'Take aim and fire' Ethan used to say.

❧◊❧

Heartbreak is doled out in increments. The surgery takes twice as long as the four hours they initially foretold. I retreat further into this private hell with every opening and closing of the waiting rooms doors, awaiting word of some kind. After eight hours, the word comes down from on high. She's alive.

And, the waiting begins. Again. The clock restarts.

I learn to appreciate the merits of lukewarm coffee and Styrofoam cups all over again. Tate and Ashleigh's wedding day comes and go. They postpone the whole thing, including their honeymoon.

There's internal bleeding. It is some unknown source for a few hours where everyone scrambles around and says things like, "we hope for the best," without any of us really believing it.

I retreat further.

⊰⊙⊱

Like I said, heartbreak is doled out in increments.

She almost loses the baby on day three. "If I have to make a choice, I choose Jordan," I tell the medical team.

A thousand times, I wonder how she'll deal with that loss, if it comes to that. A thousand times, I beg God to give her back to me. I say a little prayer for our baby girl, too, but God already knows who I would choose.

God doesn't appear to be listening.

⊰⊙⊱

"You need to go home and take a shower," Tate says on day six. "I'll call you if there's any change."

"No."

"Yes. Ashleigh's going to take you home. Your mother has food on the table. Go eat. Shower. Shave, for God's sake."

"Leave God out of this," I roar.

"Go home, Brock. I'll call you if anything changes."

Ashleigh keeps glancing at me as we make our way to my mother's. I'm reminded of Reed in another lifetime not all that long ago in Afghanistan.

"What's up?" I finally ask.

"Thank God, you guys got married. It would be a lot more complicated making all these decisions, if you two weren't married."

"She's going to hate me for not choosing that baby if she loses her."

"No. She won't. God, she loves you so much, Brock."

"Don't cry. I don't think I could take that on top of everything else."

317

I rub at my eyes and stare out at the wintry landscape. Bleak. Like me.

Ashleigh fidgets with the steering wheel and still swipes at her face every once in a while. My propensity for sympathy is at an all time low, but I give it a try.

"Ashleigh, what is it?" I ask quietly.

"We got married. Before, you guys came," she says, shaking her head. She frowns. "We just snuck away to Vegas one weekend and got married. I didn't want to wait." She tries to smile, but her eyes fill with new tears. "I knew Jordan would eventually understand. And now? I just want to be able to *tell* her." She swipes at her face, but the tears come too fast, now.

"Comas are tricky," I say slowly.

I wince at my words. They mimic Dr. Stephen Anders' so well. The brilliant surgeon has been unable to fully explain Jordan's unexpected comatose state to any of us.

Here's what we know to be true. She's alive. She's breathing on her own. She's stable. They caught the aneurysm in time, before it burst. It was some congenital condition that no one could have really known about or prevented. Benign. All good news. A full recovery is possible. Yes. All good news, except she hasn't woken up, and it's been almost seven days since that first surgery.

I reach out and pat her hand.

"Congratulations. We'll celebrate when this is over. Soon. Secret ceremonies are all the rage these days," I say with a touch of the old sarcasm.

Ashleigh laughs and gives me a grateful smile. "All the rage," she says.

CHAPTER

THIRTY-ONE

Jordan – Love, save the empty

THE VOICES COME. THEY FADE IN and out like a piece of music that seems familiar, but not quite recognizable. First, I appreciate their crescendos, but then, I encounter their despair. The musicality of their voices reaches for me, but seems to just miss me every time.

Am I the instrument being strummed? I cannot produce any sound, even when they touch me. My legs and arms are moved up and down, sideways, backwards, and forwards.

My lips form the words: 'just stop.'

'Just stop,' I long to say, but there is only the air, moving in and out of my lungs. There's no sound. All is silent, except for the breathing. It's a thousand times silent.

If I could blink, maybe, they would stop and listen and eventually say: "There she is; let's stop."

But they cannot hear me. Or, they do not listen.

Just stop.' The words roar through my mind, but there is no sound. The disconnect of my mind from my body appears permanent.

⁕

Time lapses. I am alone.

I am lifted up, floating above it all. I see it all so clearly and try to think of how to reach past the nothingness toward something, towards *anything*.

There's this hopelessness that I must battle. Despair, I suppose. It infiltrates all of me now.

Desperation sets in. 'Just stop.' I long to say.

⁂

But now, *he* is here, but just out of reach.

If I could move my hand in his and make him see me. A single finger, if I could lift a single finger, just one. Just once. I try again and again to lift a finger, just a finger, but my body does not cooperate and my mind seems reluctant to give in to such commands.

Detached? Perhaps. Defeated? Most definitely.

'Move,' I think. *'Just move.'* But nothing moves, least of all, me.

I cannot open my eyes. I cannot see him. Can he see me?

I take consolation in his presence in knowing he is here and just out of reach. It comforts me.

Somehow, I know that he waits for me. He keeps me from drowning in the despair. I will not succumb to it because he is here with me, holding my hand. I just wish I could hold his back.

The timbre of his voice consoles. It touches me, but no tears fall.

⁂

Sometimes, it feels as though I'm under water. That's it. I'm under water. Yet, I carry this firm belief that he will save me. His constant presence keeps me from drowning in these relentless, mysterious waters. Just hearing his voice keeps me afloat.

⁂

Sometimes, the sounds are too far away. I long to call out: *'I'm here.'* Yet, the sounds stay back away from me, more and more.

Frustration grows, like a runaway vine in a neglected garden, long forgotten. Hopelessness, too, it wends its way through all of my nerve endings. It holds me down. I'm its prisoner, lashed to this table.

I want to cry, but no tears fall.

Sometimes, I sense I am all alone. That's when the inner panic comes to life deep inside of me.

Coldness lurks, even though I feel the warmth as my body is constantly bathed in bright light. The light can be white, yellow, and sometimes even red and envelops all of me. But the light does not keep me from the cold and the dark that threaten from all sides.

The intensity of this prism seems prepared to set me on fire, but dark cold fear attempts to obliterate the light. It is constant.

I try to scream, but still, there is no sound.

∫∫

No movement. No sound. No life. Just this constancy of breath, in and out. That's when the terror presses downward.

My greatest fear? I'll just stop breathing one day.

My next greatest fear? That I no longer care.

Yet. It's his voice that sustains me. *His voice.*

"What do you want?" he asks.

I want to answer his question. I want to try and answer his question. I don't know the context in which he asks this of me, but I want to answer,

My lips won't move. My mind swirls, like a child's spinning top, but my body just stays disconnected from it all.

Free will ebbs away with each breath I take.

I count them. One hundred. One thousand.

Ten thousand. One hundred thousand.

I long to open my eyes and discern the nothingness for myself, ascertain the realness of this fate and test the boundaries of this prison.

Please, God. Let the nothingness end.

Acceptance settles in. I must accept my fate. This is how it will be.

Then, he whispers, "What do you want?"

He brings me back. His voice sustains me. It keeps me afloat. *His voice.*

"What do you want?" he asks again.

I cannot answer him.

But if I could, I would answer simply, *'you.'*

∫∫

Sunlight floods the room. I'm lit up by it, too. I bask in the light.

I wait it out. My mind seems to clear like a fog that, at first, occupies the shore, and then, mercifully relinquishes its grip.

Eventually, I glance at the machines to my right. My heart rate beats at a steady rate of sixty-two. I think that's good. I move my head to the left and gaze at all the horizontal lines along the papered walls. Then, I glance out the only window and see the clear blue sky.

The world appears to be in order.

And, I am here.

This rippling motion at my abdomen captivates me. Enchanted, I move my hand across this huge mound that is my abdomen.

Our baby girl is still here. Thank you, God.

My lips part and I attempt to smile. The effort is altogether exhausting.

I dwell in the haze of uncertainty and try to take it all in.

The door swings open. I turn my head in anticipation of whoever is walking in and discover I can smile more easily this time.

Joy courses through me like an incredible drug-induced high at the sight of him. He carries a Styrofoam cup of coffee in one hand and a bouquet of garden flowers in the other. So. Is it *April?*

"Oh, Lieutenant, you look so *good,*" I whisper as a single tear travels down the side of my face.

Brock drops all of it. The flowers fall to the floor, carefully chosen, it would seem, yet, forgotten in an instant. His coffee splashes everywhere. The sunlight hits his dark, wavy hair as he races over to me.

And then, he's kissing me, and I'm kissing him back.

"Do you have a toothbrush by chance?" I ask against his lips as initial joy gives way to self-conscious insecurity.

"No," he says with reverence. "No toothbrushes."

He strokes my face and fondles my hair in his amazing silent way.

I reach up and feel the left side of my head. It's short and bristles beneath the palm of my hand like an uneven crew-cut. "My hair," I murmur after a few minutes. "What happened to my hair?"

"Doesn't matter. You're here. I'm here. That's all that matters," he says, kissing me again. Then, he whispers my name over and over.

He's the one who has been here with me the whole time. I pull away and gaze up at him with intense wonder, knowing he's the miracle, not me.

"You asked me what I wanted," I finally say. "I *heard* you."

"You did?" Brock asks.

"My answer is *you.* I want you. I'm sure of only *you.*" I smile wide. "And you kept your promise," I say with a laugh.

And, that's when he starts to cry.

WITH GRATITUDE

Acknowledgements

THIS IS A SPECIAL THANK YOU to my husband Michael and my two kids, who have all put up with haphazard food preparation and too many frozen dinners to count this past year, while I wrote *When I See You* and published two other novels.

Writing is a solitary process for me with lots of starts and stops, especially with this novel, so thank you goes to all of my family and friends who have encouraged me along the way to keep going when that seemed all, but impossible.

Once again, I thank all my teachers and classmates at *The Writer's Studio* for their invaluable feedback on my writing. Their critiques also helped to shape this particular work. More than once, I had a comment from one of my writing peers, wanting to know when I was going to finish the soldier story. Well, here it is, *When I See You,* finally!

Most of all, thank you to my readers for reaching out to me and expressing such profound encouragement and praise for my novels. Thank you!

Katherine Owen

AUTHOR BIOGRAPHY

Katherine Owen

KATHERINE OWEN has been writing full-time for the past three years, after a successful career in high-tech sales and public relations. Her published novels include: *Seeing Julia*, *Not To Us*, and *When I See You*.

Owen is a graduate of the University of Washington with a Bachelor of Arts degree in Communications with a major in Editorial Journalism and a minor in English Literature. In late July of 2010, Owen won first place and the coveted Zola Award in the highly competitive romance category with her novel, *Seeing Julia*, with the Pacific Northwest Writers Association. Additionally, Owen has taken writing classes with *The Writer's Studio* for the past two years.

Owen lives near Seattle with her husband and two children. She is working on her next novel.

Also By Katherine Owen

NOT TO US
SEEING JULIA

Please visit her website: http:www.katherineowen.net
For the latest updates about her work.

Play list

I listen to a lot of music while I write, so I put together a list of songs that I played, while writing *When I See You*. As you will see, I used the song titles for most of the chapter titles. Here's that song list. Enjoy!

"Can't Help Falling In Love" - Ingrid Michaelson (Chapter 1)

"Show Me What You're Looking For" - Carolina Liar (Chapter 2)

"Wonder Woman" - Katie Todd Band (Chapter 4)

"Wreck of the Day" - Anna Nalick (Chapter 6)

"Gravity" - Sara Bareilles (Chapter 8)

"Violet Walk" - Jenny Dalton (Chapter 9)

"Hope You're Happy" - Lene Martin (Chapter 11)

"The Space Between" - Zero 7 (Chapter 12)

"Spell" - Marie Digby (Chapter 13)

"Satellite" - Ganging up on the sun Guster (Chapter 14)

"Catalyst" - Anna Nalick (Chapter 15)

"Chasing Cars" - Snow Patrol (Chapter 16)

"Crazy About This Girl" - Evan & Joran (Chapter 17)

"Give In to Me" - Garrett Hedlund; Leighton Meester (Chapter 18)

"Your Eyes Open" - Keane (Chapter 19)

"We Fall Down" - Dana Parish (Chapter 20)

"Never To Know" - Lene Martin (Chapter 21)

"You're The Storm" - The Cardigans (Chapter 22)

"Soul Meets Body" - Death Cab for Cutie (Chapter 23)

"You Lost Me" - Christina Aguilera (Chapter 24)

"A Falling Through" - Ray LaMontagne (Chapter 25)

"What I've Done" - Marie Digby (Chapter 26)

"Chances" - Five For Fighting (Chapter 27)

"Dream" - Priscilla Ahn (Chapter 28)

"Looking for Water" - Alex Parks (Chapter 29)

"Keep Breathing" - Ingrid Michaelson (Chapter 30)

"Love, Save The Empty" - Erin McCarley (Chapter 31)

Author, Author! Q & A

THIS CONTAINS SPOILERS ABOUT *WHEN I SEE YOU*. READ THIS LAST.

WHAT INSPIRED YOU TO WRITE *WHEN I SEE YOU*?

Chapter three was a scene I wrote for one of my classes at *The Writers Studio*. The story evolved from that exercise and my debut novel, Seeing Julia. I wanted to explore the idea of two people coming together after experiencing the loss of someone they had both really loved, in this story, Ethan—Jordan's husband and Brock's best friend—and how the loss of him both affects and connects them. I wanted to write a story from both points of view of the two main characters, Jordan Holloway, as well as Brock Wainwright. This proved to be a complex literary challenge for me. Readers get a sense, early on, in the book how these characters feel about one another. And yet, I think *When I See You* stretches beyond the typical love story. The novel addresses many themes including overcoming tragic loss and finding closure, but the main one is that despite all the obstacles, love will find a way.

CAN YOU TALK ABOUT JORDAN HOLLOWAY?

Jordan is such a strong character in so many ways. She's an accomplished chef, a wonderful mother, a good friend to Ashleigh and Liz. Readers get a sense of how much she loves Ethan. Yet, there are underlying hints, early on, that she's barely hanging in there on so many levels. She's carved out a life for herself, yet it almost appears to be a survivor's kind of life. The early scenes between her and Brock reveal their attraction, but also the depths of a connection that these two don't quite understand. It's there in those first conversations between them.

Readers who have read my debut novel, *Seeing Julia*, may see some similarities in Jordan's character to Julia, but I think Jordan is much more complex and emotionally stronger than my first character, Julia Hamilton. *When I See You* started out as an early version of *Seeing Julia*, but then, I moved away from the concept of a soldier story with that first book. Yet, with this novel, *When I See You*, I wanted to further explore idea of a wife left behind in Jordan Holloway and the life of a heroic soldier who is wounded and confronts a very different life upon his return in Brock Wainwright. I wanted to write about these two characters who are obviously committed to Ethan Holloway in different ways and discover how they both would deal with the loss of him and find their way back from such a loss.

I focused on writing Jordan as a true survivor and although I don't overly concentrate on Jordan's backstory, I think readers can fill it in for themselves. What Jordan Holloway has experienced in her past makes her the way she is. Her journey begins with confronting her past by herself and learning to trust in someone else and their promise and place hope in a future, however different.

I wanted to create a strong character, yet show her vulnerabilities. Yes, Jordan's an accomplished chef, but readers must ask themselves why she would choose such a career, instead of the Hollywood life she inherited from her famous parents? She likes control. She has perfectionist tendencies. She's loving and giving. She's a *foodie*. It's a safe choice. It doesn't let her down. It doesn't *die*. It was deliberate on my part to come up with a career that she could pour her heart and soul into that would reap rewards, yet, allow her to cope with all these life-changing events.

Look closely. Her relationship with Ethan is a whirlwind. Readers can sense that in the very beginning chapters. Ethan, literally, swept her off her feet. Yet, he's gone much of the time. Her life didn't really have to change all that much to let him into it. Interesting, right? Readers learn they got married because she was pregnant. They met, got married, and Ethan left with Brock for his first tour for Afghanistan within two months of their first meeting. Jordan maintains a life in L.A. and raises their three-year-old son, Max, largely by herself, because Ethan is gone so much of the time. Yet, she keeps tracks of the number of days they've actually been together, versus apart. Who does that? And, why?

Jordan and Ethan are equally focused upon building this life together that largely depends upon his return from Afghanistan for good. She's just waiting for it, waiting for it to start with his return, which, of course, doesn't ever happen. Jordan is complex. No doubt. She's one of my favorite characters. We so want things to work out for her.

Author Q & A

CAN YOU TALK ABOUT BROCK WAINWRIGHT?

Brock is set up to be the perfect hero, but he carries some intrinsic flaws and is somewhat conflicted. He's charming, yet cavalier, selfish, a real playboy. His good looks have gotten him what he wants for a number of years without any emotional entanglements with women to tie him down. Yet, within days of meeting Jordan Holloway, readers get a glimpse of the coming changes that he will have to make within himself in order to be with her. His personal journey in coming to terms with Ethan's death, battling the guilt he feels for not saving his best friend, and overcoming the guilt he has because of his feelings for Jordan—all represent his personal journey in overcoming his personal struggles and forging a different life then he had planned.

Yes, he's the hero, but so lost and so set upon personal destruction to a certain degree that he is easy to want, to save, and to love. Oh, yes! He and Jordan share some similarities in how emotionally closed off they both are and in the way they both suffer in silence with such tragic loss. It's very powerful. The connection between them was intriguing, and that is what I wanted to explore the most with this story.

WHAT ARE YOUR FAVORITE SCENES FROM *WHEN I SEE YOU*?

One of my favorite scenes is in chapter two, where Jordan is frosting the "Finding Nemo" cupcakes. The conversation between Jordan and Brock in this scene sets up the whole story, especially when he says, "So he kind of ignores the tortured soul that you are." I love that scene.

My next favorite is the one right after that where she is cutting his hair. There's a lot of subconscious wanting (subtext) in that one. What starts out as a simple favor begins to reveal the powerful connection they share.

Additionally, I really enjoyed the interaction between them when Jordan first arrives in Austin, especially in chapter fourteen, with the pancake scene late at night. Writing the Porsche scene where she lets him drive his car reveals the first sign of change in Jordan in openly placing trust in another person, and she deals so well with Brock's blindness. She is always aware of him and attempts to understand his view of the world. I think these scenes really demonstrate her own strength of character, reveal Brock's vulnerabilities, and also, how much he cares about her. My absolute favorite scene is chapter eighteen with Jordan's get-out-of-jail-free card reference. The interplay between these two was so fun to write.

Author Q & A

It was a serious challenge to write from Brock's point of view as a blind person. I had to really put myself into his head and try to view the world as he saw it from both an emotional, as well as physical, standpoint. It was not an easy thing to do or write, which is probably why it took so long to finish this novel.

What Is Your Writing Process? Where Do You Get Your Ideas?

I don't do outlines. I don't know where the story is going to go when I first start writing it. The characters, literally, take me there, on a journey. They visit me at night, or when I'm doing the dishes, or driving my car. I see scenes in my head and try to write them down when the inspiration comes to me. Sometimes, I talk to my husband and tell him what I'm thinking of. Often, he tells me to put in something with a mystery to it (kidnapping, murder, anything with a spy theme to it), and every time, I tell him no way, not my genre. Regardless, he has helped me tremendously with the plotting of all my novels. He keeps me grounded.

As I've previously shared, I've taken writing classes with *The Writer's Studio*. I cannot say enough about what I have gained in my writing craft with this amazing program. As I noted earlier, chapter three of *When I See You* was originally a scene I wrote as part of my coursework. The story started from there.

And, it's true, I steal ideas all the time: names, occupations, mannerisms, word choices, scenes, people, places, and things. I'm always on the lookout for the unusual circumstance or name for the plot line of my next novel, so watch out.

What's Next? What's The Best Way To Contact You?

I'm working on my next book. For the latest updates about my upcoming novels, please visit my website: http://www.katherineowen.net. Or, fill out the contact form, if you would like to be notified when my next novel will be out. I would love to hear from you. Most of all, thank you for reading my work!

Book Club Discussion

of

WHEN I SEE YOU

1) At the beginning of the book, it appears that there are things Brock sees and understands about Jordan that Ethan never has. When Brock says, "So he kind of ignores the tortured soul that you are," it sparks a cascade of conflicting emotions for Jordan and unleashes all these insecurities about her relationship with Ethan. Can you see why that is? Now, that you've read *When I See You*, why do you think Brock is able to recognize this in her?

2) Do you think it's possible to be in love with one person and fall in love with another? Do you think that's what happens in this story between Jordan and Brock? Or, do you think Ethan's selling of Jordan's mother's necklace is the ultimate betrayal and serves as the catalyst that allows her to move on from him to Brock? Or both?

3) Ethan kept much of his life in Austin from Jordan. Do you think this was intentional? Or, do you think, although they'd been married for almost four years, that they were apart so much of the time, they just didn't know each other all that well?

4) Why do you think Brock chose to return to Afghanistan? What do you think he's really running from?

5) The story doesn't really address Jordan's heartbreak after losing Max, beyond what Brock learns from Kate's detective work about Jordan's whereabouts, but, do you, as a reader, have a good sense of how she was coping with all of that? Why do you think she finally returned to Malibu?

6) Who is more *together* when Brock and Jordan reunite in L.A.? Brock or Jordan? Why do you think that?

7) Jordan is surrounded by a number of people who love and care about her, Ashleigh and Liz, for example. Who do you think is more grounded between those two? Ashleigh or Liz? Jordan has also had these two as friends longer than she's known Ethan. Do you have friends like that? Ones you can count on through any crisis? Do you think these two help Jordan cope with loss? In different ways? Do you think they represent family to her?

8) Jordan is immediately embraced by Brock's family, especially his mother, Janie Wainwright, and his twin sister, Diana. Do you think they recognize the connection between Brock and Jordan early on? Do you think this is another factor that draws Jordan to Brock? Why? Or, why not? Henry Wainwright is the quiet character in this story. Yet, he plays this subtle role in the changes we eventually see in Brock. Do you think he subconsciously endorsed Brock's relationship with Jordan before his death?

8) Doctor Major Kate Richards serves as the antagonist in the story. Why do you think Brock continues to pursue a friendship quasi relationship with this woman? Why do you think Kate attempts to save him from himself in the end?

9) The last scene of the book brings together these two after their heartbreaking personal journeys. Do you think they know enough about themselves and each other, now, to make their relationship work?

10) Brock finally keeps his promise to her—to stay and never leave. Do you think he's changed? Who do you think has changed the most in this story, Brock or Jordan? Did the last test on their relationship surprise you? Did you like the way it ended?

CONTACT INFORMATION

Connect with Katherine Owen in the following ways on social media:

HER WEBSITE
 http://www.katherineowen.net

TWITTER
http://twitter.com/#!/KatherineOwen01

FACEBOOK
http://www.facebook.com/KatherineOwenAuthor

GOODREADS
http://www.goodreads.com/author/show/998458.Katherine_Owen

Or, her latest obsession: *PINTEREST*
http://pinterest.com/katherine_owen/

The easiest way to find out more about her novels and other interests would be at her website: *http://www.katherineowen.net*. Come visit.

≈≈ ≈≈ ≈≈

AFTERWORD

Thank you so much for reading **When I See You**! I hope you loved reading it as much as I loved writing it.

If you enjoyed **When I See You**, I would love to ask you for a favor. Please go back to wherever you purchased this book (Amazon.com, etc...) and leave an honest review of the novel.

Authors live and die by their reviews. The few extra minutes it takes you to leave a review really helps out!

If you use Twitter, Facebook, or Goodreads, it would also really help me out if you let everyone know why you enjoyed *When I See You* as well!

And, *thank you so much* for reading my work!
Katherine Owen